KB

CRITICAL ACCLAIM FOR KAT MARTIN!

"Kat Martin keeps on getting better and better . . . A premier historical writer."　　　　　　　　—*Affaire de Coeur*

"Kat Martin dishes up sizzling passion and true love, then she serves it with savoir faire."　　　　—*Los Angeles Daily News*

"Kat Martin is pure entertainment from page one!"
　　　　　　　　　　　　　　　　　—Jill Marie Landis

"Kat Martin shimmers like a bright diamond in the genre."
　　　　　　　　　　　　　　　　　—*Romantic Times*

PERFECT SIN

A Doubleday Book Club Selection

SILK AND STEEL

"Readers who relish character-driven stories with arrogant heroes and strong-minded heroines will find this a tale to cherish."　　　　　　　　　　　　—*Romantic Times*

"I was enthralled from the beginning of Ms. Martin's latest treasure, which has a strong willful heroine who matches wits expertly with her intriguing counterpart."
　　　　　　　　　　　　　　　　　—*Rendezvous*

"If you're looking for a heroine who'll stand out from the rest, give this latest of Ms. Martin's books a try. Kathryn's dilemma will tug at your heart from the opening line, and just when you think you know what'll happen next, you find out you're wrong. I loved every page! Never a dull moment, and a most entertaining read."　　　—*Interludes*

Turn the page for more acclaim . . .

WICKED PROMISE

"Conflict dogs the steps of the protagonists while tension keeps the reader alert. Humor is like icing on a cake in this delightful tale."
—*Rendezvous*

"This is a fast-paced and passionate story; as always, Ms. Martin is wonderful."
—*Bell, Book and Candle*

DANGEROUS PASSIONS

"Ms. Martin has an excitement and edge to all the books that bring the readers back time after time."
—*Bell, Book and Candle*

"War, lust, deception, and seduction make this thrilling historical come alive as this intense romance unfolds. Graphic war passages, sensuous romantic encounters, and the quest to find an unknown traitor make this historical masterpiece unforgettable. Kat Martin has once again given us an inspiring tale of love, hope, and promise."
—*Rendezvous*

"Kat Martin weaves a tale as compelling as any she has written. This novel is un-put-downable—a non-stop read filled with excitement, tempestuous passion, betrayal, mystery and everything romance readers have come to expect from a top-notch writer."
—*Romantic Times* (4½ Stars)

NOTHING BUT VELVET

"Kat Martin draws the reader into Regency England and the lives of wealth and privilege, with the assurance of a master . . . A writer of renown who thrills us."
—*Under the Covers Book Reviews*

"NOTHING BUT VELVET is nothing but brilliant. The lead characters are super, and the villain as vile as they come. The story line is fast-paced and extremely interesting."
—*Affaire de Coeur*

"What more could a romance reader want? . . . [NOTHING BUT VELVET] is a boisterous carriage ride in which Martin shows herself to have a firm grasp on the reins."
—*Publishers Weekly*

MIDNIGHT RIDER

"Kat Martin weaves a marvelous western romance that sizzles with unbridled passion and a heated battle of wills. Readers will be enraptured by the heart-pounding adventure and warmed to their toes of the sensuality of MIDNIGHT RIDER."
—*Romantic Times*

"Another winner . . . Kat Martin keeps on getting better and better."
—*Affaire de Coeur*

"What an outlaw! Dark, daring, dangerous and delicious! MIDNIGHT RIDER is a rich panorama of old California. I couldn't put it down!"   —Georgina Gentry

DEVIL'S PRIZE

"Tempting, alluring, sensual and irresistible—destined to be a soaring success."   —*Romantic Times*

"Kat Martin is a premier historical romance author . . . and DEVIL'S PRIZE enhances her first-class reputation."
    —*Affaire de Coeur*

BOLD ANGEL

"This medieval romance is a real pleasure . . . the romance is paramount."   —*Publishers Weekly*

"BOLD ANGEL moves quickly through a bold and exciting period of history. As usual, Kat has written an excellent and entertaining novel of days gone by."
    —Heather Graham

"An excellent medieval romance . . . Readers will not only love this novel but clamor for a sequel."
    —*Affaire de Coeur*

ST. MARTIN'S PAPERBACKS TITLES BY KAT MARTIN

Gypsy Lord

Sweet Vengeance

Bold Angel

Devil's Prize

Midnight Rider

Innocence Undone

Nothing But Velvet

Dangerous Passions

Wicked Promise

Night Secrets

Silk and Steel

Perfect Sin

PERFECT SIN

KAT MARTIN

St. Martin's Paperbacks

PERFECT SIN

Copyright © 2000 by Kat Martin.

ISBN: 0-312-97564-3

Printed in the United States of America

St. Martin's Paperbacks edition / October 2000

St. Martin's Paperbacks are published by St. Martin's Press, 175 Fifth Avenue, New York, N.Y. 10010.

10 9 8 7 6 5 4 3 2 1

*To my brother, Michael,
and my sister, Patti.
Miss you guys.
Don't get to see you enough!*

PERFECT
SIN

ONE

It was the sound of her laughter, rich and melodic, sensuously feminine, that changed his life forever.

Standing beneath a crystal chandelier in the Marquess of Wester's elegant ballroom, Randall Elliott Clayton, seventh Duke of Beldon, turned in search of the sound, not the laughter of a missish young girl, but the inviting, unaffected mirth of a woman.

Rand's gaze traveled over the crush of expensively garbed men and women, his mind conjuring images of a dark sensuous beauty with heavy-lidded, black-fringed eyes, though logic told him such an open, uninhibited laugh could come only from an aging matron no longer governed by the dictates of society.

Taller than most of the men in the room, he spotted her quickly. She was younger than he had imagined, perhaps no more than twenty, not dark and exotic but exactly the opposite, with fiery, gold-tipped red hair and clear green eyes. Her skin was neither dark nor pale, but glowed as if she had spent time in the sun.

"I see you have discovered the guest of honor."

Rand turned to find his best friend, Nicholas Warring, Earl of Ravenworth, standing beside him. Black-haired and dark-skinned, nearly as tall as Rand, Nick was handsome and intelligent, but his past was nebulous, and there was an underlying toughness about him that kept people away.

"Who is she?" Rand asked, careful to keep his tone nonchalant, though it wasn't the least how he was feeling.

"Her name is Caitlin Harmon. Her father is Donovan Harmon, an American professor of antiquities."

Rand took a drink of his champagne, studying the petite woman over the rim. "American . . . yes . . ." In the course of his thirty-one years, he had bedded quite a number of them. American women didn't seem to abide by the same moral dictates as English women, not even those who were as yet unmarried. They often traveled about unchaperoned and apparently lived their lives as they saw fit, an attitude he found quite useful.

"I gather they've been living on some island off the coast of Africa for the past several years," Nick said. "You may have read about him in the newspapers."

Indeed he had. Professor Harmon and his ongoing quest for the infamous Cleopatra's Necklace. Now that he thought of it, he remembered the article also mentioned Harmon's daughter and that she worked closely with him.

Rand's probing glance found her again, small and shapely, with high, full breasts that rose above the neckline of her gown. Lovely in the extreme, he thought, feeling an unexpected heaviness in his groin. He had always liked women. Enjoyed their company, and of course their companionship in bed. He liked the looks of this one. Too easily, he could imagine stripping away the layers of her emerald silk gown and pulling the pins from all that softly curling red hair.

Inwardly, he smiled. And she was American, he reminded himself, thinking of the possibilities that might present. Perhaps he had been right about the womanly laughter. Rand hoped so. He couldn't remember when the sound of a woman's voice had affected him so profoundly.

*   *   *

Caitlin Eleanor Harmon took a sip of punch from the silver cup she held in her hand, but she didn't really taste it. All evening she had been smiling and nodding, answering the same questions over and over, repeating information about her father's upcoming expedition in an effort to help him raise the money he needed—the reason they had journeyed to England.

Cait sighed. She couldn't help thinking that in the course of the evening she had pretended interest in some of the dullest conversation she had listened to in years. Fortunately, for the moment at least, she'd been rescued by her hostess and newfound friend, Margaret Sutton, Lady Trent. Since then, Cait's thoughts had shifted from buried treasure to a far more interesting topic.

She took another sip of her punch, focusing her attention on the tall, broad-shouldered figure she watched covertly above the cup's silver rim.

"There's a man across the way," she said to Lady Trent, "the tall one beneath the chandelier. Who is he?"

Blond and blue-eyed, Maggie Sutton was five years older, but she didn't seem so. The nearly nine years she had spent in a convent had left her with an innocence that made her appear far younger. Her husband was the Marquess of Trent and it was his interest in Cait's father's project that had brought Cait and Maggie together. Considering how badly Cait had yearned for female companionship these past two years, the marchioness was truly a godsend.

Maggie's gaze followed Cait's, coming to rest on the two men conversing on the opposite side of the dance floor.

"Believe it or not, that handsome black-haired devil is my brother, Nick. Nicky is the Earl of Ravenworth and, aside from my husband, my favorite person in the world. But you are referring to the other man, are you not? The one who has been looking at you as if he would eat you with a spoon if he could."

Cait laughed. She wouldn't have phrased it quite that

way, but it was difficult not to notice such a man's interest. "The bigger man, yes. The one with the dark eyes and coffee-brown hair."

"And a set of shoulders that barely fit through the ballroom door? Along with your intelligence, it is also clear you have excellent taste in men. That, my dear, is the Duke of Beldon. Rand Clayton is perhaps the most eligible bachelor in London. He is wealthy in the extreme, certainly one of the handsomest and most charming men in the city, and also quite possibly the most dangerous—at least when it comes to women."

Cait could see exactly what Maggie meant. With his tall, muscular build, handsome profile, and faintly arrogant stance, the duke had a presence no woman—nor man for that matter—could miss. He exuded power and authority, and even from a distance, whenever he looked at her, she could feel those fierce brown eyes like a fire burning into her flesh.

It was unfortunate that he was a duke, she thought with a pang of regret. Aside from the small, select group of friends she and her father had made since their arrival, Cait had found most of the aristocracy to be arrogant, self-centered, and spoiled. Through the accident of their birth, they considered themselves above the common man. A duke, at the top of the aristocratic pyramid aside from actual royalty, would probably be worse than the rest.

From beneath her lashes, Cait studied the man, saw that he was watching her in return, felt the fire of his powerful gaze as he began to stride in her direction, and a shiver of warning ran through her. He shouldered his way through the throng of people clustered around the dance floor and strode toward her, his body moving with purpose and grace. Even at a distance, she could feel the fire shooting like sparks between them, feel the heat and the sensuous pull. The thought occurred that if she had a lick of sense, she would turn tail and run.

But then, Caitlin had never been afraid of fire, even as a child. And she loved nothing better than a challenge.

Instead, when the duke appeared in front of her a few moments later, Cait looked into that arrogant, sinfully handsome face and smiled.

"Your Grace . . ." Maggie turned to make the introductions. "I should like to present my friend, Miss Caitlin Harmon."

The duke's dark eyes held hers. She knew she was staring, had been since the moment she had seen him, but then so was he, those intense brown eyes locked with hers as if there wasn't another person in the room. She noticed they were flecked with gold, giving them an odd sort of warmth.

He bowed formally over her hand. "A pleasure, Miss Harmon. I've looked forward to making your acquaintance."

"The pleasure is mine . . . Your Grace." The last two words didn't come out as smoothly as she had intended. With the rest of the nobility, she played by the rules of British society, but somehow with Beldon, it galled her to address him as if he were better than she.

His dark eyes brightened with a trace of amusement. Clearly, he had guessed her thoughts. "You're American, I gather."

"I was born in Boston. That is about as American as it gets." Her smile held a hint of challenge. "You might remember the Boston Tea Party."

Maggie's blond eyebrows shot up. The duke merely smiled. "That was long before my time. Besides, the war is over. You might remember that, Miss Harmon."

"Yes . . . well that is certainly true. If memory serves, it ended with the passage of the Bill of Rights, making all men equal. I don't believe that sort of thinking is common in this country—or am I mistaken . . . Your Grace?"

Beldon's mouth curved up. "You're quite mistaken, Miss Harmon. Here in England we know all about equality. We simply believe some men are more equal than others." Those hot brown eyes met hers, sparkling with amusement and something more.

The beating of her heart increased to an uncomfortable pitch and the air seemed to heat between them. When his smile grew broader and a dimple formed in his left cheek, it occurred to her that, duke or not, arrogant and spoiled as she was certain he was, the Duke of Beldon was a dangerously attractive man.

Briefly, he turned to Lady Trent. "Your brother would like a word with you, Maggie. I'll be happy to keep Miss Harmon company until your return."

Maggie flashed a look at the black-haired man across the dance floor. "I trust she'll be in good hands," she said with a trace of warning.

"Undoubtedly," the duke agreed.

"I shan't be long," Maggie said to Cait. With a last pointed glance at Beldon, she took her leave, heading toward her tall, darkly handsome brother on the opposite side of the ballroom.

The duke's attention swung back to her. "Since we both agree the war is over, how about a truce, Miss Harmon?"

She couldn't help a smile. There was something about the duke that was hard to resist. "All right, a truce." The *Your Grace* went unsaid. "At least for now."

His lips twitched. He lifted a glass of champagne off a passing servant's tray and took a drink. "Rumor has it, you and your father have been living on an island off Africa for the past several years. Rather out of the social whirl, I imagine."

She recalled the primitive living conditions she had endured on Santo Amaro. "That is to say the least."

"Still, I have watched you dancing. You do so admirably for a lady who has lived away from civilization for so long. Do you also waltz, Miss Harmon?"

Cait flicked him an assessing glance. Even in America the waltz was considered somewhat daring. Though she had never actually done it, she knew the steps. Thanks to her father, she was as well educated as any man, and as far as she was concerned there was nothing the least bit scandalous about a waltz.

Still, it was clearly a challenge, perhaps a result of the slight in her form of address. Reminding herself she was there on a mission to help her father and that the duke was a potential contributor, she decided the use of his title was little price to pay.

"I believe, Your Grace, they are playing a contradance at present." She turned to survey the floor, saw that the music was just ending. As if by some hidden cue—which Cait was certain there had been—the orchestra struck up the chords of a waltz.

"Do I take that to mean you do not?" he pressed.

A smile blossomed of its own accord. "I suppose I could try—if you are willing to risk getting your very shiny shoes stepped on."

The duke laughed and flashed her a charming grin. "I believe I am willing to risk it." Leading her onto the dance floor, he placed his hand on her waist while hers found his wide shoulder, then he was sweeping her into the dance, whirling her around the floor with an ease she couldn't have imagined. For a moment, conversation seemed to slow as a dozen pairs of eyes swung in their direction. Then several other couples joined in, including Lord and Lady Trent, clearly there to lend respectability to the dance.

"I believe you've made a friend," the duke remarked as he led her into a graceful turn. "Maggie is extremely protective of those she takes under her wing. You're lucky to have won her support."

"And I am more than grateful. I think having a female friend was the thing I missed most in the years I was away."

"I gather your father and Lord Trent are also friends."

She nodded. "Lord Trent has a passionate interest in history. He and my father began corresponding several years back, when proof of the necklace first began to surface."

"Cleopatra's Necklace, as I understand it. Quite a treasure, I would guess."

"It would certainly be an important find. Including the years of study he's done, my father's been searching for the necklace for nearly four years." Cait stared into the duke's handsome face, but it was difficult to concentrate. Not when his big warm hand rode at her waist and a muscular thigh brushed intimately between her legs with every turn. He was incredibly graceful for a man of his height and build, making his steps easy to follow. She reminded herself that he was a duke and they had nothing at all in common.

Still, the music was entrancing and the rhythm of the dance began to lull her.

"It's like floating," she said, closing her eyes for a moment, absorbing the melody and the cool air rushing past her cheeks.

His hold tightened almost imperceptibly, drawing her closer still. "You dance beautifully." His eyes found hers when she looked up at him. "And fool that I am, I thought that you were a novice."

Cait smiled. "I had a dancing instructor who taught me the steps, but this is the first time I've actually tried it. My father was a stickler for education."

His mouth curved faintly, the most sensuous lips she'd ever seen. "Being a professor, I imagine he would be."

"Yes . . ." The word came out breathy and far away. She tried to tell herself she shouldn't be attracted to a man like him, but that didn't keep her heart from beating too fast or her mouth from drying to the texture of cotton. Good heavens, she had danced with men before. Still, she couldn't recall even one who'd been able to make her feel as if she had lost her wits.

When the music came to an end, she barely noticed, and oddly, neither did he. They might have gone right on dancing if it hadn't been for Lord and Lady Trent, who managed to place themselves in the duke's path at exactly the right moment to prevent them from being embarrassed.

Beldon smiled down at Lord Trent, who was shorter, well built, and also extremely good-looking.

"Sorry," the duke said. "I guess I should have been paying attention." But when he looked at Cait, she saw that he wasn't the least bit repentant, and his big hand still rode at her waist.

"It's getting late," the marquess said pointedly. "I'm afraid it's time for us to leave." Since Caitlin and her father were currently Lord Trent's houseguests, that meant she was leaving, as well. Cait felt a thread of disappointment.

She gave the duke a tentative smile. "Perhaps our paths will cross again, Your Grace."

Taking her hand, he made an elegant bow. "You may count on it, Miss Harmon." He raised her fingers to his lips and an odd little tingle ran up her arm. Cait did her best to ignore it.

But several hours later, as she lay beneath the rose silk canopy on her bed in the marquess's lavish town house, she pondered those parting words. Would she see him again, as he had said?

The sudden quickening of her pulse said how very much she wanted that to occur.

Sitting in his solicitor's oak-paneled office on Threadneedle Street, Rand Clayton, Duke of Beldon, studied the blue-inked columns in the ledger, staring at the numbers so long his vision began to blur.

He couldn't imagine a life without problems. Without duties and responsibilities. For a few brief hours last night, dancing with the stunning little American at Wester's ball, he'd had a respite from his demanding life. He'd enjoyed their playful bit of sparring and laughed as if he hadn't a care.

Ah, but that was last night and this was today. The

pressures had returned and his mind focused once more on his duties.

Hundreds of people relied on him.

It bothered him to think he had failed even one of them.

He stared back down at the ledgers, books that had formerly belonged to his youngest cousin. "Whoever it was, the bastard managed to pluck the boy clean. In less than twelve months, Jonathan invested nearly every dime of his inheritance."

His solicitor, Ephram Barclay frowned. "Young Jonathan was never satisfied. He always wanted more. He was determined to make his fortune and in doing so prove himself. In the end, his ambition was his destruction."

Rand leaned back in the deep leather chair on the opposite side of Ephram's desk and rubbed his eyes, feeling suddenly weary. "The boy was too damned trusting. If he had just come to me—"

"If he had come to you, Your Grace, you would have told him the venture was too risky. Jonathan believed that in order to make his fortune he would have to take those sorts of risks. Unfortunately, he was unprepared for the consequences."

And those consequences were severe, indeed. Being humiliated in front of his friends, losing his prized membership at Almack's, facing a mountain of debts he had no means to pay. Rather than ask for help, at the age of two and twenty, young Jonathan Randall Clayton had taken his own life. Two weeks ago, a groom had found his body hanging from the rafters in the stables of the family estate he had mortgaged and lost to his creditors.

"Whatever mistakes he might have made," Rand said, "Jonathan was a good boy. With his mother and father dead, I should have kept a closer eye on him. I can't help feeling this is partly my fault."

Ephram leaned over his desk, a tall, thin, gray-haired man who had managed Beldon affairs for the past twenty years. "You mustn't blame yourself. You had no idea what the lad was doing. The boy only came into his inheritance last year. Who would have thought he would invest it so unwisely—or that after he failed, he would take the rash course of action he did?"

But Rand still blamed himself. Jonathan was young and impressionable. For years, the boy had vowed to rebuild his fortune from the small inheritance his father, Rand's uncle, had left him. Instead he had lost what little remaining money the family still had, and fallen into such despair he had killed himself.

Rand looked back down at the account sheet. "There's no mention here of where the money went."

"No, not there." Ephram reached for another sheet, laid it over the first. "As you can see, almost all of the money went to Merriweather Shipping. It was intended for the purchase of copra from the West Indies. A successful venture would have doubled your cousin's investment. Unfortunately, the ship sank in a storm at sea with the loss of all hands, and Jonathan lost his money, all the funds he had in the world."

Rand heard something in Ephram's voice. The man had been a trusted confidant since Rand's father had died and Rand had inherited the dukedom. "All right, my friend. Obviously, there is more to all of this. You may as well tell me."

Ephram pulled off his wire-rimmed spectacles and rested them on the top of the polished oak desk. "Knowing you as I do, I thought you would want to know as much about Merriweather Shipping as I could find out. I've been doing some checking . . . not the usual sort, you understand, but the kind that involves an exchange of money into the right hands. It seems Merriweather Shipping has had more than one of their ships conveniently go down—and a number of investors have lost goodly sums of money."

Rand's muscles went tense. "What are you implying, Ephram?"

"I'm saying these cargoes were completely financed

with investors' money. If the ship didn't sink but actually landed somewhere other than England, the entire profit would have gone to the owners."

Rand leaned forward in his chair. "Are you telling me the venture was a fraud?"

"I'm saying it's possible that Merriweather Shipping may have faked the sinking, changed the name of the vessel, and landed the ship somewhere else. The profit would have been enormous."

A knot of cold fury tightened in the pit of Rand's stomach. His cousin was dead, a young man with a future that could have been bright and shiny. Instead he lay moldering in an icy grave.

Rand looked at Ephram with cold, hard purpose. "I want to know what happened to that ship. And I want to know everything there is to know about Merriweather Shipping. I want to know who runs it, and especially who raises the money for its ventures."

On the arm of his chair, his hand unconsciously fisted. "I want to know what happened to my cousin. I won't stop until I find out if Jonathan's death was simply a result of bad judgment—or if some greedy bastard took advantage of his trust and drove him to it."

TWO

❦

The man's reflection moved along the mirrored walls of the salon; Phillip Rutherford, Baron Talmadge. He was rather nondescript, Rand thought, nothing at all like he had imagined. With light brown hair and hazel eyes, he was at least four inches shorter than Rand, maybe three stone lighter, and some years older, perhaps a man of forty.

Standing just inside the door to the salon, Rand had been watching the baron since his arrival. A congenial sort, he seemed, conversing easily with those around him, apparently well liked by most of the ton.

But then, a man who swindled people out of their money to line his own pockets would likely be a man with those skills.

Rand watched him a moment more, noticing the confident way he moved, understanding how his cousin might have been taken in. He wondered why it was they hadn't chanced to meet and thought that before the evening was over, he would certainly remedy that. Then something else snagged his attention, nudging its way into the back of his mind, and his glance strayed off in another direction.

Laughter. Rich and melodic, sensuously feminine. He remembered it all too well, remembered the petite American who went with it. No other woman of his acquaintance laughed in that forthright manner and Rand felt a shot of heat that went straight to his groin.

For a moment, he forgot the man in the burgundy tailcoat, the reason he had come to the affair. Instead his gaze went in search of the woman with the fiery red hair.

Stepping out from behind a marble pillar, he saw her, her face still carrying that subtle glow, her breasts high and full above the bodice of an aqua silk gown.

"Why do I get a feeling of déjà vu?" Nick Warring walked up with a grin. "Or was it not Miss Harmon you were staring at the last time we chanced to meet?"

Rand eyed the little redhead across the way. "It was definitely she," he confirmed, but this time, along with the lust he was feeling came a tightening in the pit of his stomach. In the days since the meeting with his solicitor, he had inadvertently discovered some unsettling information about Caitlin Harmon, and more particularly her father.

Namely that Donovan Harmon was Phillip Rutherford's partner—the man Rand believed had swindled his young cousin out of his fortune and ultimately caused his death.

Rand clamped down on his jaw, burying the bitter taste of regret, wishing Cait Harmon was someone else altogether, his gaze still aimed in her direction.

"She's quite something—wouldn't you agree?" Eyeing him shrewdly, Nick took a sip of the gin he always favored.

"Indeed she is."

"She is staying with my sister, you know."

He knew all right. He also knew that her father was working with Talmadge to raise money for the professor's upcoming expedition, seeking out members of the aristocracy and soliciting funds—just as the baron had done to young Jonathan. If Caitlin Harmon worked with her father, she knew a good deal about the professor's activities. Which meant she knew something of Baron Talmadge, as well.

His assessing glance found her again, in conversation with Nick's sister, Maggie. She looked as radiant tonight as she had before, perhaps even more so. With her bright smile, glowing skin, and lush womanly figure, she made every other woman in the room look pale in comparison.

Rand's interest swelled. The lady definitely intrigued him. And with her connections to Talmadge, she might prove extremely useful. The fact that he found her so attractive only added to an already interesting equation.

With that thought in mind, along with several other, more sensual ones he tried to ignore, he started walking toward her.

"It's Rand," Maggie said softly to Cait. "I wondered when he would turn up again."

Cait wasn't sure exactly what Maggie meant, but any thought of pursuing the subject slipped away as she followed the direction of Maggie's gaze and saw the handsome Duke of Beldon bearing down on them. Long, purposeful strides carried him to the place in front of them, where he paused to make a polite greeting to Maggie, then turned his attention to Cait.

"Miss Harmon." He made a graceful bow over her hand. "It's a pleasure to see you again."

Cait smiled, her heart speeding up at the warm look in his eyes. "And you, as well, Your Grace." She meant it, she realized, surprised a bit, and then not surprised at all.

He glanced at the press of people around them, all of them gossiping, chattering about her father, whose hunt for the necklace was the reason for the fete.

"I've been reading about your money-raising exploits in the papers," he said. "If tonight is any indication, plans for the expedition should be coming along quite nicely."

Cait took a sip of her drink, watching him over the rim, feeling that same pull of attraction that she had felt before. "It's always difficult to raise the capital for such an expensive venture, but yes . . . I believe things are moving along as well as can be expected."

Maggie flicked a glance toward her husband, who stood in the group surrounding the professor. "Andrew will be hosting several events in support of Dr. Harmon's cause. We're hoping you'll be able to come."

The duke smiled indulgently. "If Miss Harmon is attending, you may be certain I will come." His glance strayed her way and an odd little tremor ran through her. His attention lingered, then moved off toward another of the men conversing with her father. "I gather Baron Talmadge is lending his assistance, as well."

Cait smiled. "We met his lordship in New York, at a fund-raising affair much like this one. Lord Talmadge was taken with the notion of finding the necklace almost from the moment he learned of its existence. When the expedition needed funding, Father wrote to the baron and he offered to help raise the money. They've been partners in the venture ever since."

Beldon's eyes seemed to darken as she spoke of the baron, then he smiled in that sensual way of his and she thought that she must have imagined it. Maggie's husband, the marquess, walked up just then.

"Sorry to interrupt," he said to his wife and the duke, "but it's getting rather late. Professor Harmon has meetings early on the morrow and Cait has a lecture to give."

The duke cocked a brow. "A lecture?"

Cait's smile turned cool. Of course a duke would frown on a young, unmarried woman speaking in public. "I'll be talking to the members of the Museum Ladies' Auxiliary. We'll be discussing Santo Amaro; my father's work; and the upcoming expedition."

"I'm impressed, Miss Harmon. I didn't realize I was talking to a scholar." Surprisingly, she detected no censure. Or at least she didn't think she did.

"Hardly a scholar," she said. "Merely a woman who has learned some interesting facts in her travels."

His mouth edged up. "Too bad I'm not a member of the auxiliary. I should like to hear what it is that you have learned." There was something in the way he said it that made the heat creep into her cheeks.

"Unlike you men—who ban us from your smoky gentlemen's clubs and insist we be constantly chaperoned—

we women are far more open-minded. There is no rule as to who may or may not attend the lecture. Perhaps you will find time to join us."

Again that faint, unreadable smile. "Perhaps." But she was certain that he would not.

He said nothing more in that vein, and they made their polite farewells. As she left the town house, she imagined that he watched her, but surely it was only her imagination.

A small fire crackled in the hearth of the low-ceilinged, wood-paneled study of the Duke of Beldon's Grosvenor Square mansion. The hour was still early and a brisk wind had risen outside, rattling against the panes.

Rand studied the two men seated on the opposite side of his desk, his solicitor, Ephram Barclay, gray-haired and dignified, and his best friend, Nicholas Warring, tall, dark, and frowning over the papers he held in a long-fingered hand. Nick was reading the report Rand had received from the Bow Street runner Ephram had hired, a man named Michael McConnell.

In the last several weeks, McConnell had unearthed a great deal. After the sinking of the *Maiden,* the ship carrying the cargo his cousin had invested in so heavily, Merriweather Shipping had gone out of business. The two men who owned the company, Dillon Sinclair and Richard Morris, had left the country. A third man had also left, though he had recently returned—Phillip Rutherford, Baron Talmadge, the man who had very discreetly raised the money for the venture.

So far no trace of the *Maiden* had been found, and Rand had been unable to prove the sinking was a fraud. But Ephram was convinced it was true, and considering the amount of money the three men had withdrawn from the Bank of England on their departure, so was Rand.

"I can see why you've been so obsessed with this," Nick said, shaking his head. "If Jonathan was duped out of his inheritance, as this report implies, his death was very nearly murder."

"Exactly so," Rand said.

Nick set the papers back on the corner of the desk. "From what I gather, you believe Talmadge is setting up another swindle, this one involving Professor Harmon."

"That's exactly what I think."

"It's a bit hard to believe. Donovan Harmon is a close friend of my brother-in-law's. If Trent didn't think quite highly of him, he would hardly invite the man into his home."

Rand turned to his solicitor. "What do you say, Ephram?"

He shoved his spectacles back up on his nose. "It's difficult to say. I've sent letters to Harvard College, where the professor taught classes on ancient Egypt, and hired an American investigator to look into the man's personal background, but it'll take weeks for a response. Harmon's professional credentials are impeccable. He's quite well respected in the antiquities community. In the matter of money, however, the story is a little different."

Rand sat up straighter in his chair. "Different in what way?"

"Ever since the death of Harmon's wife, the professor has involved himself in a series of expeditions, usually taking him out of the country. He's traveled to Egypt, sifted through the ruins in Pompeii, and spent time studying in The Hague. Each of those ventures and a number of others ended up financial disasters. Apparently, Harmon has a problem managing money. He's made a number of valuable discoveries over the years, but each time the professor returned to America in desperate financial straits."

Rand swung his attention to Nick. "The man is in need of money. That gives him a motive. It means there is every reason to believe the professor knows exactly what Talmadge has in mind."

Nick shook his head. "There is still his daughter to

consider. I met Cait Harmon only briefly, but what I saw of her I liked. She's forthright and intelligent. I can't imagine she has any knowledge of what may or may not be going on with her father and the baron—if indeed that is the case."

"I hope you're right," Rand said. "You've always had good instincts—that's why I asked you here."

"The best thing to do," Ephram added, "is to keep an open mind until all of the facts are in."

"And keep our eyes and ears open, as well," Rand said. "Nick, I'd appreciate it if you kept our conversation confidential. Both your wife and sister are close friends of Cait's and neither of them are good at deception."

Nick grinned. "Thank God for that."

Rand smiled as well; he liked both of the women. With a glance at the ornate grandfather clock across the study, he shoved back his chair and stood up.

"I really appreciate both of you taking the time to come. I'm trying to remain objective in all of this. The two of you have been a great deal of help to me."

"What's your next move?" Nick asked Rand, stepping to the door and holding it open so the men could pass.

Rand stepped out into the marble-floored hall with a smile. He tried to tell himself his eagerness to be gone had nothing to do with Caitlin Harmon, but he knew it wasn't the truth.

"I heard a rumor there is a very interesting lecture going on this morning, down at the British Museum. Perhaps if I'm lucky, I'll learn something useful."

Nick eyed him skeptically. "I don't suppose that lecture is perhaps being given by our own little bluestocking, Miss Harmon?"

Rand's smile broadened into a grin. "One never knows what sort of person one might encounter in the bowels of a museum."

THREE

Moving as quietly as possible for a man of his size, Rand seated himself in the last row of chairs in the small lecture hall where Caitlin Harmon was describing her work on Santo Amaro Island. He hadn't meant to actually go in, but when she began relating her father's search for the legendary Cleopatra's Necklace, he couldn't resist.

He'd tried to enter undetected, but as the only man in a room of nearly three dozen women there was little chance of that. In the end, his presence proved satisfyingly distracting to Cait, whose cheeks turned faintly pink and who was momentarily at a loss for words. Her confusion didn't last long. Cait Harmon was obviously a professional. After a quick review of her notes, she resumed speaking exactly where she had left off, repeating the legend of the necklace and what her father had so far unearthed.

Rand couldn't help wondering how much of it was true, and how Phillip Rutherford might fit in.

"Until recently there was little proof that such a necklace actually existed," Cait said. "But rumors of its fabulous beauty had been circulating for years. Fashioned of egg-sized diamonds, mammoth emeralds and rubies, it was said to have been commissioned by Anthony as a gift to Cleopatra. A number of Egyptian documents refer to the incredible craftsmanship of the necklace, the intricate way the stones were woven among fine strands of hammered gold. Unfortunately, it was stolen and never seen again. At least not for hundreds of years."

She looked out at the audience and smiled. "That is where my father comes in. Some years back, in the course of his research in the Dutch archives of The Hague, my father accidentally uncovered a series of documents— sworn affidavits produced by a sailor named Hans Van der Hagen nearly eighty years ago. The documents mentioned the existence of the necklace. Van der Hagan was a sailor aboard a Dutch slaver called the *Zilverijder*. He claimed that while they were capturing slaves along the Ivory Coast, they found an object of inestimable worth among one of the tribes' religious possessions. How it traveled from Egypt across the continent, no one knows, but the description he gave perfectly matches that of Cleopatra's Necklace."

For an instant the room fell silent. "What happened to the necklace after the Dutch sailors found it?" one of the women asked.

"That's the interesting part. Apparently, it was carried aboard the *Silver Rider*, but just off the remote island of Santo Amaro the ship ran into a storm. According to Dutch records, the vessel disappeared without a trace, but Van der Hagan swore it washed aground on the rocky shore of the island and three of the crew survived: the ship's first officer, Leon Metz; a sailor named Spruitenberg; and of course Hans Van der Hagen.

"According to the documents my father found, greed over the necklace finally did them in. The first officer wanted the necklace so badly he killed the other two men—or at least attempted to. Van der Hagen survived, somehow made his way back to the mainland, and eventually returned to Holland. His sworn statements claim the first officer was badly wounded in the fray. He believed the man could never have escaped the island."

"If the necklace was there," a woman in a straw bonnet asked, "why didn't he go back and get it?"

"He tried to. For years Van der Hagen worked to raise

money to return and search for the necklace, but no one ever believed his story."

"Apparently, your father did," Rand said dryly from his seat at the back of the room, turning three dozen female heads in his direction.

"Yes, he did. He raised money enough to mount the first expedition, but our supplies ran out before we had time to find the necklace. I'm sorry to say, his lack of success cost him a good deal of credibility in America and that is why we are here."

"But surely if the Americans won't support him—"

Caitlin held up a silver coin, efficiently cutting off the woman's words.

"This is a silver Dutch guilder. The date on the coin is 1724. That is the date, according to Dutch maritime records, the slaver, *Zilverijder*, went down. Two weeks before we left for England, my father unearthed this coin and a number of others just like it—on Santo Amaro Island."

A murmur rolled through the crowd. Rand felt a stirring of reluctant admiration. Whether she was telling the truth or not, Cait Harmon certainly knew how to handle an audience.

For the next few moments, she continued to answer the women's excited questions.

"I was wondering, Miss Harmon . . ." A thin, rather plain-looking woman in the front row leaned forward. "It is difficult to imagine a young woman of what . . . twenty years of age?"

"Twenty-one," Caitlin corrected.

"Yes . . . well, I am some years older, but still it is difficult to imagine living the sort of life you have lived. By the time I had reached one and twenty, I was already married and the mother of two beautiful children."

Cait smiled. "I've thought about a different sort of life. Marriage and family, the kind of things most women want. But my father's work is the most important consideration. And in truth, I value my independence more than most. As a wife, I would have to give that up—which I am completely unwilling to do."

Rand mulled over her words. Cait Harmon wasn't interested in marriage, which suited him fine, since he wasn't in the marriage mart, either. But if his instincts were correct, she was attracted to him. And in truth, he was wildly attracted to her. He needed a way to get close to Talmadge. Cait Harmon was the best way he could think of to do it.

"Santo Amaro is the farthest island in the Cape Verde chain," Cait went on. "Being closer to the equator, it has a more tropical climate than the rest. It's beautiful along the coast, but the interior is extremely hostile. So far our search has carried us no farther inland than the forest at the edge of the beach. That was the camp, we believe, of the three shipwrecked crewmen of the *Zilverijder*."

"And that, I presume, is where your father believes he will find Cleopatra's Necklace," Rand put in.

"We believe it's there," she replied in the same confident tones that had drawn him to her in the first place. "With the support of people like the ones in this room, we believe we will find Cleopatra's Necklace."

Above the heads of the women, Caitlin's bright green eyes swung to his face. Rand felt it almost as if she had reached out and touched him. His body stirred. He couldn't believe a woman could make him feel such a hot jolt of lust in the middle of a crowded hall.

The questions went on, but Rand didn't wait to hear more. Caitlin Harmon was magnificent, every bit as fiery as her hair and exactly the woman he had imagined when he had first heard the sound of her voice. It was hard to believe she was embroiled in any sort of swindle. Still, from what little he had learned so far, anything was possible.

Cait continued to answer questions as Rand made his way to the door. She laughed at something a woman said and he glanced back at her one last time. Cait was dif-

ferent, intriguing. She was intelligent and fiery and he
wanted to feel that fire.

Rand couldn't remember the last time he had wanted
a woman quite so badly.

Half an hour passed before the last of the Ladies' Auxiliary filed out of the room and Caitlin was left alone.
Busy straightening her notes and refiling them in her flat
leather satchel, she glanced up to see the Duke of Beldon
stride back through the doorway.

"Your Grace . . . I thought you had gone."

He flashed her a disarming smile. "I wanted to talk to
you in private. I wanted to tell you how much I enjoyed
your lecture, and I thought, after all that hard work, you
might be hungry. I hoped you would join me for—"

"I'm afraid Miss Harmon has a previous engagement,"
came a familiar female voice from the doorway. Cait
turned to see Elizabeth Warring and Maggie Sutton making their way down the aisle toward the podium. "Unless
you wish to join us," Elizabeth told the duke with a mis-
chievous grin.

The duke just smiled. "I may be any number of things,
but masochistic, I'm not. I've already shared Miss Harmon with three dozen women. I think that's enough for
one day." He fixed his attention on Cait and the heat in
his gaze burned all the way to her toes. "Do you like
horses, Miss Harmon?"

She eyed him with a degree of speculation, wondering
what new challenge he was about to toss out. "If you are
asking if I ride, the answer is yes, though I haven't done
so for the past several years."

"I was asking if you might enjoy attending a horse
race. I've a stallion running in a match race at Ascot day
after the morrow. I believe Lady Ravenworth and her husband are planning to attend. Is there a chance that you—
and your father, of course—might be convinced to come
along?"

Elizabeth flashed an excited smile. "Oh, do come with

us, Caitlin. It's going to be ever so much fun."

Caitlin stepped down from the podium, tucking the flat leather folder that held her notes up under her arm, careful to keep her gaze from straying toward the duke. "I've never been to a horse race, but I think I would very much enjoy it."

"Bravo!" Elizabeth clapped her hands like a delighted child. Taller and more slender than Cait, her hair several shades darker, the Countess of Ravenworth was the mother of a six-month-old son, a woman dedicated to her husband and family. On the surface, they were nothing alike, yet Cait felt a certain camaraderie with Elizabeth, as if in some underlying way they were very much the same.

"If your father can't come," Elizabeth volunteered, "Nicholas and I will be happy to escort you."

"Escort you where, my dear?" said a voice from the doorway. Slightly stooped and silver-haired, her father walked down the aisle toward the podium, the gold-rimmed monocle he wore bobbing on a chain around his neck.

Cait smiled at him warmly. "Father, I didn't expect to see you until later this afternoon. You know the ladies, of course. Have you met His Grace, the Duke of Beldon?"

Harmon turned, gave the duke a perfunctory smile. "I believe we met at Lord Chester's."

"Donovan—there you are! I wondered where you had got off to." Her father's business partner, Phillip Rutherford, stood in the open doorway. As always, he was dressed impeccably, his light brown hair newly cut and carefully groomed. He glanced at the others. "I'm sorry. I hope I'm not interrupting."

"Of course not, Phillip. Do come in."

Talmadge walked in with a smile. He was always friendly, and he was certainly enthusiastic about her father's project, yet Cait still wasn't sure exactly how she felt about him.

"I'm certain you must know everyone here," her father said.

Talmadge glanced at the others, his attention pausing for a moment on the duke. "Yes, of course."

"Lord Talmadge and I met for the first time at Lord Crutchfield's," the duke said. "Surprising that we hadn't met before."

"Actually, we met some years back," the baron corrected, "at a ball hosted by your father on the occasion of your twenty-first birthday. It was quite an affair, as I recall. With at least five hundred guests in attendance, it is hardly surprising you don't remember."

"Actually, I recall very little of what happened that night," Beldon remarked with a faint curve of his lips. "Though I have a rather strong, highly unpleasant memory of the price I paid the following day."

Cait smiled inwardly, liking the fact the duke was a man who could laugh at himself.

"I was just now in the process of inviting Miss Harmon and her father to a horse race day after the morrow," he said to the baron. "Perhaps you would join us."

"I appreciate the invitation, but the professor and I have a previous engagement."

"In that case, perhaps Caitlin could come with Lord Ravenworth and myself," Elizabeth put in smoothly.

Her father gave Cait an indulgent smile. "If that is your wish, my dear." It had been years since he had forbidden her to do anything. She was used to living life on her own and she liked it exactly that way.

"The matter, then, is settled." Beldon tossed a last smile Cait's way and her stomach did a funny little flip. "Ladies . . . until day after the morrow." Making a slight bow, he turned and strode out of the lecture hall. It was strange, the way the room seemed empty without him.

Cait luncheoned with Elizabeth and Maggie then returned to the museum to compile a list of ancient Roman texts that might contain information about the necklace.

Though she tried to work, her thoughts strayed more than once to the upcoming horse race and seeing Rand Clayton again.

She tried to tell herself she had no choice but to go. The duke was a wealthy man. If he contributed to the expedition, the sum could be substantial.

But the truth went far beyond that. Cait was attracted to Rand Clayton in a way she had never been to another man. One look from those hot brown eyes made moth wings swirl in her stomach. A single compliment in that honey-over-gravel voice and her mind turned to mush.

Those feelings were new to her and she wanted to explore them. Marriage and family were not a part of her future. With her father to think of, Cait had accepted that fact. But what would it hurt to experience a little of what it was like to be a woman?

What could it possibly hurt?

Cait ignored the shiver of warning that told her it might be more painful than she could imagine.

The April sun was unseasonably warm, shining down on the first budding flowers of spring. *The sky is nearly as blue as it is over Santo Amaro,* Cait thought. She walked beside Elizabeth Warring as they crossed an expanse of lawn, heading for the race course.

She straightened her plum silk bonnet and tugged at her kidskin gloves, enjoying the feel of such feminine clothes, so far from the simple skirt and blouse she wore on the island. She smiled to imagine what the ladies would say if they could see her working on her hands and knees in the warm tropical sun. She wondered what Beldon would say.

Then she glanced across the lawn and suffered a sudden hitch in her breath at the impressive sight of him. Dressed in a dark brown tailcoat trimmed with gold braid, tight buckskin breeches, and knee-high boots, he was the most magnificent man she had ever seen.

Elizabeth must have guessed what she was thinking for

she tossed Cait a sideways glance. "You like him, don't you?"

Cait shrugged her shoulders, doing her best to appear nonchalant. "I'm intrigued by him. I'm not certain that is the same."

"You like him," Elizabeth repeated. "Admit it."

Cait smiled. "All right, for argument's sake, let us say I like him. Is there any reason I should not?"

Elizabeth laughed. "There are at least a dozen reasons you should not, but they all have to do with being sensible and nothing at all to do with the matter of his character, which I can personally tell you is of the highest order. The problem with Rand, at least where you are concerned, is that he is not in the marriage mart. He says he isn't ready and I don't really think he is. He is obviously, however, extremely attracted to you."

A little thrill went through her that she shouldn't have felt. "I imagine he is attracted to any number of women."

"I wouldn't put it quite that way. More, I would say, any number of women are attracted to him." Elizabeth's gaze moved toward a woman approaching the duke. "Take Lady Hadleigh, for instance. She and Rand were an item of gossip for a while. She actually believed he would marry her, but I don't think he ever considered it."

Caitlin studied the woman with the thick black hair, heart-shaped face, and rosebud lips. "She's beautiful."

"Yes, she is. But she and Rand were not at all well suited. Underneath that tough exterior, Rand is extremely sensitive. Charlotte never understood that."

Sensitive. Cait pondered the word. Somehow it seemed incongruous with a powerful man like the duke.

"Normally, I would warn you away from him," Elizabeth said. "Considering the way he looks at you, that would certainly be the wiser course. But you are different from other women. I see something in you that reminds me of me. Whatever happens with Rand, I think you can handle it."

Cait hadn't time to reply for he spotted them just then,

waved a brief good-bye to Lady Hadleigh, and started striding toward them. He greeted Elizabeth briefly and made a perfect bow over Cait's hand.

"Good morning, ladies. You are both looking lovely today."

Her cheeks went warm. It was ridiculous. The man was merely being polite. It amazed her that he could cause such an instant reaction with only a few simple words.

"I expected you earlier," he said. "I had nearly given you up."

"We were running a bit behind schedule," Elizabeth explained. "Nicholas came on ahead. In fact, he should be here already." She spotted him just then, in conversation with several other men. He waved and broke away when he saw them and started walking in their direction. "Here he comes now." Elizabeth smiled brightly. "It appears we have all arrived and apparently just in time. It looks as though they are preparing to get under way."

"We'd better hurry if we don't want to miss the start." The duke extended an arm and Cait took it. Dressed in a plum silk day dress that matched her bonnet, she let him guide her up the steps into the grandstand. He settled himself beside her while Elizabeth sat next to her husband.

"They'll be running three heats," the duke explained. "Whichever horse finishes first in two out of three wins the purse."

"The purse?"

"Money put up by the horses' owners. In this case, ten thousand pounds."

Ten thousand pounds. It was a fortune. With that much money, her father could finance *several* expeditions. A stirring at the end of the race course drew her attention to the gate and two grooms appeared, each leading a prancing horse, one a gleaming black, the other a lovely, long-necked bay.

"Look! They're heading toward the starting line." Cait's pulse leapt with excitement. She had never been to a horse race, hadn't imagined it could be so rousing. She smoothed her palms over her skirt to wipe away the dampness and tried to calm her pounding heart.

"The bay is mine," the duke said, "a stallion named Sir Harry. He's running against the Earl of Mountriden's Thoroughbred, Chimera."

"He's beautiful. They both are."

Beldon smiled. "You said before that you liked to ride."

"I used to love it. My grandfather gave me a pretty little sorrel mare for my fourteenth birthday. Unfortunately, we had to leave him behind when we left Boston for Egypt."

His eyebrows drew slightly together. "Did you like it there? It's hard to imagine a girl of that age in a place so foreign as that."

"In a way, I loved it. It was like living on another, completely different planet. But women there have little freedom. I didn't enjoy that part in the least."

He chuckled softly. "You seem to value your independence more than most."

"Perhaps that was the lesson I learned in Egypt. Or perhaps I am simply used to being on my own. My mother died when I was ten. Father was devastated. He needed someone to look after him and I was the only one there. From that point on, I grew up very quickly."

"You've traveled quite extensively, I gather."

Cait just nodded. She could feel his eyes on her face, studying her in that disconcerting way of his, and suddenly it was hard to breathe.

She dragged in a steadying breath, summoned a casual smile. "Before Egypt, my father worked on excavating the ruins of Pompeii. Later he worked with a Danish scholar named Munter to translate the cuneiform scripts discovered in ancient Persepolis. That took us to the Netherlands and in a roundabout way to The Hague, which began Father's quest for the necklace."

"And eventually led to your time on the island."

"Yes."

"If I remember correctly, you were there for the past two years."

"Part of that time was spent in Dakar, the rest on Santo Amaro."

The duke said nothing, but he seemed to be weighing her words.

"Look—they've reached the starting line." She pointed at the race course simply to break free of that unrelenting gaze.

"So they have," he said, as if winning or losing ten thousand pounds concerned him not in the least. "The course is only a mile and a half long. Races can be as long as four miles, but it's awfully hard on the horses."

The animals danced and strained at their bits while riders and grooms fought to hold them back. As soon as the horses were even, the starting gun fired and they were away, manes and tails flying, pounding nose to nose over the hard-packed earth.

Cait's heart thundered along with the animals' hooves. Beside her, Elizabeth jumped up and down in her seat.

"Come on, Sir Harry, you can do it!"

Her husband squeezed her hand and his smile seemed to caress her. He leaned over and whispered in her ear—something about a ride she could look forward to when they got home—and Elizabeth's cheeks went crimson.

Cait was blushing, as well. She heard the duke's low rumble of mirth. "I don't think you were supposed to hear that."

Cait stared hard at the race course. "No, I don't suppose I was." The horses were making the first turn, running fairly even, the jockeys setting a difficult pace. As she had said, both animals were magnificent, their sleek coats glistening in the warm spring sun, their long, lean muscles rippling. They turned into the back stretch. Chimera pulled a little ahead, and Cait sat forward in her seat. Then Sir Harry shot out in front, staying ahead around the next turn, reaching for more speed with those long, powerful legs.

The jockeys urged them on, leaning over the horses' necks, moving with nearly the same grace as the animals beneath them. A good-sized crowd filled the stands and dozens of side bets were wagered. She could feel the excitement beginning to swell, the low rumble of voices growing louder. When the horses came into the final stretch, she could hear them approaching, their pounding hooves churning up the dirt, flinging it out behind them. Chimera was again in the lead, ahead by nearly a length, but Sir Harry was moving up with amazing speed.

Cait bit her lip, willing the duke's horse ahead. The jockeys took to their whips as they passed the stands, and the crowd surged to its feet. They were six lengths from the finish. Five. Four. Three.

"Sir Harry's pulling ahead!" Cait gripped the duke's solid forearm, her fingers digging into the sleeve of his coat, making the muscles bunch beneath. "He's going to win, Rand! He's going to win!"

"Yes . . ." he said, his voice deep and gruff. "It appears as though he is." But when she glanced up, he wasn't watching the race, he was staring at her lips, and the heat in those fierce brown eyes could have scorched her plum silk gown. For the first time, she realized she had used his first name, and embarrassed, she glanced away. She tried to recall if a man had ever looked at her in quite that same manner.

The horses burst over the finish line, Sir Harry winning by a nose, and Cait, Elizabeth, and half the crowd sent up a cheer.

"You did it!" Cait turned to him, laughing and grinning. "You won!"

A corner of his mouth curved faintly. "I believe Sir Harry deserves the credit. And he'll have to win again if I'm to go home with the purse." In unison they turned back to the track, watching as the jockey on Sir Harry's back rode him in circles to cool him down a little before the next heat.

Beldon watched intently, his eyebrows drawing together in a frown. "He's limping," he said, coming to his feet. "Something's happened." He left without further explanation, and she watched him walk over to an area of grooms and trainers who were standing next to the horses.

She turned to Elizabeth and Lord Ravenworth. "If his horse was limping, I certainly couldn't see it. How could Beldon tell from this far away?"

"Rand knows his horses." Ravenworth surveyed the scene on the track. "If he says there's a problem, you can bet there is."

Lord Mountriden left the stands to join the group and some sort of discussion arose between the earl and the duke. It was obvious the two owners were not in agreement. Cait chewed nervously on the end of her kidskin glove. Whatever was happening, the duke did not seem pleased. He started back to the stands but continued past them as if they weren't there, approaching a man sitting with a small group of observers in another part of the grandstand.

"He's talking to Lord Whitelaw," Ravenworth told her. "He's the man who's holding the stakes."

A few minutes later, Rand returned to Mountriden, handed him an envelope, turned, and walked away.

"We may as well go," he said as he approached where they sat. "There won't be any more racing here today."

"That's too bad," Elizabeth said with obvious disappointment. "I wanted to increase my bet."

"How's Sir Harry?" Cait asked anxiously, thinking of the beautiful, long-necked bay.

The duke arched a brow. "Sir Harry? Sir Harry is fine."

"But you said earlier that he was limping."

He smiled. "Not Sir Harry, love. Chimera was limping. He must have strained a tendon when he came into the final stretch."

"Chimera?" She swung back toward the track in search of the beautiful black. "No wonder I didn't notice. I presume Lord Mountriden was forced to forfeit the race."

The duke shook his head. "I forfeited. Chimera is one of the most incredible animals I've ever seen. Mountriden would have run him into the ground if he thought it meant winning. I didn't want that to happen."

Cait's insides seemed to melt. She could hardly believe she had heard him correctly. Ten thousand pounds to save an animal from injury? And the horse wasn't even his own. "What if Mountriden simply races him somewhere else?"

"He won't. The forfeit was made under the condition Chimera doesn't run again for at least two months. All side bets are off until then and at that time there'll be a rematch."

From beneath her lashes, Cait studied his handsome profile, Elizabeth Warring's words rising into her mind. *Rand is sensitive.* He had certainly proved he was caring today. It took a special sort of man to walk away from ten thousand pounds, especially when the odds were already in his favor.

Elizabeth reached over and squeezed her hand. "Well, Cait, what did you think? Did you enjoy your first horse race?"

Cait grinned. "As you Brits would say, it was smashing."

Elizabeth laughed and so did the duke. He walked Cait back to the carriage, and all the way there, she could feel his eyes on her, studying her in that way of his.

"I've got a couple of things to do before I leave," he said. "Since Nick's carriage is also here, we'll join you ladies a little later back at the town house." He lifted her hand and pressed his lips against the back. Cait felt the contact burning through her gloves. "I won't be long, Cait," he said pointedly, using her first name as earlier she had used his. "I promise."

Cait just nodded. Something had changed between them today. Something that reached deep down into the womanly part of her.

Warning bells went off in her head, but Cait refused to heed them.

FOUR

Nick Warring stood beside his best friend, Rand Clayton, watching his wife and Caitlin Harmon depart the track in Elizabeth's carriage. The duke's gaze followed the conveyance until it disappeared, and it was clear what was on his mind.

"Easy, my friend," Nick said. "Your intentions are showing, and if I'm correct, they are not the least bit honorable."

Rand laughed softly, not in the slightest surprised Nick had read him so well. They'd been friends since Oxford, and though Nick had been through some very rough times, Rand had never failed him. There were few secrets between them.

"I won't deny I find Cait Harmon attractive," Beldon said.

"I realize you're looking for information about Talmadge. But if you're using the girl simply as a means to an end, it is hardly fair to Cait."

"We're still not sure what part Cait Harmon is playing in all of this. She may well be involved up to her pretty little neck in the baron's latest swindle."

"You still aren't certain there is a swindle. Professor Harmon's expedition may be perfectly legitimate."

"Not a chance," Rand said as they walked over the grass toward the paddock. "You read that report. Talmadge has a history of investments that by all accounts fail, yet he and his partners seem to wind up making plenty of money. Now he has teamed up with Harmon. There can only be one reason."

"And Caitlin?"

"I'll grant it's hard to believe she has any part in this, but it's possible. And as you said, whatever her connection to Harmon and Talmadge, she could certainly prove useful."

"The girl is an innocent, Rand, and you are scarcely in the marriage mart. I believe it was you who once warned me against trifling with a young, unmarried lady."

"Caitlin is American. They approach life differently than we do."

"That's your excuse? Cait is different, therefore she's fair game?"

Rand frowned. "That's not what I meant."

"Then what do you mean?"

"For your information, I wouldn't think of taking advantage of Caitlin Harmon. On the other hand, Cait is the sort of woman who appears to do as she pleases. She seems to know what she wants out of life, and if that is the case, it may alter the situation."

"Double-talk, Rand. You want the girl and you intend to have her. I'm hardly the one to criticize, having been in a similar situation. I'm simply warning you to be careful. Cait doesn't deserve to be hurt."

Rand said nothing to that, but his dark brows pulled together. Rand was not the sort to take advantage of an innocent young girl. Though he kept his feelings well hidden, there was a gentle side to his nature. He wouldn't want to hurt Cait Harmon. On the other hand, he felt a terrible sense of failure regarding his young cousin's death and Cait Harmon might prove useful in discovering the truth of what had occurred.

Nick just hoped, where Caitlin was concerned, Rand's conscience would guide him in the proper direction.

Cait sat beside her father on the sofa in the small private salon in the suite of rooms Baron Talmadge had taken at

Grillon's Hotel in Albemarle Street. The rooms were done in the French style, in shades of olive and gold with heavy velvet draperies and marble-topped tables. Everything in England seemed incredibly ornate and elegant, but then, after the Spartan comforts of her travels, perhaps she appreciated the luxury more than most.

"What do you think, Phillip?" Her father's question interrupted her thoughts and drew her attention to the dialogue going on in the room.

"I'm afraid we are as yet some distance from our goal," Talmadge said. "Your equipment is old and outdated. We'll need money for food and supplies, preferably enough to last a year. Porters and workmen will need to be hired. We'll need money for personal expenses—clothing, boots, and other incidentals."

Sitting at a chair in front of a small French writing desk, the baron studied the list in front of him, adding an item now and then. Light from the brass oil lamp glinted against the faint traces of silver in the brown hair at his temples.

"Lord Geoffrey is new to all this," the baron said, referring to their latest supporter, Geoffrey St. Anthony, second son of the Marquess of Wester. "But as you and your daughter well know, an undertaking of this magnitude is extremely costly." Talmadge was a handsome man, Cait supposed, polished and refined. Any number of women seemed to find him attractive, though his conversations were generally boring, talk of the expedition and finding the necklace, gossip he had heard at some social affair, the latest *on dit*—as he called it—among the fashionably elite.

"How much longer do you think it will take to raise the sum you need?" Lord Geoffrey asked, leaning forward in his chair. He was perhaps twenty-five, with light blond hair and an easy smile. He was extremely good-looking, in a boyish, naïve sort of way, and so enamored with the idea of finding the treasure, he had volunteered to accompany them and pay his own expenses.

"I should hope, in perhaps another month, we shall have the funds we need," Talmadge answered. "Our cause has been steadily gaining support. Caitlin's lecture spurred several large contributions from the ladies' husbands—and it would certainly seem she is making progress with the duke."

That brought her up short. "The duke?"

"Of course, my dear. Should Beldon decide to contribute, the amount could be sizable and due directly to you."

"But I . . . I barely know the man. If you wish to approach him—"

"He seems taken with you, Cait. He attended your lecture and it was obvious he approved. Simply be nice to the man. When the time is right, I'll approach him, if you are hesitant to do so."

Geoffrey St. Anthony leapt to his feet. "It is hardly fair to ask Miss Harmon to spend time with a man like the duke simply to raise money. Why, the man has a notorious reputation. Where women are concerned, he is one of the worst rakes in London. Miss Harmon is a lady—not some sort of . . . some sort of . . ."

"We take your meaning, Lord Geoffrey." Talmadge's voice held a note of irritation. "We are not asking Caitlin to do anything she doesn't feel comfortable with, merely to lend whatever support she is able."

Cait worked to muster a smile. "I'll be happy to do what I can." As she had always done. Before Phillip Rutherford came along, she had often helped her father raise funds. Why it seemed different where Beldon was concerned, she couldn't say. She simply felt that it was.

The meeting went on. Plans were made. Lord Geoffrey volunteered to make a list of people they could contact, then began suggesting parties they might attend to gain support, but Cait's mind had begun to wander. What was it about Beldon? How could the mere mention of his name send her thoughts spinning in confusion? At times it was irritating. At other times it was intriguing.

Lord Geoffrey had called him a rake. Elizabeth had

mentioned the legion of women who constantly pursued him. It was dangerous to risk involvement with a man like that.

Her memory stirred, dredged up stories she had heard of her uncles. Unlike her father, who'd been faithful and adoring and loved his wife almost to the point of obsession, both her mother's brothers and several of her cousins were notorious when it came to women, leaving a trail of broken hearts from Boston to New York.

Rand Clayton was surely a rogue like the rest. Still, there was something that drew her, made her want to trust him. And irrationally, she wanted to see him again.

She wondered if she would hear from him or if he had already tired of his subtle pursuit and gone on to more certain quarry.

The days were slipping past, each of them precious to Cait. At Maggie's insistence, they joined Elizabeth Warring for a day of shopping. Though Cait was hardly wealthy, she had inherited a small trust fund from her grandmother, which she used for clothing and incidentals, and times when her father's money ran out, which happened far too often. The money gave her some small measure of security in a life where she'd had almost none.

In a gown of yellow silk with a matching pagoda parasol, Cait walked next to her friends along crowded Bond Street carrying an armload of packages.

"I've a quick stop to make," Elizabeth told them after they had luncheoned at the August Tea Shop, a charming little restaurant around the corner on Oxford. "I've a message for Nick from a friend, and he is only a few blocks away." She grinned at them. "Besides, I think Cait might enjoy the show."

Forgoing the carriage, which they loaded to overflowing with their purchases, Elizabeth herded them back down Bond into a red-brick building with a sign above the door—Gentleman Jackson's Parlour.

Pausing at the entrance, Maggie looked uncertain, but

Elizabeth merely laughed. The moment Cait stepped into the high-ceilinged interior, she understood why as her astonished gaze flew over an amazing assortment of sweaty, half-naked men busily pounding away at each other.

"That's Nicky and Rand," Maggie whispered, pointing toward a roped-off area on the opposite side of the room where two bare-chested men bobbed and weaved, ducking first one way and then the other, trying very hard, it appeared to Cait, to beat each other up.

"Good heavens." It was all she could think to say. She was surprised she could find words at all.

"They're sparring," Elizabeth unnecessarily explained. "They come down here to improve their boxing skills at least once a week."

Cait knew she was staring but she couldn't seem to stop herself. Nick Warring was beautifully built, tall and lean, dark complexioned and elegantly muscled, but it was the other man who captured her attention. Taller even than Lord Ravenworth and more powerfully built, with wide, heavily muscled shoulders and a chest that rippled with sinew whenever he moved, Rand Clayton was magnificent. He was covered in gleaming sweat, and a mat of damp brown chest hair glistened in the light of the lantern that hung above the ring.

He glanced up just then, spotted her standing there in her bright yellow dress, and for an instant he stopped moving. She could have sworn Lord Ravenworth grinned as he landed a solid blow to the Duke of Beldon's chin.

Elizabeth burst out laughing. "I believe you have distracted him."

"Rand isn't going to like that," Maggie said, casting a worried glance toward her brother, who was receiving for his sly blow a pounding in return.

A bell sounded just then and the round was over. Both men touched gloves and Cait could see they were grinning. "I guess they aren't hurt," she said, her own heart beating in a slightly too rapid cadence that had nothing to do with exertion and everything to do with the magnificent, half-naked duke who smiled at her from the ring.

"It's a wonder they haven't knocked themselves silly." Maggie said, rolling her pretty blue eyes. "I think anyone who enjoys getting punched in the face is a bit soft in the head."

"Too true, dear girl," Elizabeth agreed, charging forward again. "But one of them is my husband and the other my friend, so I guess I shall forgive them."

Rand ducked under the ropes that circled the ring, grabbed a linen towel off a nearby chair, and strode toward them. Fascinated, Cait stared, her gaze roaming over all that hard male flesh, past incredibly wide shoulders to a flat, ridged belly and narrow hips. He wore skintight leggings that outlined the muscles in his calves and thighs and gloved the rather substantial bulge of his sex.

Her glance lingered there a little longer than it should have. Heat rushed into her cheeks and she jerked her gaze away. When she looked at the duke, she saw amusement in his eyes and something more, something hot and intense. It was obvious he had spotted her interest in the masculine part of him any lady would have ignored, and Cait turned away, hoping to hide her embarrassment.

If Beldon sensed her discomfort, he pretended not to. "Good afternoon, ladies." He smiled at the three of them, but his eyes remained on Cait. "What a pleasant surprise."

"A surprise—yes. Apparently it was that." Lips twitching, Elizabeth reached up and touched the bruise on Rand's chin. "I believe you can blame that bit of bad luck on Cait."

He rubbed the tender spot. "Yes . . . I believe I can." His mouth curved up. "You owe me, Miss Harmon. No woman has a right to be that distracting. How shall I make you pay?"

Cait's pulse inched up a notch. "You can hardly blame me, Your Grace, for simply forgetting to duck."

Elizabeth laughed. "Come on, Maggie. We'll let them work out who's to blame. In the meantime, I believe your husband just walked in. He's over there talking to Nicholas. Shall we see if we might distract *them* a bit?"

Maggie nodded. "Good idea . . . though I doubt either of them will be pleased to see us. I don't think Andrew or Nicky consider a boxing establishment the proper place for a lady."

Elizabeth just grinned, and Cait thought how lucky she was to have made two such wonderful friends.

"Well?" The duke's seductive voice wrapped around her, returning her attention to him.

"Well what?"

"Well, how do you intend to make up for your untimely arrival?" A sleek brown eyebrow arched up. "A ride in the park, perhaps? Or better yet, a picnic. There's a lovely spot I know along the Thames, though it's a bit of a drive out of the city. I'll have Cook prepare luncheon and we'll make a day of it. What do you say?"

What she should say was a resounding no. A drive in the park was one thing, chaperoned by the dozens of people who were always about. Being alone with Rand Clayton was another matter entirely.

He used the towel to wipe the sweat from his forehead, then draped it over those impossibly broad shoulders. "Unless, of course, you're afraid."

She recognized the lure, the challenge. Almost from the start, he had sensed that about her, that a challenge was something she could rarely resist. "Should I be?"

The towel moved again, then paused at the back of his neck. "I'd never do anything, Cait, you didn't want me to do."

She wasn't sure if that was comforting or not. When it came to Rand Clayton she had every reason to be wary. But staring at his solid masculinity, her insides oddly liquid and overly warm, she was even more wary of herself.

Still, she wanted to go with him—there was no denying that. And she had never been a coward.

"All right, then, a picnic." But it wouldn't be as easy as it seemed. Her father would barely notice her departure, but Lord and Lady Trent would surely disapprove. An unchaperoned day with the duke—or any other man for that matter—was hardly an acceptable course. "I've a couple of matters to attend at the museum in the morning. Why don't you meet me there?"

He understood exactly her attempt to be discreet and his mouth curved with obvious anticipation. "I'll call for you at ten." He made a slight bow of his head and Cait wet lips that suddenly felt too dry.

"I look forward to it," she said, and it was the truth.

Rand paced back and forth in front of Ephram Barclay's desk. The room was cool. A layer of clouds had moved in, and the late afternoon had turned chilly, yet his foul temper made him overly warm. "It's damned hard to swallow, I can tell you. For a while, I actually entertained the thought the man might be an imposter."

"Sorry to disappoint you, but that doesn't appear to be the case. Phillip is the second son of Edwin Rutherford, the late Lord Talmadge. Apparently, he served as an officer in His Majesty's Navy until his older brother, Victor, died of pneumonia four years ago. He returned shortly thereafter to claim his title and inheritance."

Rand waved the papers that he had been reading, the latest Bow Street runner's report. "Which according to McConnell was in a particularly sorry state."

Ephram pulled off his wire-rimmed spectacles, unhooking them carefully from each of his slightly too large ears. "Victor had a penchant for gambling. There wasn't much money left by the time Phillip became lord. He sold the family estate in Kent to pay off debts."

Rand stopped pacing and turned to face him. "And what is the current state of his finances?"

"He has money in the bank, but not an exorbitant sum. He earned a good deal from the investments he made over the years, and of course from his association with Merriweather Shipping, but the money seems to have disappeared. Talmadge has a taste for the finer things in life. Chances are good he simply spent it."

"Which means, he is going to need more," Rand said. "What better way than fleecing members of the upper class in a swindle that appeals to their philanthropic nature—donations to what he calls 'an extremely worthy cause'?"

"Perhaps that is exactly what it is."

"And perhaps Donovan Harmon and Phillip Rutherford simply mean to take the money and run. Perhaps the good professor hasn't the slightest intention of returning to Santo Amaro Island—assuming he was actually there in the first place."

"Oh, he was there—and his daughter with him. Our man McConnell has spoken to an explorer by the name of Sir Monty Walpole. You may have read of his discoveries at Pompeii, where he also worked with the professor."

Rand sank heavily down in a chair. "I know who he is."

"Sir Monty is convinced the professor has every chance of finding Cleopatra's Necklace. In fact, there is a distinct possibility he'll be returning with the expedition. I'm sorry, Your Grace, but apparently it's legitimate."

Rand said nothing. Every instinct in his body shouted that Talmadge was a thief and a sharper. And yet there was no proof.

"It's a swindle. I know it. I just haven't figured out how it's going to work." But he was damned sure going to find out. He wasn't about to stand by and let young Jonathan's death go unavenged. Talmadge was a fraud and a cheat. One way or another, Rand intended to prove it.

With a brief farewell to Ephram, he headed for the door, his thoughts churning, swinging from Rutherford to Harmon, and eventually to Cait. She seemed too straightforward, too intelligent, to be involved in any sort of swindle. Still, her father was surely involved, and from what he had learned, Cait would do anything for him.

Nick believed she was an innocent, but Rand had his doubts. Innocent young women didn't accept unchaperoned assignations with men, yet Cait had readily accepted, even arranged matters so there would be no questions asked.

For a single brief instant, he had actually hoped she would refuse. He wanted her to be exactly as he imagined her, intelligent and charming, and not the least conniving. But she had agreed and Rand wondered why.

He hoped it was simply because she desired him, that she felt at least some measure of the hot, restless hunger he felt for her.

Tomorrow he would know more. *Tomorrow*.

A wave of anticipation rolled through him, followed by a fierce jolt of heat.

FIVE

Cait tied the strings of her wide-brimmed, coal-scuttle bonnet, waved a brief good-bye to Maggie, and stepped out on the porch of the town house. Guilt made her chest feel tight. Her palms were sweating, her heart beating a little faster than it should have been.

She hated to lie to her friends, but it was the easiest solution by far. She sighed as she crossed the paving stones and climbed aboard the carriage the marquess had provided, settling herself in for the short ride to the museum. At least they had finally resigned themselves to her "traipsing about," as they put it, without a chaperone.

She'd spent too many years on her own to succumb to that bit of nonsense.

Cait gazed out the window of the carriage as it rolled through the crowded London streets. A warm spring morning turned the sky an azure blue, yet the beautiful day did nothing to ease her nerves. She should have declined the invitation, she knew. It was the right thing, the acceptable thing to do, and the Duke of Beldon knew it. He was challenging her again—daring her to ignore social dictates—which was exactly why she had agreed.

Arriving at the museum, she sent the carriage on its way then waited out in front for the duke to appear. The breeze tugged at her mint green skirts and she adjusted her bonnet, hoping the little cluster of leaves and flowers on the brim was sitting where it should be. Beneath the brim, her gold-tipped red hair, unfashionably long, curled loosely down her back, pulled up on the sides with ivory combs she had purchased from a black-skinned street vendor in Dakar.

Her tension grew. She began to pace the marble floor beneath the portico in front of the museum. She shouldn't be there, she thought again. She should have said no, should have done what was proper—just this once—but when she glanced down the street and saw the duke striding toward her, tall and imposing and more handsome than any man should be, her heart stopped for several long seconds and suddenly she knew why she was there.

"I thought you might have come to your senses," he said with a smile when he reached her, closer to the truth than he could guess.

Cait laughed. "Actually, I did—just a few minutes ago—but I have a feeling it's too late."

The duke just grinned. "Far too late, Miss Harmon. But I promise, by the end of the day, you'll be glad you agreed to come."

Cait smiled. She was already glad, and she liked the way he looked at her as he tucked her gloved hand into the crook of his arm and started leading her away. His carriage was waiting just down the block—a smart black, high-perch phaeton with small gold wreaths painted in a delicate pattern along the sides. It was pulled by a pair of high-stepping, perfectly matched bay horses.

The rig was stylish and racy, and all Cait could think was, *Good Lord, no driver, no footman—the two of us will truly be alone.* Her nerves returned full force, making her hands faintly tremble. Mentally, she began to form some sort of protest, some plausible excuse not to go, but already he was lifting her up, settling her on the red leather seat, rounding the carriage and climbing up beside her.

He picked up the reins and wove them through his leather-gloved fingers as if he had done it a thousand times. "Ready?"

Cait swallowed hard and managed a nod. Just as she'd

feared, it was too late to turn back now. "As ready as I'll ever be, I suppose."

"Then we're off." He flicked the reins and the horses broke into a high-stepping trot. He swung the conveyance into the traffic with the same ease he held the reins, dodging freight wagons, hackney carriages, fruit vendors, and coal merchants. In a very short time, they'd reached the edge of the city and were bowling over roads bordered by open rolling fields.

At a quaint little stone-walled village, they waved to a group of schoolchildren and were chased by a barking dog. They passed a hay wagon and raced a post chaise, overtaking it in a wide spot in the road, the passengers leaning out the windows to wave them on.

Her heart was pounding, excitement spilling through her. She looked over at the duke, who threw back his head and laughed with sheer delight, and realized she was actually enjoying herself.

In truth, she was exhilarated. The fresh air, the duke's expert driving, and his obvious pleasure in her company had set her fears to rest. They spoke of casual things: the weather, the glorious countryside, his well-mannered horses.

"So what was it like?" he finally asked, returning the horses to a slower gait. "Spending so much time away from home?"

Cait leaned back against the seat, lulled by the rhythm of the wheels and the clip-clop of hooves. "That's a difficult question. In truth, I haven't had a real home in years—not since my mother died. After that, my father began to travel and I, of course, went with him. With Mother gone, foreign countries seemed to hold some special appeal for him. Solace, perhaps, escape from his grief. For me, after a few years of roaming from place to place, the strange became the norm."

The duke turned onto a less traveled road, slowed the horses to a walk, and Cait caught a glimpse of the river, a long, wide ribbon of blue that disappeared through the trees.

"From your lecture," he said, "you sounded as though you'd enjoy a respite from all this moving about. I should think you'd rather return to America than go back to Santo Amaro."

She did want that. Or at any rate, she wanted to be somewhere that she could call home—at least for a while. "What I want isn't important. My father feels certain he's going to find the necklace. If he does, it will validate everything he's worked for."

"What about you, Cait? Isn't your happiness also important?"

She shrugged her shoulders, a little uneasy with the subject. "I love him. He needs my help to achieve his goal and I intend to give it to him. I'll do everything in my power to see that he succeeds."

Beldon studied her as if there was more he wished to ask but wasn't certain he should. Then he was smiling and the moment passed. A little over an hour after they'd left the city, they turned down a narrow lane that carried them to the edge of the river. In an area of deep green grass secluded by a row of leafy willows, the Thames rolled past. Sunlight glittered in golden tones on the surface of the water and near the opposite shore, several small boats floated downstream with the current.

"It's beautiful here," she said, enchanted by her surroundings. "However did you find this place?"

He grinned and the dimple appeared. "I own it. The land is part of River Willows, an estate that was entailed to me with the dukedom." He pulled the phaeton to a halt, set the brake, and wrapped the reins around it, then jumped down and rounded the carriage. Big hands clamped around her waist and he lifted her out of the phaeton, but instead of setting her down, he lowered her slowly, holding her so close her body brushed the length of his. She could feel the hard ridges across his flat belly, the long muscles in his thighs. Goose bumps rose on her skin, and an odd, melting sensation slid into her stomach.

She tipped her head back to see his face, and her breath caught at the look in those gold-flecked brown eyes. For an instant, she thought he would kiss her. Instead, he set her firmly on her feet and stepped away.

"I hope you're hungry," he said with a casual smile that didn't quite match the husky timbre of his voice. "Cook sent enough food to feed your father's entire expedition for at least several weeks."

Cait laughed but it came out a little breathy. She could feel the heat of his hands, the brush of that hard-muscled body as if he still held her. "Thanks to you, I'm far beyond hungry. Passing that post chaise as if it were tied to a tree definitely helped work up an appetite."

The duke chuckled softly. "Most women would have been screaming for me to stop. I got the distinct impression you would have liked me to go faster."

She smiled. "I wasn't afraid. You're a very skillful driver."

He seemed pleased at the compliment, though he didn't say so. Reaching into the back of the phaeton, he drew out a soft woolen blanket and handed it over. "You carry this. I'll get the food." Plucking out a big wicker basket, he led her across the grass beneath the long drooping branches of a willow. Cait spread the blanket and the duke began to set out foodstuffs: cold roast capon, pickled salmon, sausages, boiled eggs, apples, a generous hunk of Cheshire cheese, a crusty loaf of bread, plum pudding and gingerbread for dessert.

"You're right—there's enough here for a medium-sized army."

"A regiment, at the very least." He grinned. "Shall we see if we might do it justice?"

Seating herself on the blanket, she curled her legs up beneath her, removed her hat and tossed it away. "I hate to wear the blasted things. Even when I'm working, I constantly forget to put one on. I suppose that's why my nose is so freckled."

Rand paused in the process of pulling the cork from a bottle of wine. "You look fetching in freckles, Miss Harmon—but then you'd look good in most anything." His eyes locked on her face. "Or better yet—in nothing at all."

Cait's cheeks went warm. Something fluttered in the pit of her stomach. Accepting the plate he had filled and set in front of her, she picked at the capon, ate a bit of salmon and a piece of cheese. "Everything is delicious."

"Tansy is a joy. She's been with us for nearly twenty years."

"My mother was a very good cook. We had kitchen help, of course, but Mother loved to bake—cookies, cakes, pastries. Even after all these years, I can still remember exactly how they tasted."

"My mother died of a fever just this past year," Rand said. "She was quite a woman—protective, intelligent, determined. I think of her often—and I miss her sorely."

Cait felt a tug at her heart. "My mother was beautiful, and she was the kindest woman I've ever known. She drowned during a storm when our carriage went off the road and overturned in a stream."

"You were with her at the time?"

She nodded, trying to ignore the lump beginning to rise in her throat. Eleven years had passed, yet the memory was as clear as the day it happened. "I was pinned under one of the wheels. I would have drowned if my mother hadn't been so determined. She went under again and again until I was freed. By then her strength was gone. She was washed downstream. They didn't find her body until two days later. She died saving my life."

Rand's gaze clung to hers and it was dark with sympathy. "As much as you obviously cared for her, that must have been extremely hard on you."

Cait closed her eyes for a moment, seeing old images she didn't want to see, fighting painful memories. "It was even harder on my father. He worshiped my mother from the day he met her. He was grief-stricken after the accident, completely inconsolable. The worst of it was, it was my fault she died. If she hadn't sacrificed herself for me, she would still be alive today."

The goblet of wine Rand was holding paused halfway to his lips. "Surely you don't blame yourself for what happened."

Cait looked down, toyed with the food on her plate. "How could I not?"

Astonishment roughened his voice. "Forgodsake, Cait, you were a child. Your mother was responsible for you. She loved you. Of course she would do her best to save you."

Cait trembled inside. How had they ever gotten onto this subject? "Perhaps that is so, but it was terrible for my father. After Mother was gone, he had no one to turn to, no one to help him but me. I was all he had left. In a way, I still am."

"And you are still putting his interests ahead of your own."

Cait said nothing. She owed her father. Because of her, he had lost the woman he loved. It was her fault and nothing could ever change that.

The duke reached for her hand, gave it a gentle squeeze. "I admire your dedication, Cait. But you've a life of your own to consider. You might remember that."

She dragged in a shaky breath and reached for her wine, took a sip and gazed off toward the river. They ate for a time in silence. It was something about him she liked, that they could enjoy the quiet as much as the conversation. When they finished their meal, he took her hand and urged her to her feet.

"Why don't we walk for a while?"

She nodded. "I'd like that."

Rand led her down to the river and they strolled along the bank, listening to the water lapping at the reeds. "How is the expedition progressing?" he asked.

"Better than we expected. Lord Talmadge has been a tremendous help."

His brows drew slightly together and she wondered

why it was that the baron's name always seemed to have that effect on him.

"Will he be going with you?"

"I'm not sure. I know my father would love to have him along."

"What would he do? The baron is hardly a scholar."

"We'll need men to oversee the workers, people to handle disbursement of the monies and supplies. My father has never been good at that sort of thing. He trusts Lord Talmadge. It would comfort him to have the man with us."

The duke's look seemed pensive. Cait wondered why. She started to pursue the subject, then thought better of it. Beldon knew less of Talmadge than she did. Besides, his opinion didn't really matter. It was her father's wishes that counted.

They walked a little away from the river, along an overgrown path lined with clusters of tiny white and yellow flowers, ending up in a secluded glen. With every step she took, she could feel the duke's presence beside her, all heat and drive and magnetic appeal. He drew her in that way, as if she were some malleable metal and he a powerful magnet.

Hoping her thoughts didn't show, she studied her surroundings and caught sight of a perky little bird with rust-colored wings and a long white tail. It landed on a branch above her head and her gaze lingered there.

"Do you like birds?" he asked.

"Oh, yes, I like them very much, though I don't know a whole lot about them."

"That one's a whitethroat. Pretty little thing, isn't it?"

"It's lovely." Another bird appeared a few feet away, a stumpy, short-tailed creature with a blue-gray crown. "Do you know the name of that one, as well?"

He smiled. "Nuthatch. They're tree climbers. Rather fun to watch."

Cait's brow arched up. "How is it you know so much

about birds? I wouldn't think a man in your position would take the time to learn."

Faint color rose in his cheeks. Beldon cleared his throat and looked off through the trees. "My interest is rather recent. Nick's wife, Elizabeth, has always loved birds. Once she began talking about them, pointing out the names and telling me a little about each one, I found I enjoyed them, as well."

"I think that's wonderful."

A corner of his mouth curved up. "Do you? My father would have abhorred the idea. He would have considered it unmanly to cultivate any fondness beyond shooting them. I do hunt, of course. But I also enjoy simply watching them as we are now."

A feeling of warmth settled over her. Perhaps Elizabeth was right. Perhaps the Duke of Beldon did have a sensitive nature. He was certainly not the self-centered, overblown aristocrat that she had once believed.

He looked down, studied her face. Something shifted in his features. His eyes grew dark and intense. "I enjoy watching the birds, but there is something else I'd like far more. Something I've been thinking about since the moment I saw you across the room that first night."

Her pulse took a leap. Unconsciously, she moistened her lips. "What . . . what is that?"

"I've wanted to kiss you, Cait. I've waited for just the right moment. I don't want to wait any longer." And then she was in his arms, his mouth coming down, warm and silky, and softer than she had imagined. Her stomach dropped away and her fingers curled into the lapels of his coat.

He was so incredibly tall! When he deepened the kiss, she rose on tiptoe and slid her arms around his neck. The kiss went on and on, his tongue sweeping in, making her legs feel weak. She was trembling, her heart pounding raggedly. Warmth and softness seemed to mix, growing hotter and sweeter, and a funny little moaning sound bubbled up from her throat.

Rand's hold tightened and he deepened the kiss, slanting his mouth over hers first one way and then the other. She'd been kissed before. A student at the college in Boston where her father had taught, a young British officer stationed in Dakar. Innocent kisses, demanding nothing, restrained kisses respectful of her youth and her father's position.

There was nothing of restraint in the duke's fiery kiss. There was everything of demand and need, and it burned like a wildfire through her blood. She kissed him back with the same fierce need, tentatively touched her tongue to his, and heard him groan. He tasted of sweet red wine. His mouth felt hot and male and incredibly erotic.

"God, Caitie," he whispered, breaking away to kiss the side of her neck. "Do you know how much I want you? I think about it day and night."

The words made her heart beat faster, made her insides quiver and melt. She laced her trembling fingers through his hair and opened to another passionate kiss. She could feel the hardness of his thighs, the muscles in his shoulders expanding and contracting beneath her hands. Heat swirled in her belly, sank into her bones, seeped out through her limbs.

His tongue stroked deeply, expertly, and her legs turned wobbly. She thought for an instant they might not hold her up.

Strong arms steadied her even as he took her mouth in another ravishing kiss. She never heard the sound of the buttons at the back of her dress popping open, barely felt the slight breeze against her burning skin. Her gown fell away, and he slid it off her shoulders, but it was the heat of his hand, cupping her breast through her thin lawn chemise, that alerted her to the danger.

Cait stiffened, suddenly uncertain, knowing she should stop him. Rand gentled her with soft, nibbling kisses and soothing whispered words. He massaged her nipple, worked it between his fingers, and little tugs of fire slid into her belly. Lowering his head, he took the rigid bud into his mouth, wetting the fabric, using his teeth to nip and tug. Cait was sure she would swoon.

"Rand . . ." she whispered, clinging to his neck, nearly sobbing at the pleasure rolling through her.

He kissed her again, so thoroughly her muscles turned to mush. All the while, his hands massaged her breasts, lifting and molding, testing the weight, making her numb and dizzy.

He nibbled the side of her neck, teased the lobe of an ear. "River Willows is just over the rise," he said softly. "The house is empty—only a few of the servants remain. Come with me, Cait. Let me make love to you. Let me show you how good it can be between us."

She was breathing hard, barely able to grasp what he was saying. Then the truth of her situation began to dawn. Rand had brought her here, to one of his estates. He intended to make love to her—as he had done to a score of other women. He was a rogue, a womanizer. Sweet God, what was she doing? Elizabeth had warned her, Maggie— even Geoffrey St. Anthony.

She desired him, yes. Since the day she had seen him in the boxing ring, she had thought of his beautiful body a hundred times. When he kissed her, touched her, she felt pleasure she couldn't have imagined. But it wasn't enough.

She was a woman. She wanted to know what that meant. She wanted to sample the pleasures he promised, but she refused to become just another of his meaningless conquests. She needed to trust him, to know that at least in some way she meant something special to him.

Cait shook her head. "I'm . . . I'm sorry, Rand. I can't."

His eyes were dark and fierce. "Why not? You want me. I can feel it. Let me make love to you. It's what both of us want."

She pulled away from him, drew her gown up to cover her breasts with a shaky hand. She should have been embarrassed but she wasn't. She had wanted to learn about passion and Rand Clayton had shown her a little of what it meant.

"I think you had better take me home," she said.

For a moment he just stared. Then a muscle leapt in his cheek. "Are you sure that's what you want?"

Cait shook her head, feeling the unexpected sting of tears. "I'm not sure about anything—not any more. But I know it would be best if I went home. Will you take me, Rand?"

Long, silent moments passed between them. Then he cupped her face between his palms, bent his head, and kissed her very gently on the lips. "I'll take you home."

They didn't talk along the way. Tension seemed to thrum through the duke's hard body, and a vicious ache pounded at her temples. She shouldn't have come with him. She shouldn't have let him kiss her, touch her the way he had. She shouldn't keep remembering the pleasure he'd made her feel.

She shouldn't want him to do it again.

SIX

Cait went over the list of names Geoffrey St. Anthony had just brought in, men of his acquaintance who might be interested in contributing to her father's cause. She was seated in a small, well-appointed salon in Lord Trent's town house, a room done in soft tones of yellow and russet he had outfitted as a study for her father's use while he was in London.

For the past three days, she had been working there with him, going over supply ledgers and ship's departure schedules, writing letters to contacts in Dakar. She hadn't heard from Rand, hadn't received even a note since he had returned her to the museum after their picnic. Most likely, he had realized she wasn't the easy prey he had believed and set his sights on someone else.

It's better this way, she told herself. Rand Clayton wasn't the sort of man she should involve herself with. He was an Englishman, a high-ranking member of the aristocracy. She was American, a commoner. Rand was used to women who played by society's rules. Cait lived her life as she saw fit. She'd been on her own since her mother died. She'd been places, seen things that would make the average woman swoon.

How shocked would he be if she described for him the huge phallic symbols she had seen in Pompeii, or the dozens of reliefs that graphically depicted forbidden, erotic positions of men and women making love?

At the time, she'd been puzzled by exactly what the

pictures and statues meant. Now she was older, better read. She knew full well what she had seen—and the memory of those pictures still intrigued her.

She glanced down at her hands, saw the faint spray of freckles across the back, and thought of the hours she had spent on her hands and knees in the hot island sun. An image arose of the beautiful Lady Hadleigh, and Cait tried to imagine her or any of Rand's legion of women working as she had done.

Cait was a different sort of woman than the ones he had known before. Not the sort who would appeal—beyond a quick tumble in bed—to a man like the Duke of Beldon. She was better off without him, she told herself again. Still, she couldn't stop thinking about him.

"Well, Miss Harmon, what do you say?"

Her head snapped up. She looked over to find Geoffrey St. Anthony leaning over the desk, his golden head just inches from her own. "I'm sorry, Geoffrey, what did you ask me?"

He took a step back, caught his heel on the Oriental rug, tripped, and nearly fell. "Clumsy of me." He straightened his coat, his fair complexion flooded with color. "I'm not usually such a dolt. Nervous, I suppose."

He swallowed and glanced away. "I was wondering, hoping—if you weren't previously engaged—whether you and your father might care to join me tomorrow evening for a night at the opera? They're performing *Semiramide* at the King's Theatre. I've heard the production's very good."

The professor walked in just then, his monocle lodged in one eye. "The opera, you say?" A smile of reminiscence crossed his lips. "I used to love the opera. When Marian was alive, we went as often as we could."

Cait felt the little tug of guilt she always felt when her father spoke of her mother in that adoring way. "Would you like to go, Papa? It's been years since we've attended." So long, Cait could hardly remember.

Her father turned to the young blond man who waited

with obvious anticipation. "Very kind of you to ask, Geoffrey. We would be extremely pleased to join you."

Geoffrey flashed a wide, boyish smile. "The performance begins early. I shall call for you a little before six, if that is agreeable with you."

Cait gave him a grateful smile and told him she looked forward to the evening. Geoffrey left the town house and she and her father returned to work. At least she tried to work.

It wasn't easy when memories of heated kisses and hot caresses kept creeping into her mind.

"Is there anything I can get you before I retire?" Rand's longtime valet, Percival Fox, stood beside the door of the master's suite.

"No," Rand grumbled. "I just need a good night's sleep."

"Perhaps a snifter of brandy, then. Take your mind off your troubles with the professor."

Setting the book he was reading aside, Rand shoved out of his chair and wearily gained his feet. "Perhaps you're right."

Percy smiled as he lifted the lid off a crystal decanter. Formerly a sergeant in the British Army, Percival Fox had served in India and later on the Continent. He had worked for Rand since a musketball in the chest forced him out of the service ten years ago.

In Rand's earlier years, Percy, a sort of self-appointed bodyguard, had traveled with him whenever he left the country, which he'd done quite often when his father was still alive. He had few secrets from Percy, who was more a friend than a servant.

Rand accepted the snifter of brandy and took a hefty sip. "Unfortunately, at present, it isn't the professor I find troubling, it's his daughter."

Percy said nothing, but the look in those cool gray eyes as he stepped out of the room and closed the door said, *I should have known it was a woman.*

Rand almost smiled. Instead, he set his half-full brandy snifter on the nightstand, tossed his dressing gown over the padded bench at the foot of the bed, and slid naked between the sheets. The fabric felt cool and slick, whispering sensuously against his skin, turning his thoughts to smooth, feminine flesh and making him wish he wasn't alone.

Plumping his big feather pillow, he tried to fall asleep, but instead he tossed and turned and sleep remained elusive. Staring at the gold satin canopy above his head, he listened to the clatter of the rain against the windows, the soft luffing of the wind, and thought of Caitlin Harmon.

In the three days since he had last seen her, he had determined that he would forget her. What little information she might have about her father and Talmadge wasn't worth the torment she caused him, the burning desire for her that never seemed to leave him.

Rand closed his eyes against the memory of high lush breasts perfectly formed to fit his hands, big leaf green eyes, and long, gold-tipped red hair. As it had every night, his shaft grew rigid, the familiar ache setting in, the desire for her that wouldn't go away. Last night his need had grown so strong he had gone out in search of relief.

His former mistress, Hannah Reese, an actress in Drury Lane, was always glad to see him. They were friends as well as lovers. Hannah seemed to have a sixth sense where he was concerned, and she was willing to give him solace in whatever form he needed. He had gone to the Theatre Royal to find her, but by the time he reached Catherine Street, he had realized making love to Hannah wasn't what he wanted. He wanted Caitlin Harmon and no other woman would do.

Rand sighed into the silence, heard the ticking of the ormolu clock and the gusting of the wind. Memories of Cait's soft curves teased his senses, the sweet taste of her lips, the way she trembled when he kissed her. She'd been every bit as passionate as he had imagined, and yet there was an innocence about her, a naïveté that couldn't be feigned. It was the reason he had vowed not to see her again.

In truth, there was every chance Nick Warring was right and the girl was a virgin.

Rand had no desire for marriage—at least not yet— and even if he did, the professor's too-independent, very American daughter would hardly make a suitable duchess. True, he admired her intelligence and her spirited nature. And of course there was her passion. He could hardly complain about that.

Still, from the age of ten her father had let her run wild. She ignored the dictates of society at every turn and she had no intention of mending her ways. The man she married would certainly be in for a battle. Whichever man it was would have to take her well in hand.

For some reason that thought didn't sit well with him. Cait was independent, yes. She would have to learn to bend to her husband's will, but he wouldn't want to see that bright spirit broken. His mood grew even darker as he thought of Cait Harmon in another man's bed, her small, soft body trembling with newly awakened passion.

Swearing into the darkness, he tossed back the covers, padded across his massive bedchamber, knelt, and added more coal to the fire.

It was two more hours before he finally fell asleep. When he did, he dreamed of making love to Caitlin Harmon.

Maggie Sutton stood at the rear of the small formal gardens behind her town house. Across the narrow square of manicured lawn, Cait Harmon stood in front of an ancient Greek statue that was missing an arm. Pitted with age and darkened with London soot, the piece was still lovely, and Cait obviously admired it.

"Do you know anything about this?" she asked as Maggie approached. "Where it's from? How old it might be?"

"I'm afraid not. It was here in the garden when Andrew's father, the late marquess, first acquired the property."

"You shouldn't leave it out here, you know. In time, it will weather and crumble to dust."

"I never really gave it much thought. There are statues like these in gardens all over England. I simply enjoyed its beauty—but I suppose you are right."

"So many treasures of the past have been lost. I saw it in Pompeii and also when we were in Egypt. My father went there to unearth objects that would help unlock the past. He believes the ancient treasures belong to the people—all of the people—not just the privileged and the wealthy." She glanced across at Maggie. "I hope I haven't offended you. I know it isn't a popular sentiment."

Maggie shook her head. "I am hardly offended. In fact, I couldn't agree with you more." She turned to study the sculpted head. "And I believe I shall have that beautiful statue replaced with something more modern. Perhaps the museum would be interested in having it."

Caitlin smiled brightly. "I'm certain they would. If not, we'll find one that will."

Maggie sat down on a wrought-iron bench in front of a small, bubbling fountain. She patted the place beside her, and Cait crossed to the bench and sat down.

"I saw you come out here," Maggie said. "For the past few days you've seemed distant, almost withdrawn. If there is something wrong, something you might want to discuss, Cait, you know I'm your friend. I hope you feel you can tell me."

Cait shook her head a little too quickly. "There's nothing wrong, Maggie. I've just been busy, that's all."

"Are you certain? I thought perhaps it was Rand. After the day we saw him at the boxing pavilion, I wondered if you might be hoping he would call."

Cait studied the folds of her yellow muslin skirt, pinching the fabric between her fingers then smoothing it out again. "He did call, Maggie. He invited me on a picnic. He came for me at the museum and we went out to River

Willows." Cait turned to face her. "Are you scandalized, Maggie?"

How could she be scandalized? She knew what it felt like to be attracted to a handsome man like Rand. She had felt that way about Andrew. "I'm not the least bit happy with my friend for risking your reputation that way, but I am certainly not upset with you."

"I know I shouldn't have gone. I wish I could say I was sorry."

"It's obvious you're attracted to him. And he is terribly attracted to you."

Cait's smile seemed wistful and a bit far away. "He likes birds. Did you know that, Maggie? He knows their names and his eyes light up when he watches them. It was strange, though. I think he was embarrassed about it."

Maggie sighed. "From what my brother has told me, Rand had a difficult childhood. He was an only child, you know, and apparently his father was a tyrant. From the time he was little, Rand had an appreciation for beauty. His mother once told me that as a boy, he loved to paint, but his father forbade it. He said it was a womanly pursuit."

"That's ridiculous. No wonder Rand never mentions his father—he must not have liked him very much."

"I don't think they ever got along. Not very well, at any rate. The duke pushed his son to ride and hunt. Rand was given fencing lessons, boxing lessons, and later his father introduced him to the gaming tables. Rand being Rand excelled in every one of those things. Still, for the duke it wasn't enough."

"Elizabeth says he's sensitive. I don't think that's something to be ashamed of."

"Perhaps you would if your father had taken a birch rod to you every time he caught you reading a book of poems or dabbling with a paintbrush. Rand gave up those pursuits, at least until he was grown, but no matter how hard he tried, he could never win the old duke's approval."

Cait's heart tugged oddly. Her father loved her dearly. Rand's sad childhood reminded her how lucky she was.

"Have you heard from him?" Maggie asked.

"Not since the picnic. I don't think he was happy with the way things turned out."

"Why not?"

Cait stared out at the fountain and Maggie's gaze followed. The water made a pleasant, bubbling sound, and a fine spray of mist created rainbows in the air.

"I think he believed, since I had accompanied him alone, that I would let him . . . that we would . . . make love."

"Good heavens!"

"It wasn't entirely his fault. I shouldn't have gone. I knew it wasn't the proper thing to do."

"You aren't telling me Rand took advantage? He didn't . . . he didn't force you?"

Cait's eyes widened. "No, of course not. I don't think Rand would ever do anything I didn't want him to."

Maggie released the breath she had been holding. "I didn't really think he would."

"The problem is I wanted him to."

Maggie choked on her next breath of air. "I thought you said—"

"Nothing happened, Maggie. Nothing that really mattered, at any rate. That is the point. I wouldn't let him make love to me so he is no longer interested."

Maggie pondered that, seeing an image of Rand and Cait as they had waltzed together in the ballroom. "I wish I could believe that, but I'm afraid I don't. Rand Clayton never gave up on anything he wanted. And you, dear one, he most certainly wants. The problem is, Rand isn't interested in marriage and presumably neither are you."

"I can't marry anyone—at least not now. Not while my father still needs me."

Maggie bit back words of advice her friend wouldn't want to hear. "I understand why you feel as you do about marriage," she said gently, "but in this case, those feelings could be dangerous." She reached over and took Cait's hand. "You must be very careful, my dear. Desire is a powerful force. Rand is an expert on the matter while you are only a novice. Hopefully, the duke has realized that. If he has, perhaps that is the reason you haven't heard from him."

Maggie gave Cait a hug. "I know it's difficult, but it's better for you both if he stays away. Remember that, Caitlin. And pray Rand remembers it, too."

SEVEN

For her evening at the opera, Cait chose a shot silk gown that shimmered in the same russet tones as her hair. It was cut in the Empire fashion, high-waisted and very low over the bosom, exposing a good deal of cleavage. Trimmed in wide gold braid below the bodice and along the hem, the gown had matching gold slippers and long gold gloves that extended past her elbows.

She glanced at the clock, checked the mirror one last time, stuck an extra pin into the burnished curls she wore atop her head, and headed downstairs. Her father was waiting in the entry, dressed in a burgundy tailcoat and tailored gray breeches, a gray-flecked waistcoat setting off the silver of his hair.

His clothes fit perfectly, yet it hurt Caitlin to see how much he had aged in the past few years. Donovan Harmon had once been a handsome man. Now in his sixties, his skin was thin and weathered from years of working in the sun, and his eyes had lost a bit of their sky blue luster. He'd been nearly twenty years older than her mother when they'd married. Perhaps Marian Simmons's youth and beauty were part of the reason he had fallen so deeply in love with her.

"Are you ready, my dear?"

"Yes, Father." She leaned over and kissed his wrinkled cheek, stepped back and surveyed his appearance with a discerning eye. "My, don't you look handsome this evening."

He smiled almost shyly. "Thank you, my dear."

Geoffrey St. Anthony stepped out of the shadows of the stairwell just then. She hadn't realized he was there. "And you, Miss Harmon, look ravishing."

Cait made him a deep curtsy, accepting the arm he offered. "Thank you, my lord."

They left the town house in Geoffrey's sleek black barouche, heading for the fashionable King's Theatre in the Haymarket district. It was the largest theater in London, Cait discovered, and one of the most elegant, a great horseshoe-shaped auditorium with five tiers of boxes.

Making their way up to the third floor, they entered the Marquess of Wester's private box, which Geoffrey had use of for the night. Seated on plush royal blue velvet chairs, they had an excellent view of the stage, the pit, and a gallery that seated an amazing three thousand people.

With an audience that included everyone from orange girls selling fruit and carrying messages, to garishly dressed members of the demimonde, to the top of the social elite, the place was fascinating to Cait, who could have entertained herself simply by watching the colorful assortment of onlookers.

"I'm so glad you came," Geoffrey said, breaking away from his conversation with her father and into Cait's thoughts. Dressed in a dark blue swallow-tailed coat, white waistcoat, and gray breeches, Geoffrey had garnered at least half a dozen long glances from the women who surveyed his golden good looks. "I was hoping . . . wondering if perhaps on the morrow we might—"

The music began just then and Cait was grateful. Geoffrey was one of her father's staunchest supporters. Both of them valued his help and dedication, but Cait had no interest in pursuing a relationship with him. She thought of him only as a friend.

The opera began. Cait was amazed at the rowdiness of the crowd, whose boisterous applause and cheers for Catalani, prima donna of the London opera, blotted out the sounds of the music. Eventually, the audience settled down and became absorbed in the performance, which as Geoffrey had promised was extremely good. Cait was thoroughly enjoying herself—until she happened to notice the familiar outline of a tall, well-built man seated in a box not far away. At first she thought she was mistaken. Surely the man sitting beside the beautiful brunette wasn't Rand Clayton, but as she watched his graceful, confident movements, saw the flash of even white teeth in a smile she recalled all too clearly, she knew it was, and her heart did a painful little twist.

It isn't important, she told herself. *He isn't important. You're better off without him.* But her stomach felt queasy every time he bent over to whisper in the gorgeous, dark-haired woman's ear.

When the candles were lit for intermission, Geoffrey rose from his chair and Cait gratefully took his arm.

"Join us, Father?" she asked.

"You two go on. I believe I'll stay here."

They headed downstairs for a bit of refreshment and a little fresh air, but on reaching the bottom of the stairs, nearly collided with Beldon and the attractive woman on his arm. The queasy feeling returned. Cait pasted on an overbright smile and moved a little closer to her golden-haired escort.

"Your Grace," Geoffrey said formally. "I thought I caught a glimpse of you upstairs. I had forgot you had a box near my father's."

The duke smiled thinly. "It's been a while since I've attended." He glanced at the woman on his arm. "You remember Lady Anne?"

"Of course." Geoffrey bowed over her hand.

He turned to the lovely brunette. "And the lady with him is Miss Harmon."

"Good evening." Lady Anne flashed a winsome smile at Geoffrey and smiled politely at Cait. She had a perfect complexion, and her hair, cut in short, stylishly tousled curls, gleamed like black silk in the candlelight. Cait suddenly wished she were anyplace but standing beside her.

Beldon made polite conversation for a moment, but his eyes were fixed on Cait. "Having a good time, Miss Harmon?" There was an edge to his voice she couldn't miss. Why, she couldn't imagine.

"I'm having a wonderful time." She cast a bright smile at her companion. "Geoffrey is such delightful company. I'm so glad he invited me to come."

Rand's dark brows drew together. Sparks of gold seemed to flash in his eyes. "I wasn't aware you were an aficionado of the opera. Or perhaps it is simply that you are here with an escort who is such a *delight*."

Cait ground her jaw. "I'm certain, Your Grace, there are a number of things about me of which you are not aware."

He made a slow, very thorough perusal of her body, his hot, dark eyes returning to the swell of her breasts. "That may be true. There are, however, a number of things about you of which I am very well aware."

Cait felt the heat rising into her cheeks. How dare he! It was only too obvious he was remembering the day they had spent at River Willows, recalling the shape of her breasts, how his skillful, clever hands had made her nipples grow hard, how they had quivered when he laved them with his tongue.

Embarrassment threatened to swamp her. It took a will of iron, but she forced her eyes to his face. "And you, Your Grace? Are you and Lady Anne enjoying the performance? Or perhaps there is another performance later on that you are anticipating with even greater relish."

A dark brow arched up. Then a corner of his mouth curved faintly. There was something in his manner now, something that might have been satisfaction. Had she betrayed the jealousy that was eating her up inside? Dear God, she prayed she had not.

"Actually," Rand said, "I haven't yet decided what we'll do when this ends. What about you and Lord Geoffrey? A late supper perhaps, just the two of you?"

Cait bristled. Geoffrey opened his mouth to tell him

they were hardly there alone, but Cait cut him off. "As a matter of fact that is exactly what we plan to do."

Geoffrey's face went pale, and the duke's whole body went tense.

"I believe the performance is resuming," Geoffrey said, taking Cait's arm more forcefully than she might have expected. "I think we should return to our seats. If you will excuse us, Your Grace . . ."

He made a slight bow, his eyes still snapping with fire and burning into Cait.

"You shouldn't have done that," Geoffrey whispered as they reached their third-floor box. " 'Twould be scandalous, should the rumor get out that we are spending the evening alone, and he will likely spread the lie all over London."

For some odd reason, Cait didn't believe the duke would ever stoop that low. Gossip seemed too petty for a man like him. "I'm certain he knew it was merely a jest," she said, hoping to smooth Geoffrey's rumpled feathers. Apparently it worked, for he seemed to relax and let the subject drop.

They seated themselves and the opera continued. It was obvious her father was enjoying himself, but the joy had gone out of the evening for Cait. Fighting to keep her eyes off the couple in the box across the way, midway through the next scene, she excused herself and headed for the ladies' retiring room, silently wishing the Duke of Beldon to perdition.

Rand tried to keep his mind on the performance, but again and again, his thoughts strayed to Cait. He found himself searching for her, checking the boxes until he found her. When he saw her sitting next to Geoffrey St. Anthony, a fresh shot of anger fired through him.

He had no right to the feeling, he knew. He had no hold on Caitlin Harmon. Yet the jolt he'd received at seeing her with St. Anthony was nothing short of a fist slamming into his stomach.

He had goaded her unmercifully. *A late supper? Just the two of you?*

And been paid back tenfold. *That is exactly what we intend.*

A growl of frustration slipped past his lips. His only satisfaction came from the fact that Cait hadn't been as unaffected by his appearance as she had wanted him to believe. Anne Stanwick was young and beautiful and already enamored of him. It was obvious Caitlin had noticed. Silently he cursed her, wishing he had never heard her laughter that night at the ball.

Unconsciously, his glance strayed again to the box where she sat next to St. Anthony, and for the first time he saw there was a man seated on the opposite side—her father, Donovan Harmon.

Rand swore foully. She wasn't alone with St. Anthony as she had wanted him to believe. He felt an odd combination of fury and relief.

She stood up just then, said something to her escort, and made her way out of the box.

"Excuse me, Anne. I'll be back in a moment." He mumbled an apology to Lord and Lady Bainbridge, Anne's parents, sitting in the row of seats behind them, slipped through the curtains, and followed Cait's retreating figure down the hall. With all that fiery hair, she was easy to keep in sight. He watched her disappear into the ladies' retiring room and took up a position outside the door.

When she ducked back through the heavy blue velvet curtains a few minutes later, he was lounging against the wall, trying to curb his impatience and appear nonchalant. She spotted him almost immediately and angry color flooded her cheeks. Inwardly, he smiled. Damn, but she was lovely.

"What are you doing here?" she demanded, planting her small hands on her hips.

He pushed away from the wall with a casual air he

wasn't really feeling. "You know what I'm doing. I'm waiting for you."

"What for? Isn't one woman enough for a single evening?" She tried to walk past, but he caught her arm.

"Anne Stanwick is a girl, not a woman. She is also my cousin. My very young, very impressionable cousin. The next time you are peeking into our box, you might notice that her parents are sitting in the row behind us."

Cait blinked, embarrassed to have been caught spying on him, groping for something to say. "Her parents?"

"That's right."

She cleared her throat. "Yes, well . . . I hope you all have a very pleasant evening." She started to walk away, but he didn't release her arm and instead turned her to face him.

"What about St. Anthony?"

She glanced down at the hand still holding her immobile. "What about him?"

"I saw your father sitting next to you. The two of you are not here alone."

The flush in her cheeks crept down to the soft mounds of flesh above the bodice of her gown. "You are the one who said that. I simply agreed."

"Why?"

"Because you were being extremely rude, that's why. Now please let go of my arm."

This wasn't going exactly the way he had planned. He let go of her arm but stepped in front of her, making it impossible for her to get round him. "I want to know what's going on with you and St. Anthony." He stared into those big green eyes and an awful thought occurred. It burned through him like fire and the anger he'd felt earlier scorched through him again.

"Or are you here with him because of the money? How much is he contributing to your father's expedition?"

"Lord Geoffrey's contribution is none of your business."

He took a step toward her, forcing her up against the

wall. "I imagine the amount is sizable. What would you
do for that sort of money, I wonder? How far would you
go?" He traced a finger along her jaw and felt her tremble.
"I'm a wealthy man. I might be convinced to contribute
a hefty sum if you were willing to—"

She slapped him so hard he took an unconscious step
backward, his ears ringing and his cheek burning like fire.
Cait bolted past him and raced down the hall. Rand cursed
himself and ran after her.

He caught her just as she reached the entrance to her
box, dragged her back from the curtain and into a tiny
alcove around the corner. He turned her to face him, saw
the faint shimmer of tears in her eyes, and the fury inside
him deflated like a spent balloon.

"God, Caitie, I'm sorry. I didn't mean that." He shook
his head, drew in a steadying breath. "Seeing you with St.
Anthony . . . I don't know . . . I just lost my temper." He
raised a finger to wipe away a drop of moisture that slid
down her cheek and saw that his hand was shaking. "The
truth is, I was jealous." Rand sighed, feeling like a fool,
not completely certain what had made him behave as he
had. "It isn't a feeling I'm used to."

Cait stared up at him for long, silent moments. As if
of its own accord, her hand began to move, inching slowly
upward. She touched her palm very gently to the red mark
on his cheek. Something soft and sweet rose inside him,
seemed to blossom and shimmer like threads of gold.
Rand swallowed past the tightness that swelled in his
throat.

"I'm sorry," he repeated. "I behaved like a fool. Can
you forgive me?"

Cait's eyes misted again. "I'm sorry, too. I shouldn't
have hit you. I've never hit anyone before."

Rand pulled her into his arms. For a time he just held
her. It felt so good to have her there, so right somehow.
Then she looked up at him with those big green eyes, and
he saw that she was staring at his lips. His body tightened
and inside his breeches he went hard. There was no other

choice but to kiss her. He did so with tender care, gently yet thoroughly, till her small body began to tremble.

"Send Lord Geoffrey home with your father," he whispered against her ear. "Tell them you're feeling ill, tell them you'll hire a hackney carriage, tell them anything you please, just get rid of them. I'll leave my cousin with her parents and we'll spend the rest of the evening together."

Cait stiffened and eased herself out of his arms. It was an unfair request and he knew it, but Rand no longer cared.

"I can't do that, Rand. Geoffrey was kind enough to invite me here tonight. It's a special night for my father. It wouldn't be right to treat either of them that way."

"Dammit, Cait. You know the way I feel. I want to see you—now, tonight."

She shook her head and her spine went even straighter. "I won't do it, Rand. I realize you're a duke and therefore used to getting your way, but this time it isn't going to happen."

He clamped his jaw. She was right, of course, which only irritated him further. Still, he admired her for standing up to him. Not many women did. Hell, not many men had the courage to go against him.

He took a calming breath. "All right, if not tonight then when? How about tomorrow? I'll pick you up in the morning and we'll go for a carriage ride in the park."

She worried her bottom lip, which was full and pink, and he remembered exactly how it had tasted. He had the sudden urge to suck it between his teeth, and his body went harder still. Inwardly, he groaned, wondering how one small woman could have such a damnable effect on him.

"I don't know . . ." Cait said uncertainly. "What happened tonight shouldn't have occurred. It isn't a good idea for us to see each other. Whatever is between us can only lead to trouble. You know it and so do I."

"I don't care."

"Well, I do."

He caught her chin. "Do you? I think you want to see me as badly as I want to see you. You're fiercely independent, Cait. That's the first thing I learned about you. Do what you really want, not what someone else says you should."

She glanced behind him, still unsure, and Rand held his breath. It amazed him how badly he wanted her to say yes.

"All right, but only a ride in the park. After that we'll have to see." She turned and brushed past him, and this time he let her go. He watched her hurry toward the curtain leading into her box.

"Caitie!" he called after her, stopping her just outside the door. He rubbed the red mark that still burned on his cheek and flashed her a wicked grin. "For such a little thing, you pack one hell of a wallop."

Cait laughed in that throaty way of hers, turned, and ducked out of sight behind the curtain. For several moments more, Rand stayed in the shadows, cursing the power Cait Harmon seemed to hold over him and fighting to bring his body back under control.

The balance of the evening passed in a blur for Cait. Thoughts of Rand Clayton pressed in on her and she found it impossible to concentrate. She said little on the way back to the marquess's town house, just thanked Geoffrey for a pleasant evening and started inside.

"Miss Harmon—Caitlin?" Geoffrey called after her, using her first name as he was only just beginning to.

She turned back to him while her father continued on into the house. "Yes, Geoffrey, what is it?"

"It . . . it's about Beldon."

Unease trickled through her. "What about him?"

"Be careful of him, Caitlin. The duke is a powerful man. He's used to getting what he wants. He rarely takes no for an answer."

There was nothing new in that. She had said those

same words to Rand. "I'm aware of that, Geoffrey."

"You're an innocent young woman, Caitlin. You don't know how persuasive a man like that can be."

Oh, but she did. Better than he could imagine. "I'll be careful, Geoffrey." She turned to leave, the late-night chill beginning to seep through the layers of her satin-lined cloak.

"Tell him you don't wish to see him, Caitlin. Tell him you and I are . . . well, tell him I am courting you. I should like to, you know. I should like that above all things."

Cait sighed, her breath a frosty mist in the air. "That's very flattering, Geoffrey, but I'm not interested in marriage. Not to you or anyone else—not so long as my father needs my help." She leaned down and kissed him lightly on the cheek. "But I'll give your warning some thought. Thank you for being concerned. Good night, Geoffrey."

He settled his tall beaver hat at an imposing angle on his head. "Good night, Caitlin."

Cait left him and went into the house. She climbed the stairs to her room, looking forward to the solace of sleep. It didn't come easily. Not with Geoffrey's dire warning ringing in her head. When she finally drifted off, she dreamed of Rand.

Perhaps it was recalling his contrition, or his endearing, dimpled grin when he had rubbed his reddened cheek. Whatever it was, when his image arose—against all of Geoffrey's advice—she smiled softly in her sleep.

EIGHT

Apparently, a simple jaunt through the park in the duke's fancy high-seat phaeton wasn't enough. Instead Rand sent word that Cait should dress appropriately for riding. He would be arriving in an hour, and he was bringing her a suitable mount.

A little thrill shot through her. She hadn't ridden for pleasure in years. Hurrying upstairs, she dug through a stack of clothing she hadn't worn in ages, dragged out a dark red velvet riding habit, and quickly rang for a maid. By the time the duke arrived at the town house, Cait was almost ready.

Beldon was waiting for her in the entry, sinfully handsome in his tight buckskin breeches, dark brown riding coat, and knee-high boots. He smiled when he saw her, his gaze going over her ruby habit and matching miniature top hat with obvious approval.

He led her outside where a footman waited with the horses, a big blood bay stallion and a pretty little sorrel mare much like the one she'd had as a girl. Taking note of the horse's excellent conformation and small, elegant head, she ran her hands along the animal's sleek neck.

"She's beautiful, Rand."

"You said you liked to ride. Dimples is easy to manage yet still has plenty of spirit."

She arched a brow. "Dimples? Tell me she wasn't named after you."

A flush rose in his face. "Nick Warring's idea of a

joke," he admitted a little gruffly. "I thought you would prefer this to the carriage."

She grinned up at him; she couldn't help it. "It's scary, at times, the way you seem able to read my mind."

He laughed at that, came around to help her into the sidesaddle. His hands clamped around her waist as he lifted her up, and their eyes met. Cait was the first to look away.

The duke strode to his horse and swung gracefully up into the saddle, the muscles in his powerful shoulders moving beneath his riding coat.

"Ready?" he asked, bringing his horse up beside her.

"More than ready." They set off at an easy pace, mindful of the traffic in the streets. It felt good to be mounted again, to feel the exhilarating connection between horse and rider. Rand had remembered her love of riding, and it occurred to her that he always went out of his way to please her.

It didn't take long to reach Hyde Park, which was filled with the usual morning crowd. The fashionable elite were there in force, women in silks and satins, men in tailcoats and tall beaver hats, some of them decked out like peacocks. Several times Cait found herself biting back a laugh at the extremes to which the ton would go in order to outdo one another.

"I take it you find this custom of ours somehow amusing," Rand drawled, but laughter sparkled in his golden brown eyes.

"Let's just say, some members of the aristocracy are a bit more . . . colorful than I'm used to." She cast a pointed glance at a dandy who wore a pink feather boa draped around his neck, rouge on his lips, and rice powder on his face.

Beldon followed her gaze and grinned. "Very diplomatically put, Miss Harmon. Are you telling me you are not fond of a man donning feathers?"

"I would prefer them on a hat."

"Or a bird, perhaps. As I recall, you aren't all that fond

of hats." He tossed a glance at the jaunty little top hat on her head. "Though I am rather fond of the one you are wearing today."

Cait smiled. "So am I. Perhaps that is because it is styled like a man's. It gives me a feeling of equality, even if it is short-lived."

Beldon chuckled and they started another round through the park.

From that day forward, he came for her every day, bringing small gifts on his arrival: a bouquet of roses, a box of expensive chocolates wrapped in silver paper and tied with a blue satin bow. Once he brought stuffed dates and a small porcelain music box fashioned in the shape of a heart. It played a song from the opera they had seen.

Always he acted the gentleman, his manner casual and friendly. But his eyes said something different and they seemed to burn with heat. At night, Cait saw those hot, dark eyes in her dreams, imagined his mouth on her breasts, and awakened bathed in perspiration. She knew she should end their meetings, knew the threat he posed, but in truth, seeing him was exactly what she wanted.

She was a woman. Rand made her feel like one.

And in less than three weeks, their time together would be over.

For the next two days, the duke was away on business. On Monday, he came for her again, and she realized that in the short time he'd been gone, she had missed him. The mare was fussy that morning as they set off for the park, the horse going up on its hind legs and tossing its head, but Cait soon had the animal under control. She and the mare were fast becoming friends, and riding each day had renewed her skills.

"You're an excellent horsewoman," Rand said with what sounded oddly like pride. They were circling through the park, weaving their way through the usual morning crowd. "You learned in Boston, I presume."

"On Grandfather's farm. I also rode a great deal in

Egypt, though it was more difficult there. I never got used to the heat."

Increasing the speed of their horses as they did for a while each day, they flew past an open carriage that Cait hadn't seen in the park before. Recognizing the woman inside—the beautiful Lady Hadleigh—her heart jolted sideways, set up an uncomfortable rhythm beneath her ribs. When the woman waved at Rand and motioned him to come alongside, he cast Cait an apologetic glance that begged her indulgence and complied.

He didn't stay long and returned to her side a few minutes later.

"A friend of yours, I gather," Cait said, trying to ignore the unwelcome bite of jealousy, knowing full well the woman was once his lover.

"An old friend, yes." His gaze was probing and far too perceptive. "It's over between us, Cait. I'm not interested in Lady Hadleigh. I haven't been for quite some time."

Cait studied his face, saw the sincerity. "Why are you telling me this?"

"Can't you guess? Because you are the woman I want, Cait, and I want you to know there is no one else." He reined up beneath a plane tree next to a quiet pond some distance from the milling crowd, caught her bridle and pulled her horse close to his. "We've spent a good deal of time together this past week. But there's something I have to know."

Wariness filtered through her. "What is it?"

"I know you're not yet married, but I also know you are different from other women. You've traveled widely. You live your life as you choose. Are you still a virgin, Caitlin?"

Her cheeks went warm. She knew why he was asking or at least thought she did. "Does it really make a difference?"

Something flickered in those fierce brown eyes, then it was gone. Rand shook his head. "No. I just . . . I was trying to be gallant. I want you, Cait. You have no idea how much."

"I'm not a fool, Rand. I know you've wanted any number of women. I'm not interested in becoming another of your conquests."

"Are you looking for marriage, then? At your lecture, you said you wouldn't want to give up your freedom."

"And that is exactly what I meant. There's no place in my life for a husband. Perhaps one day in the future, but certainly not now. Still, I'd like to think . . . if we made love . . . it would mean more to you than simply adding another female to your long list of lovers."

Rand swung down from his horse, went over and lifted her down. "My darling Cait. You are hardly just another female I am interested in bedding. I've never met anyone like you. I don't think I ever will. I'm mad for you, Caitie. I know you'll be leaving soon. We don't have much time left. Let's make the most of the time we have."

It was insane—the entire conversation. Rand was asking her to become his mistress and she was actually entertaining the notion!

You're a woman, part of her argued. *You deserve to know what it's like.* Marriage, she knew, if it ever occurred, would yet be years away. And even then, most likely she would end up wed to a scholar or a clergyman, or perhaps a friend of her father's, someone like Geoffrey St. Anthony. In truth, if she let this chance escape, she might never know the sort of passion that she would find with Rand.

"I don't know . . . I need time to think."

"Time, I'm afraid, is something we have very little of."

He was right, of course. The moment was here, now. If she only had the courage to grasp it. She looked into his handsome face and realized she wanted this every bit as badly as he did. "My father and Lord Talmadge will be leaving on Thursday. They'll be journeying to Bath for several days to speak to potential contributors. On Friday, Maggie and Lord Trent have invited me to join them at their country home in Sussex. The trip is all set. If I were to decline at the very last moment—"

He gripped her hand, his gaze intense. "We'll go to River Willows. You won't be sorry, Caitlin."

Cait only nodded. Her throat felt tight and a slight tremor moved down her spine. She wouldn't be sorry, she told herself. She had dedicated her life to her father and his work. She would continue to do so. But she deserved this one brief moment for herself.

She refused to listen to the tiny, niggling voice that warned her she would pay for her folly. And the price would be high, indeed.

Phillip Rutherford, Baron Talmadge sat at the small French writing desk in his suite of rooms at the Grillon Hotel in Albermarle Street. He was studying the list of men he had enticed into contributing to Professor Harmon's upcoming search for Cleopatra's Necklace. The list was lengthy. Phillip was good at his job.

For years, he'd been soliciting money from his wealthy acquaintances, ever since he'd inherited his brother's worthless title. Before that, he'd been a purser in His Majesty's Navy. He'd dabbled a bit in the black market then, diverting Navy supplies from their intended destination, selling them to the highest bidder. But the risk of getting caught was too great and the punishment too severe.

His brother's death had been a godsend—at least he'd thought so until he'd discovered that Victor had gambled away the last of the family's meager fortune and left Phillip with a mountain of debts.

Fortunately, the skills he had learned in the Navy served him even better in his new role as baron, a member of the wealthy aristocracy. Phillip smiled to think how gullible they were, amazingly so at times. Perhaps because most of them had inherited their money and had very little idea how to manage it—or even knew for certain how much they really had. When an investment he "suggested" went sour, they merely shrugged their shoulders. And of course they all believed he had lost his own money in the venture, as well.

His last project, Merriweather Shipping, had earned him a tidy sum. But alas, his partnership with Sinclair and Morris was over, the men moving on to more fertile soil. There were only so many times one could sink the same ship without raising suspicion.

Ah, but as usual, fate had been kind to him. During a brief sabbatical in America, while heat from the supposedly failed Merriweather venture died down, he had stumbled upon the professor—and of course his beautiful daughter.

That, he had believed, would be an added bonus, charming and bedding the vibrant, fiery-haired Caitlin Harmon. But Cait had shown little interest in him beyond a business association, and Phillip had resigned himself.

The fortune he intended to make was far more important.

He looked down at the column that indicated each man's contribution to the expedition. The total—for such a worthy cause—was impressive. Far more than would actually be needed. Enough that Phillip could skim off a hefty portion for himself.

A nice incentive, but in truth, he had undertaken this endeavor for a far more important reason. The necklace was priceless, of course. But rarely did the old man mention the other items that were thought to be aboard the *Zilverijder*. A hefty cache of silver coins and valuable gems the Dutch sea captain and his slave-trading crew had plundered along the African coast. The bulk of the treasure wasn't ancient—but it was worth a fortune.

If the necklace was found—and Phillip was convinced the professor was very close to finding it—it would be an added bonus. Enough so that he could disappear to some warm tropical isle in the West Indies and live like a king.

Phillip set the list he'd been reading aside and leaned back in his chair, thinking of the professor and how close he was to achieving the first step in his plan. As usual, it was amazing how completely Donovan Harmon trusted him. What was it about him, he wondered, that made them all behave like such fools?

All but Caitlin, he thought with a pang of regret. Still, once they were on the island, perhaps he could find a way to draw her interest. Or perhaps, once he had the treasure in his possession and was ready to leave, he would simply take her with him.

His body tightened at an image of Caitlin Harmon struggling beneath him, her fiery hair spread out on the bed as he forced her legs apart and drove himself inside her. Phillip smiled to himself. Why was it, he thought with the trace of a smile, so much more exciting to bed an unwilling woman than one of those who so easily gave themselves to him?

Week's end loomed ahead. Cait's mood swung from abject fear to wild anticipation. On Thursday, Lord Trent suggested they attend Lord Mortimer's fiftieth-birthday ball. Her father had left for Bath, but Rand agreed to join them. It would have been a pleasant evening if Cait hadn't been such a bundle of nerves.

From the moment the duke arrived at the town house, she could feel the heat between them like thick, hot tropical air. Though he made a point of observing the proprieties, he always seemed to be somewhere near. When he disappeared even briefly, she found her gaze restlessly searching for him.

After an extravagant midnight supper that Cait could barely eat, he had taken her hand and very firmly drawn her to her feet.

"The gardens here are lovely. Why don't we walk for a while?" It wasn't a suggestion—it was a ducal command. Still, Cait found herself smiling. Rand Clayton was a powerful man, used to giving orders, getting what he wanted, and yet she rather liked the way he took charge.

Perhaps because her father never did. Difficult decisions were usually left to her, and there was no one she could turn to for help with her burdens. Still, the Duke of Beldon would not be an easy man to live with. She had glimpsed his formidable temper the night of the opera. Whatever woman he married would find herself beneath his determined thumb if she wasn't extremely careful.

They made their way along the oyster-shell paths, Rand guiding her deeper into the lush green foliage of the garden. Up ahead, the pathway narrowed and the voices of other guests began to fade. She shouldn't have come with him, she knew. If someone saw them, the gossip-mongers would smear the news all over London. Still, there weren't many people who wished to incur the wrath of a duke, and particularly not this one.

Rand paused on the path in a secluded corner of the garden. Crickets chirped in the flower bed and the faint music of the orchestra played in the distance.

"It's lovely here," Cait said, surveying the leafy plants, daffodils, and crocuses that surrounded them. Her gaze traveled upward, into the darkness above. "So quiet and peaceful."

Rand followed her gaze, his head tipping back to look at the clear night sky. "The stars are incredible tonight, rather like a fine spray of silver. The moon seems to glow as if a million candles burned inside it."

Her eyes swung to his face. "What a lovely thing to say." She smiled. "Deep down, Your Grace, perhaps you are a poet."

Rand flushed, as she had guessed he would. She thought it was charming in a man of his size and strength. He was watching her again. A big hand gently cupped her chin, turning her face up to his. "You realize, since those few brief moments at the opera, this is the first time we've truly been alone."

A little shiver started, moved from her chest into her stomach. "I—I'm not sure we should—"

Rand silenced her with the softest, fiercest kiss she could imagine. Heat melted through her, oozed out through her limbs. He kissed the corner of her mouth, captured her lips again, and kissed her even more deeply. With a sigh of pure pleasure, Cait slid her arms around his neck and leaned into him, her breasts pressing into his chest.

Cait heard him groan. Rand kissed her again and a hot, buttery sensation curled low in her belly. He teased her bottom lip and she opened for him, allowing him to taste her, wanting him to. Her heart beat raggedly. Her body trembled. His hands slid lower, to cup her bottom and draw her more solidly against him. She could feel his hardened arousal, and a jolt of desire speared through her.

"Rand . . ." she whispered. "Rand . . ." He could set her on fire with a single kiss, a single touch. And it was only a prelude to what he would do to her tomorrow night.

He kissed her again, thoroughly, passionately, and Cait clung to his powerful shoulders. Her breath fluttered in and out; her heart thundered painfully. It was Rand who ended the kiss, pulling her into his arms and holding her against him. A faint shudder moved through his muscular frame.

"God, Caitlin, what you do to me. Tomorrow seems decades away. It's all I can do not to lift your skirts and take you right here."

Hot color flooded her cheeks. He had never spoken to her in quite that way. When she glanced down at her slippers, hoping he wouldn't see, he caught her chin, and lifted it, forcing her eyes to his face.

"I thought you said . . ." He studied the twin circles of pink she would have preferred he didn't see. "Whatever you know of men, I gather you are still rather new to all of this."

She looked away. "I . . . haven't had all that much experience." He had asked if she was a virgin. She had simply evaded the question, let him think whatever he wished. She was afraid the truth would change the way he felt about her, keep him from seeing her as a woman.

A corner of his mouth curved faintly. For some odd reason, he seemed pleased. "I'm sorry if I frightened you.

It won't happen again." When she smiled, he bent and kissed the side of her mouth. "We had better be getting back. If we don't return soon, Maggie and Andrew will be out prowling the pathways in search of us."

He trailed a finger down her cheek. "Besides, if I kiss you again, I might forget that we are not yet at River Willows."

River Willows. The tension returned with the force of a blow. Tomorrow they would go to his estate by the river. Tomorrow night she would let him make love to her. Part of her wished she didn't have to wait even one more minute.

The other part lived in terror that the hour would finally arrive.

Standing in the Oriental Salon, a high-ceilinged chamber at the rear of his house, Rand checked the clock on the black marble mantel at the far end of the room. Only ten in the morning. He'd been up for hours, unable to sleep. Damn, but the day was dragging.

He thought of the night to come and memories of his previous evening with Cait rushed to the front of his mind, an outing with two of his closest friends that had been made even more pleasant by the presence of a woman they obviously liked and admired.

In a way, it surprised him. Cait lived by her own set of rules, obeyed no master but herself. She traveled the streets unchaperoned, visiting friends and associates of her father's without so much as a lady's maid. She was outspoken and passionate in her beliefs, unafraid to speak out, particularly on the subjects that pertained to her field of study. She was vocal in regard to protecting antiquities, and staunchly against private ownership of ancient treasures.

Rand turned to study the ornate glass case that held his precious collection of Chinese jade and chuckled to himself, wondering what Caitlin would say if she saw it.

Some of the pieces were thousands of years old and had cost a small fortune.

And what of his Greek and Roman art? Statues and busts he had been purchasing over the years? They adorned the Long Gallery and their exquisite beauty pleased him every time he passed along the hall. Cait would surely believe they belonged in some moldy museum while Rand was certain the average person would find them dull and boring.

"I'm sorry to bother you, Your Grace, but a messenger has just arrived." The butler, Frederick Peterson, a thin, elegant man with wispy brown hair, stood at the door, holding a silver salver. Rand crossed the room and lifted the wax-sealed message off the top, broke the seal, and found a note from his solicitor requesting a meeting. He was fairly sure he knew what the meeting was about.

Two hours later, Ephram Barclay arrived and Rand led him into his study.

"I gather something important's come up," Rand said, both of them taking seats in deep leather chairs before the hearth.

"Yes. Or rather, yes—and no." Ephram opened the thin leather case he had placed in his lap. "Late last evening, information arrived that I thought you would wish to know. Unfortunately, it is strictly a matter of rumor, with no corroboration."

"You're saying you've news of Talmadge but you don't have any proof."

"Exactly so."

A muscle tightened in Rand's cheek. "What have you learned?"

"This morning I received a correspondence in reply to our initial query about the *Maiden*. Rumors have surfaced in South Carolina that the ship did not go down. In fact, several sailors have boasted that the *Maiden* arrived in Charleston with a load of copra under the name *Sea Nymph*."

Anger made his jaw go hard. He took the report from

Ephram's hand and scanned the first page. "Where is the *Sea Nymph* now?"

"Unfortunately, she has sailed. Our informant believes the ship may be making packet runs along the coast, but he isn't certain. He also thinks the owners may be somewhere on the eastern seaboard raising money for another ill-fated shipping venture."

Rand cursed fluently. Shoving himself out of his chair, he strode to the hearth. For a moment he stared into the flames, then he rested an arm on the mantel and turned back to Ephram. "There has to be a way to stop them."

"Oh, we'll stop them—sooner or later. The authorities will be watching for them. You have to be patient, Your Grace."

Rand's hand fisted on the mantel. "Patience is a virtue I don't have. I want those bastards to pay for what they did to Jonathan. And I don't want the same thing happening to some other poor sod."

Ephram rose and crossed the room, settled a thin, veined hand on his shoulder. "We're doing all we can. In the meantime, the best you can hope for is to discover whatever it is Phillip Rutherford is planning with Donovan Harmon."

Rand sighed. "He may be leaving the country, you know."

"If he does, there is no way you can stop him. As I said, so far there is no tangible proof."

"And getting it could take months, even years."

"The distances are formidable. Communication takes time."

"Talmadge is definitely involved in something illicit, which means Harmon is undoubtedly involved, but I no longer believe that Caitlin has any part in it."

"Perhaps not. You would know better than I."

Rand's gaze swung to Ephram, but he said nothing more. "There's something going on," Rand repeated. "I intend to find out what it is."

Ephram just nodded. If Beldon was anything, he was

tenacious, a bulldog who sank his teeth in and didn't let go. "I'd advise a bit of caution, Your Grace. The man you are dealing with has very few qualms. One never knows for certain what that sort of man will do."

It was damned good advice and Rand intended to heed it. But he wasn't going to give up. Not until Talmadge and the others paid for what they'd done.

He walked Ephram to the door and watched him depart in a hackney carriage, then returned to his study.

For the hundredth time that day, he glanced at the clock. The hours were slipping past, but none too quickly. The minute hand seemed to drag as if it was held down with lead weights.

But eventually the hour would come. Tonight he would see Caitlin Harmon. He would carry her off to River Willows, take her to one of his family estates as he had never done with another woman and make wild, passionate love to her. He would enjoy a long night of pleasure, take her until he got his fill.

His body went hard just to think of it. If he closed his eyes, he could see her lovely face, the faint spray of freckles across her nose, the full pink lips, and strong chin. He could imagine pulling the pins from her long golden-red hair, filling his hands with her high, lush breasts.

God, he wanted her so damned badly.

Rand glanced at the clock again.

NINE

"I'm sorry, Maggie. I had every intention of going with you, but I had forgotten the documents my father asked me to study over at the museum. He needs that information and it's going to take some time."

Maggie's excited posture seemed to deflate, and Cait felt like a villain. She couldn't help wondering when she had become such a competent liar—or why she was willing to go that far.

"Perhaps if you can't go," Maggie said, "Andrew and I should stay home, as well."

Cait shook her head. "Don't be silly. You told me how much you were looking forward to escaping the city. Besides, you and Andrew deserve a little time alone."

Maggie worried her bottom lip, her pale brows pulled slightly together. "I don't know . . . it doesn't seem right just to leave you here."

"I'll be fine," Cait said with a pasted-on smile, her hands slightly shaking. Perhaps lying wasn't so easy for her after all. "I have so much to do I won't even notice you're gone."

Maggie glanced down the hall toward the study, where Andrew labored to finish the last of his paperwork so they could depart. "I *was* looking forward to this. And having Andrew all to myself—" She rolled her eyes and grinned. "You can't begin to imagine."

Cait tried to smile, but her lips barely curved. Perhaps she couldn't imagine—not yet—but by morning, she would likely have a very good notion. She was extremely well read on what happened between a man and a woman, and she would never forget the pictures she had seen in Pompeii. Still, it was difficult to imagine exactly what she was letting herself in for.

She turned Maggie toward the stairs and gave her a gentle shove. "Go on, now. Go up to your room, finish your last-minute packing, and the two of you get out of here."

Impulsively, Maggie reached over and hugged her, then she turned and raced up the stairs. Watching her made Cait's guilt increase tenfold. She and Maggie had become extremely good friends. Friends didn't lie to each other.

In the entry, the ornate grandfather clock began to chime. In two more hours, she would speak to the housekeeper, Mrs. Beasley, tell her she'd received a note from Sarah Whittaker, the daughter of a friend of her father's, asking her to visit for the next several days.

"It would be best if you don't say anything to Lady Trent," Cait said to the woman when the time finally came. "You know how she frets when I go off by myself."

Mrs. Beasley merely nodded. She disapproved of Cait's independence, but she had accepted it, as the rest of the household had. "As you wish, miss," she said a bit tartly.

Twenty minutes later, Cait was dressed and on her way to the British Museum, hoping Rand's carriage would be waiting out in front. By the time she got there, her heart was hammering as if she had just run a race and her palms were sticky and damp. She clutched her tapestry traveling bag so tightly her fingers began to cramp.

The hackney came to a halt. She pulled the hood of her cloak up over her head, stepped out of the conveyance onto Great Russell Street, handed the driver a shilling, and turned to search for Rand. From the corner of her eye, she saw him, striding toward her in that purposeful way of his, tall and impossibly handsome. Her heart constricted, squeezed inside her chest.

"You came," he said, looking oddly relieved, smiling as he reached for her satchel. "I wasn't completely certain you would."

Her own smile felt wobbly. "Neither was I."

He tried to take the satchel, but her fingers wouldn't let go. He tried again—to no avail—and his eyes swung to her face.

"Good God, you're frightened to death. Your face is as white as a sheet, and you're trembling all over."

Cait wet her lips, but she felt close to fainting. "I . . . I'm fine."

"You aren't the least bit fine," he said darkly, sliding an arm around her waist and bundling her off toward a plain black carriage she hadn't seen before. "But I promise you, love, I'll make certain that you are." He helped her climb in, then followed her inside. Instead of taking a seat across from her, he sat down beside her and settled her in his lap, cradling her against him as if she were more precious than gold.

"There's no reason for you to be frightened," he said softly. "We're going to take this slow and easy. I told you once I'd never do anything you didn't want me to. I meant that, Cait. We have all the time in the world. Will you trust me to do what is right for us both?"

The shaking began to ease. She nodded against his chest. "I'm sorry. I'm behaving like a fool, I know."

"There is nothing foolish about you, Caitlin. I know you haven't had much experience. Just trust me and everything will be all right."

She did trust him, she realized. Against all her instincts, against all the advice she'd been given, she trusted him as she never had any man besides her father. The terror began to fade, her nerves to ease. She was smiling by the time they arrived at River Willows, laughing at something Rand said, beginning to look forward to the grand adventure she had embarked upon—the adventure of becoming a woman.

Rand led Caitlin inside the huge red-brick house that was River Willows, a great, sprawling mansion with gables, spires, and chimneys, the inside all dark wood and stone floors. There was nothing modern about River Willows, nothing stylish, yet he had always loved the place, which felt aged and settled, welcoming in a way none of his other houses were.

"It looks just as I imagined it would," Cait said, smiling as she stared into the darkened rafters, surveying the heavy carved furniture in the main salon with obvious delight. Done mostly in shades of dark red and blue, the sofas were slightly worn, the Oriental carpets showing their years of service. "It feels like home—a real home, you know? The sort filled with children and laughter."

Her words pleased him more than they should have. The house was old and in need of repair. He should have seen to it years ago, but somehow he liked the place exactly as it was.

"Did you ever live here, Rand?"

He shook his head. He had wanted to. How many times had he wished he could run away and live here with his aunt and uncle? "My father's brother lived on the estate. I came to visit whenever I could. I had four cousins to play with, three girls and a boy—a real treat, since at home there was only me. They were a wonderful family."

"Where are they now?"

His jaw clamped, his mood beginning to darken. "My uncle and his wife died some time back. My cousins are scattered." The girls were married. The boy, his cousin Jonathan, the youngest of the four, was dead at two and twenty, a year older than Cait. As good as murdered by Phillip Rutherford. He gave her a harder look than he meant to.

"Come on. Supper is waiting upstairs." Taking Cait's hand, he led her toward the wide oak staircase, up to the master suite. What few servants remained at the house had been dismissed for the evening, all but a footman, a cook, and a maid, who remained close by to serve them.

A fire had been laid in the hearth and it crackled pleasantly. Like the rest of the house, the room was paneled in rich, dark oak, the ceilings timbered. The furnishings were heavy and carved, the draperies fashioned of slightly faded dark blue velvet. Through the open door, he could see the huge four-poster bed where his aunt had birthed her four children.

His mood went darker still. When he had chosen to come to River Willows, it hadn't occurred to him Jonathan's ghost would be there to haunt him.

"Rand . . . ?"

He heard his name, tentatively spoken, and turned to look at Cait. She stood in front of the fire, her bonnet removed, her hair, fashioned in soft curls atop her head, the same golden red as the flames. She had draped her cloak over a chair, and the gown she wore beneath, a lovely deep green silk, displayed a generous portion of her high, full breasts. They were rising and falling far too rapidly, he saw, and realized her nervousness was returning.

It wasn't fair to direct his anger at her. It wasn't what he'd intended when he came to River Willows. Jonathan's death wasn't Caitlin's fault—he had to remember that. Taking a deep, shuddering breath, determined to force his dark mood away, he went over and took her hand.

"I'm sorry," he said, working to summon a smile. "I've been remiss in my duties as host. Would you like something to drink?" He didn't wait for her answer, simply strode to the marble-topped table beside the fireplace, lifted the stopper off a decanter of sherry and poured her a glass. He carried it over and pressed it into her hand. "I promise this will make you feel better."

Cait took a long sip of sherry and Rand returned to the sideboard. Watching her from beneath lowered lids, he poured himself a brandy, thinking how incredibly lovely she was. His mood shifted again, his body tightening, reminding him of the reason he had come.

Cait took another long drink and he studied the movement of her slender throat as she swallowed. In the light of the fire, she looked vibrant, and more beautiful than any woman he could remember. He found himself walking toward her, drawn to her as he had been the first time he had seen her. He took the glass from her hand, set it on the table. Gently, he turned her around and began to pluck the pins from her hair.

"I want to see it down," he said softly, a hairpin pinging as it hit the floor. "I want to watch the way the colors change in the firelight." When the heavy mass was finally freed, he combed his fingers through it, and silken gold-tipped curls wrapped around his hands. Desire wrapped around him as well, fierce, and nearly uncontrollable. His body tightened, went painfully hard.

Cait looked up at him, and he knew she saw the hunger he couldn't disguise, but instead of the fear he expected, he saw the same fierce need reflected in her eyes, as well.

"Caitlin . . . sweet God . . ." He had meant to go slowly, to charm and seduce. Instead he pulled her into his arms and took her mouth in a white-hot, burning kiss. His lips devoured her, impatient, greedy, taking complete control. He could feel her trembling, told himself to pull away, then her arms slid around his neck and she kissed him back, her small, sweet tongue sliding into his mouth. Rand was utterly lost.

The air seemed to heat and swirl around them. Need scorched through his veins. He tore the buttons at the back of her gown in his haste to get it undone, shoved it down her shoulders and over her hips, watched it pool at her feet. Lifting her into his arms, he carried her into the bedchamber and settled her gently in the center of the soft feather mattress.

"I promised to go slowly. You are so lovely, so incredibly tempting . . . it isn't easy, Cait."

"Rand . . ." She reached out to him and he went into

her arms, pressing her down in the mattress, his body flooding with heat. He could feel her breasts against his chest, pillowing softly, incredibly seductive. He captured her mouth, took her deeply with his tongue, and heard her tiny moan of pleasure. It fired his loins, made his body go rock hard. His hands found her breasts, massaged them through the barrier of her chemise, but it wasn't enough. He wanted to see her naked, to feel the softness of her skin, to taste the tight pink buds of her nipples.

Growling low in his throat, he shredded the chemise down the front then sat back to examine the shape and fullness of her breasts.

"Perfect . . . " he whispered, bending forward to take one into his mouth. Caitlin stopped him with a trembling hand on his chest.

"What about you?" she asked softly. "I would see you, Rand . . . if you would not mind."

Mind? Sweet God, he couldn't think of anything more erotic. He wanted her to see him, touch him, as in his dreams she had done a hundred times. "It would please me greatly, Caitlin. I would have you look your fill."

Sitting on the edge of the bed, he stripped off his boots and breeches, shed his jacket and shirt. When he turned, her eyes were fastened on his chest.

"So beautiful," she said, running her hand over the muscles along his side, sending a shudder the length of his body. "Perfectly sculpted. Like an ancient Greek statue."

He chuckled, oddly pleased, lifted her hand, and drew each of her small fingers into his mouth. "I'm glad you like what you see."

Her eyes drifted lower. Her hand followed, moving over a flat copper nipple, inspecting the ridges across his stomach, making his body tighten painfully. When her gaze reached his iron-hard erection, she went still and a tight sound came from her throat.

"You . . . you are so big. I thought . . . I thought . . ."

He couldn't help a smile. "What was it you thought, my love?"

Cait closed her eyes and shook her head. In the light of the fire, her face looked suddenly pale. "I never thought you'd be . . . I just . . . Would you kiss me, Rand?"

He came up over her, her body soft and pale and incredibly feminine beneath him. Capturing her face between his hands, he kissed her deeply, pressing her down in the feather mattress as he eased himself between her legs. He could feel her trembling, knew her nervousness had returned, and set upon a campaign of seduction. He kissed her softly, drew on her full bottom lip, kissed the corners of her mouth.

"Trust me," he whispered, nibbling the side of her neck. "Let me show you how good it can be."

He wondered fleetingly what man had taken her before, and imagined that he must have done so poorly. Rand was glad he was the man who would show her how sweet the pleasure could be. He kissed her again, this time deeply, tasting the inside of her mouth, coaxing her to taste him, as well.

His body ached. The tension in his muscles grew nearly unbearable. He massaged her breasts, tested their weight, their incredible softness, and her nipples tightened. He took first one and then the other into his mouth, laving the stiff peak with his tongue, making her moan and writhe beneath him. His own body burned. Heat seemed to scorch through his blood, burn straight into his loins. He kissed a path to the small indention at her navel, ringed it with his tongue, and unconsciously she arched upward. She trembled again, but this time from passion not from fear.

"I want you," he whispered, his hand sifting through the downy red curls at the juncture of her legs, parting the soft folds of feminine flesh and slipping a finger inside. She was hot and wet, so incredibly tight. The thought of being inside her sent a shudder ripping through him. Desire flamed. Heat scorched over his skin. He stroked her deeply, found the small bud of her womanhood and set up a rhythm that had her sobbing his name. She was slick and ready and he couldn't wait any longer, didn't want to wait a moment more.

Guiding himself to the entrance of her passage, he ravaged her mouth as he eased himself inside. He inched in farther, felt her fingers dig into the muscles across his shoulders—and the unmistakable barrier of her maidenhead.

Every muscle in his body went tense. He looked down into her big green eyes, saw the wonder and the uncertainty. "Why, Caitie? Why didn't you tell me?"

"Would we be here now if I had, Rand?"

He closed his eyes, shook his head. "In truth, I don't know."

"I want this, Rand. I want you to make love to me."

She was different, not like any other woman. He had known that from the start. Still, he had never deflowered an innocent. Caitlin must have sensed his hesitation, for she slid her arms around his neck and dragged his mouth down to hers for a kiss. Her small tongue found its way into his mouth. Rand shuddered and drove himself home.

He cursed himself as her body clenched in pain and she muffled a cry in her throat.

"I'm sorry," he said, fighting hard for control. "I didn't mean to hurt you. Are you all right?"

She released a pent-up breath, gave him a trembly smile. "The pain is receding. Mostly, I just feel filled by you. It's rather a pleasant sensation."

He almost smiled, might have if his emotions hadn't been so close to the edge. Instead he kissed her, gently yet thoroughly. He wanted this to be right for her, to be special, a night she would always remember. Easing himself out and then in, he slowly began to move.

Pleasure rolled through him, hot and intense. His shaft felt gloved in silk, surrounded by liquid warmth, and the sight of her beautiful breasts, swollen with desire, made it nearly impossible to maintain control. He increased the rhythm, moving faster, driving more deeply, Caitlin shifting restlessly, beginning to move beneath him.

He could hear her heartbeat, or perhaps it was his own. The fire in his loins grew hotter, more insistent. He wanted to be certain she was pleasured, wanted to give her something in return for the gift she'd given to him.

Again and again, he drove into her, the slickness of her passage easing the way, her urgent movements driving him nearly to frenzy. There was no stopping now, no more waiting. He wanted her too badly, had already waited too long. With a groan, he went rigid. He meant to withdraw, to insure she would be protected, but in that last moment her tight little womb contracted, the muscles constricting so sweetly around him as she reached her own release. The pleasure was so intense, so wildly erotic, he drove into her again.

His climax spiraled upward, soared till he thought it would never end. Sweet God, he couldn't remember ever feeling anything like it. Cait must have felt it, too. When the pleasure finally ebbed, she was sobbing, and he pulled her into his arms.

"Easy, love. Easy. Everything's all right. Please don't cry." She rested her cheek against his chest and he felt the wetness. He prayed he hadn't hurt her too badly.

Cait sniffed and wiped away her tears. "It wasn't in any of the pictures," she said. "There was nothing in the books."

"What wasn't in the books?" he asked softly, smoothing strands of flame-red hair away from her face.

"There was nothing about how it would feel . . . how beautiful it would be."

Something filtered through him, something soft and tender that made him want to hold her even tighter than he was already. She was so small, yet so much woman. "I know I must have hurt you. I tried to be gentle, but—"

"You were wonderful. Perfect."

That sweet feeling returned. "It only hurts the first time."

"I know," she said, and he smiled.

"You know a lot of things, Miss Harmon. By the time you return to London, you will know a great deal more about all of this."

Cait looked up at him and her lips softly curved. "I knew I was right to pick you. I knew you were the one I should choose."

He chuckled. He couldn't help it. "And here I thought I was the one who picked you."

Her fingers sifted through the curly hair on his chest. "Perhaps you were—in the beginning."

It was all the concession he would get. Enough to save his pride, he guessed. "I don't suppose it matters. What matters is what else you're going to learn."

She looked a bit surprised. "Tonight?"

"Oh, yes, my love. Definitely tonight." He frowned. "Unless, of course, you're not up to it."

Cait leaned over and kissed him. "Why don't we try it and see?"

He was hard already. He had thought she was fire the first moment he had seen her, and it pleased him to know he was right. He kissed her as he came up over her, parted her legs with his knee, and slid himself inside her.

There was so much to teach her, so much pleasure he could show her. Inwardly, he grinned, thinking how bright she was and how quickly she would learn the lessons he meant to teach.

TEN

She wouldn't think about what she had done, Cait vowed. Not now, now while everything was still so new, so full of mystery and wonder. She wouldn't worry about the lies she had told, the people who would be hurt if they found out.

She would face those problems when she returned, do as she had planned, and claim these few precious days for herself.

After a night of passionate lovemaking, Cait awakened late in the morning, her body tender in places, yet pleasantly relaxed and sated. With a sigh of contentment, she reached over to the other side of the bed, expecting to feel Rand's big, solid body, but the bed was empty, and for a moment she was confused. Then the door swung open and he strode in, a burgundy silk dressing gown flicking against his bare calves, his big hands holding a tray of food.

"I thought you might need sustenance," he said with a charming grin. *For what I have in mind*, said those sinful brown eyes.

Caitlin flushed at the memory of the intimate things they had done the night before, the way he had made her feel, and turned her attention to the food: a platter of cold roast partridge, a steaming pot of chocolate, some sweet little biscuits, sliced apples, and a hunk of Wilton cheese. A single long-stemmed rose sat on the tray in a lovely crystal bud vase.

Rand set the tray on a table in front of the hearth while Caitlin pulled on her yellow silk wrapper and joined him there. Very formally, he pulled out her chair and his dressing gown gaped open. Swirls of curly brown chest hair covered thick slabs of muscle that tightened when he bent to kiss her cheek.

Ignoring the funny little flutter in her stomach, she focused her attention on the chocolate he was pouring and discovered that indeed she did need nourishment. Especially after they had finished their meal and he shrugged off his robe and carried her back to bed.

They spent the morning making love, then took a basket of food down to the place beside the river where they had picnicked before. They watched the birds for a while, then made love on a blanket in a secluded spot protected by a copse of willow trees.

It was the most precious of days and the evening was even better, beginning with an elegant supper that this time they actually ate. They retired early and made love then fell into a pleasantly exhausted sleep.

She awakened hours later in the middle of his big four-poster bed and Cait smiled at the feel of his heavy weight curled against her. A solid wall of muscle and heat. In the darkness outside the window, she could hear the soft luffing of the wind, the faint hoot of an owl, the rustle of tall green grasses. Tomorrow Rand would be returning her to London, but it wouldn't be the old Cait who went back. It would be a new, totally different Cait Harmon.

At least she felt as if she were different. Several times during the day, she had found herself looking in the mirror to see if the way she felt inside showed somehow on her face.

It didn't, of course, not unless the healthy blush in her cheeks gave her away. She felt Rand stir behind her and gasped softly at the hardness that suddenly pressed against her. She thought of the Pompeiian stone reliefs she had seen. None of the men were so large as Rand. And the huge phallic symbols . . . perhaps they were not so out of proportion as she had guessed.

He came up on an elbow, bent his head and lightly grazed her shoulder with his teeth.

"Can't sleep?" he asked, kissing the side of her neck. She could feel the slight curve of his smile against her skin, hear the sensual hunger in his voice.

Unconsciously, she wet her lips, feeling the heat of him, knowing he would soon be inside her, wanting him there. "I just . . . no," she softly teased. "Perhaps you might know a way to help me."

Rand chuckled at that, a deep vibration in his chest. "I might." His hand found her breast, teased it gently, then he slid his fingers between her legs. He stroked her there as he kissed her throat and shoulders, making her skin feel hot and tight. She felt his maleness, hard, determined, probing. Rand adjusted her body a little, making it easier for her to accept him, then slid himself deeply inside.

Cait moaned softly. She remembered this position among the ones she had seen carved into the walls in Pompeii. At the time, she hadn't understood how the man and woman might fit so perfectly together.

One of Rand's big hands moved down from her breasts and he began to stroke her. The delicious sensations sent every other thought sliding out of her head. His hard-muscled body moved in and out with the same fluid rhythm as his hands, and in seconds she was floating, soaring upward, heading for release.

They reached the pinnacle together, their bodies intimately fused and glowing with perspiration. Afterward, she lay curled in his arms while Rand whispered soft, erotic words. How good she had felt; how tight she was. How he always seemed to want her. She drifted to sleep with his hand smoothing gently over her hair.

She might have slept as peacefully as she had the night before, but in the hours before dawn it occurred to her that in the morning they would be leaving, their idyllic time together at an end.

Now that she had given herself to Rand so completely, she could hardly imagine what life would be like without him.

And yet it must be so.

Tomorrow her father would also be returning to the city. In the days ahead, there would be a great deal of work for them to do, and little time for her and Rand.

Even if there were, in less than two more weeks she would be leaving, returning to Santo Amaro. The money had been raised; the goods and supplies had been purchased. Her father and the others were eager to continue their search for the necklace. They would be gone a year, perhaps longer. If they didn't find the necklace, there would be no reason to return. They might never come back to England.

The man sleeping beside her moved, shifting her a little in his arms, but he didn't awaken and he didn't release his hold. She could hear his even breathing, feel the rise and fall of his powerful chest. For the first time it occurred to her how much she had come to care for him. And just how much she was going to miss him.

Her heart clenched at the truth she had known all along—once she left London, there was a very good chance she would never see him again.

Maggie Sutton paused at the bottom of the steep iron stairs of the carriage, which had just arrived at the Duke of Beldon's impressive stone mansion on Grosvenor Square. She straightened her bonnet and smoothed the skirts of her apricot muslin day dress. Taking a determined breath, she squared her shoulders, climbed the front steps, and hammered on the ornately carved door.

A young blond footman clad in Beldon red and gold livery pulled it open, and the butler, a man whose name she recalled was Peterson, walked up to greet her, a thin, brown eyebrow arched in recognition. "Lady Trent? I didn't realize His Grace was expecting you."

"I'm afraid he isn't," she said a bit stiffly, stepping into the massive black-and-white marble-floored entry.

The eyebrow moved again, arching a little higher. "He's working in his study. If you would be so kind as to follow me to the Gold Salon, I'll inform him that you are here."

She did as he asked, entering a huge, white-painted room with high, molded ceilings and gilded furnishings. There were mirrors and painted vases, ornate sofas and marble-topped tables, all done in ivory and gold. Gold-framed portraits lined the walls, hanging beside gilded Italian sconces.

"Tell him it's important," Maggie called to the butler as he turned to leave. "Tell him I shall be happy to wait until such time as he is able to break free."

He made her a very formal bow. "As you wish, my lady." His posture perfectly erect, he proceeded down the hall, his footsteps slowly fading.

In his absence, Maggie began to pace, her agitation continuing to build. She'd been afraid something like this would happen. If only she had talked to Rand sooner, made him understand. If only she could have . . .

He walked in just then, impressive as always, striding through the door like a general in command of an army, turning to her with a worried look on his face. "Maggie—what is it? What's happened?"

She lifted her chin. "I'm afraid I'm not yet certain. Perhaps it is you who should tell me."

He met her gaze for several long moments, then looked away. "You are here about Caitlin."

She cast him a disapproving smile. "How very astute, Your Grace. Andrew and I leave town for a couple of days and when we return, I discover a great deal has happened."

"And that is . . . ?"

"Don't play games with me, Rand. The housekeeper informed me Caitlin left the town house just a few hours after we departed for the country. She didn't return until late Sunday evening."

Rand strode over to the sideboard. "Perhaps you should have a drink, something to calm your nerves."

"I don't want a drink. And don't you dare pour one for me anyway, as I know you are itching to do."

A corner of his mouth kicked up. "I can see why you and Caitlin have become such good friends. You are both rather strong-minded for females."

"We *are* friends, Rand. That is why I'm here. I believe Cait spent those missing several days with you. Is that where she was?"

He finished pouring himself a brandy and replaced the stopper on the crystal decanter. Lifting the glass, he took a sip, pondering the question and its ramifications.

He set the glass down very carefully, the expression on his face purposely bland. "Is that what Caitlin told you—that she was with me?"

She started to deny it, but he didn't give her the chance.

"If that is her game—if she believes she can use you to get to me, then the little vixen is in for quite a surprise. I won't be duped into marriage—not to Cait Harmon or anyone else. If that was her scheme—"

"That is quite enough, Rand Clayton!" Anger made her hands shake. Maggie fought to rein in her temper. "For your information, Caitlin has said nothing to anyone about this. She has no idea I am here."

He fell silent at that and some of the tension seemed to drain from his shoulders. "I'm sorry. I shouldn't have jumped to conclusions."

"No, you should not have. Cait Harmon would never do a thing like that. She isn't even interested in marriage. Surely you know that by now."

He sighed, raked a hand through his thick brown hair. "You're right, of course. It's just that . . . there are things you don't know . . . things that involve Cait and her father that I am not yet at liberty to discuss." Maggie wondered what those things were, but didn't ask. She could see by his dark expression he wasn't about to tell her.

He took another sip of his drink, eyeing her over the rim. "If Cait didn't send you, why did you come?"

Maggie lifted her chin, fighting a fresh round of anger. "I told you why I came. Because Cait is my friend—just as you are, Rand. With Andrew and I away, Mrs. Beasley felt responsible for Cait. When she left for the museum, Mrs. Beasley had a footman follow her, just to be certain that she arrived safely. He saw the two of you together out in front. He saw you and Caitlin climb into your carriage and drive away."

Rand swirled the brandy glass in his hand. "If you want to know where Caitlin was, why don't you simply ask her?"

"Because then she'll be forced to lie again. It can't be pleasant for her, Rand. She isn't that sort of person."

He studied the amber liquid in the bottom of his glass. "No, I don't think she is."

"You've had dozens of women, Rand. Cait is young and innocent. I don't want her getting hurt."

"Cait makes her own decisions—surely, as her friend, you are aware of that. It's a pleasant change from most of the women I've known."

"I'm sure it is. Everything about Cait Harmon is bright and refreshing. Tell me the two of you haven't . . . that you haven't . . ."

He set the heavy crystal snifter down on the table a little too hard and the glass rang into the quiet of the room. "This isn't your business, Maggie. I know you mean well, but—"

"It *is* my business. You have no intention of marrying Cait Harmon. What will happen to her if you get her with child?"

"I'm not a fool, you know—even if there are times you might think so. There are ways to prevent conception. I've been extremely careful." He must have seen the stricken look on her face, for he strode forward, reached out and took hold of her shoulders.

"It isn't as selfish as it seems. I'm mad about her, Maggie. And I think she cares a great deal for me. Unfortunately, the two of us would never suit—Cait knows that as well as I do. I'm not ready to be leg-shackled, and even if I were, Cait would never agree. She carries some ridiculous notion she's responsible for her mother's death. She'll never marry anyone—not as long as there's the slightest chance her father might need her."

Maggie's eyes filled with tears. "Oh, Rand. I'm so worried about her . . . about both of you."

"Maggie—please try to understand. Cait will be in England for less than two weeks. It's all the time we'll ever have together. We intend to make the most of it."

Maggie swallowed past the lump that had risen in her throat. She knew what it was like when two people cared for each other the way Rand and Caitlin did. The sad part was, neither of them realized the pain they would suffer once their time together was over.

Maggie looked at Rand and a soft ache rose in her chest. Neither of them had yet realized what she had discovered the night they'd been together at Lord Mortimer's birthday ball—that the two of them were falling in love.

Caitlin spent the day in the bowels of the British Museum. She hadn't lied about the texts her father had wanted her to study. She read Latin far better than he, and there were a number of old Roman manuscripts in the museum that had been taken from the ancient city of Alexandria, where Cleopatra had lived.

By late afternoon, after hours of working in the chilly underground rooms where the texts were stored, her vision was beginning to blur and her hands and feet were freezing. Her neck felt stiff and her shoulders ached, the pain inching down into her spine. So far she had uncovered several references to the fabulous necklace commissioned by Anthony as a gift to the Queen of Egypt. One account included an extensive description, mentioning the finely crafted facets of the solid gold chain, designed in the shape of a serpent, its long narrow body covered with miniature scales.

Another account mentioned the sea voyage Anthony had made from Italy to Syria, carrying the necklace to Cleopatra as a wedding gift. It was the year 32 B.C. In the city of Antioch, he and Cleopatra were married in an Egyptian ceremony, which, unlike Roman law, permitted polygamy, a necessity since Anthony was already wed.

Caitlin thought about that, wondering how the beautiful young queen could have tolerated sharing her husband with another woman. Cait couldn't help thinking of Rand. Once she was gone, how many other women would Rand take to his bed? No small number, she was sure. In that moment she was glad she would be leaving, that she would never have to know, never have to suffer the pain she would feel if she found out.

Determinedly, Cait forced Rand's image away and returned her attention to the pages of the heavy tome. All in all, it was a good day's work. Still, there were several other texts she wanted to finish before she left the museum. She rolled her head and rubbed her neck, hoping to relieve the ache, but it didn't do any good.

"You're working too hard, Caitlin."

Startled, she turned at the sight of pale, long-fingered hands settling on her shoulders. Cait looked up to see Geoffrey St. Anthony standing behind her chair. "Geoffrey—what are you doing here?"

"I came to see you, of course." He smiled and began a gentle massage, his fingers lightly digging in, working the tightness from her muscles, more skillful than she would have guessed. Her eyes slid closed as the pain began to recede. She knew what he was doing wasn't exactly proper, but she was so tired and it felt so good she let him continue.

"Better, Caitlin?"

A sigh of pleasure escaped. "Much better." Geoffrey,

she noted, was becoming bolder—at least where she was concerned—his boyish innocence disappearing beneath a growing determination. "Where did you learn to do that?"

His hands stilled, but only for an instant. "I'm not the naïve young fool you believe me to be. I'm a man, Caitlin, the same as any other."

Her eyes remained closed. "Meaning you learned it from your mistress." She wasn't surprised. In her experience, limited though it was, men were mostly the same. Rand had had any number of mistresses, including his latest—her. She pushed the unwelcome thought away.

"A valuable skill," Geoffrey said, his magical fingers working. "Wouldn't you agree?"

There was no time to answer for a familiar deep voice boomed into the room. "An extremely valuable skill," Rand drawled, and there was no mistaking the anger in his tone. Cait's eyes snapped open and the color seeped from her cheeks.

Geoffrey's hands fell away and Cait turned to the doorway. "I—I didn't hear you come in."

"Obviously not." A look of fury darkened his brown eyes nearly to black, and she remembered the night she had been with Geoffrey at the opera.

Well, she hadn't been doing anything wrong that night and she wasn't doing anything wrong today. She straightened and came to her feet. "Lord Geoffrey was merely being kind. I've been working in this icy basement for more than six hours. My entire body is stiff and sore." She flashed a tight smile at Geoffrey. "I appreciate your help, Geoffrey. I am feeling much better now, thanks to you."

"I'm certain Lord Geoffrey is quite talented," Rand said, walking purposefully toward her.

Cait ignored the sarcasm that dripped from his voice—and a ridiculous urge to run. "Yes, he is."

"I might suggest, however, that his *talent* would be put to better use on someone else." Rand stopped directly in front of her, his warning more than clear. "And since you have been working for so long, I think it is time you quit for the day."

She glanced at the stack of books on the table. "I can't quit yet. I still have work to do. I have yet to—"

"Whatever you have to do, it can wait until later." Gripping her arm, he turned her around and hauled her toward the door. "If you will excuse us, Lord Geoffrey."

To Geoffrey's credit, he placed himself in front of them, intent on blocking their way. It was a brave thing to do, considering the ferocious expression on Rand's face.

"I don't believe Miss Harmon is ready to leave."

Rand's hard gaze pinned Geoffrey where he stood. "Is that so?" The younger man's face went a little bit pale and Caitlin suddenly felt sorry for him.

She forced herself to smile. "His Grace is right, my lord. I've worked far too long for one day. I believe I could use a bit of fresh air. Thank you for stopping by. It was very kind of you."

She was propelled out the door before she had time to say more and Rand didn't stop until they had reached his carriage. He lifted her up and set her inside, climbed in and slammed the door.

Cait's temper, already near the edge, shot up a dangerous notch. "What in heaven's name do you think you're doing? You don't own me, Rand Clayton. I'm not one of your simpering women, bound to do exactly as you command."

A muscle jerked in his cheek. "And I am not some besotted young pup like Geoffrey St. Anthony. I won't stand quietly by while you throw yourself at another man."

Fury made the world turn red. "Throw myself? Throw myself! Let me out of here this instant. I refuse to listen to another word!" Though the coach was already moving, she lunged for the door, grabbing for the handle.

Rand caught her wrist, swearing as he dragged her hard

against him. "You little fool. Are you trying to get yourself killed?"

At the moment, she was far too angry to care. "Geoffrey St. Anthony had only just walked in. He saw how tired I was and—as a very good friend—was merely trying to help me."

Rand's jaw went tight. His burning gaze moved over her, pausing for an instant on her breasts, making them tighten beneath her muslin gown. "You want that sort of help, Cait? I'll be happy to see that you get it." He caught her face between his hands and his mouth crashed down over hers.

For a single, stunned instant, she was too surprised to move. Then she started to struggle, determined not to submit to his anger. Rand pinned her against his chest, holding her easily, and the taste of him, the heat of his powerful body, the sensuous movements of his mouth and tongue, slowly eroded her struggles.

Hot, hard kisses left her breathless. Wet, hungry kisses turned her insides to mush. His tongue slid into her mouth again and again, taking possession, demanding she give in to his will. Heat sank into her belly and her body began to quiver like the string of a tightly drawn bow.

The deep, drugging kisses continued. She barely noticed when he lifted her up and settled her on his lap, arranging her so she straddled his thighs. It only faintly occurred to her that the curtains were drawn and that when he parted his legs, she was open to him, vulnerable to whatever it was he wished to do.

Rand kissed her again and the taste and scent of him enveloped her. She could feel the muscles in his shoulders bunching beneath her hands and her body infused with heat. His fingers brushed her thighs beneath her skirts, probing gently, finding the wetness at her core and sliding deeply inside. A soft moan seeped from her throat.

"Rand . . ." she whispered, her fingers digging into his shoulders as the world spun away.

"I've got what you need, Cait," he said softly. "Let me give it to you."

She moistened her trembling lips. "Yes . . . Please . . ."

His body went tense. She heard the faint rustle of fabric as he unfastened his breeches, then his hardness replaced his fingers as he thrust himself deeply inside.

Cait cried out and clung to him, responding to the incredible feel, the fierce heat and slowly building rhythm. His big hands gripped her hips, holding her in place while he drove himself inside her again and again. In minutes, she was reaching her peak, her muscles contracting around him, sweet sensation rolling over her in powerful waves. At the last possible instant, he withdrew, spilling his seed outside her womb as he was always careful to do, then he pulled her tight against him, holding her gently as she began to spiral down.

He pressed soft kisses against her cheek and the side of her neck, and Cait wondered at his mood, which was different now, no longer angry, perhaps even a bit contrite.

"What is it about you, Caitlin?" he said softly. "I was never a possessive sort of man. Not until I met you."

It was an apology of sorts, all she would get from him. Oddly, it was enough. "I didn't mean to encourage him. I think of Geoffrey only as a friend."

A corner of his mouth edged up. "That may be so, but I assure you, that isn't the way he thinks of you."

She toyed with a fold of her skirt, smoothing out the creases. "Perhaps that's true. Unfortunately, whatever he does or doesn't feel, there is little I can do about it."

Rand sighed. "I shouldn't have come thundering in as I did. Somehow, where you are concerned, my calm control seems to fly right out the window."

She smiled. "I believe you demonstrated that rather clearly."

Rand chuckled. "I suppose I did. I can't say I'm sorry. I've seen you only briefly these past few days."

"I've been busy trying to get things done. I was afraid it would be this way."

All humor left his expression. "You'll be sailing soon. We haven't much time left, Cait."

She looked up at him and an ache rose in her chest. She wished he hadn't spoken the thought out loud. It was easier to pretend they could go on as they were forever.

"Father told me this morning—we sail aboard the *Merry Dolphin* in less than a week."

Rand caught her hand, brought it to his lips. "I find I am not looking forward to it."

Cait tried valiantly to smile. "Neither am I. Unfortunately, neither of us has a choice. I have my life and you have yours. They're very different lives, Rand, with different obligations."

He simply nodded. Stretching his long legs out as best he could, he leaned back against the carriage seat. "I suppose it's time I took you back. I told my driver to simply keep going until I signaled him to stop. Will I see you later on this evening?"

She shook her head. "Father has a meeting with Lord Talmadge. We'll be going over supply lists, making last-minute preparations. He has asked me to join them."

His half-smile was faintly sarcastic. "And of course you couldn't possibly disappoint him."

Cait stiffened. "As I said, I have certain obligations. I'm part of this expedition and tonight they have asked for my help."

Rand glanced away. He didn't say more, but a slight tension seemed to have settled in his shoulders. It was always that way whenever she mentioned the baron or lately even her father. As the carriage rolled over the cobbled streets, she couldn't help wondering at the cause.

ELEVEN

Dusk had fallen by the time Rand's carriage returned to the British Museum on Great Russell Street. A watchman stood out in front next to an apple seller in a dirty knit cap who hawked his wares along the paving stones. Rand meant to see Cait into a hackney, then follow the conveyance until it safely arrived at Lord Trent's town house. But first there was something he needed to do.

The coach rolled to a stop on a side street around the corner and a footman opened the door. "Give us a moment," Rand ordered. "Light the lamps and then leave us."

The footman in red and gold made a very proper bow. "As you wish, Your Grace." Pulling flint and steel from the pocket of his waistcoat, he lit a brimstone match and ignited the mirrored brass lamps inside the carriage.

Rand could see Cait's eyes, large and inquisitive in the flickering shadows, as the footman closed the door.

Her gaze fixed on his face. "Is something the matter?"

"Perhaps this isn't the time, but in truth, no time seems to be the right one. There is something I need to tell you. It involves Phillip Rutherford and your father's expedition."

She sat up a little straighter in the seat. "What is it?"

"You may find this difficult to believe, but there is every chance Lord Talmadge is involved in this expedition for reasons far more self-serving than simple philanthropy."

"What do you mean?"

"For years, the baron was part of a scheme to swindle money from wealthy aristocrats, men who invested in a shipping venture he recommended. The ship, the *Maiden*, was to sail to the West Indies and return with a cargo of copra, the sale of which was supposed to produce enough profit to double the investors' money. Instead, the ship went down with all hands and the cargo—and the profit—was lost."

"What a terrible thing to happen."

"Yes, it would have been, if the sinking had actually occurred. But rumor has it, the ship never actually went down. Instead, the vessel arrived safely in America under another name. The profit from the sale of the cargo went to the ship's two owners—and Phillip Rutherford."

For a moment Cait said nothing. Then she straightened and her chin went up. "Rumor, you said. Is there any real proof Lord Talmadge was actually involved?"

"Only the fact that he withdrew a large sum of money from his bank account shortly after the shipping company went broke. And he left the country about the same time as Dillon Sinclair and Richard Morris, the owners of the ship. That and the fact he has a rather odd history of raising money for ventures that all seem to fail, while somehow Talmadge manages to profit."

The green of her eyes seemed to have darkened in the flickering light inside the carriage. "What does Talmadge have to do with you? Were you one of the men who lost money?"

"My cousin Jonathan was among the men who invested in the *Maiden*. When he discovered he had lost the last of his family's fortune, he killed himself." The muscles in his face felt tight, his chest, as well.

Cait's small hand covered his. "I'm sorry, Rand."

"He was only two and twenty—just a year older than you, Cait. His mother and father were dead. I should have kept a closer eye on him."

"It wasn't your fault," she said gently. "You couldn't have known he would do a thing like that."

"What I should or shouldn't have known isn't the point. Talmadge is the one who convinced the boy to invest in his worthless scheme. He caused my cousin's death as surely as if he had shot him, and I'm going to see that he pays."

Cait stared at him and wariness moved across her features. "You were after Talmadge. Is that the reason you seemed so eager to meet me?"

"I admit, in the beginning, that was part of it. You worked with him. I thought that perhaps you could be useful in obtaining information. I believed—"

Angry color swept into her cheeks, and her shoulders snapped up. "I should have known you had some sort of ulterior motive. You wanted revenge against Lord Talmadge and you thought I could provide it. That's what all of this has been about, isn't it? That's the real reason you were interested in me—because you thought I might be able to give you information about Talmadge."

Her voice had risen. He hadn't meant to upset her. "As I said, in the beginning, that was part of it. But from the start I was attracted to you. That you were working with Talmadge had some bearing, but—"

"Let me out!" She stood up, bumping her head on the ceiling, saying a swear word he was surprised she knew, trying to get to the door. "Everyone tried to warn me, but I wouldn't listen. I should have known. I never should have trusted you!"

Rand wrapped his hands around her waist and pulled her back down in the seat. "That isn't the way it is, Cait— you know it isn't. I wanted you, Caitlin—from the moment I first saw you. Just looking at you now makes me want you. Your father and Talmadge had nothing to do with that."

Her angry gaze sharpened, drawing her dark auburn brows nearly together. "My father? What does my father have to do with any of this?"

Inwardly, Rand cursed. He hadn't meant to mention the professor, at least not yet. But he wasn't going to lie about it now. He took a determined breath, hoping he could make her see. "From what we've learned of Talmadge, there's a very good chance your father's expedition is nothing more than another of the baron's swindles. Which means there is also the chance your father is involved."

The color in her face grew brighter, bright flags of red in her cheeks. "You're insane."

"With your father's assistance, Phillip Rutherford has raised a great deal of money."

"That money is being used to finance our expedition. You're not suggesting my father is lying about that? Surely you aren't implying there isn't going to be an expedition?"

"Apparently, you're returning to Santo Amaro. Your father must believe there actually is a necklace and that he'll find it there. The question is, what will happen when he does? If such a valuable antiquity really exists, it would be worth a fortune. Your father needs money, Cait. A treasure like that could pose a temptation for any man."

Her small hands tightened into fists. "How do you know we need money? You've hired someone to investigate us, haven't you? Just as you did the baron. You've been prying into our lives as if we were nothing but common criminals." She lunged for the door and this time grabbed the handle before he could stop her. She was out of the carriage and down the iron stairs, Rand close behind her.

Cait whirled to face him. "Get away from me, Rand."

"Don't do this, Cait. We only have a few days left. Whatever the truth of this is, it has nothing do with you and me."

"It has everything to do with us, Rand. The kind of person you are. The kind of person you believe I am." Her eyes welled with tears. "My father is innocent of any wrongdoing. If he finds the necklace, he'll return it to London, as he has promised."

She turned and searched the street, looking for an

empty hackney carriage. He wanted to reach out and grab her, pull her into his arms and make her understand.

He knew he didn't dare. "Listen to me, Caitlin. I only told you this because I was afraid for you. Try to understand."

She spotted a carriage, waved it over, and turned to face him one last time. Rand's chest tightened at the tears streaming down her cheeks.

"Good-bye, Rand."

"Caitlin, wait—" But there was no stopping her this time. She hurried toward the hackney, gave instructions to the driver, and climbed aboard. In seconds, she was gone.

Rand swore an oath beneath his breath. He felt faintly sick to his stomach. Striding back to his carriage, he instructed his coachman to follow the hackney until Caitlin was safely back home. He wondered what she would say to her father and Talmadge, wondered how it would affect what the two men had planned. He had hoped to gain Cait's help, along with a promise of silence. Instead he had earned her contempt.

What did you expect? said a voice inside his head. *You know how she feels about her father.* But he had told her the truth—he was worried about her. If Talmadge turned out to be the unscrupulous villain he believed, he didn't want Cait anywhere near him.

The hackney arrived at the marquess's town house and Rand watched Caitlin depart and race into the house. She closed the door, disappearing from view, and his heart felt suddenly leaden. Cait would be leaving with Talmadge. What sort of danger would she be putting herself in? Perhaps in telling her his suspicions, he had somehow made things worse.

He didn't really think so. Caitlin was intelligent. Once she thought things through, she'd be wary of Phillip Rutherford and at least she would be cautious.

He had done what was best for Cait, he was sure, but in doing so he had destroyed what last few precious days they had left. *It doesn't matter,* he told himself. *In a very brief time, she'll be gone from your life for good. Today is as good as any to begin to forget her.*

But he didn't forget. And in the next few days, he realized how much he wanted to set things right between them before she went away. He sent notes to the marquess's town house asking her to meet him, begging her to let him explain.

He went to see Maggie, hoping to gain her intervention, but discovered she knew nothing of what had transpired between them.

"Cait said the two of you had had a disagreement," Maggie told him. "That is all she has said to anyone." She turned worried blue eyes to his face. "Oh, Rand, they'll be sailing day after the morrow and Cait seems so terribly unhappy. Is there nothing you can do?"

A heavy knot tightened in his chest. "Not if she won't agree to see me."

And it was clear that was exactly the way Cait meant to keep it.

Cait stowed her small amount of baggage in the cramped aft cabin she had been given aboard the *Merry Dolphin.* They were boarding the ship the night before its departure, unpacking their clothes, getting ready to sail with the early morning tide.

For the past few days, she had kept herself busy, occupying her mind with myriad details that needed to be completed before they could leave England. Going over supply lists, making certain the items they'd ordered had actually arrived. Canvas tents and folding chairs, cooking utensils, muskets, pistols, the long-bladed knives used for hacking through the jungle. There was a list that simply contained trade goods: beads and cloth, skinning knives, cooking pots.

The hours were long and tedious, and Caitlin was glad. She needed to keep busy, to work until exhaustion forced her into a restless sleep. She wanted to fill her mind so full of details there was no room for thoughts of Rand.

And yet, his image appeared, tall and commanding, and impossibly handsome. She had ignored the notes he had sent. He had accused her father of being a thief and that was the same as accusing her.

Still, she thought about him day and night, every minute that she wasn't working. Most of the time, she wished she had never met him. Other times, she longed for him, ached for him to hold her one last time. She'd been so angry before. Now it was too late.

But she couldn't simply forget the things he had said about Talmadge. What if the baron really was a thief and her father had unwittingly put his life in the man's unscrupulous hands? Her father trusted him implicitly, but Donovan Harmon had never been a particularly good judge of character.

Cait thought her own instincts far better, and she had never been overly fond of the man. Was he the sharper that Rand believed? And if he was, what should she do about it? Repeating Rand's suspicions to her father would certainly do no good. He would simply ignore them and perhaps rightly so, since there wasn't a shred of proof.

Instead of throwing out groundless accusations that would only upset her father and might alert Talmadge to Rand's suspicions, she had decided to keep her silence, to watch and listen, and remain alert. If the baron had illicit intentions, she would discover what they were. She would have to be careful, of course. A man of that sort could pose any sort of danger.

Which returned her thoughts to Rand. It galled her to think that he had been spying on them all, digging into their pasts. A man of her father's impeccable reputation surely did not deserve it. Just because he felt guilty in some way for his young cousin's death—

The notion gave Caitlin pause. She knew firsthand the terrible burden guilt could be. Her mother's death was a burden on her soul that no amount of penance could erase. Had Rand really told her his suspicions in a misguided effort to protect her? She wanted to think so. She wanted to cherish her memories of the days they'd spent together, not regret them.

The ship creaked just then, breaking into her musings. She could hear the sound of water, lapping against the hull, feel the slight nudging of the bow against the dock. It wouldn't be long before the ship departed and she wanted to be ready. Returning to the task at hand, she shook out a white cotton nightrail and hung it on the peg beside the door, then placed several chemises next to a pair of white silk stockings in the top drawer of the bureau beside her berth.

The hour grew late. There was nothing left for her to do. It was time to retire for the night, but she knew she wouldn't sleep. Instead she lay stiffly in her narrow bed, staring up at the timbers overhead, listening to the creak and groan of the ship and thinking of Rand.

She would never forget him, she knew, would always wish she could change the way they had parted. Rand had done what he believed he had to do. The man was every bit as strong-willed and determined as she. He was wrong about her father, but he couldn't know that. And he might very well be right about Phillip Rutherford.

Cait tossed and turned and finally fell asleep. She dreamed of Rand and tears dried on her cheeks.

The first faint rays of dawn filtered in through the tiny porthole in her cabin. The ship groaned and shuddered as if it were a living thing. She awakened to the shouts of sailors up on deck, hauling line and climbing into the rigging. It was just barely light, but already the crew was preparing the ship to make way.

Swinging her legs to the side of the bed, Cait sat up, stretched, and rubbed the sleep from her eyes. Padding the few short feet to the small teakwood bureau against the wall, she poured water into the porcelain basin and washed her face, then dragged her nightgown over her head and dressed in a simple brown skirt and white blouse. Stepping into a pair of sturdy brown boots, she ran a brush through her hair and headed up on deck.

Her father and Geoffrey St. Anthony stood at the rail, along with Phillip Talmadge and the explorer, Sir Monty Walpole, who had worked with her father before. Talmadge and St. Anthony had both brought valets, and there were several other servants including an English cook and a footman that the baron had insisted come along. It was a small, valiant group of travelers who were sailing together, most of whom had come up on deck to watch the ship depart English soil.

Cait made no effort to join them. Instead, she stood some distance away, her eyes fixed on the harbor. Stevedores were already at work, loading crates and barrels onto the tall-masted ships along the quay. A brisk wind flapped the canvas sails and gulls screeched overhead. In the dim gray light, she could see the towers and spires of London, poking through the mist that shrouded the streets of the city.

Cait's fingers tightened on the rail. In the short time she had been in England, she had made some wonderful friends. As she stared off toward the city, she thought of Maggie and Andrew, Nicholas and Elizabeth. She thought of Rand and her eyes welled with tears.

It was silly, she knew, but through her watery vision, in the faint gray haze of dawn, for a moment she imagined she saw him, standing near the corner of a building on the dock, watching the ship get under way. She wiped a tear from the corner of her eye, certain now the image would be gone. But when she looked again, the man was still there, and there was something familiar about him.

Her heart lurched, began to pound violently against her ribs. It wasn't Rand, she told herself. Rand was a duke. Dukes didn't stand in the shadows of the quay at this ridiculous hour to watch a past lover sail away.

But the man in the shadows remained, and the longer she watched, the more certain she was it was Rand. A painful lump rose in her throat. Her hands began to tremble. He had come to see her one last time. He hadn't approached, simply meant to watch her as the ship sailed away, certain she would refuse to see him as she had done before.

She saw him there in the dim morning light, the strongest, dearest, most masculine man she had ever known, and a tiny sob rose in her throat. He thought that she wouldn't want to see him, but he was wrong. So completely and utterly wrong. Lifting her simple cotton skirt up out of the way, she raced toward the gangplank leading down to the dock.

"Ye can't be goin' ashore, miss," a beefy sailor said, stepping into her way. "We be ready to cast off the lines."

Cait pushed past him. "Then you will just have to wait." She tore down the gangplank, saw Rand shove away from the wall and start striding toward her. The instant she reached him, he caught her up in his arms.

"I had to see you," he whispered against her ear. "Just one more time."

"I've missed you," she whispered, feeling the sharp bite of tears. "I'm so glad you came."

He held her and she clung to him, his big hands sliding into her unbound hair, cradling the back of her head as he held her tightly against him. She looked up at him through the moisture in her eyes and he bent his head and kissed her, hotly, fiercely—yet the most infinitely tender kiss she had ever known.

The lump in her throat grew more painful. She hadn't known how hard it would be to leave him. She wanted to cling to him, hold on to him forever, instead she forced the kiss to end.

"I have to go," she said. "They're about to leave." But she made no move, and neither did he, just kept holding her in the circle of his arms.

"I'm going to miss you, Cait. More than you'll ever know."

Fresh tears burned, began to roll down her cheeks. "I'll miss you, too, Rand."

"Take care of yourself, Caitlin."

"I will. I'll remember what you told me about Talmadge." He only nodded. "Stay well, Rand."

Rand kissed her again, quick and hard, then he let her go. "Good-bye, Caitie."

She tried to say good-bye, but the words got stuck in her throat. She stared at him a moment more, memorizing his features, then she turned away. She started toward the gangway, determined not to look back, hurrying faster and faster, as if she could outrun the pain that was expanding in her chest, but it only grew more fierce, eating away at her, aching deep inside.

She hoisted her skirts and climbed to the deck, returned to her place at the rail. As the ship pulled out of its mooring, she waved toward the dock, frantically searching, desperate to see him one last time, but Rand was no longer there. He was gone from her life as quickly as he had appeared, leaving only a sweetly poignant memory to carry with her through the years.

It was in that moment, her heart aching and loneliness pressing down on her in sharp, painful waves, she realized the truth she had so long denied.

That she had done the unthinkable.

And fallen desperately, hopelessly, in love with him.

TWELVE

Dressed in a burgundy tailcoat and snug black breeches, Nicholas Warring, Earl of Ravenworth, strode down the marble-floored hall into the Duke of Beldon's walnut-paneled study. Seated in a deep leather chair behind a massive rosewood desk, his forearms propped on the polished surface, Rand sat engrossed in reading a small red leather book. He glanced up when he saw Nick, closed the gilt-edged volume, and tucked it into a drawer, but not before Nick noticed it was a book of William Blake poems.

Nick didn't mention it. He knew his friend was sensitive about such matters, and having known Rand's demanding, overbearing father, the late Duke of Beldon, he understood exactly why. It seemed perfectly ridiculous to Nick, who had never known a tougher, more masculine man than Rand. But if that was the way his friend wanted it, then that was all right with Nick.

Rand smiled and rose to his feet, rounding the desk and shaking hands, at the same time clamping a big hand on Nick's shoulder. "It's good to see you, my friend. I didn't realize you were back in the city. I thought you and Elizabeth were seeking refuge from the masses at Ravenworth Hall."

"Elizabeth is still there. I don't plan on staying in London long. Actually, I came to see you."

Rand eyed him with a hint of speculation. "Why do I have the feeling this is more than a social call?"

Nick gave him a smile he hoped looked reassuring. "I suppose in a way it is. I got a rather odd note from my sister. She says you've been holed up like some sort of hermit for the past two months and she and Andrew are worried about you. She thought perhaps I could persuade you to join us at Ravenworth for a while."

Rand glanced off toward the window. Clouds had begun to move in, blocking the sun, and a slight breeze rustled the leaves on the trees at the edge of the garden.

"I suppose I have been a bit of a recluse. I don't know why exactly. I just haven't felt like getting out the way I did before."

Before what? Nick thought but didn't ask, since he was fairly certain he knew the answer. He gave Rand an inscrutable smile. "No women? No late nights at Madame Tusseau's House of Pleasure?"

Rand shook his head. "I haven't been in the mood."

"Surely you've at least paid a visit to Hannah Reese?" The actress who was once Rand's mistress was often still a favorite. Rand considered her a friend as well as a very skillful courtesan.

"Not even Hannah," he admitted, "though now that you mention it, that isn't a bad idea." His gaze swung to the ornate clock on the mantel. "The morning's already gone. By now, Cook should have luncheon prepared. Why don't you join me for something to eat?"

Nick smiled. "Sounds good to me." He waited while Rand led the way, following him out of the study and down the hall. The meal was ready and waiting for them on the terrace. Covered silver dishes sat on a linen-draped table, a bouquet of bright yellow flowers in the middle. By the time they arrived, a place had already been set for him.

"You haven't answered my question," Nick said, seating himself in a white wicker chair. "Why not come for a visit? A little time in the country might do wonders for your flagging spirits."

A footman appeared just then, lifted a silver lid off a

platter of venison pasties and began to serve the meal.

"Perhaps you're right," Rand agreed. "I've been cooped up in the city too long. Besides, I would enjoy seeing little Nicky. He must be growing by leaps and bounds."

"I swear he's getting bigger by the minute. He's such a joy, Rand. Elizabeth and Nicky are the most precious things in my life. I don't suppose you've given the matter of a wife and family any more thought of late."

He shook his head. "Not really. When I think of all those simpering little misses I'm supposed to choose from, I actually get sick to my stomach."

Nick chuckled softly, swallowed a bite of pickled salmon, and washed it down with a sip of wine. "I realize you feel a sense of duty when it comes to marriage. Your father would have expected you to choose well, but an aristocratic pedigree isn't everything. Intelligence and strength are far more important."

Rand's shrewd, dark eyes swung to his face. "You're not speaking of Caitlin Harmon?"

Nick gave a shrug of nonchalance. "It was just a thought. You seemed fond of her. It's obvious you have missed her since she has been gone."

Rand set his fork down very carefully beside his plate. "Cait and I would never suit. She is far too independent, and she is not the sort to change. She would never obey the dictates of a husband. The man who marries her will live a life of hell."

"Or perhaps one of challenge and excitement."

Rand leaned back in his chair, his mouth curving faintly. "There is no doubt of that. The girl is a veritable spitfire. She was everything I ever imagined her to be."

"And you miss her."

He sighed. "More than I would have dreamed."

Nick was a little surprised at the admission. Rand obviously cared for the girl, yet he was convinced they wouldn't suit. Nick thought perhaps it was more than that. That in truth Rand was afraid of his feelings for Cait.

"You care for her. You're a duke—you can do as you please. You could marry her, Rand."

He only shook his head. "Even if I wanted to, Cait would never agree. She lives her life only to please her father. No other man has a chance."

Nick said nothing, just swirled the wine in his goblet and took a drink. There was a very good possibility his friend was right. Cait Harmon was wildly independent. She did exactly as she pleased. And even if Rand's feelings for her were returned, odds were she wouldn't marry him. Not as long as she believed her father needed her.

"Come to Ravenworth, Rand. Spend a little time with Elizabeth and me in the country."

Rand wiped his mouth with a napkin and, amazingly, he nodded. "Perhaps I shall. A little fresh air might be good for whatever it is that ails me."

"I'm sure it will."

Rand turned to one of the numerous liveried footmen who hovered just a few feet away. "Find Percy for me, will you? Tell him I need a word with him."

Rand's valet, Percival Fox, appeared a few minutes later, crossing the terrace with a rigid military bearing suited more to the sergeant he had been than the manservant he was now.

"You were looking for me, Your Grace?" Of medium height and build, a man in his forties with long black hair slicked back in a queue, Percy Fox was lean and tough, and like Nick's own valet, Elias Moody, more a friend than an employee.

"Lord Ravenworth has extended an invitation to visit." Rand flicked a glance at Nick, turned his attention in that direction. "We'll be leaving today, I presume—considering how surly his lordship becomes when he is too long away from his Elizabeth."

Nick grinned. "That suits me—if it's all right with you."

Rand turned back to his valet. "Make the necessary arrangements, will you?"

Percy made a slight bow. "I'll take care of it, Your Grace." As quietly as he had arrived he was gone.

Rand laid his napkin down on the table beside his empty plate. "It's amazing. I haven't even left yet and already I'm beginning to feel better."

"I told you this trip is what you need." At least Nick hoped it was. But Rand's real problem was Caitlin Harmon.

And even fresh country air couldn't soothe a troubled heart.

The island was as lovely as Caitlin remembered. An azure sea that stretched to the far-off horizon, its bright blue water reflected in the vast dome of blue overhead. A warm sun shone down on a white sand beach where frothy waves washed up on the shore and a tropical breeze rolled in to cool the salty air.

Dressed in a brown cotton-twill skirt, white blouse, and sturdy leather boots, Cait crouched on her hands and knees, digging through the grains of sand with a small metal trowel, hoping to uncover another of the numerous silver Dutch guilders they had been finding since their return.

Over two months had passed since they had set sail from England. After a stop in the city of Dakar on the African coast, they'd arrived on Santo Amaro and begun to renew their search. Since the camp of the survivors of the *Zilverijder* had already been discovered—mere days before the last of the first expedition's money ran out and they had been forced to leave—their success so far had been better even than her father had expected.

Besides the silver coins that seemed to litter the beach, the corroded barrel of an old brass cannon had been found in the shallow waters of a pool just off shore. Cooking implements, tableware, broken crockery, and even a water-logged pistol had gradually joined the growing list of discoveries.

Spirits were high and everyone worked hard, never

complaining about the long hours or her father's constant prodding to do even more. Even Lord Talmadge, mostly in charge of dispensing supplies and handling the funds for paying the tall, long-boned, dark-skinned natives who worked for them, had pitched in and done some of the digging. At first, after Rand's warning, Cait had kept a wary eye on the baron, but so far nothing seemed amiss and she wondered if perhaps the duke had been wrong.

The weather had been idyllic, just the warm, even temperatures that usually graced the island and the brief tropical showers that occurred each afternoon. Everyone, and especially her father, was certain the necklace, as well as any other valuable artifacts that might have been aboard the *Silverider,* would soon be found.

Cait tried to muster the same excitement as the other members of the expedition, and she might have—if she hadn't recently discovered that she carried Rand's babe.

The trowel trembled in her hand. Worry blossomed in the middle of her chest. She tightened her grip on the handle and began to dig again, carefully spreading the sand away from the edge of what appeared to be a weathered, brass-cornered box. Then a shadow fell across the sand and she glanced up, pushing her flat-brimmed straw hat back with a finger to see who it was.

"You look pale, Caitlin." Geoffrey St. Anthony stood on the beach just a few feet away, a look of concern on his face. With the hours he had spent in the sun, his hair was even blonder than it was when he had left England, but his skin was no longer pale, and the healthy color made him look older and more attractive.

"You shouldn't be working so hard. I know you've been ill for some time. I asked Maruba about it and she said you've been unable to keep anything in your stomach for the past several weeks."

Maruba was the young black woman they had hired to help Hester Wilmot, the English cook who had come along.

"I'm not ill," Cait argued, though at that very moment

nausea rolled in her stomach. "I ate something bad, that's all. It happens sometimes out here. I'll be fine in a day or two."

"Does your father know? I doubt it. The only thing he notices are how much sand has been dug and what items have been unearthed at the end of the day."

"My father has enough on his mind. He doesn't need to worry about a silly little thing like what I should or shouldn't eat."

"Even so, I don't think you should be out here working in the sun until you are feeling better."

Cait shaded her face with her hand and looked up into his face. It was a nice face, with its clean contours, straight nose, and pale brows, and at present it was lined with worry. In a way, she supposed it was nice to have someone concerned about her. She wasn't used to it. Rand had been a protective sort of man, but—

Cait ended the thought before it was finished, shoving Rand's image and the painful memory away.

"I appreciate your concern, Geoffrey, I really do. You've become a very dear friend, but really I am fine."

Geoffrey scowled but didn't argue, just stared down at her, grumbled something she couldn't hear, and stalked away. That night, she ate heartily and made certain that he saw her. In the morning, she was sick again, but this time she took care that he didn't see. The days crept past. The morning sickness continued, but if she watched what she ate, it only lasted a couple of hours.

It wasn't the continuing nausea that worried her. It was what she was going to do about the babe.

Sitting in front of the campfire that night, watching the orange and yellow flames spiral into the darkness above the clearing and listening to the whir of insects, Cait surveyed her primitive surroundings. Half a dozen canvas tents had been pitched in a circle in a clearing at the edge of the beach. Her own tent sheltered a narrow cot with a chamber pot beneath, a folding chair, and a crudely fashioned table. A basin and pitcher of water perched on top, next to a tiny, silver-framed portrait of her mother.

Lord Talmadge had a tent, Lord Geoffrey, Sir Monty, and of course her father. The cook shared a tent with Maruba while the rest of the servants slept on pallets on the ground outside. The natives they employed had their own campfire a little distance away, where they grouped together to cook and eat.

Sitting on an empty, overturned barrel that served as a chair, Cait watched the fire and unconsciously her hand moved over her still-flat stomach. In a few more months, her pregnancy would begin to show. Already her breasts had plumped a little and her nipples were faintly swollen. The island was miles from nowhere and there was no one to help birth the babe.

Dear God, what would she do?

She thought of Rand as she had a thousand times since she had left England. She had missed him more than she ever could have guessed yet she knew that their parting had been for the best.

Rand wasn't ready for marriage. She wasn't sure whether, even if she told him about the babe, he would offer her marriage. And even if he did, she would hardly make a suitable duchess. Living the sort of stuffy, socially demanding existence expected of an aristocrat's wife was the last thing she wanted. She treasured her freedom and she would lose it if she married a domineering, demanding man like Rand.

They were completely ill-suited, as both of them had known from the beginning.

And there was her father to think of. He needed her now more than ever—she couldn't simply abandon him.

Feeling a painful lump in her throat, Cait silently raged at herself. How could she have allowed herself to fall in love with him? She had known the danger he posed, had recognized his lethal charm from the moment she had met him—she should have been more careful.

Instead, in the dead of night as she lay on her narrow cot, she ached for him. She remembered his kisses and she yearned for the hot, sweet taste of his mouth over hers, the delicious, heavy warmth of having him inside her.

What would he say if he knew about the babe? What would he do?

A thin, chill shiver ran through her, trickling uncomfortably down her spine. If the Duke of Beldon knew she carried his babe, perhaps a son who would one day be heir to the dukedom, would he demand that she marry him?

Or simply find some way to take the child away from her?

Cait shuddered again, recognizing a fearful possibility she had never acknowledged, and in that moment she silently vowed that she would never tell him. It was wrong, she knew, but even the rush of guilt she felt at denying Rand his child was not enough to deter her.

Still, she had to do something. Dear Lord, her father would be devastated to learn she carried a nameless babe. The scandal would ruin his spotless reputation. Everything he had worked for, all the years he had studied and labored, would be overshadowed by his daughter's fall from grace. And what would it do to the poor, innocent babe? The child would be born a bastard, shunned from society at every turn.

Cait felt suddenly cold, though the night was still and pleasantly warm. If only she had someone to talk to, someone she could ask for advice. Maggie Sutton's laughing blue eyes swept into her mind, and Cait wished more than anything she could talk to the woman she considered her dearest friend. But Maggie was nowhere near and there was no one else she would turn to.

I'll think of something, Cait told herself firmly. *I'll do whatever I have to.* She wanted this child—more than she could have imagined. She had always loved children. Until fate stepped in, she had never really believed she would be lucky enough to have one. She loved this babe already, and some way, somehow, she would find a way to protect it.

Ignoring the knot of tension that formed in her stomach, Cait made her way across the camp to her small canvas tent. She paused for a moment outside, staring up at the blanket of stars overhead, chips of crystal against the blackness of the night.

She couldn't help wondering what Rand was doing on a starry night like this, if he thought of her from time to time, or if he even remembered her name.

Maggie read and reread the letter that had just arrived from Santo Amaro, pacing up and down the floor of the bright yellow morning room that faced the garden at the rear of the town house.

It had taken a month by ship for the letter to reach her, and when the messenger carrying it had arrived, Maggie had been so excited she'd torn it open and read it at once. The first part was friendly and cheerful: the weather on the island had been pleasant as it usually was, a number of items had been recovered from the wreckage of the *Silverider*, which meant chances of finding the necklace were good.

It was the last paragraph, written in a slightly shaky hand, that made Maggie's stomach clench with worry for her friend.

I pen this last to you, my dearest Maggie, as my closest friend and confidante. I ask that you keep my secret, on your honor as a woman and your happiness as Andrew's wife. I would not ask you to bear such a burden, but I am desperate and have no one else to turn to.

Maggie sank down on a yellow striped chair as she read the next line. *I am going to have Rand's child.*

Her hand trembled, ruffling the pages, making the fine blue script hard to read. The letter went on to say Caitlin had decided not to tell Rand and explained her reasons, including the fact that Rand did not wish to wed any more than she did. She spoke of how poorly suited they were, and mentioned her father's aging years and continuing need of her help.

I beg you not to judge either of us too harshly. I believe, in his way, Rand cared for me, as I cared very much for him. It was simply not meant to be.

She added that she already loved the babe and was certain she would find a way to work things out.

Thank you for listening, my dear Maggie, she finished. *You will never know how much your friendship has meant to me.* It was signed, *With greatest affection, Caitlin Harmon.*

Maggie didn't realize she was crying until a tear slipped down her cheek. She brushed it away with the back of her hand and dragged in a shaky breath of air. Dear God, she had been so afraid something like this would happen. Now Caitlin was miles away with no one to help her. Why couldn't Rand have listened!

Because Rand was in love with Cait and she was in love with him—Maggie knew it, even if they were too blind to see. In a few more months a child would be born out of that love, and because of the parents' stubbornness, the babe would never know his father.

Maggie reread the last part of the letter one more time, sick at heart and aching for Caitlin, wishing there was something she could do.

But her dear friend had written her in strictest confidence, trusting Maggie with her most intimate secret. If Maggie went to Rand, it would be a betrayal of the very worst sort. She wasn't at liberty to discuss it even with Andrew.

The awful truth was, except for writing to Cait in the hope she could persuade her friend to change her mind and tell the duke, there was nothing at all she could do.

Rand felt restless as he often did of late. In the past few months, he'd grown bored with the endless rounds of parties and meaningless flirtations that he had once enjoyed. Since his return from Ravenworth Hall several weeks past, he had decided that perhaps it was time he settled down. Watching Nick and Elizabeth with their infant son, he had wondered if perhaps he should think about fulfilling his obligations as duke, marrying and getting himself an heir. Perhaps a family would somehow add meaning to his boring, jaded existence.

The difficulty, he discovered, lay in finding a suitable wife. As he had suspected, none of the young women currently in the marriage mart seemed to capture his interest. Margaret Foxmoor, a willowy, pale-skinned blond who was the current rage of the ton, and Vera Petersmith, a doe-eyed brunette whose father was the Marquess of Clifton and would make a very handsome settlement were they to wed, best seemed to fit his requirements. Both were from excellent families and well schooled as ladies of quality. They were quiet and docile, would obey his every command, yet in some way he found each of them lacking.

Rand sighed as he stood at the edge of the dance floor in the Earl of Dryden's town house, watching Lady Margaret enjoying a contradance with the Viscount Brimford. Since he had decided to enter the marriage mart, he had been on his best behavior. Now he found himself chafing for a night of debauchery at Madame Tusseau's where, at least for a while, he could completely forget himself and his future obligations.

Instead, he watched the members of the ton from behind an insipid smile and tried not to compare the women in the room to Caitlin Harmon. If he did, he had discovered, they failed miserably in the comparison. As he had a thousand times, he wondered where she was, hoped she was well and safe. Hoped she'd encountered no trouble from Phillip Rutherford.

Several meetings with his solicitor, Ephram Barclay, had proved fruitless in that regard. They were no closer to proving the baron's duplicity than they were when he had left with Donovan Harmon for Santo Amaro.

Rand's jaw tightened in frustration. Surely, sooner or

later, something would break. But even if it did, with Talmadge thousands of miles away or perhaps already fled to parts unknown, the effort would likely prove futile.

"Good evening, Your Grace. I was hoping I would find you here."

Rand glanced down, cocked a brow as he caught sight of Maggie Sutton, standing just a few feet away. "Good evening, Maggie. You were looking for me?"

Her lips curved briefly but there was no smile in her eyes and there was something unsettling about the tension in her face. "Actually, I dropped by your house a little earlier in the evening. The butler informed your valet I was looking for you. Mr. Fox told me he believed you might be attending the earl's soirée."

"Where is Andrew?" he asked, glancing around the ballroom but not seeing him, sensing something was very wrong, indeed.

"Andrew is playing cards at his club. I came by myself. I need to speak to you, Rand. Alone. I've been trying to work up my courage for days. With Andrew out for the evening, I thought perhaps tonight would suffice." Maggie made another attempt to smile but failed even worse than before. Noticing she had begun to tremble, Rand took her arm, settled a firm hand at her waist, and led her out the door to the terrace.

The wide brick balcony overlooking the garden was mostly deserted. Guiding her to a quiet corner beneath a flaming torch, he gently turned her to face him.

"I can see that you're upset. If there is anything I can do to help, you know I will. What is it, Maggie?"

"It's . . . it's about Caitlin, Rand."

Something clenched hard in his stomach. "Caitlin? Has something happened to her? She isn't in some sort of trouble?"

"Actually, Rand, Caitlin is in very serious trouble. She swore me to secrecy, but in good conscience, I simply cannot keep silent. Not when I believe that in doing so

I'll be ruining the lives of two people I care very much about."

His heart was hammering. He drew in a breath and steeled himself. "Tell me what's wrong."

"Caitlin is carrying your child, Rand."

The air seemed to whoosh from his lungs. "You're mistaken. I was careful. It isn't possible."

Maggie's head snapped up. "It isn't possible? Are you actually going to stand there and deny that the child she carries is yours?"

His hands shook. He took hold of the balustrade to steady himself, searching to find the right words. "That isn't what I meant. I just thought I had been . . . it doesn't matter. Is she certain, then?"

"It's been nearly four months, Rand. In that length of time, a woman would know for sure."

He dragged in a calming breath, shoved a hand through his hair, raking it back from his forehead. He wasn't sure what he was feeling, but it wasn't the horror he would have expected. It was more of a stirring, a coming to life, as if he were just now waking from a long, unpleasant dream.

"When will she be returning to England?"

A flood of color rushed into Maggie's cheeks. "You still don't understand, do you? You think Caitlin is coming back, that she expects you to marry her. Well, you're mistaken. She doesn't even plan to tell you. She made me swear I wouldn't. She says she loves the child already. She says she'll find a way to handle the situation by herself."

For the first time, Maggie's words began to sink in. "You're not saying . . . you're not telling me she doesn't intend for us to wed?"

Maggie's chin inched up. "That is exactly what I'm saying—and from the way you are behaving I don't blame her." She turned and started to walk away, but Rand caught her arm.

"Maggie, please—you don't understand. It's just that

this is all happening so fast." He blew out a breath, fighting to collect his thoughts. "Cait Harmon means a great deal to me. If she is having a child, there is no doubt that it is mine." A corner of his mouth edged up. "And now that I am over the shock, I am rather pleased about it."

She stared up at him, her eyes widening in disbelief. "You are?"

Rand smiled. "Yes, I am. Cait may be a little headstrong and she is not exactly ideally suited for the role of duchess, but at least she will never be dull. She is beautiful and intelligent—and she is going to marry me, whether she likes it or not."

Maggie laughed then, the sound filled with relief and a hint of tears. Rand reached out and took her hand, felt how cold it was, carried it to his lips. "You are a very dear friend, Maggie Sutton, and I shall always be indebted to you for the risk you have taken in coming to me this way."

Her smile slipped away. "I hope I'm doing what's right for Caitlin, as well as what's right for you."

Rand's smile also slid away. "Leave Cait Harmon to me. I am not the least bit happy that she planned to keep my child from me, but knowing her as I do, I suppose I can understand the reason she is behaving as she is."

"She cares for you, Rand. And I believe she'll make you a very fine duchess."

Rand just nodded. He wasn't sure about that, but he was certain about one thing. Cait Harmon would soon be the mother of his child. That made her his, and Rand was a man who kept what belonged to him.

It occurred to him that the only real mistake he had made was in letting her leave in the first place.

THIRTEEN

The days slid past, grew into another month. Cait was over her morning sickness, but other problems had surfaced. Twice in the middle of the afternoon and again this morning, she had grown dizzy and light-headed, and fainted dead away.

Geoffrey had witnessed the humiliating occurrence and come to her rescue, though thankfully she had been working in a sheltered spot away from the others. Geoffrey had watched her with worried eyes and intense speculation, and she was terrified he would say something about it to her father.

Instead, as night began to fall and the supper hour ended, he approached where she sat on a long driftwood log in front of the fire, next to the explorer, Sir Monty Walpole.

"This is all so exciting," Sir Monty said. "Rather like the time I was in India, searching for the lost city of Ramaka." He was a small, fit man in his forties, with sunfaded bright red hair and parchmentlike skin that was heavily freckled and weathered from his numerous outdoor adventures. "Unfortunately, we never found the place. Never really proved it even existed. Ah, but this time . . . this time is going to be different. I can feel it in here." He raised a fist and set it over his heart. "Can't you, my dear?"

Cait took a sip from the tin cup of thick black coffee she cradled between her hands. "I believe my father is right. I think if we persevere, we shall find the necklace."

"And perhaps more silver and other treasure, as well. Your father says the *Silverider* plundered the African coast for hundreds of miles before it sank off Santo Amaro."

"Yes, well, that is mainly speculation, though my father believes it is true and he is quite an expert on those sorts of things."

The professor walked up just then, the firelight reflecting on his thinning gray hair. He smiled as he held up the heavy silver ingot that was their latest and most exciting discovery so far. "A moment, Sir Monty, if you please. There's something I'd like to show you."

Cait watched the two men walk away, chatting good-naturedly, and frowned at the stooped spine and sagging shoulders that altered her father's once erect bearing. He was getting older, the years of hard work taking their toll. She was worried about him—but then she had worried about him for as long as she could remember.

Geoffrey's voice interrupted her thoughts. She had forgotten he was there. "I need to speak to you, Caitlin. I was hoping we might find someplace quiet where we could be alone."

Caitlin gazed up at him. At his serious expression, her nerve endings went on alert. He had seen her swoon that morning, and another time, as well. What was he thinking? Dear God, she wished she knew.

She moistened her suddenly dry lips. "What . . . what did you wish to discuss?"

Instead of answering, he simply took her arm, urging her up off the log, then started guiding her across the beach toward the firm, damp sand at the edge of the surf.

"What is it, Geoffrey?" Cait asked as they strolled along and he made no more effort to speak. Her nerves were continuing to build and Geoffrey seemed nervous, too, his shoulders tense, the muscles taut beneath his cotton jacket.

Some distance from the camp, he stopped and turned.

"I don't exactly know where or how to begin. What I'm going to say will remain between the two of us. Please understand I am saying this as your friend, and if I am wrong, you have my foremost apologies."

Her heart speeded up, clanked uncomfortably against her ribs. There was something in his eyes that made her stomach quiver. "Go on."

"I know you were ill for quite some time. Lately, you've begun to have dizzy spells. I think . . . I believe I may know what is wrong, and if I am correct, I would like to offer a solution."

She searched his face, but his eyes now were hooded, his expression mostly in shadow. "Geoffrey, what are you trying to say?"

He took her hand, cradled it between both of his. "In my inept, roundabout way, I am asking you to marry me. Considering your current situation—"

She stiffened. "Which is?"

"Are you with child, Caitlin? I've had little experience in such matters, but I know that when a woman falls ill in the mornings, as you did, when she swoons for no apparent cause, it can mean she is going to have a babe."

For an instant, Cait stood frozen. She had prayed no one would guess, hoped she would have more time to think things through. She blinked but her eyes filled with tears. The game was up. There was no more use pretending.

"Geoffrey . . . I know what you must think. I didn't . . . I never meant . . ." He turned her, took her in his arms, and held her as she cried against his shoulder.

"It isn't your fault," he said softly. "The child is Beldon's, is it not?"

She nodded into his shoulder and felt his body stiffen.

"The man is an outrage." He drew back to look at her. "He took advantage of your innocence. No decent man would have done such a thing."

She brushed away the wetness on her cheeks. "It wasn't that way. I can't let you believe that it was."

"You were a virgin, Caitlin. You had no knowledge of men. Beldon is a lecher of the very worst sort."

Cait shook her head. "Don't say that. It isn't true. If you are truly a friend, you'll believe that what happened between us was my idea as well as his. I wanted to learn about passion, to know what it meant to be a woman. I was afraid I would never have the chance to find out."

"And now he has abandoned you. I assume you have written, told him about the child."

A sliver of guilt speared through her. Cait determinedly forced it away. "I haven't told him, and I never will. My life is here, with my father. He needs me and I intend to stay with him as long as he does."

Geoffrey tipped her chin up with his hand, his long thin fingers warm against her skin. "Then marry me. We'll stay with your father as long as you like. Forever, if that is your wish. You know how much I admire the professor. His passion for knowledge, his dedication to uncovering the secrets of the past—I have pledged him my loyalty and my help, and I mean to continue."

"My father thinks a great deal of you, Geoffrey."

"If that is the case, then he will consent to the marriage. The three of us could be a family, Caitlin."

She looked into his hopeful face, her heart squeezing painfully. The answer to her prayers was standing right in front of her. For weeks she had agonized, trying to decide what to do. Now the way was clear. Her father's reputation would be protected. Her child would have a name, not be scorned as a nameless bastard, and yet . . . "What of the babe, Geoffrey?"

"I would raise him as my own."

Cait's eyes slid closed on a wave of pain. It wasn't what she wanted. She wasn't in love with Geoffrey St. Anthony. She doubted she could ever love him in the same way she had loved Rand. But he was a decent young man and the professor certainly approved of him. She could stay here in Santo Amaro, take care of her father as she always had, raise the child as she saw fit. Geoffrey would be a manageable husband. With his genteel, agreeable nature, the freedom and independence she'd always known would not be at risk.

Rand's image, tall and commanding, exuding power and authority, rushed into her mind, nearly blinding in its intensity. If she had told him about the babe, would he have married her? And even if he had, did she want a husband who would wed her out of a sense of obligation?

"I appreciate your offer, Geoffrey. It is extremely generous of you, but I . . . I need a little more time."

"How long, Caitlin? The child was conceived some months back."

She glanced off toward the water, saw a wave curling up, watched it wash up on the sand. "You're right. I have to think what's best for the babe." She turned to face him, forced herself to smile. "If you are certain this is what you want, I would be honored to marry you, Geoffrey. And I promise you, I'll do my very best to be a good wife."

Geoffrey grinned like a schoolboy and dragged her into his arms. "You won't be sorry, Caitlin." Then his mouth crushed down so hard their teeth met and cut into her lip. Geoffrey thrust his tongue inside, and the warm slickness made her stomach roll. She closed her eyes, hoping she would feel something, anything but repulsion. There was nothing but the unfamiliar sensation of having his long, lean frame pressed against her.

He ended the kiss so abruptly she stumbled and nearly fell. Geoffrey caught her arm to steady her.

"We'll tell your father tomorrow morning," he said. "We'll wed as soon as it can be arranged."

Cait just nodded. A painful lump had risen in her throat and embarrassing tears threatened behind her eyes. "We'd better be getting back," she whispered. "Father will begin to worry."

She thought he meant to argue and braced herself for another unwanted kiss, but instead he glanced back toward the campfire, saw that her father and Sir Monty had returned, set a long-boned hand at her waist, and began to guide her in that direction. When they reached the clearing, she said good-night and left him, crossing to the place where her father sat silently smoking a pipe.

"Off to bed already?" he asked.

Caitlin bent and kissed his weathered cheek. "I'm a bit tired tonight. I'll see you in the morning."

"Big day, tomorrow, Caitlin. We're close now—I can feel it."

Cait tried to smile, felt it falter. "I'm sure we are." But in truth, she no longer cared. In a very short time, she'd be married to Geoffrey St. Anthony. In her wildest dreams, she'd never imagined making love to Rand Clayton would force her life upon such a drastic course.

Rand stood at the rail of the small, double-masted schooner *Moroto,* the Portuguese word for *rascal,* that traveled between the mainland African seaport of Dakar and the Cape Verde island chain that included Santo Amaro. The packet usually made this run only once a month, but for a substantial sum of gold guineas, she was making a special trip for Rand.

Traveling with his valet, Percy Fox, he'd been gone from England nearly four weeks, sailing first aboard the passenger ship *Madrigal,* out of London, now aboard the *Moroto.* It was a long, tension-filled journey, but it was almost over. Today he would arrive at Santo Amaro.

Standing on deck in the first yellow rays of dawn, a damp, salty wind rifling through his hair, his feet splayed against the roll of the ship, Rand could see the cloud-encircled peak of the towering volcano, Pico de Maligno—Malevolent Peak—that dominated the island. The captain of the *Moroto,* a Portuguese seaman from São Vicente on the northern end of the Verdes, had delivered the professor and his party to the island. The *Moroto* would anchor offshore of the expedition's campsite and he and Percy would be taken to land by dinghy.

Rand's mouth curved into a hard, grim smile. Before

noon today, he would encounter the lady he had traveled so far to see. He couldn't begin to imagine the greeting he would receive. Nor was he quite certain what his own feelings would be.

Cait Harmon had deceived him. If it hadn't been for Maggie Sutton, she would have denied him a child of his own blood. Though he tried to understand the reasons that Cait would do such a thing, whenever he thought about it, he got angry all over again.

Still, he was certain, once they were together, she would tell him. In the meantime, though he wasn't a patient man, he would wait.

And there was another benefit to his journey. Assuming Phillip Rutherford was still among the members of the expedition, Rand would be able to watch him. With Percy's help, perhaps he would discover what had happened to the money Rutherford had raised. Perhaps they could discover how the baron meant to carry out his swindle, and whether or not Caitlin's father was involved.

It wasn't why he was there, of course. His friend Nick Warring had made him see reason on that score.

"If you marry Caitlin and have a child, they have to be your first concern. Revenge against Talmadge is no longer important, not when you have a family to consider. Believe me, I know."

It galled him to think that Talmadge might never pay for his sins, but after mulling over what Nick had said, Rand knew his friend was right. As long as he was there on the island he would learn what he could, but Cait and the child had to come first.

The island grew nearer. Rand could just make out the white sand beaches along the shore and the dense green foliage at the edge of the sand that grew even thicker as it progressed inland, climbing up the sides of the mountains until it disappeared into the murky ring of clouds that covered the summit of Pico de Maligno.

As they rounded a promontory at the far south end, he spotted the professor's campsite in a small sheltered cove, and his heart increased its sluggish beat until it was fairly drumming.

His gaze skimmed over several men in European dress, and a group of brightly garbed, brown-skinned natives working to haul buckets of sand away from the pit where they were digging. One of the members of the group worked on his knees, sifting through the sand in an area off from the rest. When the man lifted his hat to blot the sweat from his brow, Rand caught a glimpse of fiery red hair and knew it was Caitlin Harmon.

His mouth felt suddenly dry. He might be angry at her, but he was also eager to see her. Amazingly so. His palms felt damp. It was ridiculous. He was hardly a callow schoolboy, and yet in truth, he was nervous.

"Well, we are finally arrived." Percy stood beside him at the rail. Rand never heard his approach. He was the quietest man Rand had ever known.

"Yes, at last we are here. Let us hope our visit will be a brief one."

Percy eyed him the length of his long, narrow nose. "I suppose that depends upon your lady."

"To a point," Rand said, a muscle clamping down in his jaw. "If she doesn't come round soon enough, I may have to take more drastic measures." He didn't want to stay any longer than he had to, only time enough for Cait to come to her senses, tell him about the child, and accept his offer of marriage.

Until he knew what Cait had told her father, he would simply explain that in the months since the expedition had departed, his curiosity had overcome him. He needed a little diversion, a little adventure in his life, and he thought that perhaps he would find it on Santo Amaro. And of course he was willing to pay for the privilege.

He didn't doubt for a moment that Talmadge would gladly accept his funds.

The captain anchored the schooner some distance off-shore and a wooden dinghy was lowered. Percy settled himself in the bow, Rand sat on a gunwale in the middle, and a sailor took up the oars at the aft end of the boat. Their crate of gear had already been loaded aboard. A seaman on the deck of the *Moroto* tossed down Rand's big leather satchel along with Percy's canvas portmanteau. Rand caught them both, gave the sailor a grateful wave, and they were off, the dinghy cutting more gracefully through the waves than he would have guessed.

As the little boat headed for shore, Rand watched the island looming nearer and found himself smiling.

He could hardly wait to see the look on Cait Harmon's face when she realized exactly who it was that had come to call.

The sun beat down, far hotter than it had been the day before. Or at least it felt that way to Cait. Lifting the flat-brimmed, flat-crowned man's straw hat she wore, she mopped her brow with the white linen handkerchief she had purchased in a quaint little shop in St. James's. The small pink initials embroidered in the corner brought a mist of tears to her eyes, and a shot of irritation trickled through her. Jamming her hat back down on her head, she stuffed the handkerchief back in the pocket of her blouse, wishing the silly little thing didn't remind her of London and the friends she had come to miss so much.

She wished the darned thing didn't remind her of England and the days she had spent with Rand. Cait sighed and returned to her digging. Since she had accepted Geoffrey's proposal two weeks ago, she had missed Rand more than ever. She tried not to compare the two men, but when Geoffrey walked with her in the moonlight, when he pulled her into his arms and kissed her, she simply couldn't help it.

Geoffrey St. Anthony, she'd discovered, was even less like the duke than she had thought. With Geoffrey, there was no fire, no grand passion—and yet she was sure she was doing what was best. They would be married by the captain of the sailing packet that came to the island with supplies once a month. It was due in two more weeks.

Far too soon to suit Cait, and yet it wasn't fair to the child to put off the deed any longer.

From the corner of her eye, she caught sight of a sail in the waters just off shore. When she turned for a better look, she saw it was the *Moroto*. Dear God—Captain Baptiste had come early! For an instant her stomach turned upside down and completely inside out.

But the captain, she saw, was still standing on the bridge, not coming ashore in the dinghy as he usually did, and the little wooden boat was already heading back toward the ship. Wondering why the schooner had returned to the island, Cait tossed her trowel down on the sand and dusted her hands. When she looked up, a pair of heavy leather boots appeared in her field of vision. Buff-colored cotton twill trousers were tucked into the tops. Her gaze moved the length of two long legs, past narrow hips to a wide, powerful chest that looked amazingly familiar.

"Hello, Caitlin."

A shock wave rippled through her. Cait gasped at that deep, rumbling voice, and her head snapped up. With the sun at his back, his broad shoulders and lean hips were outlined in the light, while his face remained shadowed beneath the brim of a flat-brimmed canvas hat.

"Rand . . ." The word came out choked and a little bit ragged. Her heart was trying with all its might to pound its way out of her chest. For a single, sweet, heart-stopping moment, she thought that he had come for her, that in the months that she had been gone, he had discovered that he loved her. That they should be together.

Then reality set in. He hadn't come for her—Rand Clayton would never do that. He was a duke, she merely the daughter of a lowly professor. They would never suit and both of them knew it. No, Rand hadn't come for her; he had come for Talmadge—and for her father.

An icy shiver ran through her, making her cold even in the warm island sun. The Duke of Beldon would make a formidable opponent. She prayed her father was not in jeopardy, and wondered exactly what Rand meant to do.

She tried to stand, stumbled, and nearly fell. Rand caught her wrist and helped her to her feet. It felt as if a lightning bolt had sizzled up her arm.

"All right?" he asked, and she nodded, steeling herself and her resolve.

"I was just a little surprised, is all. You are possibly the last person I ever expected to see on Santo Amaro."

A corner of his mouth edged up. "You told me more than once how beautiful it was. Perhaps I simply wanted to see for myself."

She tipped her head back and her hat fell off. With a smile, Rand caught it and handed it over. "I know you hate them, but this sun is terribly bright. I'm glad to see you are wearing one out here."

"What are you doing on the island? Then again, I suppose I know."

A coffee brown eyebrow arched up. "Do you?"

Her heart was thumping too hard. Her palms had begun to sweat. Damn him to Hades—why did he have to come? And why now? Just before she was to marry? "You're here for Talmadge," she said, unable to keep a trace of bitterness out of her voice.

"How do you know I am not here for you?"

She didn't have time to answer for her father and Geoffrey walked up just then. Geoffrey continued past the duke, stopping close beside her, settling a proprietary hand at her waist.

Rand said nothing, but a muscle tightened in his cheek. Her father extended a hand and Rand shook it. "It's good to see you, Professor."

"Beldon—what on earth brings you way out here?"

The question sent a tingle of alarm down her spine. For the first time it occurred to her that perhaps he had found out about the babe. No—she didn't believe it. Maggie was her dearest friend. She would never, ever, betray her.

Rand smiled blandly. "The truth is, I was simply bored. I found myself wondering what it might be like to get away from England for a while, to discover a bit of adventure. I remembered you said you could use as many men as you could get. And of course, I'll be happy to make a sizable contribution to your efforts."

Geoffrey scowled, but her father smiled. "Well, then, if adventure is what you want, that is what you shall have, my boy. We're grateful for whatever help you can give us. Isn't that right, Geoffrey?"

"Actually, I thought we'd been doing quite well on our own," Geoffrey said with a trace of hostility. "I can't imagine digging up old coins and broken bits of pottery would hold much interest for a duke."

Rand's grin was feral. "That just shows how little you know of dukes. This one enjoys the out-of-doors more than most, and of course any chance to escape one's mundane existence for a while."

Geoffrey glanced off toward the ship. "I had hoped Captain Baptiste would be coming ashore," he said, but the vessel's sails had already been hoisted, the boat plunging through the sea, heading back toward the mainland. Caitlin tried to suppress a feeling of relief.

Rand followed Geoffrey's gaze out to sea. "The captain was pressed for time, I'm afraid. I gather he's due back in two weeks."

"Yes . . . two weeks." Geoffrey drew her a little bit closer. Cait fought the urge to shove him away. "Once he returns, Caitlin and I plan to be married."

Rand's dark eyes locked with hers and any hint of warmth they had held was replaced with bitter anger. "Is that right, Miss Harmon? You and Lord Geoffrey are to wed?"

She moistened her lips. She wondered if she would be able to force out even a single word. "Yes."

Rand's mouth edged up in the coldest smile she had ever seen. "Congratulations . . . to both of you."

Turning away, he started speaking to her father, asking where he and his valet might pitch their tents and unload their gear. Walking together, the two men left Geoffrey standing beside her and headed back toward the clearing, where Rand's black-haired valet, Percy Fox, stood waiting in the shade of a palm tree.

"I thought you said he didn't know." The accusation in Geoffrey's voice grated like a shiver down her spine.

"He doesn't. I don't know why he's here," she lied, certain he had come for Talmadge. "Perhaps what he said was the truth."

"And perhaps he has come here for you. Perhaps he expects the two of you to take up where you left off. If he wants you to share his bed again, Caitlin, what will you do?"

A fine spark of anger flared. She worked to snuff it out. "I'll do exactly what I've agreed to do, Geoffrey. What happened with the duke is over and done. When the captain arrives in two weeks, I'll marry you—if that is still your wish."

Some of the tightness vanished from his face. He took both of her hands in his. "You know it is. I shouldn't have doubted you. I just don't like having him here—especially not now."

"Neither do I, but there is nothing we can do. I'm sure he won't stay long. As you said, digging in the dirt and sleeping on a cot are hardly the sort of comforts he is used to."

But as Cait's attention swung to the tall, powerfully built man beside her father, she thought that he didn't look the least bit out of place, as she had imagined he would. In fact, he looked as though he had been on a thousand such adventures, as though he knew exactly what he was about.

It galled her that he should appear as commanding and attractive here on the island as he had in the glittering ballrooms of London's *haut ton*.

And it galled her even more that she was still as drawn to him as she had been before. And still very much in love with him.

FOURTEEN

Standing at the edge of the clearing, Rand finished speaking to the professor, who pointed toward a place where they could pitch their tents.

"That spot should do, I think. Give you a little privacy, as well."

"Yes, thank you, that looks fine."

Professor Harmon smiled. He seemed different here, more relaxed, as if he was finally in a place he belonged. His monocle was missing. Rand supposed he didn't need it way out here.

"I'd best be getting back," he said. "Take your time and get settled in. There is food in the cook tents. We'll see you at supper." He looked frailer than Rand remembered, but in truth he hadn't paid all that much attention. The gray-haired man walked away and Rand's gaze followed, but his thoughts were no longer on the professor.

They'd returned with a vengeance to Caitlin Harmon and anger boiled like hot oil through his blood. He glanced up to see Percy walking toward him, balancing the wooden crate that held their gear on his shoulder. Rand helped him lower the box to the ground.

"So how did it go with your lady?" Percy asked.

Unconsciously, Rand's hand balled into a fist. "I can hardly believe it. I travel thousands of miles only to discover she is marrying that preening coxcomb Geoffrey St. Anthony—or at least she thinks she is."

Percy lifted a long iron crowbar he had somehow managed to procure and began prying the lid off the crate. "So I heard," he said in his typical, few-words fashion.

Rand didn't ask him how he knew. There were a number of English servants among the members of the expedition and Percy had a knack for gleaning information.

"I swear it is all I can do not to throttle her."

Percy's lean features curved in a slight, knowing smile. "After all this time, I imagine that isn't the only thing you would like to do."

No, it wasn't. Just seeing her had made him hard. He'd wanted to tear her away from St. Anthony, drag her off down the beach, and make passionate love to her for hours on end. Instead, he stood there, frustrated and angry, uncertain whether he wanted to kiss her or strangle her.

Percy pried off the wooden lid and set it on the ground. "They're to marry when Captain Baptiste returns," he said. "Obviously, you intend to stop them. What will you do?"

Rand ground his jaw. "Whatever it takes. That woman is carrying my child. She is badly in need of a husband, and like it or not, the man she marries is going to be me."

"Perhaps that's what you should tell her."

"I will if I have to. At present, I prefer a more subtle course. I want to know what's been going on in that pretty little head of hers. I want to know what is happening with her and St. Anthony and if her feelings for me have changed—not that it will make a whit of difference."

Percy chuckled, leaned into the box, lifted out a heavy canvas tent and set it on the ground. Wordlessly, Rand turned to help him, dragging out the tent stakes, a coil of rope, and a heavy box of tools. This wasn't the first trip of this sort that they had made together. Before his father died, Rand had gone on a number of adventures—mountain climbing in the Alps, stag hunting on the Scottish moors, tiger hunting in India—and Percy had usually accompanied him.

Mostly he had done those things to prove himself to his father. It hadn't worked, of course, but he had gained a great deal of knowledge and experience, the sort that often came in handy, even in the civilized world of the London ton.

He meant to use that experience as he hunted a different sort of prey this time—one that was far more important than any he had ever gone after before.

Rand smiled grimly. As he worked to set up the tents and stow his gear, he began to plan his campaign.

Cait tossed and turned, unable to sleep. The narrow cot seemed harder than it ever had before. When she finally dozed off sometime in the late hours just before dawn, she dreamed of Rand and awakened with her heart pounding madly. Most of the dream was nothing but mindless bits and pieces, but she remembered the end—Rand raging at her for denying him his child. If she closed her eyes, she could still see his face, a mottled angry red as he reached into the small wooden cradle sitting at the end of her cot, picked up the babe, and stormed out of the tent, shaking his fist and swearing she would never see her child again.

Cait shivered and hugged herself. Would Rand really do such a thing? He was arrogant and demanding, used to getting his way, but he had never been cruel.

As she dressed and brushed her hair, her mind slipped back to the days they had spent at River Willows, precious days, days she would always treasure. She thought of the fury in Rand's expression when Geoffrey had told him they were to marry.

Rand had been possessive of her before, but that had been months ago. Surely he didn't still have feelings for her? Then again, remembering the look in those cold dark eyes when he had stared at Geoffrey, perhaps he did. Cait tried to suppress the little thrill she had no right to feel.

It was ridiculous, she knew. It could never work between them. Even if he loved her it didn't matter. They were simply too different. And there was her father to think of, as well as the commitment that she had made to

Geoffrey. As she lifted the tent flap and ducked outside, she caught a glimpse of her lightly freckled hands against the brown of her cotton twill skirt. Her boots were scuffed, the pockets of her well-worn white blouse slightly frayed.

How far from an English lady she must look to Rand. The man was a duke, for heaven's sake. He was used to women in silk and lace, not scuffed boots and cotton twill. Now that he had seen the real Cait Harmon, there wasn't the slightest chance he would still be interested in her.

The notion brought a soft ache to the area around her heart and darkened her already dismal mood.

"I see you start work early." Rand's voice, coming from the corner of the tent, startled her from her musings.

She thought again what a dreadful sight she must be and her head came up. "That's right—work. That's what I do. I don't imagine you know much about that sort of thing. Which reminds me—what job has my father decided you should do during the brief time you'll be here?"

A corner of his mouth curved up, but there wasn't a drop of humor in his smile. "You believe I'll find this place too strenuous for my delicate constitution?"

"I didn't say that, but . . . yes, I suppose I do."

"What gave you that impression? Certainly not my lack of stamina in bed. I believe in that regard, I accounted myself rather well."

Cait's mouth dropped open, then snapped shut. She was certain her hair must have turned a brighter shade of red. "It—it is hardly gentlemanly of you to make mention of something that happened between us in the past. Besides, that isn't what I meant and you know it. I was merely pointing out that you are hardly used to a life of deprivation. We live simply here. Our clothes are not fancy." She didn't mean to glance down, but she did, filling her vision with plain brown cotton and dusty, work-stained boots.

She felt the brush of his hand on her cheek and her eyes shot up to his face.

"I told you once that you would look good in just about anything. I meant it, Cait. I still do."

Cait turned away, her heart raggedly pounding. "Please . . . you mustn't say those sorts of things. Not any more."

"Why? You don't like to remember the times we shared, the hours we spent making love?" When she didn't reply, the lines of his face turned hard. "Or is it because it might disturb your precious betrothed? Pardon me if I am not overly concerned."

"Geoffrey and I are to marry. For that reason alone, you shouldn't—"

"Does he know about us, Caitlin? Does he have any idea of the intimate things we did? The way I touched you? The way you touched me?"

Her cheeks went scarlet, and something else was happening. Something warm and liquid moved through her, something she couldn't allow. "He knows that at one time we were . . . physically involved. It would hardly be fair if he didn't."

"And one thing you are is fair. Isn't that right, Caitlin?"

She didn't answer. She wasn't being fair, not to him. Her chest felt painfully tight and her bottom lip dangerously close to trembling. "I have to go. As I said, some of us have work to do."

Rand said nothing, just stood there as she walked away. She could feel those hot brown eyes burning into her back all the way across the beach.

Geoffrey St. Anthony spotted the duke and his valet standing next to Sir Monty Walpole, who was nodding and smiling at something Beldon said. God, he hated the bastard. As much for his arrogance as for what he had done to Caitlin. As Sir Monty walked away, Geoffrey set his jaw and started forward.

"I see you're still with us," he said, drawing the duke's attention. "I thought perhaps a single night spent on something other than a feather bed would be enough for you. Then again, I suppose, now that you're here, you have no choice but to stay—at least until the *Moroto* returns."

A muscle ticked in Beldon's cheek. "You know, St. Anthony, one of these days you're going to open that mouth of yours one time too many and find a fist planted in it."

Geoffrey blanched. Beldon had a devilish reputation as a pugilist. He might despise the man, but he scarcely wanted a physical confrontation.

"Is there something you need?" the duke asked. "Or are you merely being charming?"

"Actually, I thought there was a slight chance that you really meant what you said and came here to help. If that is the case, there is some heavy digging over in the pit that needs to be done. It is rather specialized work, so the natives have been called away. I can show you—"

"Beldon! There you are, my boy. I wondered where you had taken yourself off to." The professor strolled up just then, alongside the baron, who was smiling at the duke in a way that seemed sincere, though Geoffrey had noticed that when Beldon was near, Talmadge always seemed a bit uneasy. Then again, the bastard had a way of doing that.

"Sorry," the duke said to the professor. "I was just sorting things out a bit, taking a look around. I was attempting to discover where I might be most helpful. After supper last night and what was fed to us this morning, I thought—"

"I told you this would scarcely be the sort of thing you were used to," Geoffrey interrupted. "Our supplies are limited. We do the best we can."

Beldon's cold-eyed stare seemed to slice right through him. He felt the ridiculous urge to run. He hated himself for it, but the feeling was there just the same. When the duke returned his attention to the professor, he felt like sighing with relief.

"As I was saying, I thought that perhaps the best way I could help would be to bring the camp some fresh meat. There are tracks in the woods, deer and small feral pigs.

There are a number of birds on the island. Several species would probably be very good to eat."

Professor Harmon looked uncertain. "That would be extremely helpful, Your Grace, but I'm afraid it is simply too dangerous. Beyond the beach, the forest gets exceedingly jungle-like and dense. The mountains harbor all sorts of perils."

"Let me worry about that. I'm not unfamiliar with this sort of country."

"I don't know . . ."

"I assure you I'll be careful."

The professor lifted his canvas hat and scratched his gray head. "Well . . . if you're certain . . ."

"I am."

Donovan Harmon beamed. "It would certainly be appreciated—don't you agree, Phillip? We could all use something to eat besides fish and jerked beef."

Talmadge smiled in that enigmatic way of his. "Fresh game would certainly suit us all. In fact, it would be a godsend."

Beldon returned the baron's smile, but his eyes remained oddly distant. "Consider it done, then."

"If this works out," the professor said, "your arrival could prove timely, indeed."

"Perhaps it will," said Beldon.

Caitlin walked up just then, passing Geoffrey and stopping beside her father as she always did. Geoffrey felt a trickle of annoyance, especially since Beldon noticed and appeared smugly pleased. He wondered if she would continue her ridiculous devotion to her father even after they were married. Sooner or later, he vowed, he would demand that same respect. He had been lenient with her thus far, but once they were wed, he would expect her affections to belong to him.

"You sent for me, Father?" she asked.

"Yes, yes, I almost forgot. We are about to unearth what appears to be a very interesting, early medieval brass urn. We aren't yet certain where it's from or how it got aboard the ship, but I thought you might wish to be there when it was brought up."

"Yes, of course I would." She glanced up at Beldon as if she thought that he might be interested, as well.

"His Grace is going hunting, my dear," her father said. "He and Mr. Fox will be in charge of bringing in fresh meat."

Cait's face turned a little bit pale. She stared up at the duke as if she couldn't quite believe what she had heard. "But it's dangerous out there. Once you get back into the woods, the terrain changes dramatically. There are dense jungles, raging rivers, swamps filled with poisonous snakes—on the last expedition we even saw a leopard. Father, you mustn't let him go out there."

The duke was looking at her in a way he hadn't before and there was a softness in his expression that Geoffrey found extremely annoying.

"I appreciate your concern, Caitlin, but Percy and I have hunted this sort of terrain before."

"You—you have?"

He gave her an indulgent smile. "In India and also in Africa."

Geoffrey hated the way Cait was staring, with a look of amazement mixed with admiration. Geoffrey's features tightened in outrage. It was time for this bloody charade to end.

He started walking toward her, reached out and caught her arm. "Come along, Caitlin. I believe the professor has something he wishes us to see." His lips curled unpleasantly. "And I'm certain His Grace is eager to get on with his hunt."

Beldon turned, made a slight bow to Cait. "Good luck with your treasure," he said.

"Good luck with your hunting," said Cait. Geoffrey tightened his hold on her arm and fairly dragged her toward the opposite end of the beach, all the while silently raining down curses upon the head of the man who so confidently strode away.

*   *   *

The camp was mostly asleep. Rand sat in the darkness in front of the nearly dead campfire, the glowing coals all that remained in the circle of round gray stones. In the distance he could hear the faint chatter of a monkey that had made its way down from the inland mountains into one of the trees close to the beach.

Earlier in the evening, the group had eaten their fill of the venison he and Percy had brought in that afternoon. Both of them had successfully downed one of the small reddish deer that lived on the island, enough meat to last several days, and everyone's spirits were high.

Well, perhaps not everyone. His own mood was grim. After supper had ended, St. Anthony had taken Cait for a walk along the beach. They had disappeared in the darkness and it had been too damned long before they returned. When they did, Cait had refused to look at him, heading instead straight for her tent.

His hands fisted. It was all he could do not to storm in there and demand to know what was going on between them. He was halfway to her tent before he realized he was actually on his feet. By the time he did, he no longer cared.

With a quick glance around to be certain he wasn't seen, he jerked open the tent flap and stepped into the darkness.

Her soft gasp told him she wasn't asleep. Cait bolted upright on her cot, a light woolen blanket clutched over her breasts. "What do you think you're doing? You can't come in here."

"Apparently I can, since I am here."

She stiffened. Drawing the blanket around her, she swung her legs to the side of the cot and stood up. Behind the tent, the natives' campfire blazed, casting enough light through the canvas he could see that she wore a long white nightrail and had plaited her hair into a single thick braid. It hung over one shoulder, teasing a full, pink-tipped breast that Rand remembered only too well. Inside his cotton trousers, he went hard.

"What do you want?" Cait's voice broke into his wayward thoughts.

"I want to know what's going on between you and St. Anthony. Are you sleeping with him?"

She cast a glance toward her narrow bunk. "Does it look like I'm sleeping with him? There is hardly room on that cot for me."

"That isn't what I meant."

"Not that it's any of your business, but no . . . I am not sleeping with Geoffrey. I never have."

"But you will be—once you are married."

She swallowed. He watched her throat move up and down. "I'll be his wife, Rand."

No you won't, he thought, biting hard on his tongue to keep from saying it. *Not as long as I am here to stop you.* Instead he moved closer, reached out and caught the end of her braid, felt the silky strands slide through his fingers.

God, she was lovely, so vibrant and full of life. Seeing her here only made her seem more so. He had been drawn to her from the moment he had heard the sound of her voice. Since then, his attraction had grown, and now that he was here, he wanted her beyond anything he could have imagined.

"You aren't married to him yet," he said softly, his eyes searching her face. Her tongue edged out to moisten her lips and Rand's whole body tightened. Reaching down, he captured her face between his palms, holding her immobile, then his mouth came down over hers.

For an instant, Cait stood frozen, then she began to struggle, her hands pressing hard against his chest. Rand only deepened the kiss. He could feel the war within her, the battle not to give in. She was pledged to St. Anthony. She wasn't a woman who gave her word lightly. But Rand had also made a vow and he intended to see it fulfilled. His kiss grew gentle, turned to soft little butterfly caresses at the corners of her mouth, then he kissed her deeply again. Her lips softened, her body turned pliant. With a faint sigh of surrender, she melted against him.

"God, Caitie . . ." He had forgotten how good it felt to kiss her, how incredible she tasted, how her breasts pillowed so sweetly against his chest. He kissed her again, more thoroughly this time, and she opened to him, accepting the sweep of his tongue, entangling it with her own. He was hard and throbbing, aching for her, wanting her the way he always did. His hands moved over her rib cage, testing each indentation, moving upward to capture her breasts.

He began to gently caress them, to test their fullness, slightly larger now, nearly spilling out of his hands. He used his thumb to abrade a nipple, felt it stiffen and swell, and Caitlin went rigid in his arms.

Jerking away from him, she stepped back into the shadows, her breathing too fast, her body faintly trembling. "That—that shouldn't have happened."

"No? I think that is exactly what should have happened—only it should have happened sooner."

"Get out of here, Rand. It's over between us. Don't come back in here again."

He clamped his jaw. He wanted to shout at her, to tell her he had every intention of coming back, that soon she would be his wife and he would kiss her until she was dizzy, make love to her until she begged him to stop. Instead, he watched her trembling, saw the faint glitter of tears on her cheeks, and held his silence.

Cursing, he turned away. Storming out of the tent and into the cool tropical night, he dragged in deep, calming breaths of air. He told himself to be patient, that there was still time. He had missed her even more than he had realized, but he wanted her to come to him, tell him the truth about the babe. If she didn't . . . well, he would worry about that then.

For the present, his questions had been answered. She wasn't sleeping with St. Anthony, wasn't in love with the man. And her body said what Caitlin wouldn't. That she was still attracted to him.

That she still wanted him.

God knew how badly he wanted her.

Sitting behind a stack of upturned crates that served as a desk in his tent, Phillip Rutherford finished the entry he was making in his ledger. Handling all of the expenditures for the expedition was more of a job than he had bargained for. Since most of the natives spoke a combination of French and Portuguese, and he spoke French very well, his job had expanded, requiring more time and effort than he had expended in years.

It also provided a greater opportunity.

Phillip inwardly smiled. Handling all of the money himself, including the payroll, he knew exactly what items had be paid and where he could shave off money for himself. He knew which supplies they couldn't do without and those that were extras, goods that might have provided the camp with a small bit of luxury, but weren't really crucial.

Donovan Harmon—naïve old fool that he was—trusted him implicitly, which meant the other members of the expedition did, as well. All but Caitlin. Even after all these months, the girl remained wary where he was concerned.

In the first few weeks after they left England, he had set out once more to charm her, but with each of his overtures, she seemed to withdraw even further. Most women found him attractive, and it annoyed him that Caitlin seemed immune. In the end he'd decided—at least for the present—Cait Harmon was more trouble than she was worth.

He had turned his attention to someone more willing to accommodate his needs, a woman who did exactly as he commanded. She saw to his care and made his life on this miserable island bearable. She would do for the relatively short time he meant to be there.

In that regard, things were also progressing well. Already they'd amassed quite an assortment of valuable items: more silver coins, ten silver ingots, a solid gold crucifix encrusted with emeralds and rubies, a golden goblet, several valuable silver chains, an ornate golden jewelry box—and these were merely items they had discovered buried in the sand, articles stowed in disintegrating wooden crates that washed up on shore when the ship broke apart on the reef.

The chest holding Cleopatra's Necklace had yet to be unearthed. Even if they never found it, the items they had discovered thus far were worth a small fortune.

He smiled to think those items sat carefully packed in a box in the corner of his tent.

The only fly in the ointment he could see thus far was the duke's untimely arrival. So far Beldon had only begun to settle in. He had no idea what they had already found. Unlike the others, once he knew, perhaps he would become suspicious. Phillip had never liked the man. He didn't trust him and it was obvious the feeling was mutual.

Still, there was no reason to believe the duke would stay long. He scarcely needed the money, and the adventure of being in such a remote place didn't take long to wear thin. As long as Phillip was careful, there was really no reason to worry.

He pulled his watch fob from the pocket of his coat, flipped open the lid of his solid gold watch, and checked the time. Almost midnight. He closed the ledger, blew out the lamp, and the tent fell into darkness. Outside, the camp was silent. He could hear the hum of cicadas and the soft rustle of palm fronds.

The canvas flap whispered open. A slim, dark silhouette stepped into the quiet inside the tent.

"Bwana Phillip," she called softly. She was willowy and supple, her skin exquisitely smooth, the color of chocolate mixed with cream. Her breasts were small and pert, her buttocks as round as twin moons.

"I've been waiting," he said sternly. "Where have you been?"

"But you said come when the lamp went out—"

"I don't like to be kept waiting, Maruba. You know that." His tone was firm, yet held a note of anticipation. "I'll expect you to make amends."

She understood then that he was playing a game, and her smile was so feline it looked as if she might purr. "Yes, Bwana. Maruba sorry. She only wish to please."

Kneeling in front of him, her nimble fingers found and worked the buttons at the front of his trousers. She pulled open the fabric and his shaft sprang into her waiting hands.

"Such a big mon," she said, lightly stroking him, knowing he wanted to hear it though it wasn't really the truth. Still, what he lacked in size he made up for in inventiveness. That always seemed to please the women.

"Put it in your mouth," he commanded and she did so without reservation, her tongue sliding along his flesh with expert skill. His muscles tightened, his body coming alive with sensation. It didn't take her long to bring him to climax. He did so with a grinding hiss, plunging his hardness between her lips again and again.

When he was finished, she used the hem of her red sarong to clean him up, then led him over to the cot and began to undress him. He let her help, removing his coat and trousers, taking off his boots, rolling down his stockings, though in truth, he would have preferred she simply leave. But women liked to think they were useful, liked to believe that they were needed and that you enjoyed their attentions.

If the damnable cot hadn't been so small he might have let her have him again.

Instead, he pressed a kiss on the corner of her mouth and motioned for her to leave.

"Come again tomorrow night, Bwana Phillip?"

He nodded and smiled, giving her a flash of white in the darkness. She left as quietly as she had come, pausing only long enough to retrieve the silver coin he had left for her at the foot of the bed.

Phillip forced down a faint trace of anger that was aimed at Cait Harmon. If the bitch had been more co-operative, he would be getting it for free, instead of having to pay for it.

FIFTEEN

Moving quietly along a game trail, Rand and Percival Fox headed deeper into the forest, each of them carrying a long-barreled musket in his hand. At the edge of a rushing stream that cascaded down out of the mountains, they paused, leaning their weapons against the base of an acacia tree.

"We're safe here," Rand said. "The others aren't about to come this far into the woods." He knelt and scooped up a handful of water, enjoying the cold against his skin, drinking until he'd had his fill. "So what about Talmadge?" he called over his shoulder. "Have you had a chance to learn anything useful?"

Percy smiled. "Actually, I have. The cook—the widow Mrs. Wilmot—has been extremely informative."

"For example?"

"Did you know the baron has control of the supply ledgers?"

Rand frowned.

"He has complete control of the money, and he has the treasure."

"Treasure? What treasure?" Rand turned away from the stream to face his friend more squarely. "You aren't saying they've found the necklace?"

"No, not the necklace, at least not yet. But their discoveries so far have been quite significant. A jeweled crucifix, at least ten silver ingots, a solid gold jewelry box set with diamonds and emeralds, that sort of thing. At least two thousand silver Dutch guilders were uncovered in a single cache."

Rand blew out a breath. It wasn't at all what he had expected. "Did the professor anticipate finding this stuff? I don't recall him mentioning any other treasure outside the necklace."

"Apparently he thought there was a chance. He wasn't really interested in finding anything except the necklace and he didn't want to make promises he wasn't certain he could keep."

"But Talmadge must have known. And he must have been convinced the professor would succeed. And now you are telling me Talmadge has these items in his possession. The professor must be insane."

"Naïve, I think. Apparently he trusts the baron completely. I'm beginning to think the man is innocent of your suspicions. I don't think Professor Harmon has enough guile to be involved in any sort of swindle."

A thread of relief filtered through him. "I hope you're right. I'm beginning to like the old man."

"According to Mrs. Wilmot, who apparently overheard their conversations, Miss Harmon has tried on several occasions to persuade her father to be a bit more circumspect where the baron is concerned. Obviously, it hasn't done any good."

"If Talmadge has won Harmon's trust so completely, he must have done so some time back." Rand clamped a hand on Percy's shoulder. "Perhaps, my friend, you have just uncovered the baron's scheme. The professor's finds thus far must be worth a great deal of money. It never occurred to me the man's goal was so simple. Raise the money, use it to find the treasure—then simply steal it. If his plan succeeds, he'll never have to work again."

Percy looked uncertain. "If that was his intention, the risk of failing would have been high. There was no guarantee the professor would find anything at all on the island."

"True. And Talmadge isn't a man given to taking

risks." He rubbed the side of his jaw. "Still, the money was hardly his own. He had nothing to lose but time— and a fortune in gold and jewels to gain should the venture prove successful."

"Assuming you're correct, how do we prove it? And what do we do to stop him?"

"That, my friend, is a very good question." Rand hefted his musket and Percy did the same. As they started along the trail, Percy's voice floated forward from behind him.

"You might also be interested to know he is seeing the servant girl, Maruba. Apparently, they have an arrangement of sorts."

Rand stopped and turned. "My, you are a wealth of information today. An interesting tidbit. Perhaps in some way it might prove useful. At present, however, even catching Talmadge isn't my main concern. I'm far more interested in how I'm going to convince Cait Harmon she is better off with me than with Geoffrey St. Anthony."

Percy's laughter echoed into the forest. "Your Miss Harmon appears to be a very smart woman. Given a choice between you and St. Anthony . . . surely the decision will be easy."

Rand grumbled a curse. "It bloody well should be. If Caitlin wasn't so damned stubborn—"

"If she wasn't such a strong young woman, you probably wouldn't like her as much as you do."

Rand's mouth edged up. "Perhaps that's true. At any rate, she had better come to her senses and soon." The *or else* was left unsaid, but Percy would know it was there. In less than two weeks, Cait Harmon was going to become Rand's wife, the next Duchess of Beldon. They were leaving this blessed island, going back to a civilized place where she could safely birth his babe.

He would do whatever it took to insure that happened. Whether Caitlin wished it or not.

A weak sun rode low on the horizon, muted by a thin layer of clouds. Cait watched Rand stride out of the forest into the clearing, a brace of plump birds draped over his shoulder. He'd been hunting for more than a week, and each time he left, she'd grown tense and uneasy. Now, seeing him safely returned, she felt a wave of relief.

Dammit to Hades, she shouldn't be worried about him. Rand Clayton meant nothing to her—not any more. In less than a week, Geoffrey St. Anthony would become her husband. It was Geoffrey who deserved her concern. But the jungles on the island were dense and inhospitable. Danger lurked around every turn. During their first expedition to Santo Amaro, two of the native porters in their party had been killed when they ventured inland in search of game.

Cait took a last glance at Rand, saw him slide the birds off his shoulder onto the sand. Then he looked across the camp, directly at her, and a tingle of awareness slid through her. She had tried to forget the night he had barged into her tent and kissed her, but every time he smiled, she remembered the feel of those firm male lips moving so hotly over hers, remembered his big hands caressing her breasts.

She tried not to feel guilty for keeping the child she carried a secret, told herself she had no choice, but a hundred times she had thought of going to him, telling him the truth. She thought what it might be like if she were marrying him instead of Geoffrey St. Anthony.

Unfortunately, there was too much at risk. She wasn't even certain he would marry her if he knew. But she hadn't the slightest doubt that he would want the babe.

Turning away from Rand's steady gaze, determined to ignore him, she scooped up the wicker basket she had gotten from the cook and started down the beach. It was getting late and she wanted to pick a few of the wild grapes that grew over the cliffs in a cove not far away.

Soon the tide would be coming in, blocking her way around the promontory she needed to pass in order to reach it, and she didn't want that to happen.

It didn't take long to reach the sandy inlet, the next

cove to the south of where they were camped. It was crescent shaped, and a steep slope rose at the rear, flattening into a ledge halfway up, forming a shelf where the wild grapes could be reached, the long vines cascading down from the top of the cliff. As she had done a dozen times, she climbed up the steep slope, using jagged rocks and narrow ledges to make her way toward the shallow plateau that provided sound footing.

In less than an hour, her basket was filled with succulent purple grapes and Cait was ready to make her way back down. The sea had begun to rise and she wanted to be gone long before it filled the cove.

She had almost made it when her hold on a crumbling piece of rock broke loose and she started to slide. Cait screamed as a portion of the ledge gave way and she landed on the rocks several feet below, knocking the breath from her lungs.

For a moment, she just lay there, fighting to catch her breath. She was all right, not really hurt. As her heartbeat began to slow, she spotted the basket of grapes, which had landed just a few feet away. With a smile of relief that her hard work would not be in vain, she reached for it. Unfortunately, when she did, another piece of the ledge broke off and she slid downward again, her skirt billowing up in front of her face, the rough rock abrading the skin on the backs of her legs. The ground rose up with alarming speed and Cait thrust out a hand to slow her fall, but something went wrong and her head smacked painfully against an outcropping of rock.

For a moment her ears rang and her vision went blurry. She blinked to try to clear it, but even that slight movement made her dizzy. Cait fought down her panic and battled against the darkness that loomed behind her eyes, terrified that if she lost consciousness, she would never get out of the cove before the tide came in and swept her out to sea.

It was her last coherent thought as the pain in her head

grew more fierce, her eyes slid closed, and she sank into darkness.

Rand stared up the beach. Dusk was beginning to fall and Caitlin had not yet returned. Where the devil was she? He glanced around the camp. And where was that sniveling fool St. Anthony?

A muscle knotted in his jaw. By God, if the two of them had gone off somewhere together—

He never finished the thought for the blond man stepped out of the forest just then. Several seconds later, a little farther up the beach, the pretty little serving girl, Maruba, also slipped out of the trees. Interesting, Rand thought, wondering if the girl had been entertaining Geoffrey in the same manner that she had the baron.

Then his thoughts slid away from St. Anthony and returned to Cait, and he was torn between worry and relief. Worry won out. If she wasn't with St. Anthony, where the devil was she?

He asked around, but no one in camp seemed to have seen her.

"She went to pick grapes," Hester Wilmot said, a hefty, rather abrasive woman with sagging cheeks and broad hips. "Does it a couple a times a week. No need to worry. She'll be back before it gets dark."

But he *was* worried. His sixth sense was jabbing him in the back of the neck and it was a feeling he rarely ignored. "Where does she go to get these grapes?"

"A little ways down the beach. There's another cove just past this one. The grapes grow down over the cliff."

The tension he was feeling inched up a notch. There was something about the word *cliff* he didn't like the sound of. "Thank you. I'll just go and check on her, make sure she gets back safely."

Hester Wilmot gave him a look that said he was wasting his time, wiped her hands on the apron tied over her skirt, and returned to stirring the big kettle of soup she was cooking.

Telling himself he was a fool, that Caitlin was perfectly capable of taking care of herself, Rand strode off down the beach. He might be worrying for nothing, but there was the babe to consider, and in truth, he rather liked the idea of catching her alone.

If he hadn't been so worried, he might have smiled. He wanted to take up where they had left off in her tent. If he was lucky, perhaps this would provide the occasion he had been seeking.

Unfortunately, when he reached the promontory that separated the two coves, he saw that the waves had already begun to roll in. He would have to wade knee deep in the water to reach the other side, which meant Cait would have to do the same in order to get out.

He didn't like the notion. The waves were growing larger and Caitlin wasn't very big. One wrong step and she could be swept out to sea. Damn the little witch. If she was too reckless to think of herself, she might at least consider the child.

Cursing her and headstrong women in general, Rand unlaced his boots and set them away, rolled up his trouser legs, and waded into the water. When a wave rolled in, the water came nearly to the tops of his thighs and real concern for Cait began to set in.

She might be willful and a little bit reckless, but Cait wasn't a fool. He didn't believe she would take this sort of risk on purpose. His pulse kicked up as he grew more and more certain that something must have happened.

"Cait!" he called out above the crash of the surf. "Caitie, can you hear me?" Rounding the promontory, he sloshed toward the shore. "Caitlin! Cait, where are you?" But he didn't get an answer and his heartbeat increased along with his fear.

"Caitlin! Answer me!" He scanned the cliffs, saw the lush growth of vines cascading down from the top. It was getting dark, and the rocks were little more than faint black shapes, misleading in the fading sunlight. It was difficult to see, but . . . Damn! Up on the ledge—it had to be Cait. He was sure he could see a portion of her brown twill skirt draped over a ledge about halfway up the steep slope leading up to the top.

The sharp edge of fear knifed through him. She wasn't moving. *God, don't let her be hurt.* Rand steeled himself and began to climb, slowly making his way up the slope. Hand over hand, placing each bare foot carefully, wishing he had worn his boots, he moved upward. By the time he reached the ledge, he could see Cait's motionless body, the pale hue of her face against the black volcanic rock.

Emotion streaked into his chest and it tightened. For an instant, it was hard to breathe. Rand steadied himself, forced in a lungful of cooling sea air. There wasn't time for fear, not yet. He had to remain clear-headed.

He continued to climb and when he reached the ledge, he knelt beside her, lifted her hand and squeezed her fingers. "Caitlin? Caitlin, can you hear me?"

He heard a faint moan. Her eyelids fluttered and finally opened. "Rand . . . ?"

His hands were shaking. He forced himself under control. "Everything's going to be fine. Tell me where you're hurt."

She moistened her lips, swallowed. "My head . . . I . . . I must have hit my head."

"You fell? You fell off the ledge?" Worry for Cait expanded, compounded by his worry for the babe.

"It crumbled and I slipped. I didn't . . . didn't fall far. I just hit my head."

"Lie still. I want to be sure nothing's broken." He made a quick search of her limbs, looking for fractures, finding none, feeling a trace of relief.

"The tide, Rand." She jerked upward too quickly, grimaced as pain shot into her head, and Rand eased her back down. "We have to leave," she said. "We have to get out of here before the tide comes in."

"I know, love. Just take it easy. I want you to try and sit up, but this time I want you to do it slowly. Think you can manage?"

She nodded. "I think so." She did so carefully and with obvious discomfort. But once she was sitting, she smiled. Rand couldn't help it—he bent over and very lightly kissed her.

"Come on. Let's get out of here."

Cait gripped his hand and he helped her to her feet. Cait took a tentative step, stumbled, and he caught her. "Just my luck," she said. "I think I may have twisted my ankle."

Rand swore an oath he hoped she didn't hear. "It's all right. It may take us a little bit longer, but we'll get down. Just lean on me."

Slowly, methodically, one awkward step at a time, Rand helped Cait make her way down the cliff. When they reached the bottom, her legs were shaking and he scooped her up in his arms.

"Hold on to my neck. Just don't let go and I'll get you home."

She did as he said, bracing herself against his chest. He could feel the warmth of her body seeping into his clothes, smell the salty sea spray in her hair. He tightened his hold protectively and silently thanked God he'd come after her when he did.

Still, time was slipping away. When they crossed the beach to the promontory at the side of the cove, they discovered the water had risen dangerously high.

"I'm afraid we're going to get wet."

Cait's arms tightened around his neck. "I'm frightened, Rand. I'm not a very good swimmer."

He mustered a confident smile. "Trust me. I'm not going to let anything happen to you."

Cait studied the incoming surf, the white foam shooting up from the rocks. "But the water—I've never seen it so high."

"We'll make it, Caitie, I promise. Just hang on and enjoy the ride."

He waded in, deeper and deeper, till the sea was chest-high and waves were hitting him in the face. He could feel Cait trembling, feel the tension in her small body. Step by cautious step, he sloshed forward, leaning into the waves, fighting the pull of the surf, using his weight to hold him steady. By the time they rounded the promontory and waded up onto the dry sand on the opposite side, his muscles felt like overcooked mutton and he was exhausted.

With a grateful sigh, he set his light burden down on the dry sand away from the water then sank down wearily beside her.

"We made it," she said with a sigh of relief.

"How's your head?"

"It hurts like the devil, but I think I'll be all right."

"And the ankle?"

She tested it gently, winced a little. "Just lightly sprained, I think. I'm not much good at doctoring, but hopefully it'll be fine in a couple of days."

"You aren't hurt anywhere else? When you fell, you didn't . . . you didn't injure yourself in some other way?"

Cait eyed him with a trace of suspicion. "I told you I am fine."

Rand raked a hand through his hair, shoving the wet brown locks back from his face. "Dammit, Cait, you shouldn't have been out there in the first place. What if I hadn't come along when I did?"

She glanced off toward the water. It was nearly dark, the last faint rays of sunlight fading to purple at the edge of the horizon. "How did you know where I was?"

"Mrs. Wilmot told me."

"Why did you come after me?"

"Because I was worried about you. You aren't invincible, you know. Even if you happen to think so."

Cait reached over and took his hand. Her skin was damp and chill yet his fingers warmed where she touched. "Thank you, Rand. You probably saved my life."

He wanted to draw her into his arms, let her know that she was safe. The timing wasn't right. Not with her father and St. Anthony just down the beach. "If I actually saved you, would it mean that you belong to me? That's what the Chinese believe."

In the shadowy light, he could barely see her face. "Would you want me to?"

For an instant, his heart stopped beating. "Yes, Cait, I would."

She only shook her head. "I can't be your mistress any longer, Rand. I'm going to marry Geoffrey."

He lifted her hand to his lips, pressed a kiss against the back. "Marry *me*, Caitie."

For an instant she just stared, her green eyes widened in disbelief. "You don't mean that," she finally said. "You know it would never work. Our lives are simply too different."

"We could make it work, Cait. Tell St. Anthony you've changed your mind. Tell him I'm the man you're going to marry."

She studied him for long, silent moments, and he thought he saw tears in her eyes. Then shouts erupted from down the beach and both of them came to their feet, Cait leaning against him to take the weight off her injured ankle.

"Caitlin!" Geoffrey St. Anthony raced forward. "Where in God's name have you been? You were supposed to be back before dark." He tossed an accusing look at Rand, who slanted a dark look right back. "It's your father. Something's happened. You've got to get back to camp at once."

"Oh, dear God." Before she could take a step, Rand scooped her back in his arms.

"She's twisted an ankle," he said to St. Anthony as he strode off toward the yellow-orange flames of the campfire barely visible in the distance. "Get my boots," he called over his shoulder, and heard St. Anthony curse.

SIXTEEN

"Father! Dear Lord, what happened?" Cait squirmed frantically against Rand's chest and he set her on her feet next to the blanket her father lay on beside the fire. Sir Monty and the baron stood beside him, their expressions worried and grim.

Kneeling, Cait rested a shaky hand on his forehead, which was drenched in perspiration, his face as white as the sand on the beach.

"I'm sure it's nothing serious, my dear." He mustered a shaky smile. "Just a bit too much sun, I imagine."

She turned worriedly to Sir Monty. "What happened?"

"He was working over in the pit. All of a sudden, he simply keeled over."

She bit down on her trembling lip, praying it wasn't his heart. He was getting older. It was the sort of thing that happened when people began to age. She reached out and clasped his hand, felt a weak squeeze in return. "How are you feeling?"

"A little weak, is all. I'm sure it isn't anything for you to worry about." But she *was* worried. She was terrified. Her father was getting more frail every year. She thought of Rand's unexpected offer of marriage and felt a soft ache in her heart. Then she looked down at her father's pale face and knew it was impossible. He needed her now more than ever.

"You need to rest for a couple of days," she told him. "No sun, no physical labor. Just rest and get your strength back." Instead of arguing as he normally would have, he simply nodded, and Cait was more worried than ever.

"I'm sure he'll be all right," Geoffrey said. He tossed a meaningful glance at Cait. "With both of us here to look after him."

Cait simply nodded. She couldn't look at Rand, could not possibly. He had been worried about her, had saved her life in the cove. He had asked her to marry him and for one insane, shining moment, she had actually thought to agree.

Mrs. Wilmot appeared with a bowl of water and a damp cloth. "Thank you." Cait took them from her gratefully, dampened the cloth, and placed it across her father's forehead. She could feel Rand standing behind her, feel his hard gaze cutting through her. He knew her so well. The moment he had seen her father lying there on the blanket, he had known that she would say no to his offer of marriage.

When she turned to look up at him, tears burned her eyes. Rand saw them, knew they confirmed exactly what he had been thinking, turned and stalked away. Her watery gaze followed his tall retreating figure till he disappeared into the shadows and she swallowed past the painful lump in her throat.

Her father made a movement on the blanket. Cait's thoughts swung back to him. Wringing out the cloth, she replaced it on his forehead, which was covered with sweat and overly warm.

"We'll need to keep an eye on him for a couple of days," Lord Talmadge said. "As weak as he is, it might be some sort of jungle fever. We ought to keep him away from the others—just in case it's contagious."

He was right, but still it rankled. Why was it the baron's suggestions always seemed most advantageous to the baron? "Move his tent off from the others. I'll stay with him for the next few days."

And so she did. Their meals were left outside the tent. Still hobbling a bit, Cait brought them in and helped him eat. She had her cot brought into the tent and stayed there at night so that she could take care of him. She sat with him while he slept, which was most of the day, and read to him when he was awake. His fever remained high, but not life-threateningly so.

Three days later, he was on his feet and nearly back to normal. The weakness he had suffered began to fade and his strength slowly returned. Since no other cases of sickness appeared, his tent was returned to the camp and he rejoined the others at meals. Still, Cait worried about him. There was no way to know what had happened to him, or if it might strike him down again.

Rand had come to check on her several times, but once the professor was on the mend and she had things under control, she hadn't seen him again.

It was just as well, she told herself. The day after the morrow, the *Moroto* was due to return and she and Geoffrey would wed. It wasn't what she wanted, wasn't the way she had imagined her life to be. Still, her father seemed more pleased than she would have guessed.

"I was afraid when I fell ill I'd be unable to attend your wedding." Sitting on a log in front of the fire, he reached over and took her hand. "I haven't really told you how pleased I am about your decision. Every year I get older. I've been worried about your future, Caitlin. With Geoffrey to care for you, you'll be protected and looked after. And one day you'll have children. I know you'll be a very good mother. Just as your own mother was."

Cait just nodded. Her throat had closed up and it was impossible to speak. From the corner of her eye, she saw Rand standing there in the shadows and his rigid posture said he had heard their conversation. She brushed at a drop of moisture that clung to her lashes and smiled at her father. When she turned to look at Rand, she saw that he was gone.

A hot afternoon sun beat down, stabbing relentlessly through the leaves of the trees, scorching the sand and the workers on the beach. Though most of the days had been pleasant, these past few had been abnormally warm, still and airless, without even the relief of a breeze.

Rand watched Caitlin from behind a copse of trees, watched her leave the dig site, as she had nearly every day since his arrival. She grabbed a linen towel from inside her tent, and make her way a short distance inland.

Today Rand followed, knowing she was headed for a natural pool in the rocks formed at the foot of a gently flowing waterfall. It was a beautiful, isolated spot that Cait made nearly daily use of, the perfect place to implement the plan he had already set in motion.

Rand smiled grimly, torn between anticipation and regret. The course of action he was taking was not what he had wanted. He had hoped that Caitlin would come to him, tell him about the babe. Even though she'd remained silent, his fear for her that day in the cove had driven him to offer marriage.

For a moment, in the darkness there on the beach, he had believed she would accept, that she was about to tell him about the babe. Then news had arrived of her father's illness and the moment had been lost. It appeared it wouldn't come again.

Tomorrow she intended to marry Geoffrey St. Anthony. If her decision up till now had been the least bit uncertain, worry for her father had strengthened her resolve. But Donovan Harmon had already lived a goodly portion of his life and Cait's had only just begun. She would soon be the mother of Rand's child, and that child deserved to be raised by its parents. Both of its parents.

Rand meant to see that was exactly what occurred.

Moving off in the same direction Caitlin had taken, he skirted the camp, remaining out of sight, and disappeared into the trees. When he reached the pool, he watched Cait shed the last of her garments, pull the pins from her long, gold-tipped red hair, and pad naked into the pool beneath the falls.

His stomach muscles tightened. It wasn't the happenstance he would have chosen, but there was no doubt his body approved of the plan.

Sinking down in the water with a sigh of contentment, Cait stroked out toward the middle of the pool and rolled onto her back, her long red hair streaming out behind her. Rand could see the tips of her breasts, the triangle of burnished hair at the apex of her thighs, the faint swell of her stomach that was his child.

A surge of emotion rose inside him, colliding with a raw wave of desire. He wanted her. God knew he wanted her. But it was more than that. He wanted Caitlin for herself, for the woman she was, for the passion and strength she carried inside her. It was a feeling he hadn't expected, one he didn't really want to feel, and it made him suddenly uneasy.

Still, he was there for a purpose and he meant to see it done. Making his way down the embankment, he stopped at the side of the pool, sat down on a rock, pulled off his boots, and began to unbutton his trousers.

Cait closed her eyes and let the cool, clear water stream through her hair. It slipped over her skin and swirled through her fingers, washing away the afternoon heat, easing her troubles, at least for a while. Tomorrow she would marry Geoffrey St. Anthony. Tomorrow she would become the wife of a man she considered merely a friend, and her life would never be the same again.

Images of Rand rose up, memories of the worry on his face when he had found her lying unconscious in the cove, of the desire in his eyes when he had kissed her in the tent. They were useless thoughts, she knew, dangerous thoughts she worked to force away.

Her father needed her, now even more than the day her mother had died. He was frail and his health was fragile. She couldn't possibly leave him.

A rustling sound at the edge of the water drew her attention and her eyes snapped open, swung in that direction. Rand was standing there, magnificently naked, his eyes dark and glowing with sensual heat. Her gaze moved over his powerful chest, down his flat-muscled belly, and she saw he was fiercely aroused.

Her heart kicked up in warning. She swam away from him, toward the far side of the pool, until her feet touched the sandy bottom and she turned to face him. "What . . . what do you think you're doing? You can't come in here. Not . . . not like that."

"As I said before, I believe I can, since I am already here." He stepped into the water, which rushed up his calves, curled around his thighs, splashed against his buttocks. Sinking lower, he made several slow strokes that knifed through the water and brought him up beside her.

Her heart was hammering, her mouth felt dry, though she stood shoulder-deep in the water. She wanted to turn and run, but her legs refused to move. His feet touched the bottom and he stood up beside her, exposing his incredible chest, those wide, hard-muscled shoulders.

Cait swallowed, tried not to notice the tiny drops of spray that clung to each of his curly brown chest hairs. "Rand, please. Someone might see us. Someone might think that . . . that—I'm asking you . . . as a friend . . . to leave."

His mouth curved faintly, seductively. "But you don't really want me to—do you, Caitie?"

It was woefully wrong, but no, dear God, she didn't want him to leave. She wanted him to stay right where he was. She wanted him to kiss her, touch her, make love to her, the way she remembered in her dreams.

She tossed a long wet strand of hair over her shoulder. "I'm marrying Geoffrey. The captain of the *Moroto* will be here tomorrow to see it done."

His eyes traveled over her face, down her throat and across the tops of her breasts. "But that is tomorrow and this is today." His hands went around her waist, big hands, strong and warm, holding her gently in place. "Today you remain unwed. You are still Cait Harmon, and we have one more day."

She shook her head, felt the wet strands moving across her shoulders. Her throat felt tight. It was impossible to swallow. "It wouldn't be right, Rand. He's going to be my husband."

His palms came up, molded themselves over her breasts. The pads of his thumbs rasped slowly, skillfully, over her nipples. "You want me, Cait. Can you deny it?"

Back and forth, back and forth, insistent, relentless, her nipples tightening, throbbing. Desire curled in her stomach. Slick wet heat slid into her core. Could she deny it? She could try, but Rand would know it for the lie it was.

"We deserve this, Cait—this one last time together. Say you want me, Caitlin. Admit you want me to touch you, come inside you."

She bit down on her trembling lip, determined to hold back the words. His hands slid lower, down her back, over her buttocks, cupping them, pulling her closer, into his heavy erection. He parted her legs, lifted her up and wrapped them around his waist. His fingers found her from behind, parted her sex, slid inside her.

"You're hot, Caitie, so incredibly hot. I remember how tight you are, how good you feel."

She made a little sound in her throat as he gently began to stroke her. She told herself she had to stop him, but heat and need made her mind go fuzzy and her limbs feel weak.

"Say it, Caitie. Tell me you want me." Those skillful fingers slid into her again and again. She was trembling, her body tightening around them. It had been so long. So long. And she was in love with him.

She was perched on the brink, near the edge of release, when he stopped his determined assault. Arching toward him in frustration, she bit back a sob.

"Tell me what you want," he softly pressed. "Tell me, Cait, and I'll give it to you."

"Oh, God, Rand . . . I need you so much. I want you so badly."

He kissed her hard and plunged himself deeply inside.

Gripping her hips, he held her in place while he drove into her again and again. Long, powerful strokes, the heavy thrust and drag of his shaft. Pleasure washed over her. Gooseflesh skipped over her skin. Her fingers dug into the muscles across his shoulders and her head fell back, her long hair heavy with the weight of the water. She was dizzy with desire, awash with heat and need and love for him.

"Come with me, Caitie." Several more hard, penetrating strokes and she splintered, her body flying off in a thousand different directions all at once. She couldn't seem to think, couldn't quite catch her breath and didn't care. Rand followed her to climax and she clung to him, her thoughts far away and drifting with the water, Rand holding her, his hardness still buried deep inside.

As they began to spiral down, he carried her to the riverbank, but didn't climb out. A rock ledge formed a chair and they sat there together, his arm around her waist, her head against his shoulder. She wasn't sure how long they sat that way, seconds only, minutes perhaps.

Longer than they should have.

Not nearly long enough.

She tensed at the sound of voices, began to scramble up from her rocky perch, but Rand's hands clamped around her waist and he dragged her back into the cover of the water.

"Someone's coming! We have to get dressed!"

His mouth flattened into an unsympathetic line, and her blood went cold at the look of satisfaction on his face. "It's too late, Cait. They're already here."

Just then Rand's valet, Percival Fox, stepped out of the trees. Two steps behind him stood her father.

"Good God! Caitlin—what on earth?" He glanced from Rand's bare chest to Cait's exposed shoulders, and it was more than apparent that both of them were naked. "What the devil is going on?"

Cait slid lower into the water, wishing she could vanish into the hot tropical air, blinded by tears and cursing her own reckless nature. She swallowed and tried to speak, but no words would come.

"Give us a moment, Professor," Rand put in smoothly. "As soon as we're dressed, we can straighten all of this out."

"That you will, sir—I assure you."

Caitlin couldn't remember her father ever speaking in quite that tone of voice. She watched him turn away and walk back in the opposite direction, Percival Fox right beside him.

"Come on, Cait," Rand said gently. "Surely marrying me can't be all that bad."

She didn't answer, just sat there numbly. She told herself to get out of the water, that she had to get dressed, but her legs felt too rubbery to move. She felt Rand's arm around her, urging her out of the pool. They sloshed toward the shore together and he handed her the linen towel she had brought along. Rand dried himself with the tail of his shirt, then shrugged it on and pulled on his trousers. As she stepped into her skirt and fastened the tabs, he tied the laces on his boots.

They said nothing along the path back to camp, but when they arrived, her father was waiting. His eyes swung straight to hers and she thought he had never looked more weary. Her heart went out to him, and in that moment she hated the Duke of Beldon.

"All right, young lady. Let's hear it. What do you have to say?"

Tears burned, rolled down her cheeks. Rand spoke up before she had time to answer.

"This isn't exactly as it seems, Professor. Your daughter and I have had . . . feelings for each other for some time. I realize she has pledged herself to Lord Geoffrey, but I believe she would rather marry me."

Cait couldn't help it. She turned on him with fire in her eyes. "Are you that sure of yourself . . . *Your Grace*? Do you think you are the only man who could possibly appeal to me?"

Rand's expression hardened. He tossed her a glance that told her she had just lost the chance to accept defeat gracefully. "Your daughter is carrying my child," he said flatly. "I think that is reason enough for us to wed."

If he had hit her with his fist, the blow could not have been more painful. She should have guessed he knew about the babe. She should have known the instant he set foot on the island. If she had shared her secret with anyone but Maggie, she would have. But she had been so sure her friend would not betray her.

She glanced at Rand and a painful knot rose in her throat. He had known about the child from the start. He didn't want her. He never had. He only wanted the babe.

Her father's troubled blue eyes swung to her face. "Is that true, Caitlin? Are you with child?"

She moistened her lips, anger and resentment destroying the last of her composure. "It doesn't matter. Geoffrey knows everything. He has asked me to marry and I have agreed."

The gold in Rand's dark eyes seemed to ignite with an inward heat. "The child is mine. I won't have him raised by some sniveling milksop."

Caitlin hoisted her chin. She knew her lips were trembling. "I won't marry you. I don't even like you."

Her father's sharp tone cut between them. "You liked him well enough this afternoon when I discovered the two of you together in the pool." For an instant he faltered, but his stance remained unbending. "Since your mother died, I haven't been a very good father. I've allowed you too much freedom, given you your own way too often. But you will not have your way in this. When Captain Baptiste arrives on the morrow, you will be married to the man who fathered your child. You will wed the Duke of Beldon."

"B-but, Father—"

"That is the end of it, Caitlin. We'll talk no more about it. Now I suggest you speak to young Geoffrey and tell him you have changed your mind."

She stood her ground, fighting the trembling that moved through her body. "Father, you don't understand. If I marry the duke I'll have to leave Santo Amaro. I can't do that. You need me. I can't just—"

He reached out and caught her shoulders. "Listen to me, Caitlin. I'm an old man. I've lived a long, rewarding life. I know you don't believe it, and perhaps it pleased me to allow you the illusion, but in truth, I'm very capable of taking care of myself."

"But you've been ill. You might be sick again. I couldn't—"

"I might fall ill, yes. So might you. So might the duke. That is not the question." His hand cupped her cheek. "You know I love you, Caitlin. If I didn't believe your marriage to the duke was the best thing for you, I wouldn't insist. Considering the circumstances—and what transpired this afternoon—I believe His Grace is the best man for you."

Cait said nothing, but her heart felt leaden. Ice seemed to flow through her veins. She glanced at Rand, certain he would appear triumphant, but gentle concern softened his features.

"Trust me, Caitlin," he said. "You've trusted me before and you haven't been sorry."

She didn't answer. Rand had seduced her, forced her into marriage. He was taking her away from her father when he needed her most. There was no possible way she could trust him.

Still, deep down inside, she wanted to. She wanted to so very much.

SEVENTEEN

"You're nervous." Percy Fox grinned, eyeing the big man who had been his friend and employer for the past ten years, watching him fiddle with the wide white stock around his neck, tug on the cuffs beneath his tailored brown coat. "You knew you would wed the lass, sooner or later. You were determined to have her. I can scarcely credit that you would be nervous."

"What did you expect? Until I learned about the child, marriage was hardly my plan. Now I'm about to become a father as well as a husband. Tell me you wouldn't be nervous."

Percy laughed. "All right, I concede. I suppose it's natural when a man's about to become leg-shackled. If it makes you feel any better, I gather your lady isn't taking this any better than you are."

The duke merely grunted and continued to wrestle with his stock, fighting to tie it properly.

"Here—let me do it. You are only going to make a mess of it." Percy tied the neckcloth with his usual efficiency, then stepped back to admire his handiwork. The duke looked quite elegant in a dark brown jacket and beige waistcoat shot with a fine gold thread. His breeches were beige and his shoes had shiny gold buckles.

"I'm afraid you may be a bit overdressed," Percy told him. "Rumor has it your Miss Harmon means to wed you in plain brown twill."

Rand made a rude sound in his throat. "I'm not surprised. Fortunately, I don't give a damn what the lady wears as long as we end up married."

"Captain Baptiste is getting things ready. It won't be long now, I don't imagine."

The duke plucked a nonexistent piece of lint from the sleeve of his perfectly tailored coat. "The sooner the better," he grumbled.

Percy looked at him and bit back a smile, thinking that beneath that gruff façade, behind the nerves and the bluster, what the Duke of Beldon was mostly feeling was a profound sense of relief. The lady would finally be his, and though he might not even realize it himself, it was exactly what he'd wanted all along.

It was time for her wedding. Never in her wildest dreams had Cait imagined anything like this. Not a bride, but a fallen woman, tricked into marriage by the man whose child she carried.

Standing in front of her tent, she stood waiting for her father to arrive, resigned to her fate, but still not happy about it. She was wearing her cotton twill skirt, simple white blouse, and scuffed brown boots. If the Duke of Beldon was determined to marry her, by heaven, he would take her exactly as she was!

"Missie Harmon?" Maruba stepped into the clearing, willowy slim, with a pleasant smile and softly feminine features. "Cook say you no have dress for wedding. Maruba bring this." Cait glanced down at the bright swathe of red flowered material draped over Maruba's dark-skinned arm.

"It isn't exactly that I don't have a dress. It's more that I would rather dress as I am."

"No, no, missie. Today wedding day. Must look pretty for your mon." She held up a red sarong of the sort the native women wore. "Look pretty in this—a gift for you from the women."

She was shaking her head, trying to think of a polite way to refuse, when her father walked up.

"Why aren't you dressed?" He studied her work clothes with obvious disapproval. "Tell me you do not intend to wear what you have on."

Her chin hiked up. "If he wants me, he'll have to take me the way I am."

Her father's pale blue eyes moistened with sympathy. He touched a weathered hand to her cheek. "I know you are resentful of the way things came about, but I can't believe you don't have feelings for him. You aren't the sort of woman who would give herself to a man if she didn't care for him greatly."

Cait glanced down. Of course she cared. She was in love with him. But Rand wasn't in love with her, and he didn't have the right to simply ignore her feelings, her wishes.

"Today is your wedding day, Caitlin. It's a special day, one you will both remember for the rest of your lives. Twenty years from now, do you want your husband to remember that his bride came to him dressed in the garb of a peasant? Do you want to remember yourself that way?"

Cait bit down on her lip. Twenty years. Would Rand really remember? She knew that whatever happened between them, it was a day she would certainly never forget. She looked down at her threadbare skirt, saw the scuffed toes of her boots peeping from beneath the hem.

With a sigh of defeat, she turned to the dark-skinned girl. "I appreciate your gift. I would be honored to wear the dress, Maruba."

White teeth flashed against the smooth, creamy darkness of her skin. "Come. I help you put on. Then we pick flowers for your hair."

It didn't take long to strip off her work clothes and put on the colorful red sarong. She wondered what Rand would think when he saw it, wondered if he would approve of the split that showed a portion of her thigh when she walked, the shoulder the sarong left bare. Deciding to go native all the way and forgo even a pair of kidskin slippers, she stood by patiently while Maruba and one of the other women pinned a purple-throated, ruffled white orchid in her hair.

Outside the tent, her father was waiting and this time when he saw her he smiled.

"Now that is more like it. You look lovely, my dear. And I believe you will still make your point. The woman Beldon is marrying is unique, not like any other woman. Your duke had best remember that."

Cait's throat went tight. She went up on tiptoe and kissed his wrinkled cheek. "I wish I didn't have to leave you."

Her father patted her hand. "It's time for you to fly, little bird. It has been for quite some time."

Cait brushed away a tear that slipped down her cheek. "I love you, Father."

"I'm so proud of you, Caitlin. Always remember that. You're the best daughter a man could ever have." Taking her hand, he started toward the arbor that had been fashioned for the occasion at the edge of the sand. Made of broad green leaves, it was decorated with the same wild orchids as the one she wore in her hair.

Rand stood beneath it. Her gaze clung to his tall, broad-shouldered figure as he watched her approach, and she couldn't miss the possessive gleam in his eyes. When she stopped beside him, she could feel his assessing gaze moving over her, taking in the clinging red sarong and the bare skin it displayed.

A corner of his mouth edged up. "It isn't exactly the way I would have imagined my bride to dress, but I believe I prefer it to cotton twill and scuffed leather boots."

She eyed him darkly. She hadn't forgotten the way he had tricked her, or the reason he was marrying her. "I'm glad you approve."

"Oh, I do," he said with a slight edge to his voice. "Only the next time you wear it, it won't be in public. You'll be wearing it for me in the confines of our bedchamber."

Cait's temper cranked up a notch. How dare he begin giving orders even before they were married! She opened her mouth to tell him she would dress as she pleased, that marrying him didn't mean he was now her keeper.

But the captain stepped in front of them just then. "It appears that everyone is here. Are we ready?"

She wished he hadn't asked. She felt less ready for this than anything she had undertaken in her life. Cait surveyed the small group gathered in a half-circle around them: Sir Monty and her father, Lord Talmadge, the workers and the servants. Geoffrey St. Anthony stood there stiffly, his jaw so tight a muscle flinched in his cheek.

Cait stared at him a little longer than she should have, suffering a momentary pang of conscience. She had never meant to hurt Geoffrey. She had never meant to hurt her father or anyone else.

"You may begin, Captain Baptiste," Rand said a bit darkly, his gaze moving between her and Geoffrey, taking a firm grip on her arm.

"Dearly beloved," the captain began, reading from a marriage text in his thick Portuguese accent. "We are gathered here on the island today . . ." Cait's mind went fuzzy as he launched into a somewhat strange rendition of the wedding ceremony, and only faintly heard the words. From the moment he started, her nerves seemed to swell.

Dear God, she was marrying a man who didn't love her. A domineering, demanding man used to getting exactly what he wanted. He had learned about the babe and traveled thousands of miles determined they would wed. How would he treat her? What about his legions of women? What would her life be like once they returned to England?

They were questions without answers and unconsciously Cait shivered.

"Are you, Caitlin Harmon, willing to accept this man, Randall Clayton, Duke of Beldon, as your husband, lawfully wedded?" She swallowed hard. Rand nudged her and she squeaked out a yes.

The question was asked of Rand and he answered with a note of authority and a hard glance at Cait. It was obvious that he wasn't happy with her lack of enthusiasm, nor her sympathy for Geoffrey.

Too bad. He should have thought of that before he embarrassed her in front of her father and the members of the expedition, and tricked her into marriage.

The ceremony was over in a matter of minutes. When the captain gave permission for Rand to kiss his bride, he did so thoroughly, almost savagely. That he was angry was apparent. Perhaps he had imagined that once the decision to marry him was made, she would meekly resign herself. Well, it wasn't going to happen—not that way.

"The captain will be leaving within the hour," Rand said as the others moved off toward the scant feast that had been cooked in honor of the occasion. "I presume you are packed and ready to leave."

"I'm packed. I'm hardly ready to leave. You know very well I would prefer to remain here with my father."

"And you—Your Grace—know very well that isn't going to happen."

Her stomach tightened at the pointed reminder that she now belonged to him. "What about Talmadge?"

Rand's brows pulled together. "What about him?"

"If he has done the things you say, there is no telling what he might do to get the treasure. I realize you don't believe it, but my father is innocent of your suspicions. He might be in some sort of danger."

Rand seemed to ponder that. "I'm no longer convinced your father is involved in Talmadge's scheme. I'll speak to him before I leave, tell him my suspicions. At least he'll know enough to be wary."

"But shouldn't we stay and—"

"We're leaving, Cait. I want you back in England where you can safely birth my child. For the present, that is all that matters."

Cait didn't argue. In a way he was right. She didn't want to have her babe here in this primitive landscape with no one to help her. In regard to Talmadge, for all she knew, Rand's suspicions were merely that—unfounded suspicions. So far the baron had done nothing improper. Without proof of his supposed crimes, there was no reason for her father not to trust him.

Still, a good deal of treasure had already been unearthed. Enough to interest the greedy self-serving sort of man Rand believed Talmadge was. It was one more worry to add to a growing list.

Their departure was a teary occasion, at least on Caitlin's part, one that almost made Rand feel guilty. Almost, but not quite. Cait Harmon—Cait Harmon Clayton, he corrected, newly titled Duchess of Beldon, wasn't in love with Geoffrey St. Anthony. And she didn't owe her father the balance of her life.

In a way he had saved her from a dismal fate. Marriage to St. Anthony would hardly suit an intelligent, strong-willed woman like Cait. And spending the rest of her life moving from place to place with her father was hardly a future to look forward to, no matter what Caitlin said.

He had saved her, married her, given her child its rightful name. She should be grateful, dammit. Instead, she had hardly spoken to him since they had left Santo Amaro. For the past ten days, she'd been moody and withdrawn.

And he still hadn't consummated the marriage, which galled him most of all.

"You're brooding again," Percy said as he joined Rand at the rail of the *Swift Venture,* the ship they had boarded in Dakar. Upon their arrival, they'd fortuitously discovered a vessel bound for England, set to sail the end of the week. "Marital problems already?"

"You know very well the problem I am having. I've been sleeping in your cabin for the past ten days. Not exactly what I had in mind when I got married."

"Remind me—why is it you're not sharing your pretty wife's bed? Whatever reason you gave was so poor it seems to have slipped my mind."

"I am trying to give her time, dammit. I want her to accept this marriage and resign herself to being my wife."

"And you think staying away from her will accomplish that end?"

"Are you saying it will not?"

"I'm saying the lady succumbed quite readily to your rather dubious charms the day you seduced her at the pool. If it worked once, perhaps it will do so again."

Rand stared at his friend, remembering that day all too clearly, wondering if, indeed, the tactic might work again. His scowl slid into a grin. "By God, Percy, I believe you may be right. The little witch has had her way long enough. She has a husband to think of now. She might as well get used to the notion."

"Exactly so," Percy agreed.

Rand turned back toward the rail, his gaze going out to the horizon. It was hours yet till dark. For ten miserable days, he had stayed away from her, denied himself the comfort of her sweet little body. Now that his decision was made, he wanted to storm into the cabin, drag her down on the mattress, and make passionate love to her.

He wouldn't, of course. He would wait till after supper, wait until she retired, then join her in bed, as he should have done on his wedding night aboard the *Moroto*. Rand glanced back toward the ladder leading down to her cabin. He would wait, he told himself. Until it was time to retire.

But as soon as the sun dipped below the horizon and darkness enveloped the ship, he found himself striding toward Caitlin's cabin door.

Ten days, Cait thought, disgruntled. Ten days and Rand had yet to share her bed. She'd been certain he would come to her, claim his husbandly rights that first night, and she had been determined to deny him. Instead, she had tossed and turned, barely slept at all, and Rand had not come. She had wondered how he would treat her, now that she was his wife. She wouldn't have guessed that he would completely ignore her.

She glanced out the porthole. Nothing but endless sea and white-capped waves. The sun was just down. Soon she would have to dress for supper in one of the few decent gowns she had brought with her from England. Rand would come for her, as he did each evening, escort her down to the dining room to join the captain and other passengers, then make polite conversation about every subject but those that interested her.

He wouldn't discuss her father, wouldn't talk about Talmadge, wouldn't even mention the days he'd spent on Santo Amaro. He never spoke of the babe, their marriage, or the future.

He seemed to go out of his way not to broach a subject that might upset her.

Well, she certainly wasn't upset. She was well and truly bored. She never would have guessed that marrying Rand Clayton would be the least bit boring.

With a sigh, she picked up her embroidery hoop, flounced down on the bed, and began to work tiny stitches into the fabric. It wasn't something she particularly liked to do, but it was too early to change for supper and she had gown weary of reading.

She glanced toward the porthole again, saw that the sun was completely down and it was dark outside except for a faint glow at the edge of the horizon. A few seconds later footsteps sounded in the passageway outside the cabin, the door swung open without a knock, and Rand stormed in.

Her fingers tightened around the hoop. She plunged the needle through the cloth with a little too much force. "It's early yet for supper. What is it you want?"

His jaw tightened. "What is it I want?" he repeated, a muscle bunching in his cheek. "You have to ask me what I want?"

There was something in his stance, the way he stood

with his legs slightly splayed, his hands unconsciously fisting. And the look in his eyes—no longer bland indifference but the same burning desire she had seen in Santo Amaro. Her pulse took a leap, started a too-rapid clatter.

"For the past ten days I've stayed away from you," he said. "I've given you time to adjust. I hoped that in doing so you would come to accept our marriage. It's obvious that hasn't occurred."

Caitlin slid backward on the bed as Rand stalked toward her, hard purpose there in his face. He pulled the embroidery hoop out of her hand, jerked her to her feet, and into his arms.

"You're my wife," he growled. "It's time you knew it." Whatever reply she might have made was silenced by a scorching hot kiss. For a single stunned instant, she thought that she should fight him. He was her husband, yes, but that didn't give him the right to barge in and make demands!

Then the truth rushed in with staggering force. She wanted Rand to kiss her. She wanted him to touch her, make love to her. He captured her face between his hands and deepened the kiss, and a funny little whimper came from her throat. Her lips softened under his and she opened to him, accepting the hot sweep of his tongue. Her own touched his, fenced with it, entangled it. She thought she heard him groan.

Her hands were trembling as she slid them beneath his jacket, forcing it off his shoulders. She could feel his muscles moving, tightening, as she undid the buttons on his waistcoat and shoved it off, urged him to drag his white linen shirt off over his head then pressed her mouth against his naked chest.

"Caitie . . . God . . . It's been torture without you. I've missed you so damned much." His big hands tangled in her hair, dragging her mouth back to his. He tore open her blouse, fumbled with the binding she wore to help support her breasts, finally found the end and jerked it loose, and they spilled into his hands.

Cait tore his breeches in her frenzy to unfasten the buttons, brushed his hardened arousal where it pressed against the cloth, and heard his quick intake of breath. Rand pushed her fingers aside and quickly finished the task, his thick shaft springing free, hot as it arched into her hand.

She locked her fingers around it, tested the thickness, the length, and he groaned.

They were both naked to the waist, their breathing hard and urgent. Rand eased her down on the bed and shoved up her skirts, settled himself between her legs and started kissing her breasts. She felt the warmth of his breath against her skin, the wetness of his kisses as he trailed them lower, over her rib cage, the rounded swell of her stomach, then his mouth fastened gently at her core.

Cait gasped at the swift shot of pleasure and the burning blaze of heat. Desire engulfed her, roared through her blood. He stroked her with his hands and his tongue, laved her deeply and with expert skill. Her back arched upward and her fingers curled into his wavy dark brown hair. Her muscles tightened. Her body clenched in pleasure and she wildly came undone.

She was sobbing his name when he came up over her, sliding himself inside in a single deep thrust, filling her to the limit with his thick, heavy hardness. Easing out, he began to move, slowly at first, then faster, deeper, harder. Again and again he thrust into her, as if he took possession, as if he couldn't get enough.

She came again, but he didn't let up, driving into her with purpose, forcing her to peak once more.

"Caitie . . ." he ground out as he joined her in climax, his muscles contracting, his body going rigid with the pleasure that burned through him. He kissed her softly one last time, and his heartbeat began to slow, his breathing became more even. He settled himself beside her and pulled her into his arms.

For a while they lay in silence, listening to the creak

of timbers, absorbing the roll and sway of the ship as it knifed through the water.

Cait smiled into his shoulder. "I'm beginning to think you should have done that sooner."

The edge of his mouth curved up. "Yes, I can see that now." He turned, reached out and cupped her cheek. "I never meant to force the marriage, Cait. I hoped you would come to me, tell me about the babe."

"I wanted to. A dozen times I almost did."

"It doesn't matter now. We're married. For the child's sake, that is what counts."

For the child's sake. She had known the truth in her heart, yet it hurt to hear him say it.

"Considering what just happened . . ." His smile looked slightly smug. "Do you think we might call a truce? I believe we did that fairly successfully once before."

A truce. Yes, she supposed she could give him that. They were married now. She didn't really have any other choice. But the hurt was still there, the knowledge that he didn't love her, that if it hadn't been for the child, they never would have wed.

And so many problems still lay between them. What would happen once they reached London? What would her life be like?

Cait wished she could see into the future.

And she was very glad she could not.

They spent a little over a month at sea. After they made love that first night, Rand moved into the cabin and, as Cait might have guessed, the trip went from boring to wildly exciting. He was just that sort of man.

Little by little, Rand began to speak more freely and no topic was forbidden. They talked about the child, tossing out names, planning the nursery Rand was determined to fashion at Beldon Hall, his country estate in Buckinghamshire where he determined they would spend most of their time.

"It's lovely in the extreme," he told her, "a big sprawling house made of stone surrounded by green rolling hills. It's away from the noise and dirt of the city, a good place to raise a child."

They argued about Geoffrey St. Anthony, Caitlin defending him, Rand convinced he would have made her a very poor husband.

"You would have chewed him up and spit him out in little pieces." He gave her a devilish grin. "It takes a man to handle you, Caitie. Not a little boy."

Cait fought not to smile. Rand was a man—that was certain. And she wasn't completely sure he was wrong. She had never found Geoffrey the least bit attractive, and their conversations were rarely inspired. Still, it was great fun to watch the possessive light come into Rand's eyes when she spoke of another man.

In truth, they didn't always agree, but she liked that about him—that they could argue and shout and still the attraction remained. And making up was often the best part. The last time Rand decided their feuding had gone on long enough, he had scooped her into his arms, carried her down to the cabin, tossed her onto the bed and made love to her with furious intent.

They talked about the baron, Rand relaying the latest information he had received from his Bow Street runner, as well as the conversation he'd had with her father just before they'd left Santo Amaro.

"Where Talmadge is concerned, your father is quite unreasonable," he said with a sigh. "He's determined the man is a saint, and there is no convincing him it might not be so. Perhaps after the child is born, we can return to the island and make certain the professor is safe."

She loved him for that, for understanding her fears and wanting to allay them. But then she loved him a little more every day. And whatever care Rand felt for her also seemed to be growing. For the first time since they had sailed from the island, her hopes began to rise. Perhaps they could be happy after all. Perhaps he might even come to love her.

Then they reached London, and every hope for the future she had nurtured aboard the ship grew dim and slowly faded away.

EIGHTEEN

Rand strode into the foyer of Beldon Hall. They had been in residence for only a week and already the house seemed different, warmer than it ever had before. He paused in the entry, heard the sound of Cait's laughter coming from upstairs, followed it up the sweeping marble staircase.

She was working with a drapery seller, choosing fabrics to complete the nursery. "A bright, sunny yellow," she had insisted, though he had been determined the color should be royal blue. "You might be wrong," she said. "It might very well be a girl."

"It's a boy," he'd argued with such determination that Caitlin had laughed in that throaty way of hers. "But you may paint it yellow if you wish." They were no longer sleeping together. His wife was nearly seven months pregnant and he was concerned that their intimacy might somehow hurt the babe.

Considering how round she had grown, most men wouldn't have cared. Rand found himself more fascinated with his little wife's body than he'd ever been before. He wanted to touch her, hold her, feel the movements of his child in her belly. And he wanted to be inside her, wanted to make love to her, just as he always did.

It frightened him, these feelings that came over him with such unbearable force. Whatever Caitlin asked for, he wanted to give her—perhaps because she rarely asked for anything at all. Whatever she wanted to do, he wanted to agree. Not that he did, of course.

As the Duchess of Beldon, there were rules she must learn to follow and he meant to see that she did. No more running about by herself, as she was determined to do. Pregnant women simply did not go out. No more public speaking, and certainly not some outlandish diatribe against supposed crimes of which he, himself, was guilty.

Like the subject of his valuable jade collection. Or his private collection of ancient Roman and Hellenistic busts.

"I can't believe it," she'd once told him, aghast when she first discovered the beautiful Chinese jade in a cabinet in the Oriental Salon. "You of all people! Hoarding away such magnificent objects. You knew how I felt about that sort of thing yet you never said a word!"

He found himself grinning. "That was because I knew how you felt about that sort of thing."

"Ohhhh, you are maddening!"

"And you think you are not? Once our son is born, I swear I shall extract a penance for all the sleepless nights you've been responsible for—considering you no longer share my bed."

She flushed prettily and Rand thought for the hundredth time how much of his heart she had captured. In truth, he adored her, and it terrified him to feel that way. There wasn't a man of his acquaintance—except, of course, Nick Warring—who felt such a ridiculously strong attraction to his wife.

His father would have laughed at him, called him ten kinds of a fool. "Women are for swiving—pleasuring a man, and giving him sons. That is all they are good for, and any man who forgets that isn't a man at all."

And the way he felt about the child. He already thought of his offspring as a living, breathing part of the family. Little Jonathan Randall—the name they had chosen if the infant were a boy, which Rand was sure it would be— was as real to him as if he already lay upstairs in the nursery, a tiny, brown-haired version of himself. Or perhaps a boy with freckles and fiery auburn hair like its mother. He would be smart like Cait and strong like his father.

Rand smiled at the image, deciding he would like a whole house full of children. Then the smile slid away.

What the devil was he doing? Women were supposed to sit around mooning over babies, acting like lovesick fools—not men. He shuddered to think what his father would say if he knew.

"Rand? Is that you?" Caitlin came out of the nursery and stood looking down over the banister at the top of the stairs. She gave him one of her sunny smiles and an odd lump rose in his throat. Damn but she was beautiful, even more so now that she carried his child. With her clear skin and the bright bloom in her cheeks, she had never looked more attractive, at least not to him.

"Why don't you come up and help me choose the fabric? The draper says the silk I've picked is too bright, but I disagree. We could certainly use your help."

He wanted to. He was good with colors and textures. He always had been. It was the reason he had so loved to paint. Using colors and textures to re-create the world as he saw it in sparkling, vibrant hues. It was a pastime he would have pursued as a youth if his father hadn't forbade it.

He looked up at Cait and shook his head. "I'm afraid you'll have to make do without me. I've got work to do in my study."

It was the truth, of course. He always had work to do, responsibilities he needed to see to. But the truth was, he was afraid. Every day he spent with Caitlin, every hour, every minute, he was becoming more and more enamored of her. He was losing his senses where she was concerned, turning ridiculously soft and weak-willed. He was wildly afraid he was falling in love with her.

And that, Rand was determined, he simply would not do.

*   *   *

Through the window of the Red Room, Cait watched her husband working with the gardener, giving him instructions, helping him lay out the winter garden.

"It should have been done already," he'd told her last night at supper, the one occasion she could count on spending time with him. "But I like to do it a little differently each year, and since I was away and didn't leave any instructions, the gardener simply waited for my return."

Gardening was another of his many interests, one, like poetry or birds, he seemed loath to acknowledge. But Cait had merely smiled her approval when he'd mentioned the topiary leopard he had ordered fashioned in the hedge, from what had previously been a mammoth bear. She had asked him to break away from his work for a while and join her for luncheon, but he had refused. It saddened her to think how much he had done that lately.

She told herself she shouldn't mind. He was busy, she knew. Since her arrival at Beldon Hall, she had discovered just how hard a duke was expected to work. He had estates to manage, people whose livelihood depended upon him. And Rand was a man who took his responsibilities to heart.

But lately, she feared it was more than simple duty that kept him away.

It seemed Rand was purposely avoiding her. He no longer came to her bed, though the doctor assured them both it was still safe to do so, and the evenings they had once spent playing cards or chess, he now often spent in his study.

She didn't know what was wrong, worried that perhaps her cumbersome bulk made her repulsive to him. Rand never said so, of course. In fact, he often made comment on how pretty she looked, but Cait wasn't sure she believed him.

She watched him now through the window, watched him leave the garden and head off toward the stables. The autumn day was clear and bright, just a few wispy clouds overhead and a soft, faint breeze. She thought that he would go riding, perhaps make calls on some of his tenants. Though she longed to join him, she'd been forced to forgo the luxury of riding as her girth continued to swell.

Still, she'd been cooped up in the house far too long and a walk would surely do her good. Fetching her cashmere shawl from her bedchamber, she left the house, heading off toward the little stream that wound its way across the rolling fields.

The wind was brisker than she had thought as it ruffled her hair but the sun was warm where it filtered down through the leafless trees. She thought that perhaps she should have worn a hat, but quickly discarded the notion. If a freckled duchess wasn't exactly the mode, well that was simply too bad. She had bent to Rand's will on too many occasions already. She was who she was. Rand had known that before he married her.

She climbed a small knoll and was surprised to find him standing on the opposite side, just out of view of the house. He was holding a watercolor palette, awash with bright fall colors, and a three-legged easel stood in front of him. He was painting a lovely scene that depicted both the copse of naked sycamores in front of him and the clear little stream that meandered along at the base of the trees.

Cait drew closer, eager to view the work, trying to peer over his shoulder without disturbing him. He must have sensed her presence for he whirled in her direction, saw who it was, and the color drained from his face.

"What the devil are you doing out here? Can't I have even a single moment's peace? Must you follow me about like some overgrown puppy?"

The words stung. For a moment, she felt at a loss for words. "You're painting," she pointed out needlessly, stupidly, upset and embarrassed all at once.

His face went from pale to flushed. "I was just passing time—dabbling a bit, that's all." Reaching toward the paper, he snatched it off the easel. Cait gasped as he neatly ripped the picture in two. "As you can see, now I am through." In amazement, Cait watched as he released the two halves of the painting, which fluttered to the ground, then turned and stormed back toward the house.

She bent and picked up the pieces, studied the firm, clear lines, admired the way he had captured the light shining down through the trees. It was amazingly good and it saddened her that he had destroyed it.

Good Lord, what was the matter with him?

But in her heart she knew. She remembered the words Maggie had said, remembered how his father had ridiculed his efforts, even beat him for pursuing what the duke called "womanly pursuits." Staring after him, she lifted her skirts and started running as best she could, catching up with him just as he reached the garden.

"Rand! Wait a minute!" He heard her but kept on walking, striding in that purposeful way of his. "Rand! I only want to talk to you . . . please . . . ?"

At her softly spoken words, his pace began to slow. He stopped at the side of a hedge, dragged in a deep, shuddering breath. "What is it you want? There's work I need to do."

"Listen to me, Rand." She held out the two halves of the picture. "Your painting . . . it's lovely . . . wonderful, in fact. If you are embarrassed about it, you shouldn't be. You're a very talented artist. You should be proud of the work you've done."

His eyes, turbulent and dark, searched her face. He found no mockery, no disapproval as he seemed certain he would. "It's only a hobby," he said defensively.

"It doesn't matter why you do it, as long as it gives you pleasure. And the painting really is beautiful. I would love to see what else you've done."

Some of the stiffness eased from his body. "I only began again earlier this year."

"But you painted as a child," she gently pressed, hoping he would tell her about it.

"Yes. It pleased my mother, and I loved doing it. My father, of course, disapproved."

"He thought a man who painted wasn't much of a man."

Rand shrugged his shoulders. "He caned me for it. More than once. My mother tried to intercede, but it didn't do any good. She was younger then, not the strong sort of woman she became after he was gone. I put my paints away. As I said, I only started dabbling again this year."

Cait smiled. "You're the strongest man I've ever known, Rand. But I love this side of you, too. I love that you are sensitive and gentle."

Rand cleared his throat, glanced away. "I'm sorry I said what I did. I didn't mean it, you know."

Something sweet sifted through her. "I didn't follow you. I didn't even know you were out there."

He smiled, took her hand, pressed the back against his lips. There was so much warmth in his expression, so much tenderness. He stared at her for several moments more, and she saw the rise of emotion, the swell of turbulence that wiped the smile away.

"We had better be getting back," he said a bit gruffly. "I really do have work to do."

"I'm not . . . not yet ready to go in. You go ahead."

He looked at her and simply nodded. Whatever softness had passed between them was over and done. His expression was closed again, as unreadable as it usually was. Turning away, he left her standing just outside the garden and returned to the house. Feeling more alone than she had since she left the island, Cait walked back toward the copse of trees and the little meandering stream.

Maggie Sutton, Countess of Trent, arrived with her husband at Beldon Hall two weeks after the duke and his bride returned to England. Rand knew they were coming, had encouraged the visit. Apparently, he had decided against informing Cait, and the greeting Maggie received was cool if not downright cold.

Maggie sighed as she left the pretty blue bedchamber she and Andrew shared. After destroying Cait's trust as she had, she couldn't really blame her. And yet she was determined to breach the gap of what Cait saw as a friend's blatant betrayal.

While Rand and Andrew went hunting, Maggie sought Cait out in the nursery, a sunny little room just down the hall from the duchess's private apartments. The walls were painted a soft lemon yellow, and ornate white plaster moldings decorated the ceilings and outlined the doors. The cradle was white, as well as the furniture, and there was a colorful yellow quilt draped over the cushions in the window seat.

Cait turned at Maggie's approach and her chin inched up. "I thought you were reading in your room."

"I didn't travel all the way from London merely to sit and read. I came to see you, Cait. I want to know how you are." *I want to know how Rand is treating you. I want to know if I've ruined your life.*

"As you can see, I'm doing quite well. The babe will be born in a couple of months. Rand takes care of anything I might need."

Cait's hostility knifed into Maggie. "I know how you feel about me, Cait, but I never meant to betray you. I wouldn't have done that for the world. You'll never know how I agonized over my decision to go to Rand. I wouldn't have—I swear I wouldn't—if I hadn't truly believed the two of you loved each other."

Something shifted, moved across Cait's features. "You thought that Rand loved me?"

"I could see it whenever you were together . . . the way you looked at him . . . the way he looked at you. I wanted you to have a chance to find the happiness I've found with Andrew."

The muscles in Cait's throat constricted. Tears sprang into her eyes. "Oh, Maggie—I'm sorry. I didn't understand." Then they were hugging each other, both of them crying, holding on to each other. "You were my dearest friend in the world. It broke my heart when I realized you had told Rand the secret I had trusted only with you."

Maggie sat down on a small yellow upholstered sofa along the wall and Cait sat down beside her. "I only wanted what was best for you and Rand, best for the child. Tell me what happened when he got there . . . how the two of you wound up getting married."

Wiping away her tears, Cait told her the whole amazing story, ending with the way Rand had seduced her in the pool and arranged for her father to find out. By the time she was finished, Maggie was shaking her head.

"He's in love with you, Cait. I know he is."

"You're wrong, Maggie. Rand is sorry he ever married me. I think if it weren't for the child, he would leave and return to London."

Maggie reached over and clasped her hand. "Give him time, Cait. Whatever he's feeling is new to him. Rand is a man of deep, powerful emotions—he always has been. But he's afraid of them, afraid his feelings will control him and not the other way around."

"I don't know, Maggie."

"Do you love him?"

Cait gave her a miserable nod. "I love him. That's why this is so hard."

"He wouldn't be an easy man to live with."

"He's hard-headed and domineering. He issues orders as if he commands an army instead of merely a wife."

"But you love him."

She smiled with a hint of sadness. "I love him."

"Then I am not sorry I did what I did. I just hope in time it will all work out and you will be able to forgive me."

Caitlin leaned over and hugged her. "Now that I understand, there is nothing to forgive."

"So . . . you're about to become a father." Sitting in a chair in front of the fire in Rand's walnut-paneled study, Andrew Sutton accepted the cigar he offered. "How does it feel?" Andrew was a strong man, Rand knew, and just the right man for Maggie.

The Marquess of Trent knew exactly who he was and what he wanted out of life. There was a solidarity about him, an acceptance of self that Rand envied.

"To tell you the truth, I wasn't really prepared for all of this. You and Maggie have been married for a while. Until Cait came bounding into my life, I'd thought children were yet years away. Still, I have to admit, I'm eager to greet my son."

"And if it's a daughter?"

Rand grinned. "Then I'll shoot the first man who tries to hold her hand."

Andrew laughed and Rand chuckled. Maggie and Cait walked into the study just then, and the laughter slowly faded.

"All right . . . what are you two laughing about?" Cait raised a questioning brow in Rand's direction.

"A bit of male humor, is all," he said. "Considering the circumstances of our marriage, I don't believe you would find the conversation humorous in the least."

Cait let the subject drop, for which he was grateful. "We just stopped by to let you know we're going out," she said. "We've been invited to Lady Harriman's for tea. We'll be back by late afternoon."

Rand frowned. "I don't think that's a good idea. It's chilly outside. The roads are muddy. I would prefer that you remained here."

Cait's smile went tight. "It isn't far to Harriman Park, only a few miles down the road. Lady Harriman and I are of an age. I enjoyed meeting her when she came to pay her respects last week. I would like to cultivate her friendship."

Rand leaned toward the fire, lit the end of his cigar, took several slow puffs. "Perhaps after our guests have departed, I can find time to take you. Until then—"

"I'm going, Rand. I realize you are a duke, but thanks to our marriage, I am now a duchess. I can do as I wish.

If you think it unseemly for your pregnant wife to be seen in public, that is simply too bad. I shall see you this afternoon." Cait started toward the door and Rand shot to his feet.

"Dammit, Caitlin—you are seven months gone with child. Anything could happen. The road is bumpy. A wheel might break on the carriage. The weather is chill— you might catch an ague. I will not stand by and allow you to put yourself or my son in danger."

Before Cait could argue, Maggie stepped into the breach. "Perhaps Rand is right," she said gently. "Another time might be better, when the weather is less inclement."

Cait's face turned a faint shade of pink. "Perhaps . . . Your Grace . . . we might have a word in private?" Rand nodded stiffly and followed her down the hall into the Oriental Salon.

Cait turned to face him the moment he closed the door. "I don't know what you're thinking, Rand, but the truth is I'm a normal, healthy woman—the fact I am carrying your child notwithstanding. I should like to ask how long you intend to continue giving orders like some sort of imperial emperor? Because if you go on much longer, I will simply pack my bags and return to London."

Rand's eyes went wide. "You can't possibly do that."

"I will, Rand, I swear it. We're married. That doesn't give you license to control my every thought, my every move. If that is how you imagined this marriage to be then you are sorely mistaken."

For a moment, he just stood there, anger mixed with chagrin. She was right, of course. He had caged her in the house in an effort to protect her. He was afraid for her, afraid something might happen to the child. With a woman like Cait, he should have known it wouldn't work.

A heavy sigh escaped. "All right, dammit. You may go to Lady Harriman's. But I'm sending a pair of footmen in case there is any sort of trouble. And I intend to caution the driver to be careful of the bumps on the road."

A faint smile softened her features. Cait walked over

and kissed him lightly on the mouth. Rand felt the contact like a hot iron pressed to his loins. "I'll be fine, Rand. I won't do anything to injure your child, I promise."

He merely nodded. He was giving in to her again, but with Cait, it was nearly impossible to say no. Perhaps it wasn't important, since she never asked for more than she was due.

Still it bothered him, the power she seemed to hold over him. He wished he knew what to do.

NINETEEN

Maggie's bags were packed and sitting next to Andrew's in the foyer, ready to be loaded into the carriage. They were preparing to leave, saying their farewells to Rand in the Red Room, when a pale Cait arrived in the doorway, several hours later than she was expected.

"What's happened?" Rand asked, his expression suddenly worried as he crossed to where she stood in the opening. "I thought you had merely overslept, but you're as white as a ghost."

"Something's wrong. Perhaps . . . perhaps we should call Dr. Denis. When I awakened, there was . . ." Her face colored with anxiety and embarrassment. "This morning there was . . . blood on the sheets."

Rand said something beneath his breath, drew her over to the sofa, gently eased her down, then strode out the door, shouting for the butler, instructing him to send a footman to bring the physician in all haste.

"It wasn't . . . it wasn't the journey to Harriman Park," Cait told him when he returned, her eyes fixed on his face. "Nothing happened—not even a bump in the road—I swear it."

Rand leaned over, pressed a kiss on her forehead. "Take it easy, love. I'm sure it's nothing to worry about. I'll take you back upstairs, the doctor will have a look at you, and everything will be all right."

Dr. Denis arrived several hours later and headed straight up to the duchess's bedchamber, shooing everyone else away. By then Cait was feeling better. Still, the doctor insisted on strict bed rest for the next several days, and grudgingly Cait agreed.

Andrew returned to London, but at Rand's request, Maggie agreed to stay until Caitlin was feeling better. In fact, within days, she seemed to be. Enough so she'd begun to complain about being confined to bed, and reluctantly Rand agreed to a few hours each day in the garden.

"He's so protective," Maggie said with a smile as they sat in the comfortable overstuffed chairs the footman had carried outside for them. "I've never seen him behave quite this way."

Cait's hand moved down to her swollen stomach, round with Rand's child. "He wants this child. I think he loves it already. He'll make a wonderful father."

"He remembers his own childhood. The old duke treated him badly. He wants this child's life to be different."

Cait smiled. "It will be. We'll both make certain that it is." The babe moved just then and she smiled. She started to tell Maggie when an unexpected pain jabbed into her stomach and she sat up a little straighter in her chair.

"What is it? What's the matter?"

Another sharp pain speared through her. Cait sucked in several panting breaths. "Something's wrong, Maggie. The babe is moving inside me, stirring around somehow." Sweat popped out on her forehead. "My God, what's happening?"

Maggie leaped to her feet. "Don't move. Just stay right here." Shouting for Rand, she rushed out of the garden and back inside the house. The moment she was gone, Cait doubled over in pain. Beads of perspiration soaked into the hair at her temples and her hands started shaking.

Oh, dear God, not the babe. Not so soon. Not yet. Not yet. More pain slammed into her, knives of steel that thrust into her belly, forcing the bile up her throat. Nausea washed over her in sickening waves, and Cait slid off the chair, sinking down on her knees, bending forward to retch into the grass. At the same moment, a flood of water gushed from between her legs; it was followed by a surge of bright red blood. Cait felt the sticky wetness and her heart shuddered in horror.

From the corner of her eye, she saw Rand rushing toward her, knew he heard the scream of denial that ripped from her throat. Then darkness ate at the edges of her vision, more pain struck her, blackness rushed in, and she slumped forward onto the grass.

When she awakened, she was lying in her bedchamber, still swamped in pain, drowning in a sea of agony that would not go away.

"It's all right," Rand said, gently shoving damp hair back from her forehead. He looked as pale as she, and across the room, Maggie's eyes glistened with tears. "The doctor's on his way. Just hang on for a little while longer."

But she couldn't hang on, couldn't keep from crying in fear, couldn't hold the pain at bay. For hours, she labored, knowing it was too soon, knowing that if the child were born, it likely would not live.

The doctor arrived and Rand left for a while, not long. As soon as the next wave of pain washed over her and she bit back a moan, he jerked open the door and strode in.

"Can't you see she's hurting?" he said to the physician. "Give her something to ease the pain."

The doctor shook his head. "We need her awake. It'll be over soon."

Rand sank down in the chair beside the bed. "Over?" he repeated numbly, and the doctor confirmed the dreaded news. The child was coming. It was far too soon. Odds were, the babe would not live.

Rand's eyes slid closed. Caitlin screamed again, her body contracting, pressing to expel the child. When she turned her head to look at Rand, she saw that there were tears on his cheeks.

It was several hours later that the infant finally came. A little boy, the doctor said. It lived only minutes, long enough for Rand to see that the child was perfectly formed, a miniature of the son he had so desperately wanted.

Cait turned her head and wept into the pillow. The pain was even greater now, no longer a physical ache, but an unbearable pain of the heart.

Rand stood beside Caitlin at the top of the frost-covered hill. An icy wind whipped the thin, bare branches overhead, blew brittle, dead leaves against the low wrought-iron fence that enclosed the tombstones and vaults, the graves of his Clayton family for seven generations. Some were more recent than others, his uncle and aunt, his father and mother, his recently deceased young cousin.

His newborn son, Jonathan Randall Clayton.

Rand's stomach knotted as he read the inscription on the granite headstone that marked the child's grave. *Beloved son of his mother and father, the Duke and Duchess of Beldon.* His eyes burned. He was afraid he would openly weep. He blinked several times and for a while the burning eased.

Beside him, Cait stood rigid, tearless and staring at the mound of damp black earth. She had cried for days, wept until she had no more tears. The chill wind tugged at her stark black bonnet, molded the skirts of her high-waisted black mourning gown against her legs. She didn't seem to feel it, not the wind, nor the chill. She stared down at the grave, and he could feel her numbness, the heavy weight of her grief.

It increased his own until it was nearly unbearable. He agonized inside, not just for his son, but for Cait. For each of her tears, he silently cried a hundredfold. Her pain was his, compounded by his own. He felt mired in sadness, surrounded by it, consumed by it.

That she blamed herself, he knew. "It must have been

the fall," she'd told him, ". . . that day on the island . . . I shouldn't have gone after the grapes."

"It wasn't your fault," he'd said gently, though there were times he wished he could blame her, direct his unreasonable anger at someone other than God. "Sometimes things just happen. It's simply the way life is."

"Perhaps he's punishing us. Just like Adam and Eve. Perhaps this is the price of our sin."

He had tried to argue, to convince her it wasn't the truth, but he knew she hadn't listened.

The vicar completed the service, and the small group of mourners started back down the hill—Nicholas and Elizabeth, Maggie and Andrew, a few friends from neighboring estates. Caitlin walked beside him, but she never touched him. Instead, she kept herself carefully closed away.

From that day forward he watched her withdraw, grow more and more remote. He felt frustrated and angry. There was nothing he could do and he felt helpless and out of control.

Little by little it was killing him, the pain she felt, the grief he could not heal. His own unending grief for his lost son.

The holidays came and went. There was no celebration at Beldon Hall, no Christmas cheer, no Yule log, no Twelfth Day gifts to share. Caitlin would not allow it, and Rand couldn't bear to go against her wishes, not when she looked at him with those big sorrowful green eyes and he watched them well with tears.

The days crept past and the distance between them grew. It cut into his heart until he simply could not bear it. It was destroying him, this well of emotion he could not conquer, and more frightening than any foe he had ever faced. It was making him weak and confused, castrating him in a way he couldn't have imagined. He was no longer himself, no longer the man he once was, and he hated himself for it.

Every time he saw Caitlin's sad, too-thin face, emotion

curled around him, made him feel powerless, filled him
with a even deeper grief. He was becoming the weakling
his father had predicted and it terrified Rand in a way he
had never been afraid before.

He had to do something, had to save himself. If he
didn't, he would lose himself completely. He would never
again be the strong, capable man he once was, the man
he was determined to be again.

There was only one way, he knew. He had to leave
Caitlin, leave Beldon Hall. He would return to his life in
the city, bring his emotions back under control, and he
knew exactly how to go about it. He would return things
to the way they were before, back to the days he'd felt
only friendship for Cait and a strong physical attraction.
It was more than most married couples shared.

It was enough for Rand.

It would be enough for Cait.

Rand had been gone from the country for more than a
month before Cait roused herself from her sorrow. It was
a day in late February, the air still cold, but the sky a
clear, crystalline blue, without a cloud on the horizon.
Perhaps it was the brilliance of the sun on that day, or the
warmth of its rays that finally broke through the shell she
had built around her, began to thaw the heart that felt
frozen in her chest.

The pain was still there, the loss of her son still a fresh
wound inside her. But on that bright, hopeful day, for the
first time in weeks, she realized that she had lost something besides her child, something equally precious.

Rand was gone and her world felt empty without him.

Perhaps it was her fault, Cait thought as she walked
through the garden, admiring the topiary leopard Rand
had designed and ordered built. Surely he had felt much
of the same grief she had at the loss of his son, and yet
he had seemed so stoic, so strong, it hadn't occurred to
her at the time.

In the back of her mind, she thought that he should

have stayed, shouldn't have abandoned her when she needed him so badly. His occasional notes had been politely formal, with none of the warmth she remembered. Still, he was her husband, she missed him, ached to be with him. He might not love her, but she loved him, and in these past few days, she began to realize exactly how much. It was time to rouse herself from her despair and begin to put her life back in order.

With that goal in mind, she sent a note to Woodland, Maggie and Lord Trent's country house in Sussex, only a short ride from London, asking if she might join them for a visit on her way to the city. Maggie was ecstatic at the notion. The note Cait received in return relayed the news that Elizabeth and Lord Ravenworth would be visiting at that time, as well.

We are so looking forward to all of us being together again, and especially to seeing you and Rand.

It surprised Cait to discover that neither of them knew that Rand was no longer at Beldon Hall, but for weeks had been living in London. It worried her to think that he had not confided in his friends and a niggling fear began to gnaw at her insides. She loved Rand and she missed him. She wanted to be with him. When she responded to Maggie's note, she didn't bother to tell her friend that she would be coming to Woodland alone. She desperately needed Maggie's advice. She had to discover a way to mend the rift between her and Rand.

And Lord Ravenworth would be there, as well. Only Nick Warring knew her husband better than Maggie. Perhaps he could also be of help.

It was time to think of the future, and now that Cait had put her grief behind her, Rand was all she thought of. She remembered every smile, every gentle touch. She remembered the way it had felt when he had made love to her and she wanted him to do it again.

Rand might not love her, but he was her husband. They were married, with years together ahead of them. The doctor had said there was every chance she could bear him a healthy child, that perhaps this one had simply not taken root as well as it should have. Once Rand came home, they could try again, and this time, she vowed, they would succeed. She was determined they could make a future together.

All Cait had to do was convince her husband to come home.

Rand drew on his kidskin gloves, stood in the foyer of his London mansion, waited as the butler draped a satin-lined cloak around his shoulders, and headed out the door. It was a glorious night in London, the sky clear for a change, the stars shining like sparkling gems down on the streets of the city. Earlier a light snow had fallen, blanketing the dirt and papers in the gutters, making the whole world look clear and clean.

That was how it felt to Rand. Clean and fresh, his life back to normal. His world was here now, once again the dancing and glitter, the laughter and gaiety of the wealthy London aristocracy. Since his arrival in the city, he had immersed himself in that life with relentless, driving purpose—to forget the pain of his disastrous marriage, forget the loss of his beloved son, and the lady who had, without the least intent, practically unmanned him.

Determined to succeed in his goal, he rarely returned to the house before dawn, usually mildly drunk, the evening a pleasant blur. Friends from his past reappeared: Lord Anthony Miles, second son of the Marquess of Wilburn; Raymond de Young, a former school chum; the Viscount St. Ives, a handsome, dedicated rogue he had known for years; others he barely knew but who seemed content to tag along in company with a duke and his friends, most of them bachelors, but a few of them married.

They drank hard, gamed hard, played hard, and so did Rand—and he was beginning to succeed in his purpose.

The pain was behind him, Rand was sure. He was happy again, those dark days bottled away deep inside him where he never had to think about them, never had to confront them. An occasional, dutiful letter to Cait was enough for the present. Perhaps at a later date, he would pay her a visit, see how she fared. Not now. For the time being, he was content as he was, frequenting the darker, slightly debauched side of London.

And resuming his pleasant, past liaison with Hannah Reese.

He was heading there later in the evening as he usually did. Since his return, he had provided her with new quarters, more luxurious accommodations where they could be more comfortable. First he would spend a few hours at Whites, playing whist or loo and undoubtedly winning, then make the rounds of whatever parties his friends suggested.

Afterward, Hannah would be waiting. She was blond and fair, slenderly built, with small, cone-shaped breasts. She was nothing at all like the petite little redhead who hovered at the edges of his mind whenever he wasn't careful, threatening to destroy his comfortable world.

Hannah was as different from Caitlin as the moon was from the sun. That he missed that warmth, that shining brightness, was something he fiercely denied. But even as he immersed himself in the world he had thought to abandon, a flicker of yearning remained, even in the hardest, most chilling recesses of his heart.

Winning several hundred pounds from his old racing rival, Lord Mountriden, which he took with considerable glee, Rand left Boodles just after midnight and proceeded to Hannah's comfortable town house in a quiet yet suitable Mayfair neighborhood. She was waiting, of course, in the sheer French silk nightgown he had bought her several years ago, greeting him with a snifter of brandy, leading him directly into her bedchamber.

"I thought you would be here earlier," she said with a bit of a pout, though Hannah rarely complained. "You mentioned we might go out for supper."

He hadn't really wanted to go out. It wasn't conversation he wanted from Hannah, just the simple comfort of her body, a way to keep his thoughts occupied for at least another night.

"Time slipped away. There's a new opera opening at the Surrey. Why don't I take you there sometime this week?" It was more a farce than a true opera, but that better suited Hannah. And the theater was smaller, less well attended, the sort of place a man took his mistress. An image of Caitlin appeared the night he had kissed her at the King's Theatre, beautiful and fiery tempered, standing up to him with spirit and courage. Making him want her as he never had another woman. Rand clamped his jaw and ruthlessly shoved the memory away.

"Come here, Hannah."

She did as he said, her movements graceful in the nearly transparent lavender silk. For as long as he could remember, she had been there to console him when he needed it, times his world threatened to crumble around him, when his duties became too weighty, when there was no one else to whom he could turn.

She slid her hands up the lapels of his coat and pulled his mouth down to hers for a kiss. Rand ended it before she was ready.

There was something too intimate about a kiss, or at least he had come to think so. It was something that had to do with tenderness and longing, emotions he had never really shared with Hannah. Instead, he massaged her breasts, ran his hands over her body, absently began to stroke her. His body slowly responded, but it took far longer than it should have. It bothered him to realize he felt less and less pleasure in their mating.

Tonight, he simply wanted it over and done. Pressing her down on the bed, he unbuttoned his breeches and nudged her legs apart. Hannah gasped as he thrust himself inside her. He took her swiftly and without his usual care, knowing he should wait until she reached her peak, but somehow unwilling to.

When they were finished, he pulled away, got up, and began to straighten his clothes.

Curling up on the bed, Hannah lay watching from beneath her golden lashes. "It's her, isn't it? You were thinking about your wife."

He glanced in her direction, looked at her hard. "I never think of my wife."

Hannah cocked a brow. "Don't you? I think she's there inside you all the time. I think it's her you wanted, not me. I think you pretend you don't miss her but you do. She's your wife. Why don't you simply go back to her?"

Something moved through him, an emotion he couldn't name. A familiar, unwanted heaviness crept into his chest. He tightened his jaw to banish it. "I don't want to talk about my wife. As long as I'm paying the rent, I expect you to respect my wishes."

He could feel her eyes on his face. She was an actress. It was her job to understand how people behaved and she was good at it, too discerning by half. She watched as he wiped a trace of rouge off his cheek with an embroidered white handkerchief and started toward the door.

"You're not staying?" she said with obvious surprise. "But you only just arrived."

True, but tonight it didn't matter. He had to get out of there, needed to get away from those knowing blue eyes. "I'll be back in a couple of days. We'll go to the opera, as I promised."

Hannah said nothing and Rand continued out the door, closing it quietly behind him. Trying to ignore a feeling of relief.

Lord Trent was hosting a ball. Cait hadn't imagined anything of the sort when she had written to Maggie, but Woodland Hills was close to London, and though the Season was not yet upon them, the ton was ready for a bit of celebration. The occasion of Lady Trent's birthday— or just about anything else—was as good an excuse as any.

Caitlin arrived at the stately brick mansion in the middle of the morning, rolling up in the carriage Rand had left at the hall for her use. Maggie had been surprised to discover she was traveling alone, even more surprised to learn that Rand was already in London.

"I can't believe we didn't know. He hasn't even been in touch with Nick." They were seated in a comfortable salon that looked out over the wooded fields behind the house, sipping tea from gold-rimmed porcelain cups. "That isn't like him."

"I don't know what to do, Maggie. I wish I knew what he was thinking. I'm afraid he's still hurting. I need to see him, talk to him, find out what's wrong, but I'm afraid he won't tell me even if I ask."

"I know he took the loss of his son extremely hard. I noticed it the day we came to Beldon Hall for the service. I've never seen him so distraught."

Cait set her teacup down with an unsteady hand. "He always seems so strong. Dear God, he was hurting and I was so buried in grief I couldn't see."

"I think you should go straight to Grosvenor Square. Find out what he's feeling. Make him listen to what you have to say."

Cait glanced down at the black silk faille mourning gown she wore. "This is the last time I'm wearing this. My sorrow drove him away. I don't intend to let it keep us apart any longer."

Maggie smiled. "Good girl! You may as well begin your transformation tonight. I hope you brought something pretty to wear."

Cait set her cup and saucer down on the table. "Actually, I brought several trunks of clothes. I wasn't sure how long I was going to be in London." A determined glint came into her eyes. "However long it takes, I suppose."

Maggie reached over and squeezed her hand. "Your room is ready. Why don't you go upstairs and rest for a while? In a couple of hours, I'll send a maid up to help you bathe and change."

Caitlin nodded and came to her feet. She wasn't really looking forward to the ball, but she had made up her mind to return to the world of the living. Tonight was a good time to start.

Standing on the black-and-white marble floor in the third-floor ballroom of Woodland Hills, Elizabeth Warring spoke with her sister-in-law Maggie Sutton. Across the way, Rand's wife, the recently titled Duchess of Beldon, dressed in a high-waisted gown of emerald silk, pleasantly conversed with William St. Anthony, Marquess of Wester, whose second son, Geoffrey, remained yet on Santo Amaro Island, part of Cait's father's expedition.

"I think Rand underestimates her," Maggie said, following Elizabeth's gaze toward their petite friend. "Her forthright manner is the very thing people like about her. I don't know of anyone who has ever found Cait's plain-speaking offensive."

"It's the very thing he likes about her. Why shouldn't other people like it, as well?"

"I wonder what he's doing? It isn't like him to go off the way he has. Cait says he's been living in the city for more than a month."

"If I were in her shoes, I'd be on my way to London. I'd be finding out for myself."

"That is exactly what she plans to do. As a matter of fact, she's decided to shorten her visit and leave for London in the morning."

Nodding her approval, Elizabeth flicked open the plum silk fan that matched her gown and stirred the air in front of her face. She liked the duchess and she carried a warm spot in her heart for Rand, whose unflagging loyalty had once saved her husband's life.

But Rand was different from Nick. He was a man of strong emotions who had never quite come to grips with them. She hoped those emotions didn't lead him into trouble where Caitlin was concerned. In her own way, Cait was as every bit as strong as he. And, Elizabeth suspected, could be equally unforgiving should she be treated unfairly.

From behind the fan, Elizabeth watched her friend across the way, saw Lady Hadleigh approach in a seductive whirl of white and silver-shot silk, her hair swept up into stylish black curls. Elizabeth frowned. Why would Rand's former lover possibly wish to seek Caitlin out? Elizabeth didn't know, but instinct told her whatever the woman had to say would not be good.

The conversation went on a little too long for Elizabeth's liking. A few minutes later, Cait turned and walked away, the spray of freckles across her forehead standing out against the paleness of her face, her hands faintly trembling as she moved with purpose across the ballroom and out through the high double doors. Worried and uncertain, Elizabeth followed her, praying her instincts were wrong. Hoping Lady Hadleigh, jealous of Rand's marriage to Cait, hadn't said something to hurt her.

Elizabeth searched the hallway to no avail. She went down the stairs to the main floor of the house, looked in the gaming rooms, the several salons that were overflowing with guests, searched the terrace and the gardens. By the time she headed toward the stairs leading up to the east wing where the guest chambers were, Caitlin was making her way back down, a fur-lined cloak draped over her shoulders.

"Caitlin! Forheavensake—where are you going?"

Cait's bottom lip trembled and Elizabeth's worry swelled. "Tell Maggie I appreciate her hospitality. Tell her something came up and I had to leave for London."

"Now? At this time of night? It'll be midnight before you can get there."

"It doesn't matter. I've already sent for the carriage. It should be waiting out in front. Tell Maggie I'll send for my things once I arrive."

"Please, Cait, tell me what's wrong."

Cait blinked back a sudden sheen of tears. "I don't know for certain—not yet. But I intend to find out." Turning away, she disappeared out the door.

Frantic with concern for Cait, Elizabeth raced off in search of Maggie. Whatever had happened, she prayed that Rand's wife would safely reach London.

And that Rand, in his terrible grief, had not done what Elizabeth had a very strong suspicion he might have.

TWENTY

Still dressed in her emerald silk gown, Cait arrived at the ducal mansion on Grosvenor Square just before midnight.

To her utter disappointment, Rand wasn't there.

It shouldn't have surprised her, but it did. In some innocent, naïve corner of her mind, she had imagined him in London pining away, grieving for his child just as she had done in the country. But it appeared Rand was long past his sorrow.

What if Lavinia Wentworth, Lady Hadleigh, had been telling her the truth? What if Rand was once again consorting with his longtime mistress, Hannah Reese? Of course the woman hadn't come right out and said so, not at first. In the beginning, there had just been simple innuendoes, speculation, a hint of gossip she mentioned she had heard.

Caitlin shook her head, forcing away the ugly memory.

"I'm sorry, but you are mistaken," she had said. "My husband is in London on business." Cait had turned and walked away, leaving the woman standing there alone. But the memory of her smug, self-satisfied smile stayed with her all the way to London.

I don't believe it, Cait told herself. *I won't.* Rand had followed her all the way to Santo Amaro, insisted on the marriage—actually tricked her and forced her to agree. If he wanted the marriage so badly, surely he wouldn't destroy it.

But in truth, she had known from the start that it was

the child he had wanted. Now that child was gone. Her heart ached to think of it.

Leaving a sleepy-eyed Frederick staring after her at the door, Cait climbed the stairs to their second-floor suite of rooms, fighting a tightness in her chest that hadn't been there since the awful days after she had lost her son.

She had defended Rand to the viscountess, been certain the woman was wrong. She had traveled all the way to London to see him. Now she had to know the truth.

Bypassing her own suite of rooms, she continued on down the hall to the master's suite. The room was in mild disarray as it rarely was, Rand's clothes strewn across the bed, not neatly put away as they usually were. Then she remembered it was Thursday, Percival Fox's evening off.

Percy had apparently gone out, but where was Rand? She started to walk away, knowing she would have to wait until he returned. Then she saw the hasty note Rand had scribbled and left for his valet.

Picking up the slip of paper on the rosewood bureau, Cait read the words, her hands beginning to tremble. *Going to the opera, then to Chatelaine's. Home late. Won't be needing you until tomorrow.*

Percy always worried. Rand had obviously meant to alleviate his concern. Whatever explanation Cait had wished to believe, it was obvious Rand was enjoying himself. Was he merely out with friends, as she desperately prayed he was? Or was he with his mistress?

She swallowed past the ache that had risen in her throat and squared her shoulders, determined to find out.

Heading back down the stairs, she paused to retrieve her cloak from the butler and made her way toward the stables at the rear of the house. The coachman had just begun to unharness the horses. Cait told him he would have to wait, that she would be needing the carriage once again.

"Aye, Your Grace," the man said a bit wearily. "Just be a moment." She climbed aboard and settled against the seat, and a few minutes later he stuck his head inside the door. "Wherebouts we be off to, Duchess?"

"A place called Chatelaine's. Have you heard of it?"

In the lantern light, she thought the man flushed. "Yes, ma'am, I have."

"Do you know where it is?"

He nodded somewhat stiffly. It was obvious the coachman had driven Rand there before.

"All right, then. That is the place I wish to go."

He hesitated only a moment, then climbed up on the seat, shaking his head as if he would never understand the nobility. A few minutes later they were bowling down Picadilly, passing St. James's, heading in the direction of Covent Gardens. In the lamplight inside the carriage, Caitlin said another silent prayer. Rand was the strongest, kindest man she had ever known. He would never do anything to hurt her.

But her heart constricted with fear that she had been wrong about him, and she was terrified her prayers were too late.

Hannah Reese sat across from the Duke of Beldon in the main dining room of Chatelaine's, an intimate restaurant in Covent Gardens that was famous for its chef, a Frenchman named Pierre Dumont whose cooking Rand had always been fond of.

He ordered a second bottle of wine, an expensive twenty-year-old French Bordeaux, and the waiter popped the cork. Rand drank deeply, as he had been doing all night. Since his return to London, he had been drinking more heavily than she had ever seen him, trying to bury his troubles, Hannah believed.

She knew about the death of his son. They were friends of a sort, as well as lovers. She knew he had married an American woman, though his marriage was the single subject he refused to discuss.

Hannah thought she knew why.

For nearly ten years, Hannah had been in love with Rand Clayton. Because she knew the symptoms, knew exactly how painful loving someone could be, she was convinced that the duke was in love with his wife.

"I thought you were hungry," he said, staring down at her nearly full plate. "You've hardly eaten a bite."

She lifted her fork, took a taste of the delicate turbot in lobster sauce she had ordered. "It's very good, really. I suppose I'm just a bit tired after such a long performance." He had taken her to the opera as he had promised, but seemed distracted and unable to enjoy himself.

He made some reply and looked away. It was obvious his mind was not on the conversation, as earlier it had not been on the performance onstage. He hadn't been himself since his return to the city, though he tried very hard to convince himself he was exactly the same man he was before.

The waiter appeared and they ordered dessert, though Hannah didn't really want it, and Rand seemed not to care. She wanted simply to be with him for as long as she could, and she was afraid that once he took her home, he might not stay. Even if he did, she suspected their lovemaking would be as unfulfilling tonight as it had been for the past several weeks. His heart simply wasn't in it. And Hannah meant that literally.

Though she wanted more than anything for Rand to spend the night with her making wildly passionate love, the deepest part of her believed that no matter the problems he would have to conquer, he would be far better off simply going home.

She wondered what his wife had done to hurt him so badly, how she could have driven him away so completely.

Perhaps in time, he would tell her.

Hannah wanted that to happen, wanted him to turn away from the woman he had married and trust in her instead. No matter the pain he had caused her, Rand was worth it. She would do whatever it took to make that happen.

*   *   *

Rand toyed with his dessert, his mind far away, numbed a little by the wine he had consumed. Hannah sat across from him, wearing the apricot silk gown he had bought her when he'd first returned to London. It complemented her upswept blond hair, deep blue eyes, and pale skin. The neckline revealed a glimpse of her elegant, pointed breasts, but they only made him think of others, high and lush, spilling like ripe fruit into his hands.

Hannah was lovely, each of her movements quietly seductive. Half the men in London fought to have her in their beds, yet when he touched her, made love to her, he felt nothing. For days, he had known it was over between them, had come to regret he had sought her out in the first place. Tonight he meant to do something about it.

Thoughts of Caitlin surfaced, along with a painful shot of guilt, and he could no longer shut them out. He never should have left her, never should have abandoned her at a time when she needed him so badly.

It wasn't like him—not at all. He'd never been a coward. He had just been so confused. And the pain . . . so much pain. No matter how hard he had tried, he could not make it end. For a while, here in London, he'd been able to bury it. He had come to grips with the loss of his son, but now a new despair gripped him.

Need for Caitlin haunted him, the burning desire to see her again, hold her, touch her, simply be with her. He was in love with her, he knew, had accepted the fact at last, though he had tried long and fiercely to deny it. He was in love with her, and he had begun to think that instead of a terrible weakness, what he had discovered with Cait was an incredible gift.

His father wouldn't have thought so. He would have laughed, ridiculed him for his feelings.

"You're a fool," he would have said, "not a fit man to follow in my shoes." But when Rand thought of the way she made him feel, the joy he couldn't begin to find with anyone else, he believed that his father was wrong.

Why couldn't he see it until now? Why had it taken

so long? Why had it been so hard for him to admit the truth?

A fresh shot of guilt rose up, along with a deep, abiding regret. He never should have betrayed his wife with Hannah, never should have left her in the first place. God, whatever had possessed him?

Hannah made a comment he didn't quite catch. He turned, tried to muster a smile. "I'm sorry . . . what did you say?"

She sighed and shook her head. "Nothing important." She gave him a falsely bright smile and laid her napkin down beside her plate. "Since neither of us seems hungry, I suppose we might as well leave."

He wanted to—God knew, he hadn't wanted to come in the first place. But he needed to settle things between them, and he thought he owed her at least this much.

Hannah waited till he helped her rise from her chair, then took his arm. They had almost reached the door when a servant pulled it open and a woman stepped inside the candlelit, low-ceilinged room. She was gowned in emerald silk, just a shade darker than her eyes, her hair an unusual gold-tipped red. Rand saw her and his mouth went dry. She was everything he remembered and more, everything he had fallen in love with and been too frightened to accept.

She stopped just a few feet inside the door and he noticed her gown was slightly wrinkled and in faint disarray, the loose curls at the top of her head beginning to come undone, one wayward lock dangling softly against the side of her neck. She stood frozen in the hallway, her eyes locked with his, her face bleak with pain, and his heart crumbled to pieces inside his chest.

For a moment she said nothing and neither did he. She looked as if she wanted to turn and run, yet her spine remained straight and she stayed right where she was.

Rand swallowed past the hard lump rising in his throat, and the sudden, indisputable knowledge that everything he had ever wanted stood in front of him. And he was about to lose it all. "Caitlin . . ."

"Good evening, Rand."

He couldn't find his voice, couldn't make a single sound. When he finally spoke, the words came out thick and rough. "I thought you were in the country. What are you doing in London?"

A film of tears welled in her pretty green eyes. "I wanted to surprise you. It's obvious that I have."

The pain on her face made a sharp ache throb beneath his breastbone. Every heartbeat seemed a burden. He couldn't quite get enough air. "Caitie . . . please . . . you don't understand."

Her chin remained high, but she blinked and a tear rolled down her cheek. "Oh, but I do, Rand. I understand completely."

The muscles in his throat constricted, moved up and down, but the words remained locked inside. There were no words for what he had done, no excuses. And he would not humiliate her by trying to invent one.

"Whatever you are thinking," he said softly, gravely, "I never meant to hurt you." *I love you. And I was such a fool.*

Her gaze swung to Hannah, then back to his face. More tears washed down her cheeks. "Whatever your intentions were or were not is no longer important." She swallowed, moistened her trembling lips. Teardrops sparkled on her thick dark lashes, forming wet, damp spikes, making the ache in his chest spread out through his limbs.

"Good-bye, Rand." Her voice broke as she said his name. Turning, she walked away, shoulders straight, her head held high. Her steps grew faster as she approached the door, shoved it open, moved down the front stairs. She was running by the time she reached the street.

Rand turned to Hannah and he saw that she understood, perhaps had always understood. "I have to go. I'll leave the carriage. Will you be all right?"

Hannah nodded, tried to smile. He looked in her eyes,

saw pain there, as well, realized he had hurt her, too, and his own pain rose up again, crushing in on him with leaden force. Turning away, he raced out the door and into the street, calling Cait's name, trying to catch up with the carriage, but already it was pulling into traffic, disappearing among a sea of others, moving off at a rapid pace. Frantic now, he ran in search of a passing hack but couldn't find one.

Eventually he did, climbing aboard, giving directions to his house on Grosvenor Square, knowing that even when he reached it, there was nothing he could say that would make the least amount of difference.

Knowing one thing for certain.

The stark truth he had only recently admitted had become crystal clear the moment he had seen Caitlin walk through the door. He was completely, utterly, hopelessly, in love with her.

It was in that moment that he finally knew what he had been searching for, what he had wanted all along.

And now that he knew—it was too late.

Cait wasn't there at the house when he burst through the ornate front doors and thundered up the stairs, shouting her name. She had been there earlier, Frederick told him, which explained how she had been able to find him at Chatelaine's. The note he had left for Percy sat in a slightly different place on his rosewood bureau, a little more crumpled than when he had left it. On the edge near the corner, the ink was blurred in the shape of a tear.

Pain moved through him, a fresh, hot, jabbing ache even more fierce than the sort he had suffered before. His son was gone. He had thought that nothing could fill him with such sorrow. The pain of losing Cait was a thousand times worse.

Worry for her surfaced along with the pain. Where had she gone? What would she do? Would she come back to the house at all?

In the days that followed he searched for her, sending

footmen to scour every London hotel, finally giving that notion up and returning, himself, to Beldon Hall, certain she must have fled to the country.

She wasn't at the house and hadn't been since the morning she set off for Woodland Hills.

Maggie! He should have guessed Cait would go to her friend.

He got there as quickly as he could, the wheels of the carriage tossing up gravel as it careened up the drive. He grabbed the handle on the door and threw it open before the vehicle had come to a halt, striding up the front stairs in the same clothes he had worn the day before, his hair unkempt, a day's growth of beard on his face.

Andrew greeted him in the entry, his expression dark and faintly disapproving.

"Where is she?" Rand asked, his gaze frantically searching, praying she was there and that she was safe.

"I'm sorry, Rand. Caitlin has already gone."

His eyes slid closed. Weariness threatened to overwhelm him. He hadn't slept for the past three nights, hadn't had anything to eat or drink but several cups of strong, black coffee. "But she *was* here? She's all right?"

"No, Rand, she isn't all right." Maggie's voice rang from the hall as she made her way in his direction. "Your lovely wife is crushed. Her heart is broken. Time and time again, she has given you her trust and you have done nothing but hurt her."

He didn't bother to deny it. He deserved every bit of her scorn. "Where is she?"

"She came to get her clothes, trunks she planned to take with her when she joined you in the city. She wanted to straighten things out between you. She was worried about you." Maggie's soft mouth curved into a bitter smile. "But you didn't deserve her worry, did you, Rand? You had someone else to worry about you."

His eyes burned with tears. He blinked. God, he didn't want them to see. "No . . ." he said softly. "I didn't deserve her worry."

"You didn't need Cait—why would you? You had Hannah, always Hannah. Whenever you had a problem, Hannah was there. You lost your son, but instead of staying with Cait when she needed you so badly, you ran away—straight into the arms of your mistress."

It was true, every harsh, painful word, and instead of turning away, he punished himself by listening.

"Your father was right, Rand. You aren't a real man. A real man would never have acted the way you did. A real man would never have left the woman he loved."

Pain lanced through him, cut into his heart. His eyes slid closed for a moment knowing that was exactly the awful thing he had done. "I was . . . a coward."

Maggie stared at him and her brows drew faintly together. Suddenly the harshness drained from her features. "Oh, my God." Tears sprang into her gentle blue eyes. "You didn't know, did you? All this time, I thought it just didn't matter, that you were more like your father than you believed. But that isn't it, is it, Rand?"

She reached out, rested a trembling hand against the rough stubble on his cheek. "Dear God—all this time, you've been lying to yourself. You were afraid of your feelings, so you simply denied them. That's it, isn't it? You left Caitlin at Beldon Hall because you couldn't understand what was happening to you. You didn't know you were in love with her."

Rand said nothing. It was too hard to speak.

"You're exhausted," Andrew said gently, leading him farther into the house. "You need to rest and have something to eat."

Rand shook his head. "I've got to find her, at least make certain she is safe."

Tears slipped down Maggie's cheeks. "Caitlin is gone, Rand. I'm not sure where she is now, but she'll be leaving England soon to join her father. I don't think you should go after her. She doesn't want to see you. I don't think . . . I don't think she will ever forgive you."

He simply nodded. He had known that, of course,

known it the moment he had seen her walk through the doors of Chatelaine's and seen him with Hannah Reese. Caitlin was good and loyal and she would never betray the man she had married. She expected that same loyalty from him. No matter the reason he gave for his actions, she would never understand, and she would never forgive him.

"She'll write to you," he said gruffly. "I'd appreciate it if you'd let me know how she fares. I'd like to send her money, make certain she's well cared for. I'm not sure she'll accept it."

"I don't . . . don't think she will. She has a little money of her own . . . enough to take care of herself."

"The baron is there. He may be dangerous. There is no way to know what he might do."

"You still have no proof he is anything other than what he seems," Andrew put in gently. "And even if you are right about him, the man is a swindler, not a killer."

"Andrew is right," Maggie agreed. "You mustn't worry yourself about that."

Rand nodded, hoping they were right. Then he thought of Cait and a soft, sad smile edged up. "She was something, wasn't she, Maggie? There'll never be anyone like her . . . not for me."

Maggie turned her head into her husband's shoulder and quietly began to weep. Rand simply turned and started for the door.

"Rand?" He turned at the sound of Andrew's voice. "Perhaps in time . . ."

The soft, sad smile reappeared. "Perhaps . . ." he agreed for Andrew's sake, knowing it was a lie. Cait Harmon was gone from his life for good. He had no one to blame but himself.

He had lost her.

And his life, his world, would be bleak and empty without her.

*   *   *

Cait dug into the earth with furious intent, the hot sand flying out behind her. When her progress wasn't fast enough, she tossed the trowel aside and started scooping the burning sand away with her hands. The day was overly warm. Perspiration ran down the sides of her face, drawing tiny gnats that buzzed beside her ears.

She'd been back at Santo Amaro for only a week, yet it seemed like a month. She had forgotten how confined she felt on the island, how each day blended with the next until they all seemed the same, how much she missed her friends.

Things had changed very little in the nearly six months she'd been away. No more treasure had surfaced and no sign of the necklace had been found. They had, however, discovered a new cache of items buried in the sand farther in toward the trees, including personal possessions her father believed had belonged to the three sailors who had been shipwrecked on the island. A small oak chest, a brass looking glass, a soggy, nearly disintegrated Bible printed in Dutch.

Which meant that spirits remained high.

They had all, of course, been amazed to see her the day she arrived aboard the *Moroto*. Both Geoffrey and Phillip Rutherford had been effusive in their greetings, Sir Monty had been politely formal, while her father had been both glad and concerned. He was saddened by the loss of her babe, the failure of her marriage, and the consequences that were so clearly evidenced by the weary sadness in her face.

Rand's betrayal had scourged her mind and heart, and as hard as she tried to forget it, she simply was not able.

She had loved him so much.

She wondered if he remained yet with his mistress, or if he had already tired of her and moved on to fresher quarry. Perhaps a young woman like herself, with shining ideals and a dogged belief in the duke's sincerity.

If so, that young woman was bound for heartache more painful than she could imagine.

Cait glanced up as a shadow fell over the place where she worked. Her father stooped down, then squatted beside her. "You missed the midday meal again today. It worries me, Caitlin, to see you so thin." He extended the long-fingered, veined hand that held a linen-wrapped parcel. "I brought you a bit of bread and cheese."

Cait shook her head. "Thank you, Father, but I'm not really hungry."

"You need to eat, Cait. You'll fall ill if you don't."

She stared into his face, saw the worry, the concern. She came to her feet and so did he. "You're right, of course." She forced herself to smile. "I just got so involved time slipped away."

He pressed the food into her hand. "I know how badly you've been hurt. That man broke your heart and I can't help but feel responsible. If I hadn't forced the marriage—"

"It wasn't your fault. In my heart, I wanted to marry him more than anything in the world. I was in love with him. I couldn't see the man he really was."

"He fooled me, as well. I saw something in him—or at least thought I did—something I believed was strong and good. I was convinced he was more than half in love with you. I never thought he would hurt you the way he did."

Cait just nodded. Her throat had closed up and tears burned the backs of her eyes. She had cried all the tears she intended to cry on the journey here from England. She refused to cry for Rand again.

"I'll be all right, Father. It will just take a little more time, is all."

"Geoffrey is pleased you are back. He wanted to marry you. Perhaps we can find a way to set aside the marriage. In time, perhaps the two of you could find a way to be happy."

She only shook her head. "I'd rather not talk about that now, if you don't mind. It's very painful for me, and at any rate, it's far too soon to think of marrying again."

And years down the road, it would still be too soon. She had walked that path once in her life with disastrous results. She knew in her heart she would never marry again.

"Come sit in the shade for a while," her father softly coaxed, patting her shoulder like a child. "Eat your bread and cheese."

She did as he asked, but only to please him. Perhaps if she took better care of herself, he would stop feeling guilty and end his pursuit of the painful topic of marriage.

As far as Cait was concerned, the subject was closed. It was her single aim in life to reach the point where she never thought of Rand Clayton again.

TWENTY-ONE

Nick Warring climbed the front porch stairs and rapped on the ornate wooden doors of the Duke of Beldon's mansion on Grosvenor Square. The butler, Frederick Peterson, saw him through the peephole and hurriedly pulled it open.

"Please come in, your lordship. We . . . all of us . . . appreciate your coming, particularly on such short notice."

At his town house that morning, Nick had received a note from Rand's valet asking him to come as soon as it was convenient. He had made it convenient. He was worried about Rand and it appeared Percival Fox and the rest of Rand's staff were also concerned.

"I hope I can be of help. Where's Percy?"

"Right here, my lord." Rand's lean, hawk-nosed valet strode toward him, the shoulder-length black hair he wore queued back with a ribbon bobbing against his back. "As Frederick said, we appreciate your coming."

"Rand is my friend. I just hope I can be of some help."

"So do I," Percy agreed, the worried look on his face making him look older than his forty years. The valet led him into a small, well-appointed salon where they could be private and quietly closed the door.

"What appears to be the problem?" Nick asked as soon as Percy turned to face him.

The valet sighed. "I don't know exactly how to say this. I realize the two of you are best of friends. That is the reason I sent the message. I hope you won't be offended, but . . . well, simply put—His Grace has turned into a madman."

Nick might have laughed if Percy hadn't been so serious. "I presume this has something to do with the departure of his wife."

"For the first several weeks, he went into a sort of decline. He was drinking hard, keeping himself locked away. He was filled with self-loathing. I have never seen him so bitter, not even after the loss of his son. Then one day, something changed. I suppose he figured he couldn't go on the way he was, I don't know. He stopped drinking, which was good. Unfortunately, now he goes from day to day in a mild sort of rage."

"He has always had a formidable temper."

"This goes far beyond that, I'm afraid. He is constantly on edge, prone to fits of violence. Two days ago, he fired an upstairs maid because she didn't get the pillows straight on his bed. Yesterday he threw his dinner plate clear across the dining room because he said the gravy wasn't hot enough. And this morning—good God, this morning, the man went into some kind of fit because the morning newspaper wasn't exactly in the right position on the table beside the chair in his study. He is in there now, sitting at his desk, practically daring one of us to come in."

"I haven't seen him since the trouble with his wife. My sister told me what happened and I knew he was taking it hard, but I had no idea about this. I'm glad you sent for me, Percy."

The valet simply nodded. Nick knew how much Rand's friendship meant to Percy, knew the courage it had taken for him to intrude on Rand's privacy and send for Nick.

Leaving the small salon, he headed down the hall to Rand's study, heard the sound of breaking glass, and quietly opened the door. Across the way, Rand sat in the chair behind his desk, which had been swept clean of every item that had been atop it. On the floor beside it, a pile of overturned books, a pair of silver plumed pens, an upside-down ink blotter, and a shattered crystal ashtray lay among the ruins. The rest of the study looked nearly as bad. Evidence of Rand's rage could be seen from one end of the room to the other.

Nick stepped quietly inside and closed the door. At the slight click, Rand glanced up and spotted him. "Well, what do *you* want?"

Slowly, purposely, he let his gaze travel over the jumble in the room. He looked at Rand and cocked a black eyebrow. "Don't you think you've wallowed in self-pity long enough?"

Rand's face turned red and a muscle jerked in his cheek. For a moment, he said nothing. Then he shoved back his chair and surged to his feet, his big hands balling into fists. "What are you talking about?"

"I'm talking about sitting in here feeling sorry for yourself. I'm talking about taking out your ill temper on everyone in the household when the truth is the only person you're mad at is yourself."

Rand glared at him for several long moments, then dropped like a stone back into his chair. "If I am—what the devil business is it of yours?"

"None, I suppose. Other than the fact you're my friend and I care about you. It just doesn't sit well with me to see you behaving like some sort of raging bull when you ought to be getting off your arse and going after your wife."

Rand's posture deflated even more, all the rage going out of him at once. He dragged in a shaky breath of air. "Don't you think I would if I believed it would do an ounce of good? I've thought of nothing else for weeks. After what I've done, Caitlin will never forgive me."

Nick shrugged. "*Never* is a pretty strong word. I've known you for a goodly number of years, Rand. I've never known you to give up when there was something you really wanted. You do want her, don't you? That's what all of this is about?" He cocked his head toward the broken crockery and general havoc Rand had created.

He sighed. "I want her. I'm hopelessly in love with her. That's what caused the problem in the first place. I began to realize how much I cared for her and it scared me half to death."

Nick smiled. "If that is the case, then go after her. Tell her what you just told me. Tell her you behaved like a bloody damned fool but you won't do it again."

Rand braced his elbows on the table, raked his hands through his unkempt, slightly shaggy dark brown hair. "You make it sound so simple."

Nick moved farther into the room, stepping around an overturned piecrust table that was now missing part of a leg, past a fringed pillow leaking feathers.

"I don't think winning Cait Harmon's trust again is going to be simple. I think it may be the hardest thing you've ever done. But I also think she's worth it. And if anyone can do it, you can."

Rand shook his head. "I don't know. What I did to her . . . if she had done that to me, I don't think I could ever forgive her."

"Perhaps you could—if you understood why it happened. We all make mistakes, Rand. Before Elizabeth and I were married, I hurt her time and again, and it was the last thing I wanted to do."

Something passed over Rand's features. Nick recognized it as the first faint glimmer of hope. "Do you really think there's a chance?"

"There is always a chance. Cait loves you. That's the reason you hurt her so badly. Now get out of that chair and get moving. Sooner or later, there's bound to be a ship on its way to the African coast. If you're smart, you'll be on it."

Rand actually grinned. The expression, so long unused, must have felt somehow foreign for it slowly slipped away. How long had it been since Rand had allowed himself to smile in that way? Surely it must have been weeks.

"By God, I'll do it," Rand said, the hope beginning to glow in his face, rising through the darkness that had been so long inside him. "I'll find a ship. You may be certain I'll be on it—and I won't come back without my wife."

Nick smiled at the fierce determination that had replaced his friend's despair. He knew the happiness loving the right woman could bring and he wanted that happiness for Rand. He only hoped Caitlin was smart enough to know that when a man like Rand committed himself to her so completely, she could count on him with her life.

And no matter what happened, he would never fail her again.

"Caitlin! Caitlin, come quickly!" It was her father's voice and it rang with such excitement she knew something important had happened. Tossing down her trowel, she sprinted toward the group of people hovering around the pit where the workers had been digging, all of them chattering excitedly.

"What is it, Father? What's happened?"

"Look, Caitlin. It must have belonged to Leonard Metz, himself—the last man alive on the island. His initials are carved into that tree."

She glanced up, saw the odd mark that had been cut into the trunk of the huge palm—the initials *LEM*. Leonard Emery Metz, first mate aboard the *Silverider*. The letters were weathered and hard to read. The tree had grown, pushing the carving up above their heads. Until now, no one had noticed it.

"That's wonderful." She reached out to touch the small inlaid box that had just been unearthed, tracing the smooth geometric ivory patterns.

With a freckled hand, Sir Monty flipped open the lid. "Not nearly as wonderful as what is inside," he said with a grin, his leathery skin so dark he looked like a native. "It's a map, Caitlin."

"And it shows the exact location of Cleopatra's Necklace." That from a grinning Geoffrey St. Anthony, whose hair had paled so much from the hot island sun it was nearly platinum.

Cait sucked in a breath as she stared down at the neatly folded piece of yellowed cloth that had been drawn on and carefully placed in the box, then her gaze swung to her father. "Is the necklace here—on the island?"

Her father nodded, though with a little less enthusiasm than before.

"That is the good news," Phillip Rutherford said, drawing her attention to him. It was amazing, considering the primitive conditions in which they lived, he could always appear so perfectly groomed. His brown twill trousers showed only the slightest wear and his white lawn shirt didn't have a single wrinkle.

"The necklace is here and definitely within our reach," he confirmed. "Unfortunately, to insure its safety, Mr. Metz apparently carried it inland. We will have to journey into the interior in order to retrieve it."

A ripple of uncertainty slid down her spine. It would be a dangerous endeavor, and surely something they had hoped to avoid. Still, it could be done, and even Cait began to get caught up in the excitement.

"It seems all of your hard work is about to pay off," she said to the small group gathered around the inlaid box. "When do we leave?"

"I'm afraid it isn't that simple," the baron said. "We'll need additional supplies and equipment, and of course someone to guide us. And money will no doubt be a problem."

"But I thought we had raised more than enough."

He frowned and shook his head. "The expedition has been more costly than we initially imagined. Still, I'm certain we'll be able to scrape up enough."

And so it was decided that as soon as the *Moroto* arrived with the next load of supplies, the baron would return with the schooner to Dakar and obtain the items they would need.

That night they celebrated what they were certain

would be the final leg of their mission. As soon as the baron returned with the needed gear, they would set off in search of the necklace.

Darkness settled over the island. Phillip left the revelers to their meager celebration: the freshly caught fish the natives had cooked wrapped in seaweed and roasted over a slow-burning fire, the wild grapes and melons that had been scavenged to accompany the boiled potatoes they ate at nearly every meal.

Returning to his tent, Phillip lit the oil lamp and sat down at his makeshift desk. A quick study of the ledgers that sat on top and he saw what he had already known—that the expedition money was almost gone.

At least the money he had set aside for the expedition.

Grumbling a curse, he left his chair and moved to the corner, dug into his steamer trunk and pulled out the smaller set of ledgers he kept for himself. It galled him to give back any of the money he had socked away with such skill and patience. It hadn't been easy to know exactly where to cut, which items were absolutely necessary and those he could safely ignore. He sighed to think of the hours he had spent, the planning he had done.

If he were smart, he would simply take what he had skimmed, along with whatever portion of the treasure he could manage to hide in the belongings he took with him to Dakar, leave on the *Moroto,* and never return.

It was the wise thing to do, the sane thing. But the lure of finding the necklace was simply too great. Why settle for a portion of the riches when he could have it all?

As usual, it wouldn't be easy. In the beginning, he had planned to simply make arrangements for a boat to be waiting one night, sneak aboard with the treasure, and leave. He could live handsomely in the West Indies, or wherever else he might choose. But there was always a risk in leaving loose ends. Once the necklace was found, the better plan would be to get rid of the professor, Sir Monty, and Lord Geoffrey.

After all—accidents happened in this sort of rough, uncivilized country.

Caitlin wouldn't be a problem. He would simply take her with him as he had intended to do from the start. She would go along more readily once her father was out of the way and there was no one here to help her.

His groin tightened with anticipation.

Phillip glanced at his watch, knew it would soon be time for Maruba to appear and the ache in his groin began to strengthen. He had summoned her every night since Caitlin's return. The red-haired woman had a way of whetting his appetite, or perhaps it was simply that he hadn't had her yet and his imagination had been working for months, forming delicious images of what it would be like to bring her to heel.

Whatever the reason, he wanted her and soon she would be his.

A slight noise outside the tent drew his attention, and his body hardened, certain it was Maruba and relief was about to arrive. He waited for the tent flap to open. When it didn't, he headed for the front of the tent to see who was out there.

Phillip lifted the flap but saw only darkness. He glanced around, concerned now, wondering if perhaps a wild animal had been sniffing about. Perhaps even a leopard might have come down from the interior of the island. Instead, he caught a movement among the trees, a flash of white in the blackness, saw the hem of a brown twill skirt as someone hurried away.

Phillip frowned, certain it was Cait, wondering what she had wanted, why she had been spying on him. Then he remembered the ledgers. In the lamplight glowing through the tent, she could have seen him working. Surely it was too dark to see much of anything else.

Still, he wondered. Several times since her return, Cait had seemed to be watching him more closely than she should have been. Then again, perhaps he had simply piqued her interest. Phillip smiled. Cait was a married woman now. A mature young woman had needs and Cait no longer had a husband. Perhaps she had finally realized the pleasure they might share.

He hoped so.

More than that, he hoped she hadn't been spying on him. He would hate for one of those terrible "accidents" to happen to Cait.

Rand stood next to Percy Fox on the bow of the *Moroto*. As the ship sliced through the water, he could see the island of Santo Amaro up ahead, the familiar cloud-encircled summit of Pico de Maligno, the dense, dark green foliage leading down the mountain toward the broad white sand beach.

As the schooner drew near, he could make out the circle of tents that was the expedition campsite, and even that first glimpse gave him a sense of relief. The professor was still there, as Captain Baptiste had assured him, along with his daughter, whom the captain had delivered to Santo Amaro a little over a month ago.

Rand watched the island emerge and thought for the hundredth time what he would say when he arrived, what he would do. Telling Cait he was sorry, throwing himself at her feet and begging her forgiveness had occurred to him. If he believed for an instant it would work, he might actually consider doing it.

Unfortunately, he was completely certain Caitlin would laugh in his face and simply walk away. No, Cait wasn't going to forgive him so easily. He would have to prove himself, earn the trust he had so carelessly destroyed. How, he wasn't quite sure. He only knew that somehow he would succeed.

Failure wasn't an option.

Not when he loved her so much.

"We're almost there," Percy said, breaking into his thoughts. Thin black brows drew faintly together as Percy studied the spot where they intended to go ashore. "Take a look there." He pointed toward a group of people clustered together, watching the ship come in. "Wonder what's going on."

Rand followed the line of his gaze. "They're waiting for the boat. Probably expecting supplies."

"Baptiste didn't mention it. He charged us for an unscheduled charter, remember?"

Rand frowned, his pulse inching up. "True. I hope to hell nothing's wrong."

Percy laughed softly. "Your wife has sailed several thousand miles from England to get away from you. She'll probably run you through the minute she lays eyes on you. What could possibly be wrong?"

Rand chuckled softly. "Put that way, I see what you mean." But still, he wondered why work had been stopped and the entire expedition had gathered on the beach.

By the time they'd boarded the dinghy and were on their way to shore, he could clearly make out the professor's thin, slightly stooped frame, Geoffrey St. Anthony's pale blond hair, Sir Monty's freckled, weathered face, and Talmadge's perfectly groomed appearance. The instant Cait stepped out from behind her father, he recognized her simple brown skirt and white blouse, the wide-brimmed straw hat that covered most of her bright hair.

His heart kicked up, began a dull cadence beneath his ribs. His mouth felt dry, his chest tight. It occurred to him he was afraid. *So much to lose,* he thought. *So much at stake.* But he'd been a coward before. He wouldn't be again.

"Well, Percival. I believe we have a greeting party waiting for us on shore."

Percy grunted. "I'm sure they'll be delighted to see us."

Rand turned, smiled. "Maybe they'll be hungry for a little fresh game. They probably haven't had much of that since we left six months ago."

"One can always hope."

Rand said nothing more and neither did Percy. They simply stared off at the rapidly approaching shoreline, Rand silently praying he wouldn't be shot on sight.

*   *   *

Standing next to her father, Cait watched the dinghy cut through the waves, making its way toward the beach. She blinked, certain the image she was seeing would disappear, praying that it would. But her heart tripped wildly, slamming hard inside her chest, and the tall, broad-shouldered man sitting in the center of the dinghy continued to keep his gaze riveted in her direction. There was no mistaking who it was.

"Good God!" Her father's face hardened as he recognized the big man in the boat. "Surely it can't be him."

But it was, of course. He was dressed as he had been the first time he had come, in beige twill trousers tucked into high leather boots, a simple white linen shirt, and a wide-brimmed canvas hat. He looked muscled and fit and more handsome than she had ever seen him.

Anger washed over her, fury that he would dare to come after her again, and another elusive emotion she refused to name. Cait gripped her father's arm to steady her suddenly shaking legs. They stood waiting while the dinghy beached on the sand, then Rand jumped into the water, hoisted his gear up onto those incredibly broad shoulders, and sloshed ashore.

Crossing the distance to where they stood waiting, he tossed his burden down on the sand, cast a glance at Cait's pale, bloodless face, then turned his attention to her father.

"Greetings, Professor."

"You have a great deal of gall, young man, coming back here after what you've done."

Rand looked at Cait and something moved across his features, something soft and sad and eminently regretful. Cait blinked, certain that she had imagined it.

"There's something here that belongs to me."

Geoffrey stepped toward him, his legs splayed in a belligerent stance. "Not anymore there isn't. Cait doesn't want you or she wouldn't have left England."

Rand simply ignored him. "I realize there are . . . problems between Cait and me that need straightening out. I came here hoping—"

"You aren't welcome here," Cait said, finally finding her voice. "Not now, not ever again."

Her father protectively eased her a little behind him. "My daughter doesn't want you here. That is good enough for me."

Rand didn't budge. She had forgotten how tall he was, how incredibly imposing he could be. "I'm sorry, Professor. This island doesn't belong strictly to you. I've come a long way to get here and I'm staying. You had both better get used to it."

Anger tightened Cait's jaw. "I realize that legally I'm still your wife. If you came here with the intention of dragging me back to England, you can forget it. I'm not going back and there is no way you can make me."

His eyes swung to hers. She could feel the warmth in his look, the gentleness she now knew was a lie.

"I didn't come here to force you to do anything you don't want to, Cait."

"Then why are you here?"

"Let's just say I came to check on your welfare. As you said, you're my wife—no matter how distasteful you may find that circumstance to be."

Cait turned away from those dark, probing eyes that still had the power to move her. No wonder she had succumbed. Rand exuded a combination of tough and gentle, hard and vulnerable, that was nearly irresistible. It was a complete and utter façade, she now knew and she wasn't about to be swayed by it. "Father, please . . . can't you make him leave."

"It isn't that easy, my dear. As the duke correctly pointed out, he has as much right to be here as we do."

"Besides," Rand drawled, "I can make it worth your while."

Talmadge stepped into the circle, Sir Monty at his side. "In what way worth our while?" the baron asked. "Are you saying . . . if we allow you to remain . . . you'd be willing to make a contribution, as you did when you came here before?"

Rand's gaze remained on Cait. "More than that. I'm willing to finance the entire expedition—anything and everything you need from now until you find the necklace—or decide to give up and go home."

Talmadge whirled toward her father. "Did you hear that, Professor? Perhaps this will turn out to be our lucky day. With the duke's arrival, our problems are suddenly solved."

"I don't care," Cait protested, fury burning into the nape of her neck. "I don't want him here! I want him to get on that boat and go back where he came from!"

"What problems?" Rand asked softly, ignoring her as if she weren't there.

"Tell him, Professor," the baron insisted. "We've worked so hard, come so far. With Beldon's money, we could finally succeed."

Her father glanced her way, his face full of emotion, then he sighed. "Four days ago, we unearthed a small ivory-inlaid chest. It was buried among the personal possessions that belonged—we believe—to Leonard Metz, the first mate aboard the *Silverider*—the last survivor left on Santo Amaro."

"Go on."

"Apparently. Metz must have realized that one of the other crewmen, a man named Hans Van der Hagen that he believed he had killed, had actually survived and escaped the island. He was afraid the man would return and that if he did, he would steal the treasure. According to the map we found inside the box, Metz carried the treasure inland. The drawing he made shows the exact location of Cleopatra's Necklace."

Rand seemed to mull that over. "And of course you intend to go after it."

"Yes."

"That's the reason we were all here waiting for the *Moroto*," Talmadge put in. "We didn't expect the ship to arrive for another two weeks and, as you might imagine, we are eager to get on with our search. We need additional supplies and equipment, and porters who are willing to help carry it inland. When we saw the schooner headed this way, we hoped to speed things up a bit."

"It's a difficult journey," the professor said. "We need an experienced guide to lead us. There are several capable men in Dakar, men who know the island. Phillip is going back with the ship to obtain what we need in order for us to get started."

Rand flashed a hard look at Talmadge. It was obvious he still didn't trust the man and, after all that Rand had told her, neither did Cait. She had been watching him since her return, determined to protect her father should the man prove unworthy. She wondered if Rand had uncovered some new evidence against him and if, perhaps, it wasn't she but Talmadge who was the reason he had returned.

Her stomach tightened at the thought. It was ridiculous to care why Rand had come. He was there and that was the last thing she wanted. The thought of seeing him every day, of remembering the way he had charmed her, won her heart so completely, then tossed her aside like an unwanted bit of rubbish and returned to his mistress was simply too much to bear.

"The supplies you need are going to be costly," Rand was saying. "I can take care of it for you, make the whole endeavor financially painless."

Talmadge tossed a beseeching look at her father. According to the baron, their money was all but gone. There was enough for a last, feeble attempt to journey inland, but supplies would be limited, they would have to make do with their worn equipment, and they couldn't afford to hire the guide they so badly needed.

Her father turned his attention to Cait. She could read the hope that had risen in his face. "I'm afraid, considering the circumstances, I'll have to leave the final decision to my daughter."

She closed her eyes, fought not to sway on her feet. She wanted to say no, to tell Rand to go back to England and never come near her again. If she did, her father would likely fail. If she let Rand stay, they would have the money they so desperately needed and there was a very good chance he would succeed.

Her father's dream would become a reality at last, a gift more precious than anything she could give him.

She wet her lips and noticed that they trembled. "All right, he can stay—on one condition."

Rand's eyes touched her face. "Which is?" She tried not to notice how warm they felt, the way they moved over her like a caress.

"Which is that you stay away from me. You don't come anywhere near me."

Rand simply shook his head. "Sorry, I won't agree to that."

"If you have any intention of demanding your husbandly rights—"

"I don't. I know the way you feel, the way you have every right to feel."

She frowned, the words catching her a little off guard. "I don't like this—not one bit. But the truth is we need your money. You can stay if you want. But you had better keep your distance—I'm warning you."

The edge of his sensuous mouth curved up. "You don't make things easy, do you, Cait?"

Not for you, she thought, but didn't say so.

Talmadge smiled and took the reins. "All right, it's settled, then. I'll be leaving with the *Moroto* as we planned."

"Fine," Rand agreed. "But Mr. Fox will go with you. There are banks in Dakar. He'll be carrying a draft for whatever monies you may need."

Cait said nothing. From beneath her lashes, her gaze strayed to Rand. She was certain his interest would be centered on Talmadge, but instead his eyes were fixed on her, and there was the softest, most tender expression she had ever seen on his face.

Danger signals went off in her head. Dear God, surely she was over him. Surely, after all he had done, all she had suffered, she had learned her lesson. Cait took a last look into those compelling dark eyes and hardened her heart.

She was through with the Duke of Beldon.

And there was nothing he could do or say that could ever change her mind.

TWENTY-TWO

Rand staked a tent for himself and one for Percy, who had left aboard the *Moroto,* a ways away from the others in a small copse of trees. Still, he could see the campfire, watch the people gathered round it.

He could see his wife, and the ache for her he had managed to conquer on the long ocean voyage throbbed softly to life inside his chest. The moment he had spotted her on the beach, he had experienced such a fierce jolt a lump had risen in his throat. He'd wanted to hold her, kiss her, tell her how sorry he was.

It amazed him now that he could ever have gone to Hannah, ever been so foolish as to risk all that he had. But as Nick Warring had said, people made mistakes. He had made a colossal one, but he wasn't going to let it ruin his life—ruin both of their lives. He would find a way to make things right, a way to win Cait's trust once more, and he would guard that trust with every ounce of his being.

And never do anything to destroy it again.

Time was the key. He would take things slowly, be more patient than he had ever been. It wouldn't be easy. He wasn't a patient man. Still, he was determined.

Over the next two weeks, he discovered exactly how difficult it was. He forced himself to stay away from her, saw her only at meals and whenever he happened to accidentally stumble upon her.

Once he ran into her on the trail leading away from

camp and she stood there warily, watching him from beneath her thick fringe of dark auburn lashes. Reading her thoughts, he inwardly grinned and said the words she was thinking before she had the chance.

"You're not following me, are you, Cait?"

Her eyebrows shot up. "Following you! Why in God's name would I be following you?"

He shrugged his shoulders. "You're my wife. If there is something you want from me, you have every right to ask." His mouth curved faintly. "Conjugal rights work both ways, you know."

Hot color rushed into her cheeks. "Conjugal rights? If you think for a moment I am interested in . . . in . . . ever doing that sort of thing with you again—"

"I only wish you were."

Cait said nothing, but she studied him for several long moments. "I have to get back. If you will please step aside and let me pass—"

He didn't move, just remained where he was, lounging against a large granite boulder. Cait blew out a breath, moving a burnished lock of hair that had fallen over her forehead. "There was a time, Rand, I wanted a great deal from you. Far more than just a physical relationship. That time is past." She started to go around him, but he gently caught her arm.

"Perhaps that day will come again. If it does, you won't have to ask. I'll give you everything you want and more."

"If you're talking about money, it means nothing to me. Surely you know that."

"I wasn't speaking of money. What I have to give you now comes from in here." He laid a hand over his heart. "It took a while, but I finally learned that it's worth far more than just about anything in the world."

Cait said nothing, but several different emotions flickered across her face. Then she jerked her arm away and continued past him along the trail.

More days passed. Percy and Talmadge returned from

Dakar, along with the supplies, equipment, and the necessary porters. Rand had wondered if perhaps the baron had intended to leave the island with a portion of the treasure they had already unearthed and simply not return. It was one of the reasons he'd sent Percy along. Apparently the lure of even greater wealth was simply too much to pass up.

A third man returned with them, as well, a big, barrel-chested, blond-haired German named Max von Schnell. He wore a bushy mustache that curled up at the ends, and he swaggered more than walked. Rand didn't like him from the start.

"He wasn't my first choice, either," Percy told him as they sat in front of the small fire they had made in front of their tents. "Most of the best guides are French. Unfortunately, none of them were available and there was no one else who knew the island the way he did. Apparently, von Schnell lived here with his native wife until she died a couple of years ago. He says he knows every trail, rock, and canyon, and the best route up the mountain."

The man appeared capable enough, Rand had to admit. Tough as nails and a competent woodsman. But Rand didn't like the way he looked at the women. Even Maruba, who for a price willingly entertained his sort, seemed nervous around von Schnell.

Caitlin must have felt the same, for she rarely went anywhere near him, which was exactly the way Rand wanted it.

Three days after the baron and Percy returned, the gear was assembled, the equipment loaded into packs, the porters made ready, and they were off.

As they walked single file through the dense tropical foliage, Rand took up a position behind Cait. When she realized he was there, she stopped and turned, then marched back down the trail.

"What do you think you're doing? I told you to leave me alone."

"I've hunted these forests, Cait. You said yourself how dangerous they are."

"I can take care of myself."

"I know you can, but not as well as I can—especially not out here. I'm staying right behind you. You might as well get used to it."

"Why? What do you care what happens to me? You never cared before."

He reached out, gently caught her chin. "You're wrong, Cait. I've always cared. I was just afraid to admit how much—even to myself."

Cait said nothing, just studied him in that way she had begun to of late, turned and walked away.

That night they made camp in a clearing at the bottom of a sheer rock wall cliff face littered with granite scree. A turbulent dark gray sky threatened overhead, boding a tropical storm. But the rain didn't come, and after a meal of jerked venison and hard biscuits, they settled into their bedrolls and tried to fall asleep.

Rand had placed his blankets not far from Cait's, and though she glared at him, she didn't protest and instead simply ignored him, rolling up in her bedroll and turning her back in his direction. Not yet sleepy, Rand sat a little longer watching the fire that had burned to glowing coals, listening to the screech of bats and the hum of insects. Mostly, he simply watched Cait.

Moments they had shared slipped through his head, days they had spent at River Willows, the grief they had suffered when she had lost the babe, making love here on the island in the pool beneath the falls. He thought of the joyful times they'd shared aboard the ship on the journey home, remembered the feel of her body next to his, the exact shape of her breasts. He thought of how incredibly good it had felt to be inside her, and his groin tightened, began to feel thick and heavy.

He wanted her as he always did, ached with wanting her. But now he wanted so much more.

He heard her stir, knew that though she pretended, she

wasn't really asleep. Then he saw it, the scaly, thin green body sliding down off the branch of a tree, slipping silently closer till it hung less than a foot from her cheek. He knew by the shovel-shaped head that the snake was poisonous, and icy fear collected in his stomach.

"Don't move, Cait." She started to do just that. "Forgodsake, just this once do what I say." Her body went rigid and he knew she sensed danger, had heard it in his voice. Reaching behind him, toward the leather sheath he carried at his waist, he slowly pulled his thin-bladed knife and eased toward her.

"It's all right," he soothed. "Just take it easy. Don't make any sudden moves."

An involuntary shudder ran through her and the snake's head came up. The forked tongue slid out, the hinged jaw opened with a sharp, deadly hiss, the long fangs glistening in the faint light of the fire. Rand dove forward, striking out with the knife the same instant he slammed into Cait, knocking her out of danger.

The snake's head flew from its body, severed neatly, and Cait threw her arms around his neck. "Rand! Rand—oh, God—it nearly bit me."

He tightened his hold, felt her small body trembling.

"You're safe, love—I've got you. The snake is dead. There's nothing more to be afraid of." She only shook harder, her frame pressed to his. His eyes slid closed. God, it felt so good to hold her. He wished he could hold her this way forever, protect her and keep her safe. His jaw hardened. The damnable snake had come far too close.

The commotion had the camp on its feet. The professor and Geoffrey came racing up to Cait, who realized she was wrapped in his arms and clinging to his neck. Embarrassed, she pulled away.

"Caitlin! What the devil . . . ?" The professor saw the snake and the color bled from his face. "Good God—a green makimbo!"

"At least that's what the natives call it," Sir Monty put in. "They're deadly poisonous."

The professor's glance strayed to Rand. "Thank God you were here."

Rand just nodded. He had already thanked God more than once.

"Perhaps Cait should put her bedroll next to mine," St. Anthony suggested, tossing him a hostile glare. "I can look after her as well as he can."

Rand just shook his head. "She stays where she is."

For once Cait didn't argue. He imagined she was still too shaken to put up much of a protest.

"Now that the ex-zite-ment is past," the big German said, "vee all need to get zome sleep. You've a good eye—eh, English? Perhaps you vill be of some use on this trip after all."

Rand said nothing. It was obvious the German didn't like him much, either. Rand suspected it was because he was keeping such a close eye on Cait.

He returned to his bedroll, but didn't fall asleep. Every time he closed his eyes, he kept seeing the green snake's deadly fangs, just inches away from Cait's face.

They traveled upward, moving most of the time beside a swiftly falling river that emptied into the sea, the trail becoming steeper, more rugged. They crossed jagged gullies and deep ravines, passing out of bright sunlight into deep shade, the spray from the river making the boulders slick and soaking into their clothes. In one spot, fearsome cliffs dropped off on one side of the trail, in another, odd-shaped needles of volcanic rock rose up, carved by wind and rain.

With each step she took, Cait could feel Rand's presence behind her. It annoyed her to admit she found it comforting. Last night, he had probably saved her life. She owed him for that, and being in his debt was the last thing she wanted.

When they stopped to make camp that night, she ignored her screaming muscles, the fatigue that had settled into nearly every part of her body, and went in search of him.

"He's gone hunting," her father said, when she asked where he was. "I don't think he intended to go far." She passed one of the natives carrying a brace of birds, then found Rand a little while later, squatting as he cleaned his gun. He set the musket away when he saw her, came to his feet, and crossed to where she stood nearly lost among the dark green jungle foliage.

"Were you looking for me?"

She nodded and wet her lips, which felt drier than they should have. "I came to thank you . . . for what you did last night."

"You don't need to thank me. I'm your husband. It's my duty to keep you safe."

She stiffened. *Husband.* Once she had thought of him that way, been proud to call him that. Not anymore. Now when she looked at him, she remembered how he had abandoned her, left her for his mistress. "Husbands have any number of duties, Rand. They didn't concern you before."

"They should have. I didn't understand that then."

"And now, I suppose, you do. You understand your obligations."

He looked her square in the face. "Yes."

Cait cleared her throat, uncomfortable beneath that penetrating stare, refusing to be swayed by such a simple word. "At any rate, I owe you and I want to repay you."

"Repay me? How?"

"With information."

He cocked a brow. "What sort of information?"

"Exactly the kind you've been looking for. When I returned to the island, I was worried about the things you'd told me about the baron. I wasn't completely certain they were true, but I was concerned for my father. I never really trusted the man, but my father does. I started watching him. I wanted to know if he was the sort of man you believed he was."

"And?"

"One night I watched him working over the ledgers in his tent. He did that a great deal, but something he did that night caught my attention. I could see his shadow against the canvas in the light of the oil lantern that was burning inside. He was digging in his trunk and it got me wondering what might be in there. After you arrived on the island, while Talmadge was away in Dakar, I went into his tent and found out what it was."

Rand's jaw tightened. "You shouldn't have done that. The man could be dangerous. I don't want you—"

"Wouldn't you like to know what I found?"

He sighed. "All right, what did you find?"

"A second set of ledgers. They show how much money he has been stealing from the expedition's funds. So you see, you were correct. If you came here for Talmadge—"

"I didn't come for Talmadge. Revenge against Talmadge is no longer important. Not if it means losing you."

Her eyes swung to his face. Anger mixed with hurt and dark, ugly memories of his betrayal. "You lost me months ago, Rand. The day you climbed back into bed with Hannah Reese." She started to turn away, but Rand caught her arm.

"I was a fool, Cait. I knew it even before the night you found me at Chatelaine's. Do you have any idea how much I regret what I've done?" His hand stroked softly along her arm, moving the fabric against her skin, making it tingle. Sadly, he shook his head. "I don't think so. There is no way on earth you could possibly know how badly I wish I could change what I did."

"Let go of me, Rand."

He didn't want to—she could see it in his eyes. Dragging in a breath, he released her arm and stepped away. "Thank you for telling me about the baron," he said.

"Are you going to tell my father?"

"Not yet. There are too many dangers here. Too many things could go wrong. There's no reason to alert Talmadge until we're safely back down from the mountain."

"Yes . . . that was my thought, as well." Her eyes remained on his face. Such a handsome face. Once so beloved. With a force of will, she turned and started walking.

"Good night, Cait." The soft sound of his voice followed her up the trail. Cait made no reply, just swallowed past the aching lump that rose in her throat and continued along the path back to camp.

The next day mirrored the one before, only this time they hiked beneath flat purple clouds and drizzling rain. The porters were strung out in a line that stretched along the river so far von Schnell began raging at them to hurry their pace.

Late in the afternoon, the sun came out and the weather grew hot and steamy. The river plunged into a gorge, exploding into great clouds of spray when it hit the bottom, and von Schnell decided it was too late in the day to make the crossing. One of the porters scaled the gorge and climbed up on the opposite side. A line weighted with a rock and tied to a thicker, heavier rope they would use for the bridge was thrown to him, then several more. He anchored the rope to a stout tree on the far side of the gorge and the men set to work, weaving a sort of makeshift suspension bridge.

Cait spotted Rand among them. He dragged off his shirt and bent to the task, working naked to the waist like the porters. She couldn't help admiring the flex of muscle over bone, the thick bands moving across his shoulders, the sinew that tightened across his ribs. The muscles in his back carved deep, sensuous valleys that changed shape as he worked with the rope. She remembered how it had felt to touch them, to press her mouth against that smooth, warm flesh. She remembered how his tight round buttocks felt in her palms, how it moved as he drove himself inside her.

Desire rose up, curled seductively in her belly. Anger rose with it, determination to drive it away.

By dusk, a sturdy rope bridge had been created and the men sat around the campfire pleased with their efforts. During the day, Percy Fox had shot a feral pig. The porters had brought it back to camp and everyone was looking forward to the meal.

Everyone but Rand, who seemed to have disappeared. Some inner demon drove her to look for him, some odd niggling at the back of her neck, or perhaps it was simply worry for a man she once had loved. Whatever the case, she wandered a short ways into the jungle, hoping to spot him, and eventually she did. He was lounging against a tree, his shoulders propped against it, his musket leaning there beside him.

"You were hunting?" she asked, catching his attention. He saw her, came away from the tree, and a soft smile curved his lips. It made her insides tighten in that old familiar way and suddenly she wished she hadn't come.

"I was doing a bit of scouting. Von Schnell seems to know what he's doing, but it never hurts to be sure."

She glanced toward the musket.

"I don't like to go off without it. Too much can happen out here." His expression darkened. "Which reminds me— what the devil are you doing out here alone? After what happened with the snake, you, better than anyone, ought to know it isn't safe."

She glanced around, saw that she had come a good deal farther than she'd meant to. "Sorry. I didn't realize I had come quite this far."

"Why did you?"

What could she say? That some sixth sense had prodded her to come? That she had been worried about him? Even if it were true, she would never tell him. "I don't know. Perhaps I needed some air."

"The next time you need air, you had better find it closer to camp."

Cait started to tell him she no longer had to follow his commands when she happened to glance up into the tree. The blood drained from her face while her heart dropped into her stomach. Rand must have noticed for he went completely still.

"What is it?" Slowly, instinctively, he reached for his weapon.

"Leopard," she whispered as he wrapped his hand around the long metal barrel and eased the musket toward him. "He is crouched on the branch just to your right. His fangs are showing. Oh, God, Rand, he's going to—"

Rand jerked up the musket and spun at the same instant the leopard leapt toward him. He fired the rifle and Cait screamed. Rand's body went down beneath the heavy weight of spotted yellow fur, long, bared teeth, and razor-sharp claws.

Cait whirled and began a frantic search of the undergrowth for some sort of weapon, her heart threatening to pound its way through her chest. Grabbing a heavy log, she spun toward the leopard, bringing the club down with all her strength across its head. The leopard didn't stir, but neither did Rand.

"Rand! Rand!" On shaking legs, she used the club to pry the leopard's heavy weight off him, then knelt at his side and pressed her cheek against his chest. She heard his steady heartbeat, felt the rise and fall of his breathing, then heard him groan.

"Rand! Are you all right?"

He sat up slowly, shoving the leopard off him, easing himself out from beneath the heavy weight. He was breathing hard, shaking his head as if to clear it. "Knocked the air out of my lungs. I banged my head when I hit the ground, but other than that, I think I'm all right." He looked up, into her worried face. "Thanks to you."

"Thanks to me?" She studied the stick she still held in a death grip, tossed it aside, and blushed. "The leopard was already dead when I hit it."

Slowly, unsteadily, he came to his feet. "You didn't know that at the time."

"No, but—"

"If you hadn't seen him, he would have been on me

before I could reach my weapon. If you hadn't been here, that leopard would likely have killed me."

Cait shuddered to think of it. She looked over at Rand, saw the torn sleeve of his shirt and the deep scratches on his biceps marked bright red with blood. Seeing how close he had come to being seriously injured, a wave of dizziness washed over her. It was all she could do not to throw herself against him and weep in relief.

It was stupid, utterly ridiculous, that she should still have such strong feelings for him.

Where was her self-respect?

What kind of woman continued to care about a man who had betrayed her with another woman?

"Your arm needs tending," she said blandly, though she wasn't feeling nearly so calm. "We had better be getting back to camp."

Rand just nodded. But he kept his eyes on her all the way back and she knew he was still wondering, asking himself why it was that she had come.

She prayed he didn't figure it out.

TWENTY-THREE

As the members of the expedition gathered around the campfire for supper, Rand mulled over what had happened earlier in the day. Was it just coincidence that Cait had come upon him when she did? Or was she looking for him? And if she was, what did she want?

He wanted to believe she had gone in search of him. Perhaps unconsciously, she simply wanted to see him, the way he ached every moment to see her. It heartened him to think it might be so and renewed his strength of will. Somehow, someway, he would find a means of reaching her, convincing her he was a different man than he was before.

He saw her sitting next to Geoffrey St. Anthony and a fine thread of tension filtered through him. As usual he didn't hear Percy's silent approach.

"St. Anthony means nothing to her," he said, following the line of his gaze. "I've watched them together. She appreciates his friendship, nothing more."

"He wanted to marry her."

"And she wanted to marry you—whether she is willing to admit it or not."

"Well, we are married—for all the good it has done. As a husband, I was a complete and utter failure."

"*Was* is the crucial word here. I've known you, been your friend, for more than ten years. Once your mind is set on a course of action, you do not fail. You are determined to make Cait Harmon a good and faithful husband. I believe you will do just that."

"That's assuming she'll give me the chance."

Percy gave a noncommittal shrug. "Unfortunately, that is the case. In the meantime, supper is ready. Why don't we eat?"

The boar Percy had shot had been skinned and prepared and was roasting in great hunks on a spit above the fire. Succulent juice hissed onto the glowing coals, and the delicious aroma drifted over the camp, making Rand's stomach growl. He picked up a tin plate from a stack that sat on a rock near the fire and lined up behind Percy and the professor.

All three men loaded their plates with meat, potatoes, wild onions, and unleavened bread, and Rand found a spot on a flat rock to eat. To his surprise, the professor took up a place beside him.

"How's the arm?" Donovan Harmon asked, taking a bite of the succulent meat.

Unconsciously, Rand's hand massaged the bandages beneath his shirt that covered the painful claw marks the leopard had made. "Hurts like the devil, but the scratches aren't all that deep. Your daughter cleaned and bound it for me. Assuming there's no putrefaction, in a few days I'll be fine."

The professor swallowed, took a sip from his tin mug of coffee. "It's hard on her . . . your being here. I must say, I wasn't too keen on the notion myself."

"I regret the pain I've caused her—more than you can imagine. I intend to make it up to her."

"My daughter isn't a woman who trusts easily. After her mother died, she learned to guard her emotions. Over the years, she has rarely made deep friendships. She knew that sooner or later we would be leaving wherever we were living at the time. Losing a close friend was simply too painful. She thought it was better to keep her distance and so she did."

"She shared a close friendship with Margaret Sutton,

and I believe she considered Elizabeth Warring a very good friend, as well."

"Yes. Perhaps it was merely that Caitlin has spent so much time alone. Or that she was becoming a woman and felt she was ready to take another risk. Then she met you and let down her guard even more. In the end, she paid for it dearly."

Rand swallowed the chunk of pork he had been chewing, though it tried to stick in his throat. He looked down at the food beginning to congeal on his plate and set it aside, his appetite suddenly gone. "I want to make things right between us. I made a mistake—a bad one. But I've paid for it, just as she has. Cait is my wife. I'm not leaving here without her."

The professor studied Rand's face, saw the determination and, Rand prayed, the sincerity. He started to reply, but stopped when Geoffrey St. Anthony walked up with Phillip Rutherford.

"We heard about the leopard," Talmadge said. "One of the porters brought in the hide. Magnificent specimen. Sounds as if Caitlin is a bona fide hero."

Rand eyed the baron, feeling the same distaste he always did. "As far as I'm concerned, she is."

"Considering the way you treated her," Geoffrey said snidely, "I'm surprised she didn't let the bugger eat you."

The muscles in Rand's face went tight. "Sorry to disappoint you, St. Anthony. I'm alive and I intend to stay that way."

"I'm sure Geoffrey didn't mean anything," Talmadge, ever the diplomat, put in. Rand itched to confront the bastard, tell him he knew he had been stealing from the expedition funds, robbing them just as he had done his young cousin—and God knew how many others. But now was not the time, not when there was a chance it might put Caitlin in danger.

Percy and Sir Monty strode into the group, distracting Rand from the bitter train of his thoughts.

"Good show, old man." That from Sir Monty, who

grinned and clapped Rand on the back, sending a sharp pain vibrating into his injured arm. "Saw the leopard skin. Big blighter, I can tell you. Wonder he didn't do more damage than he did."

"He would have if it hadn't been for Cait."

"So I heard. Good thing she went looking for you. She asked me if I had seen you and I told her I thought you went off in that direction."

Rand's gaze swung directly to St. Anthony, whose mouth went thin at the news. Rand flashed him a satisfied grin, feeling a shot of hope that Cait had been seeking him out. "Yes, it was extremely fortunate for me."

The two men stared at each other until Sir Monty tipped his head toward the person approaching and pointedly cleared his throat. "Good evening, Caitlin."

She arrived in the circle and stopped next to her father. "Good evening, gentlemen."

"We were just discussing your heroics."

"My heroics? What heroics?"

Rand flashed her a smile. "You mean you don't consider saving my worthless hide heroic?"

Cait glanced his way and her lips twitched. "I merely spotted the leopard a few seconds before you would have."

"A few seconds before I would have been leopard food, you mean."

Everyone laughed, even Cait. "I suppose it could have been a great deal worse."

"A very great deal," he said. "Considering how highly I value all four of my limbs."

Another round of chuckles, all but St. Anthony.

"I didn't mean to intrude." She smiled at Percy. "I just wanted to thank Mr. Fox for the wonderful supper he provided. It's been a long time since I've tasted anything quite so delicious."

Percy made a gallant bow. "I assure you it was my pleasure, Your Grace."

Cait blanched as if he had struck her. The smile remained in place, but the color leached from her cheeks. It was rare that anyone called her that and the pointed reminder apparently did not sit well. Rand silently cursed. Bloody hell, just the notion of being married to him completely overset her. Cait took a last look around the circle of men, excused herself, and quietly slipped away.

As the group dispersed, some to play cards, others to read before retiring, Rand went in search of her, finding her alone at the edge of camp. She was sitting on a fallen log darning one of her father's linen shirts beneath the light of a hanging oil lamp.

"How has he been these past few months?" Rand asked as he walked up beside her. "No more bouts of illness, I hope."

She glanced up, saw him, and sat up a little straighter on the log. "None so far. He seems healthy enough, I'm happy to say."

He nodded. "I'm glad."

She rested her needlework in her lap. "Was there something you wanted?"

Something he wanted? God, did he. Just looking at her there in the lamp light made him ache with longing. Every moment near her was an agony of the very worst sort, yet being apart from her was worse.

"I came to thank you again . . . for what you did today." It was as good an excuse as any. "If it hadn't been for you, I could have been killed."

She shook her head. "Somehow I don't think so. You've proven yourself extremely capable in this country. I never would have believed it, but you are."

He smiled. "India, remember? And hunting big game in Africa. The terrain there in places is very much the same."

"You've learned to take care of yourself. Though I imagine you only did it to impress your father."

"I suppose at the time I did. But in some ways, I'm grateful to my father. The things he taught me have often come in handy."

"I'm sure they have." She picked up her sewing, jabbed the needle a bit too forcefully through the linen. "He insisted you learn the manly arts. Did he also teach you a man should have a mistress as well as a wife?"

Those clear green eyes fixed on his face and guilt knifed through him, cutting like a dull-edged blade. "By example, I suppose he did. In that, I discovered he was wrong."

An auburn brow arched upward. "Wrong? You're not saying if you had it to do over, that you would remain faithful to me?"

"I'm saying that if you would agree to be my wife again, there would never be another woman."

Cait stared up at him. She blinked several times, and in the distant firelight, he caught the unmistakable shimmer of tears. "I don't . . . I don't believe you, Rand."

"I've made mistakes, Cait, but I've never lied to you. I'm not lying about something as important as this."

She only shook her head. Shoving to her feet as if she couldn't bear the sight of him a moment more, the shirt clutched in front of her, her back rigidly straight, she made her way back to the camp.

Rand watched her go, the claw marks aching in his arm, his insides knotted with a different, far more painful ache. How could he ever convince her?

But no answer came.

With a defeated sigh, he returned to the camp and tossed down his bedroll a few feet away from Cait's, another long night ahead of him.

At the first light of dawn, they assembled beside the river to cross the rope suspension bridge they had built the day before. Beneath it, the river fell in great white sheets into the narrow, rugged canyon seventy feet below.

"It is called Angels' Gorge," von Schnell said to the small group surrounding him, the professor and Geoffrey St. Anthony, Sir Monty Walpole, Caitlin, and Rand. "Gargantua de Anjos in Portuguese." He grinned beneath his bushy blond mustache. "If you fall, you vill join with the angels."

Rand said nothing, but he noticed Caitlin shivered.

Von Schnell saw the movement, too. His pale blue eyes ran over her, assessing her womanly curves, lingering a moment on her breasts, sliding down over her hips. It was all Rand could do not to hit him. He didn't like von Schnell, didn't like him looking at Cait with that hungry gleam in his eyes.

Still, the professor needed the beefy German to guide them to the top, and Rand wasn't about to do anything that might destroy what Cait and her father had worked so long and hard to accomplish. He would simply do as he had been and keep a very close eye on them both.

Von Schnell made the crossing first, his heavy frame causing the bridge to swing in the wind, but he arrived safely on the opposite side and the others began the same journey. Cait stood waiting next to St. Anthony, who seemed determined to give her advice.

"I'll go first," he told her, "then wait for you on the other side. Just remember, don't look down."

For the first time, Rand realized how pale she was, her usually sun-warmed skin bleached to the color of sand. As soon as St. Anthony headed for the bridge, he walked up beside her.

"Tell me you aren't afraid of heights."

She shrugged her small shoulders. "It doesn't matter. I have to go across and I will."

He glanced at the bridge then into the craggy gorge, and swore a soft curse. "If the bridge could take the weight, I'd carry you across. I don't think it's a good idea. Damn, I wish you were home and safe. I can't stand to watch you day after day, putting yourself in danger."

"No one asked you to come here, Rand."

He gazed down into her face. "I had to, Cait."

"Why?"

Because I love you. But he didn't say it. He knew she wouldn't believe him. Someone shouted that it was Cait's turn next and she turned to go, moving woodenly toward the narrow suspension bridge. The wind had come up and the bridge swung precariously. Seventy feet below, the river crashed against the jagged rocks and ignited into white plumes of foamy spray.

Rand caught up with her just before she started across. "For once St. Anthony is right. Don't look down. Just hold on to the ropes and keep walking. Keep your eyes on Geoffrey. He's waiting for you on the opposite side."

Cait moistened her lips, then she nodded. "I'll see you over there."

Rand smiled and Cait gave him a brave, tremulous smile in return. Something passed between them, something sweet they had shared before, and Rand wanted desperately to hold onto it. Bending toward her, he gave her a quick, hard kiss on the mouth.

"Get going," he said gruffly. "Don't think about anything but putting one foot in front of the other."

She looked up at him, unconsciously touched her fingers to her lips. Taking a long deep breath, she turned and took hold of the ropes. Little by little she edged forward, step by hesitant step. A gust of wind caught the bridge, whipping it back and forth, and Rand's stomach tightened.

"Hold on, Cait," he whispered, afraid to shout for fear it might frighten her. Two thirds of the way across, she paused. He could feel the tension thrumming through her as if it were his own. "Go on, love," he quietly urged, "you can make it."

She started again and this time her steps were stronger, more confident. Rand's eyes slid closed on a wave of relief the moment she reached the opposite side. He didn't even care that St. Anthony had pulled her into his arms.

The rest of the porters crossed, more confident after watching Caitlin. The two native women who did the cooking crossed next, then Maruba, on the journey, Rand suspected, to take care of the baron's needs. Hester Wilmot, the English cook, had stayed with the two valets and the footman at the base camp.

Rand was the last to go over.

The wind was gusting hard now, making the crossing treacherous. Bits of dirt and leaves flew into his eyes, and it was difficult to see. As he reached the middle of the bridge, he looked down at the frothy water below and realized how terrified Caitlin must have been. Silently, he saluted her courage.

He could see her as he drew near, and there was no mistaking the worry on her face. She cared about him—he was sure of it. She belonged to him and, no matter what it took, he meant to make her his wife again.

She was smiling when he reached the other side, nearly as relieved as he had been.

"All right?" he asked as they started up the trail.

"Fine. I just hope there's another way down."

The corners of his mouth edged up. "To tell you the truth, so do I."

She didn't say more, and the warmth in her expression slowly faded. Turning away, she started up the path with the others and Rand fell into his usual place behind her. He recalled the fear he had felt as he'd watched her cross the swinging bridge. He'd be bloody well glad when they reached the top.

They climbed all day, making slow but steady progress. Late in the morning, they encountered the heavy ring of clouds that encircled the upper slopes of Pico de Maligno, and disappeared into the thick gray mist. By late afternoon, they had emerged once more into sunlight, growing ever closer to the summit of the huge volcanic peak.

Two more days and they would reach the place on the map that marked the spot where Leonard Metz had hidden Cleopatra's Necklace—or at least they hoped he had. They had reached a crossroads on the mountain yesterday morning and begun to follow the trail Metz had described on the map her father kept constantly with him.

After days of climbing, Cait's legs had grown stronger, but the muscles in her arms and back still ached from dawn to dusk. Rubbing a crick in her neck, she was grateful when von Schnell called a halt for the travelers to relieve themselves and catch their breath. She had just returned from the forest when she spotted Rand speaking to the big beefy German. They said something she couldn't hear and von Schnell stalked away. Rand turned toward the trail just as Maruba walked up to him.

Cait stood frozen, a knot of tension forming in her stomach. Maruba was lovely, willowy, dark, and exotic, and Cait knew she had been involved with Phillip Rutherford. Twice she had seen the girl with Geoffrey St. Anthony, and Cait wondered if perhaps he had also been seduced by her charms.

It bothered her a little to believe it was so, since he still pressed her to think of marriage. What was it about her that the men in her life always seemed to need other women?

Cait watched Maruba, who gazed up at Rand and gave him a slow, seductive smile, and a sickening wave of nausea rolled through her. The girl ran a long dark finger down the open vee of his shirt and inched even closer. Going up on tiptoe, Maruba whispered something in his ear, and Cait felt a nearly unbearable pain spear into her heart.

Then Rand caught Maruba's hand, gently pushed her away, and firmly shook his head. Without a backward glance, he turned and walked away, leaving Maruba staring after him.

Cait watched his tall figure retreating up the trail, the pain beginning to fade, her heart no longer aching. Then her attention swung back to Maruba. The slender girl was walking directly toward her, and there wasn't a hint of guilt on her pretty, cocoa-skinned face. She stopped a few feet in front of her.

Maruba tipped her head toward Rand, whose broad

shoulders continued up the trail. "You husband . . . he a good mon."

Cait just stared.

Maruba gave her a knowing, womanly smile that ended almost in a grin and continued on her way. With a shot of clarity, Cait realized that the girl must have known from the start that she was watching. But Rand hadn't known. What had happened between husband and wife was hardly a secret. There were few secrets in a group that lived so closely together.

Perhaps Maruba had been testing him in some way. The fact that Rand hadn't accepted what the lovely girl had so obviously offered sent a shot of relief pulsing through her, and stirred an odd feeling of warmth.

It was ridiculous. It meant nothing. Perhaps he simply did not desire her.

Still, the warm feeling would not go away.

Supper came early, a meal of unleavened bread and a watery stew fashioned of wild herbs and an array of small game. Cait didn't know exactly what meat she was eating and wisely didn't ask. Afterward she took a walk, simply to work the kinks from her sore muscles, careful not to stray too far.

She was standing in the shadows, watching the distant campfire, when she heard the rustle of leaves and heavy footfalls behind her. Certain it was Rand, her heartbeat increased. She started to turn, when a big callused hand clamped over her mouth and the excitement she had tried not to feel turned into a sudden shot of fear.

Cait grabbed the hand, tried to pry it free, but a thick arm clamped around her waist. The big German lifted her easily and began to drag her farther back into the foliage. Her heart pounded fiercely, crashing against the walls of her chest. Cait struggled, kicked out with her heavy leather boots, and got a moment's satisfaction at his husky grunt of pain.

Von Schnell jerked her around and shoved her hard

against a tree. "You vill behave yourself, if you know vhat is good for you."

"You had better let me go—if you know what is good for you."

Beneath his blond mustache, his mouth curved up in the semblance of a smile. "I do not mean you harm." His hand ran along her neck, slid down over a breast, and Cait shivered. She wanted to run, but he was big and strong, and she might only have one chance.

"What do you want?"

He meaningfully squeezed a breast, and nausea rolled in her stomach. "You are married but you do not sleep vith your husband. I am attracted to you. I could give you vhat he does not."

"I'm not interested in anything you have to give, von Schnell. I'm telling you to let me go."

"One kiss—that is all I ask. One little kiss and I vill let you leave." Von Schnell lowered his head, but Cait turned her face away. She tried to jerk free, but he held her fast, pressing her into the rough bark of the tree.

"I'll scream," she warned.

"Not if you vish to reach the summit. Your father needs me to get him there and you know it." His hand tightened over her breast. "I vill give him his treasure and you vill give me vhat it is that *I* need."

As his head dipped down, Cait struggled in outrage and tried to twist free. An instant later, his heavy weight was simply gone. She heard a grunt, the sound of a fist slamming into flesh, and whirled to see von Schnell's big body crashing to the ground a few feet away. Rand stood over him, long legs splayed, his hands balled into shaking fists.

"Come near her again, von Schnell, and I swear by all that's holy—I'll kill you."

"You are threatening me?"

"That's not a threat—it's a promise."

Von Schnell grunted and rolled to his feet, a big, knotty hand rubbing the bruise on his jaw. "Do not make promises, English, you cannot possibly keep." He gave Rand an icy glare, brushed off his clothes, and disappeared into the forest, sending several small rodents scurrying out of his way as he stomped along.

Rand's hard gaze swung to Cait. "I thought I told you to stay close to camp."

She straightened, forced a stiffness into her trembling limbs. "I don't take orders from you anymore—in case you have forgotten."

"What were you doing out here with von Schnell?"

"I assure you I didn't come willingly."

He rubbed a hand over his face, fighting to collect himself, then the tension seeped from his body. "I'm sorry." Releasing a weary breath, he started toward her. "I just . . ." He might have reached for her, drawn her into his arms, if she hadn't stepped away. "I realized you were gone and I got worried. It appears my concern was not misplaced."

"I could have handled von Schnell." That was a lie. She was darned glad Rand had arrived when he did, but she wasn't about to tell him. "You didn't have to interfere."

A muscle tightened in his cheek. "You're my wife, Cait—whether you're willing to accept the fact or not. No man puts his hands on you. Not now, not ever."

A strange sense of elation mixed with a burst of anger. Anger won out. "No man but you, is that what you mean?" She knew she was pushing him, knew the heat of battle still burned through his blood, but she couldn't seem to resist.

She caught the blaze of heat in his eyes, the flash of undisguised hunger, just before his arm shot out and he hauled her against him. "That is exactly what I mean."

Claiming her mouth in a ravaging kiss, he held her immobile, locked in his arms and unable—or unwilling—to move. For a moment, Cait just stood there, fighting the heat that spilled through her like warm tropical rain, the terrible yearning she had suffered for so long.

Rand's lips softened over hers, moving with exquisite care, his mouth brushing back and forth, tasting her slowly, gently, then pressing into her more deeply, his tongue parting her lips then sliding inside. Fierce tenderness coupled with fiery demand, a kiss so wildly passionate, so achingly sweet, that tears sprang into her eyes. Longing welled up, overrode logic and caution, and for a single brief moment she kissed him back. Love for him flowed through her, poured into her heart.

He was her world, her love, the only man who could satisfy this wild craving that burned in her blood.

Then the past rose up, memories of the night she had found him with Hannah Reese, imaginary images of Rand making love to the woman, caressing her, touching Hannah as intimately as he had once touched her. She remembered the terrible days after she had left him, the unbearable ache of loss, the pain of betrayal, shedding an ocean of tears. Cait broke away.

"Don't . . ." she whispered, trembling all over, her breath coming ragged and fast. "Don't, Rand, I beg you . . ."

One big hand cupped her cheek. "Why not, Caitie? You're my wife. I have every right to kiss you."

She only shook her head and backed away. "Not . . . not any more."

"Tell me you don't care about me. Tell me you can look at me, kiss me, and feel none of the things you felt before. Tell me, and I'll go away and never bother you again."

She wanted to tell him just that. She wanted to hurt him as he had hurt her. She tried to force out the words, but the lie wouldn't come. Instead, she backed even farther away. Turning, she raced off toward the fire, Rand's stormy, regretful gaze following her all the way there.

Phillip Rutherford waited impatiently behind an outcropping of boulders some distance from the clearing. It was late. Most of the camp was already asleep. Heavy gray clouds blocked the moon, rolling in above a white-capped sea.

"Bwana Phillip? Bwana Phillip, are you here?" Maruba stifled a squeak of surprise when he gripped her arm and dragged her into a break in the forest protected by thick green jungle foliage.

"I don't like to be kept waiting—you know that, Maruba."

She bit down on her pouty lower lip, watching him from beneath lowered lashes. "I am sorry. I did not realize it was so late."

"You did not realize? Perhaps that is because you were busy entertaining His Grace, the bloody Duke of Beldon. I saw you with him earlier." His mouth curled harshly. "I saw what you offered. It was plain for anyone to see."

Maruba shook her head. "No, no—you do not understand. It was only a game. I only wished to see—"

He wrenched her arm up behind her and she made a slight gasp of pain. "You only wished to see what? If the bastard is as big as he looks? If he can swive you better than I can?" He whirled her around, forcing her belly-down over a rock, and began to shove up her sarong. "Why don't we see?"

Moving behind her, he began to rub her nipples, stroke between her legs, but not for long. He was tired of playing games with her, tired of pretending she wasn't a whore. He urged her legs apart, unfastened his trousers, and freed himself. A few more strokes and her flesh grew faintly damp. He felt her stiffen at his rough entry, but he didn't care.

With a grunt, he gripped her hips and began to ram himself inside her, pounding hard again and again. He liked the sound of flesh slapping against flesh, and his body grew hot and slick with sweat. It didn't take long to reach his peak. His muscles tightened, contracted even more, and he shuddered as the pleasure washed over him.

He stood there a moment, the warm tropical air cooling his heated skin. Once the sensations had faded, he withdrew, allowed her to turn and straighten her clothes. Maruba glanced toward the rock, saw no money had been left for her as there should have been, turned uncertain eyes to his face.

"Tonight you earned nothing, little whore. You've displeased me, Maruba." He reached out and caught her chin. "Stay away from Beldon—and St. Anthony. Until I tell you otherwise, your body belongs to me."

She flinched as he squeezed her jaw, her black eyes widening with a trace of fear.

"Do you understand me?"

She nodded vigorously. "Yes, Bwana." Phillip let her go and she made her way silently back to where she slept with the other women.

Phillip waited a little longer, then returned to his own bedroll and stretched out on top of it. A rock poked into his back and he grimaced, reached under the blanket and removed it, thought, *At least there aren't any mosquitoes.*

It hadn't been so bad on the beach, but he was sick and tired of this damnable jungle. Sick of the dampness and the heat. He yearned for the taste of good wine, the softness of a feather bed, the smell of clean, freshly washed sheets. He could hardly wait to get off this bloody island, and in a few more days, he intended to do just that.

He smiled to think of the plans he had made in Dakar. In a few more days, the boat he had hired would be waiting in a secluded cove near the base camp. Once he had the necklace, he would return to the camp, pick up the rest of the treasure, and simply leave.

He wasn't worried about the natives who'd stayed behind or the few English servants. It was the professor and the others—and that arrogant bastard Beldon. The man had been a thorn in his side from the start. It was just his luck, the fool had decided to give up his English whore and come after his wife. It was going to be the biggest—and last—mistake of his life.

Phillip felt the evening drizzle begin to settle over him

and inwardly he cursed, wishing he was gone already. He wasn't exactly certain how he would dispense with Beldon and the others, but for a portion of the booty, von Schnell had agreed to help him. His weary little band would come to a fitting end on this hellishly primitive island, and he would have the riches he deserved.

And something to amuse him, as well.

He thought of Caitlin Harmon, peacefully sleeping back in camp. His worry over Cait's spying had faded. Apparently, she had learned nothing that would do him any harm. He thought of her full breasts and beautiful body, finally under his command, thought of doing to her what he had just done to Maruba—and he smiled.

TWENTY-FOUR

Cait was dusty and hot and determined that today, after they had made camp, she would find a place in the river to bathe and wash her clothes.

Von Schnell chose a campsite in a rocky flat next to the river that was protected from the wind, which blew harder this high up on the mountain. There was less jungle here, less chance of running into danger. While the camp was being set up, she draped a linen towel over her shoulder, took a clean change of clothes, and headed downstream to a place she had spotted just before they'd stopped for the day.

Unfortunately, when she got there, she found someone else had beaten her to it. Irritation warred with a voyeur's urge to watch. The river formed swirling pools along the shore, a long, gently flowing chain of them, and Rand knifed cleanly through the water, diving under, then surfacing with a foamy spray and rolling over onto his back. He was naked, she saw, beautifully, splendidly naked, and she could no more look away than she could spread wings and soar over Angels' Gorge.

Hidden in the cover of the trees, she allowed herself to study his magnificent form. She remembered it only too well, the solid indentations beneath each of his ribs, the iron-hard slabs of muscle across his shoulders, the springy texture of his curly brown chest hair. She missed the intimacies they had shared, the closeness of touching him, having him touch her, feeling him inside her. The thought caused a quickening in her blood and a slight hitch in her breathing.

He stood up for a moment in waist-deep water and glistening droplets cascaded down his massive shoulders, over his muscled chest.

He slicked back wet brown hair from his forehead and sinew contracted across his flat belly. Cait's insides contracted with it, her pulse speeding up once more. Desire curled softly, sank in its claws and wouldn't let go. Her hands trembled with the need to touch that smooth, damp skin, feel those thick, hard muscles, run her tongue across a flat copper nipple.

Soft heat unfurled, began to slip through her body, settle low in her belly. It seeped lower, tugged at her womb, throbbed in her private woman's place. He dove beneath the water and the muscles in his buttocks tightened. Long muscles bunched in his thighs. Her nipples went hard, began to pulse softly beneath her cotton blouse. Desire made her woman's passage slick and she cursed Rand Clayton for the power he still held.

But she didn't turn away, couldn't make herself move. Mesmerized, she watched him swim toward shore and slowly climb out of the water. He was looking toward the trees where she hid and she sucked in a breath, praying he wouldn't see her.

As he neared the bank, the water dropped below his hips, his thighs, his ankles, and she saw that he was fully aroused, his long shaft thick and rigid, standing high and hard against his belly. He was staring straight at her— had seen her after all. The edge of his mouth curved up.

Walking with long, purposeful strides and not the least degree of modesty, he began to close the distance between them.

Cait's senses went on alert. Still, she watched him a moment longer than she should have. When she turned and started to run, Rand caught her before she got three paces, swinging her around, bringing her hard against his chest.

"I hope you liked what you saw, little voyeur."

"Let me go!"

"I knew you were there. I saw you watching." Hot brown eyes moved slowly, purposefully, over her from head to foot. His wet body dampened her blouse, making it nearly transparent, and the dark pink areolas of her nipples shone through. His fierce gaze burned her there, turning the crests pebble hard.

His arousal leapt against her, hot even through her clothes. "See what you do to me, Cait? What you've always been able to do?" He pulled a little away and she glanced down, saw how big and hard he was, how badly he wanted her, and heat raced beneath her skin.

She started to reply but her lips felt tight and refused to move. He stood just inches away, close enough she could feel the heat radiating off his big body. His skin was wet and slick and glistening in the sunlight spilling down through the branches of the trees. He was male and beautiful, magnificent in his nakedness. Her hands trembled where they pressed against his chest.

"I—I came for a bath. I was just . . . just waiting for you to leave."

A soft chuckle, the sound of utter disbelief. He knew why she had stayed, recognized the desire she could not hide. His hand came out, gently cupped a breast. His thumb brushed softly across a stiff nipple, rasping gently, seductively, and a funny little sound came from her throat.

"It's always been this way between us. It always will be, Cait." He began to knead her breasts and they swelled into his palms. His gaze fixed on her lips. He saw her tongue slide out to moisten them, certain now what she was thinking. He caressed her softly, skillfully, and she heard herself moan.

Rand bent his head, pressed his lips to the side of her neck, trailed kisses along her jaw, kissed the pulse beating fiercely at the base of her throat. He pulled the string on her blouse, parted the opening at the neck, and eased it down, then settled his mouth on her breast.

Cait swayed against him, her hands sliding up to clutch his shoulders. He circled her nipple with his tongue, suckled gently, then more deeply, taking the fullness into his mouth, and her knees nearly buckled beneath her.

Dear God, she couldn't be doing this! She didn't dare take the risk. But her body refused to listen. He was her husband. A woman had needs the same as a man. What did it matter if she took something—just this once—for herself?

A hard arm slid around her waist and he eased her down among the soft green grasses. He drew off her blouse, unfastened the tabs on her skirt and eased it off, then lifted her chemise gently over her shoulders. Bending his head, he kissed her breasts, trailed kisses down over her stomach, ringed her navel with his tongue then moved lower, settling his mouth on the damp, aching spot between her legs. He suckled her there and fierce sensation rocked her. Heat crushed in on her in thick, overpowering waves.

It wasn't enough.

"Tell me you want me," he whispered, pressing his mouth against the inside of her thigh, laving it with his tongue. "Tell me you need me the way I need you."

She needed him. Like a flower needed rain. But she couldn't say the words, couldn't afford to give him that hold over her. "I want to feel you inside me," she said instead, the words soft and shaky. "I have to. Now, Rand, this minute."

He came up over her in a single smooth motion and her arms went around his neck. He kissed her wildly, thoroughly, his tongue sweeping in, stroking the inside of her mouth, taking her with skill and determination. It was a kiss of savage demand, yet there was gentleness, too, and an aching tenderness that tore straight into her heart.

Tears burned behind her eyes as her fingers slid into

his wet brown hair. She wanted him. She wanted him so badly. And dear God, she loved him still.

"Caitie . . ." he whispered. "My beloved Caitie, I've missed you so much."

Tears leaked from beneath her lashes. Beautiful words. Such incredibly beautiful words. Still, they were nothing more than that and they really didn't matter. Truth or lies. None of it mattered. Not now. Need was all-important. The deep, uncontrollable yearning to be joined with this man once more.

Her breasts pressed into his chest and each diamond-hard tip seemed to burn. He laved them with his tongue as if he understood, as if he could soothe the fiery ache that flamed straight into her core. She could feel his hard-ness pressing against her and ached to feel it inside.

"Please . . ." she whispered, her body arching upward. "Please, Rand, I need you . . ."

He hesitated only a moment, his dark gaze intent and filled with some emotion she could not name. Then he found the entrance to her passage and gently eased him-self inside.

"Caitie . . ." he whispered, sliding in more deeply, until she was fully impaled. He slid out and then filled her with a single hard stroke, claiming her in some primitive fash-ion. His movements quickened, became more seductive, more erotic.

Cait refused to think of it, to admit that those long, deep, penetrating strokes were meant to possess her. In-stead, she reveled in the heat and the pleasure, gloried in the passion they hadn't shared in so long.

Her hands dug into his shoulders while her body arched upward to take more of him. Rand drove into her again and again, the pleasure expanding, swelling, filling her senses completely. Out and then in, each penetrating thrust carrying her higher than before. She wrapped her legs around him, took him deeper still, and spiraled even higher.

Rand whispered her name, and an instant later, pleasure tore through her in great rippling waves. Cait bit back the cry of his name as a second spasm shook her. Rand drove into her two more times then his whole body tightened. His muscles contracted, and he shuddered with the power of his release. He held her tightly against him as he began to spiral down, resting his head against her shoulder. Cait clung to him, breathing in his scent, savoring the hard, sleek muscles beneath his damp skin, the river-clean fragrance of his hair.

For a while they remained locked together, savoring the moment, the sweetness. Cait wished they could stay that way forever. That the world would simply stop exactly where it was now.

But the world waited for no one, she knew, and finally, wordlessly, Rand came to his feet. Bending down, he slid his arms beneath her, lifted her against his chest, and carried her into the stream, sinking deeper, until the cool water gently rushed over them.

The river soothed her weary muscles, washed the heat away, left her body cleaned and refreshed, but it also cleared her senses. She and Rand were naked and she had just made love to him.

Dear God, what had she done?

Standing behind her in the shoulder-deep water, Rand slid his arms around her waist and pulled her back against his chest.

"Say you'll forgive me," he said softly. "Say you'll come home and be my wife."

She wanted to. Dear God, for the very first time she realized just how badly she wanted to do just that. But Rand was Rand, one of the handsomest, most charming men in England, and no matter what he said, one woman would never be enough for him.

A painful lump rose in Cait's throat. She had made a mistake in giving herself to him, and yet she didn't regret it. She eased out of the protective circle of his arms, then shivered at the sudden loss of his warmth.

"I'm sorry, Rand. What we did just now . . . it . . . it

never should have happened. It's over between us. It has been since the night I followed you to Chatelaine's."

A muscle flexed in his jaw. "Your body doesn't seem to agree." His eyes moved boldly over her naked breasts and unconsciously her hands came up to cover them. "You wanted me," he said. "Just as much as I wanted you. Surely you don't deny it."

She slowly shook her head. "Sometimes wanting isn't enough. That was the mistake I made when we first met. I wanted you so much I didn't consider the consequences. Now I know better. I don't trust you, Rand. I never will again."

A dozen different emotions passed over his face. Cait could only read one of them. It was difficult not to recognize despair.

Her heart clenched hard inside her. Cait forced the emotion away. With it went the flicker of hope that begged her to believe in him again. She couldn't do that—not ever. She couldn't afford to take the risk. If she did and he failed her, she would never survive that terrible pain again.

Turning, she sloshed toward the shore and retrieved the towel she had brought. She dried herself as best she could and stepped into her clean skirt and blouse. She sensed him behind her, turned to find him fully dressed, as well.

Rand lifted damp hair away from her cheek, guided it back into place over her shoulder. "You don't believe me," he said, parroting her words, "and you don't trust me. Not the best foundation for a marriage, is it, Cait?"

Cait didn't answer. There was nothing she could say.

"But if I were telling the truth . . . if I were a man worthy of your trust, we could be happy. We could be a family. We could have everything, couldn't we, Cait?"

The ache returned to her throat. *Everything*. If she could trust him, Rand would be the sort of man she had once foolishly believed he was. The strongest, kindest, most gentle man she had ever known. If that were true, they could make a wonderful marriage, the sort she had once imagined. But still, she wouldn't have everything.

Not unless she also had his love.

Rand rose from his bedroll to the excited sounds of the early-breaking camp. Everyone knew that the long weeks of searching, all the hopes and dreams the members of the expedition had carried with them for so long, would be answered on this one single day. If the necklace wasn't where the Dutch sailor's map indicated it should be, they would probably never find it.

They would have wasted hours of backbreaking labor and they would have failed.

Rand took up his usual place behind Cait, who walked with renewed energy today. She wore her flat-brimmed straw hat down low over her forehead and a single thick red braid bobbed against her back, the gold-tipped ends shining in the bright rays of the sun. He watched the sway of her hips and couldn't help thinking about what had happened at the stream.

Cait might believe it was over between them, but Rand wasn't convinced—not by a long shot. Not when he could still make her body respond with such incredible passion, not when being inside her felt so perfectly, completely right.

One of the porters who had been scouting ahead with von Schnell rushed back to the professor and pointed excitedly up the trail. Donovan Harmon nodded and started walking even faster, and the others stepped up their pace, as well. Even Rand couldn't resist the pull of excitement involved in discovering an ancient object of such incredible worth.

It would be a telling day, no matter what they found, but not a day to let his guard down. Greed did strange things to men. If by some miracle the necklace was actually found, it would have to be transported back down the mountain to the base camp. With men like Talmadge and von Schnell among them, the return might be far more perilous than the climb to the summit.

The trail grew steeper, but eventually widened out, the river no more than a trickling stream, splashing gently over smooth, lichen-covered rocks. A sky of cerulean blue whitened by a few wispy clouds stretched overhead, and the wind blew in cooling gusts up the steep ravines. Colorful birds, bright red and yellow, screeched from high in the trees and several times Rand stopped to watch them.

They rounded a high rock wall, and up ahead he saw von Schnell waiting at the edge of a copse of trees. Talmadge and the professor broke away and hurried toward him, followed by Sir Monty and Lord Geoffrey. Cait glanced at Rand over her shoulder, then lifted her skirts and raced ahead to join them. Apparently this was it.

Rand's hold tightened on his musket, which rarely left his side these days. With the other hand, he reached behind him to check the knife he carried in a sheath at his waist. Perhaps he was being overly cautious, but he knew for certain the baron was a thief, and his scuffle with von Schnell had confirmed his suspicions about the big German, as well.

Better to be safe than sorry.

He strode up next to Cait, set the butt of the musket down on the grass, but kept a hand on the barrel. "I gather this is the place."

"The map indicated certain markings. We knew it was just below the summit on this side of the mountain. Yesterday we passed the first indicator, a rock in the shape of a mushroom. Father told von Schnell to stop as soon as he could see a notch in the crater of the volcano, another spot indicated on the map." She pointed. "You can see it right through there."

Her father was poring over the scrap of cloth marked in faded ink, checking for the rest of the landmarks. With each confirmation, he flashed a grin at Cait and pointed to where it was.

"We've come to the right place," he said. "This is the spot Metz describes. According to the map, the necklace should be buried not far off the trail, beneath a tree marked with the sign of a cross."

They all spread out in search of it, Rand staying close beside Cait, who carefully examined the trunk of each tree. An hour passed. Still no sign of it. They moved deeper into the leafy forest. It was damper and hotter in here, and sweat broke out on Rand's forehead. He couldn't help remembering the deadly green snake, and when Cait leaned down to examine one tree more closely, Rand caught her arm and gently hauled her back to safety.

"You've got to be more careful, Cait. This place could be dangerous. The light's not good and there is way too much foliage. Remember the snake that nearly bit you? This is the sort of place you might run across another."

An involuntary shudder ran through her.

"Keep that in mind and your eyes wide open."

Cait nodded, began to pick her way more carefully through the dense green cover of the tropical forest. The afternoon slipped away and still no sign of the tree with a cross marked on it.

The porters began to set up camp for another night on the mountain, and spirits began to droop.

"Why the devil isn't it here?" Talmadge strode up to where Cait and Rand searched next to her father. Instead of his usual meticulous appearance, for once the baron looked completely done in. His light cotton trousers were wrinkled and his shirt undone, exposing the salt-and-pepper hair on his chest. "You said we'd find it," he railed at the professor. "You told us all it would be here."

"I'm sorry, Phillip. I imagined, once we had the map, it would be easy." He glanced around, saw only thick jungle foliage. "It's here. I know it. We mustn't give up."

The baron jerked a handkerchief from a pocket in the seam of his trousers and mopped the back of his neck. "It had better be here. After all you've put me through, it had damn well better be."

Donovan Harmon frowned at the harsh tone of voice. "We'll find it, Phillip. We won't leave until we do."

But they didn't find it that afternoon and darkness set in, postponing the search. No one said much that evening. Although Percy and one of the porters brought in a small red deer and the venison supper was tender and delicious, the men kept mostly to themselves.

Cait sat through the meal next to her father, working to bolster his flagging spirits, but several times, Rand caught her watching him when she thought he couldn't see. He wondered if she was thinking of making love beside the stream and prayed that she was. If seduction was his only course, then that was the path he would take. He would start his pursuit again, as soon as they were safely down the mountain.

Though the rest of the party remained silent and brooding, Rand's spirits suddenly lifted.

The members of the expedition were up before dawn, resuming their search of the heavily wooded tropical forest. As their efforts spread in an ever-growing circle, the jungle thickened and it was more and more difficult to make way. Finally von Schnell was forced to resort to the heavy, long-bladed knives they had brought to cut through the vines and leaves.

High above their heads, monkeys chattered in the treetops, and Cait found herself watching them, smiling at their antics as they leaped from branch to branch, each long prehensile tail acting like an extra hand. A small brown monkey with a round white face caught a branch too thin to support its weight. The branch cracked and the monkey fell, landing in a rolling tumble on the ground at her feet.

Cait laughed out loud and the little monkey scampered away, looking slightly indignant.

"Cute little devils, aren't they?" Rand's deep voice sent a warm shiver over her skin.

"We didn't see many of them down at the other camp," Cait said. "Apparently, they like it better up here."

"Apparently." He smiled, took her hand, began to tow

her through a break in the undergrowth. "I've found something you need to see." Cait hesitated only a moment. They were all in this together, after a fashion, and even the slightest clue might be of help.

Cait let Rand lead her along a game trail that led back toward the main path in a roundabout way.

Before they reached it, he paused. "Take a look at those two trees."

Cait stared through the dense, dimly lit foliage, but saw only faint sunlight slanting down through leafy vegetation, smelling of damp earth and wet leaves. She could hear the trickle of the nearby stream.

"I don't see anything."

"Not there." He pointed slightly to the left. "Over there." Cait strained to see through the undergrowth and suddenly she saw it—two trees, their trunks interwoven, the one on the right growing almost perpendicular to the one on the left. From a distance, the trees formed a natural cross.

"Oh, my God! You don't think Metz could have meant the crossed trees instead of the cross on the tree?"

He grinned. "I think that's exactly what he meant. Come and see."

She followed him eagerly now, pausing at the base of the tree to discover a hole Rand had dug with his hands. A small metal box lay rusting in the bottom. Cait dropped to her knees in front of the box, reached down eagerly, and extracted it. Setting it gently on the ground, she carefully flipped open the lid.

Her shoulders sagged. Except for the remnants of a moldy cloth bag that had rotted into bits and pieces, the box was empty.

Her disappointment built, grew into a painful ache for her father and all his lost dreams. Then she felt it, the heavy length of finely hammered gold Rand draped around her neck. Her fingers brushed the scales of an exquisitely fashioned golden snake set with perfectly faceted jewels—Cleopatra's Necklace.

"You've found it, Cait," he said softly. "You and your father. It's everything you ever said it would be."

She swallowed against the painful ache that rose in her throat. Lifting the necklace away with trembling hands, she held it up to examine it. Even in the dim light of the forest, it glittered as if it were lit by a thousand suns, sparkled with the brilliance of blood-red rubies, diamonds, and the exquisite gleam of emeralds.

"It's . . . magnificent."

"Yes . . ." he said, but when she looked at him, his eyes were on her face. "Magnificent."

Her gaze remained locked with his, her fingers tightening around the necklace until the glittering jewels cut into her palms. Finally, she glanced away. "We have to get my father. We have to show him what we've found and where we found it."

He nodded. Grabbing his musket, he took her hand and they started back the way they had come.

"The necklace!" someone shouted, spotting the glint of gold and jewels she cradled protectively against her chest. "Sweet Lord, she's found the necklace!" She recognized Sir Monty's voice and saw him running toward her. Geoffrey fell in behind him, then Talmadge and von Schnell, and finally, her father.

His face was red from the hours of exertion, but he was smiling, and his eyes had never looked so clear and blue.

"My dear, sweet girl, you've found it!"

Cait smiled and pressed it into his hands. They were shaking, she saw, just as hers had been, and when she looked up at him, tears were streaming from his eyes. "They said it wasn't real. They said it was only a myth, but I always knew it was true. I swore one day I would find it. I would prove to the world it existed." He brushed away the wetness on his cheeks. "Where in God's name was it buried?"

Cait grinned and took his hand. "Come on. I'll show you." The entire group made its way back into the woods, stopping in front of the two crossed trees. "Rand figured it out. He saw the trees and guessed that was what Metz had really meant—two crossed trees instead of a cross carved into a tree. He found it exactly where it was supposed to be." She watched as her father dropped down to his knees and carefully examined the rusty box.

Perhaps there were clues about Metz and the necklace in that box, or in the bits of rotting cloth it had been wrapped in, lost information about the past. Perhaps one day, archaeologists would discover ways of ferreting out those clues.

For now, Cait was simply glad that they had found so magnificent a treasure and would be able to share it with the world.

It was passed to each member of the expedition, including von Schnell, and each man chattered excitedly as he examined the exquisite work. When Phillip Rutherford received his turn, he studied each precious gem and stroked it almost lovingly.

"I'll put it in my pack until we return to the base camp," he said. "That way we'll be certain it gets there safely."

Behind her, she felt Rand stiffen. He might have said something, but her father reached over and slipped the necklace out of his partner's hands.

"I believe I shall keep it with me for a while. That way I'll be able to study it more closely."

Talmadge clamped his jaw, but Cait breathed a sigh of relief.

"Vee vill start down the mountain at first light," von Schnell said. "The sooner vee are out of this place, the better it vill be for all of us."

Cait definitely agreed. She wanted to be safely returned to the base camp, away from the threat of dangerous animals, treacherous terrain, and deadly snakes. From there they would return the necklace to England and her father would receive the accolades his fine mind and hard work had long deserved.

They walked in single file back along the game trail to camp, where they would spend their final night before beginning their journey down the mountain to the safety of the beach. All the way there, she felt Rand's presence behind her and couldn't help remembering the instant when he had draped the necklace around her throat.

No matter how long she lived, the tender look on his face in that moment would never leave her. He was giving her the most precious gift she would ever receive—a gift she had wanted for her father more than anything in this world.

She thought of the other gifts he had given her, the beautiful roses, the lovely music box, the pretty little sorrel he had bought for her to ride, thoughtful gifts chosen especially to please her. She remembered the kindness he had shown the injured horse the day of the race, remembered his shyness over his painting, his love of beautiful birds.

The words he had said rose into her mind once more. *I've never lied to you, Cait.*

It was a truth she couldn't deny. In the past few days that truth had surfaced again and again, nagging at her subconscious, pleading with her to believe it.

She had never been a coward, but just how brave was she? Was she willing to risk herself as she had before?

She heard Rand's footsteps on the trail behind her, protecting her as he had from the moment of his arrival. What if his promise of fidelity were true? What if she could trust him, as she had once believed?

The questions haunted her.

She knew they would nag her relentlessly all the way back down the mountain.

TWENTY-FIVE

Chanting filled the air, the wild yips and shouts of the porters celebrating the expedition's success. Tonight there would be feasting: a big fresh-water turtle roasted in its shell, an abundant supply of fish that had been wrapped in plate-sized leaves then buried beneath rocks and burning coals, nuts and fruits gathered in the forest. The fat larvae of moths nearly six inches long were an extra special delicacy, though Rand imagined most of the expedition members would pass on the treat.

The mood was high and it continued that way on into the evening. Talk had turned to the trip back to England. The treasures that had been found would be presented to the British Museum, as the professor had promised, and everyone was happy to be returning victorious to London.

Everyone, Rand thought, but Cait.

Once the meal was finished and the revelry began to diminish, the members of the expedition started making their way to their respective bedrolls to settle in for the night. Unlike the others, Cait moved quietly off by herself.

Rand followed a few minutes later, and she turned at the muffled sound of his footsteps in the soft, mossy earth.

"Why is it I feel as if I've had a living, breathing shadow since the day I started on this trip?"

A corner of his mouth kicked up. "Because that's exactly what I am—exactly what I intend to remain until you are safely returned to England."

She gazed out into the darkness, the rasp of cicadas

cutting into the still night air. "I have to go back. My father has commitments, and he deserves the glory he'll receive once we arrive. But our stay there will only be brief." She slowly turned to face him. "When we're finished, we'll be returning to America, Rand."

In the light of the moon slanting down through the leaves, he tried to read her features, a painful knot tightening in his chest. "You're my wife, Cait. A wife belongs with her husband."

"We never should have married. We only did it because of the child."

"Are you certain of that?"

"Of course I am. After I lost . . . our child, you went back to the life you really wanted. A life that didn't include me."

"You think I returned to London because I wanted the life I had before?"

"Didn't you?"

"I went to London because I was afraid."

Cait scoffed, a tight, unpleasant sound. "What in God's name would you have to be afraid of?"

Rand took a long, deep breath, trying to find the words. He raked a hand through his hair, leaving it slightly disheveled. "It's hard to explain. It took months before I understood it completely myself. I can only say that when you lost the child, something completely unexpected happened to me. I saw a side of myself I'd never seen before, a frighteningly soft side, Cait. At the time, I viewed it as a weakness. I'd fought against those sorts of emotions since I was a boy. Later I realized I was simply afraid of my feelings for you—and for the child we would have had. And I couldn't bear the pain. Mine or yours. I couldn't stand to watch you suffering and not be able to do anything about it. Instead I ran away."

Cait stared up at him searching for the truth, her expression troubled and dark with uncertainty. In her simple clothes and sturdy shoes, with her nose slightly sunburned and her hair coming loose from its braid, he thought there wasn't a woman in London who could possibly compare. He ached to go to her, pull her into his arms, beg her to forgive him. He wanted to kiss her until she pleaded with him to make love to her, as she had done that day at the stream.

It took sheer force of will to remain where he was, to ignore the hot sweep of desire coursing through him, and the deep feelings of love.

Cait walked away from him, reached out and plucked a small red blossom from one of the leafy plants that grew in wild profusion around them. "I'd like very much to believe there was a reason for your leaving besides the urge to sleep with another woman." She plucked a petal from the blossom, smoothed it between her fingers. "But even if you're telling the truth, it doesn't matter. It never would have worked between us. We're simply too different."

"In what way, different?"

She let the flower fall to the ground and turned to face him. "Take your collection of Chinese jade, for instance. You believe you're protecting it by locking it away in your mansion. I think it's a sin for you to keep such beauty to yourself. It's a treasure everyone should be able to enjoy."

He grinned. He couldn't help it. "Maybe that is the reason I donated the collection to the museum—along with my Greek and Roman busts—in your name."

Her eyes widened. "You did that?"

"I'm not an ogre, Cait. I could see the merit in your thinking, though at the time I didn't agree. It was important to you, and that made it important to me." He moved toward her, reached out and caught her shoulders in his hands. "I can't undo the past, Cait. I wish I could but I can't. But I can make it up to you. If you'll only give me the chance."

She looked up at him, her eyes dark with emotion, but she simply shook her head. "I wish I had the strength to try again. I really do. But you see, Rand, now I am the one who's afraid."

His hold tightened on her shoulders. He wanted to shake her, force her to understand. "You care for me—I know you do. I can see it in your eyes, feel it whenever I kiss you."

He couldn't mistake the pain in her face. His chest felt heavy with regret as her eyes filled with tears.

"I cared for you once," she said softly. "I loved you, Rand. I loved you so much." For several long moments she just stood there, her gaze locked with his, staring at the stricken look on his face. Brushing the wetness from her cheeks, she turned and started walking back to camp.

Though he yearned to go after her, Rand remained where he was, his whole body frozen in place. *I loved you, Rand. I loved you so much.* Something burned at the back of his eyes. In the past he would have been embarrassed. Now he no longer cared. His wife had loved him. Other people had said so, Maggie and Nick, even Percy believed it, but Cait had never spoken the words, and she was so strong, so independent, it had never occurred to him it might actually be true.

Why would it? He had been too blind to recognize his own feelings—how could he possibly recognize those feelings in Cait? Instead he had run away, betrayed her with Hannah, and completely destroyed the love she once had felt for him.

For the first time since he had come to the island, Rand felt doomed to fail. He didn't deserve a wife like Cait, not after the way he had treated her. And he wasn't going to press her any longer. He would see her safely returned to England, afterward, if that was what she truly wanted, he would help her and her father go back to America.

Perhaps it was fitting penance that he pay for his sins by losing the only woman he would ever love.

They set out early down the mountain, traveling the exact same trail they'd come up, much to Cait's chagrin. For two full days, she dreaded the moment they would reach the suspension bridge. She told herself she had made it once and she could do it again. Still, she was quiet and a bit withdrawn all the way down the trail.

But then so was Rand.

Though he stayed close by, since their last conversation, he had rarely spoken. He never came near until he dropped down on his bedroll late at night and, as she did, tried with little success to fall asleep.

She had surprised him, she knew, with her declaration of love. Did he really not know? Or perhaps he didn't want to hear the truth. Perhaps the confession of her once-deep feelings for him had frightened him again. If that was so, perhaps now, finally, he would return to England and leave her in peace.

The thought should have been comforting.

It was not.

Instead, despair throbbed like a wound in her chest and would not go away.

It came to her with stunning force that she had wanted to believe in him again, had actually begun to think that perhaps they might truly be able to start over. Now her doubts returned full measure and she was no longer sure what to believe.

Cait hitched the small pack she carried higher on her shoulder. The going was far easier heading down the mountain, which meant their pace was much faster. In the afternoon of the second day, they reached the suspension bridge. A slight drizzle had begun to fall and mud on the path sucked at their boots.

"The bridge vill be vet and a little bit slippery," the big German warned.

And during the night it had rained higher up on the mountain. The water was higher, not that it mattered since the river ran through the gorge so far below, but she could see the foamy spray shooting upward, splashing against the rocks, looking even more ominous than it had before.

Von Schnell crossed over first, his grip firm on the

rope, his footsteps sure, making it look almost easy. Talmadge followed, then Maruba and the women. Her father and Geoffrey approached where Cait stood faintly trembling.

"Will you be all right?" Geoffrey asked.

She flashed him an overbright smile. "Of course. I made it the first time, didn't I?"

Her father squeezed her hand. "That's my girl."

"Go ahead, Professor," Geoffrey said, "I'll stay with Cait." Her father nodded and started across. His steps weren't nearly as sure as some of the others' and it took him a whole lot longer, but in time he made it to the opposite side.

"I'll be waiting for you," Geoffrey told her. "Just like before." With a brief, reassuring smile, he stepped out on the bridge and crossed without a problem.

Now it was Cait's turn. She found her gaze searching for Rand, who strode up just then.

"There isn't much wind today," he said. "That should make the crossing somewhat easier." His eyes, dark with worry and compassion, moved over her too-pale face. "Do exactly as you did before. Just put one foot in front of the other, and remember not to look down."

"Will you be crossing behind me?"

He gave her a reassuring smile. "Percy will follow you over. I'll stay behind, make sure everyone gets across safely."

Cait just nodded. She remembered only too well the difficult crossing he had made the last time they had approached the gorge. Taking a long, shaky breath, she stepped out onto the bridge. As Rand had advised, she kept her eyes on Geoffrey, battled down her terror, and placed one foot in front of the other until she had made it to the opposite side. It didn't seem nearly as hard the second time.

Rand herded the other porters across and they arrived without a problem, all but two, who remained behind with Rand and Sir Monty. The little explorer said something that was lost in the rush of raging water, motioned for Rand to go on ahead, then he and the porters started back up the trail the way they had come.

Rand conquered the bridge with his usual competence, and once he reached safety, Cait breathed a sigh of relief.

"Apparently Walpole's journal fell out of his pack," he told her, joining her at the edge of the gorge to await the explorer's return. "He thinks it may have happened when he climbed over that downed tree a little ways back. He took a couple of the porters along to help him search."

They kept watch up the path leading into the forest until Sir Monty reappeared a few minutes later, grinning and waving a red leather volume in the air. As soon as he reached the bridge, he stuffed it into his pack and readied himself to make the crossing. The remaining two porters waved him on and he made the journey safely. Then the last two started across, the first arriving safely.

The second man had just reached the middle of the gorge when it happened. Cait didn't know what went wrong, only stood there frozen, watching in horror as the rope tied to the tree on her side of the gorge suddenly began to fray and unravel, then snapped in two. Someone shouted to the thin, cocoa-skinned porter, telling him to grab hold of the rope, but it was already too late.

Cait screamed as the flimsy rope bridge dropped away beneath the man's bare feet and he began to fall, his body tumbling end over end, plunging toward the foaming river below, his anguished wail echoing off the steep rock walls of the gorge, then slamming against the jagged boulders at the bottom. A sob caught in Cait's throat and she turned away.

She felt Rand's arms around her, pulling her trembling body into his, pressing her face into his coat, holding her while she wept against his shoulder. For minutes that seemed like hours, no one said a word. There was only the sound of rushing water, the echo of the wind through the canyon, and the hollow refrain of Cait's weeping, mingled with the keening of the native women.

"There always seems to be a price," Rand said gently, smoothing back strands of her hair. "Nothing of consequence ever comes cheap in this world."

A shudder passed through her. She thought how true were his words and began to sniff back her tears. Her father came up just then, his eyes bleak, his face haggard, as if he had aged ten years in the past two minutes.

"He was a good man," he said, shaking his head. "A good worker. It's a shame . . . a terrible, terrible shame."

Cait looked up at Rand and an awful thought occurred. "It could have been you," she whispered, her eyes fixed on his face. "You meant to go last. If Sir Monty hadn't lost his journal, it's you who would be dead."

While the others reassembled to continue the journey, Rand glanced off toward the bridge. Walking to the tree that had been used to secure it, he picked up the broken length of rope and examined the end. It was frayed and uneven, but it was obvious that a portion of the fibers had been cut.

Rand swore foully, his hand tightening around the sturdy length of hemp.

"What . . . what does it mean?" Cait asked, coming up beside him.

Rand held up the rope, turning it slowly between his fingers. "It means someone didn't want all of us to get across." He pointed to the blunt edge made by the blade of a knife. "It wasn't cut completely in two. Whoever did it would have wanted to be certain the bridge remained intact long enough for him to distance himself. He probably didn't do it until after the professor crossed safely, since he was carrying the necklace. Did you happen to notice anyone standing in this area?"

Cait shook her head. "No, I . . . I didn't see anyone. We were all paying attention to the crossing."

Rand studied the end of the rope. "There was no exact way to calculate when the bridge would actually break— or if it would break at all. I think whoever was responsible just hoped to eliminate at least one of us. Probably me."

A faint shudder passed over Cait's body. "Do you think it was the baron?"

"Perhaps. But von Schnell is at least as likely. In truth, even one of the porters might have done it. Everyone saw the necklace. Perhaps one of the natives is hoping to wind up with it."

He caught the shrewd look in her eyes. "But you don't really think so, do you?"

"No."

"If you're right, my father could be in grave danger."

Rand shook his head. "On the contrary—I think carrying the necklace will help insure his safety—at least until we reach the base camp."

"I don't like this, Rand."

"Neither do I. But until we discover for certain who is responsible, there isn't a damned thing we can do."

That was the truth, Rand thought, frustrating though it was. They were all of them in danger—and Caitlin smack in the middle of it. Silently, he cursed. For the second time in his life he was helpless where she was concerned.

He had failed her the first time.

He didn't intend to do it again.

The journey continued, the group somber and silent as it moved down the trail, now that a man was dead. Cait kept thinking of the rope Rand had shown her, seeing an image of the helpless porter crashing to a savage death, knowing now that it was murder.

Rand said nothing to the others of his suspicions, though after they stopped for the night, he reminded her father and the others they were carrying a valuable cargo and they all should remain alert.

Unfortunately, his warning proved futile. That night Sir Monty and three of the porters fell ill.

It occurred just after supper, the little man suddenly breaking into a sweat, growing light-headed and weak, then beginning to shake all over. Sitting down on a fallen log, he asked Rand for a drink of water, then fell unconscious with the wooden canteen still pressed to his lips.

"Oh, dear God!" Cait rushed to the fallen man's aid, quickly kneeling beside him. She reached out and touched his forehead, which was hot and damp, the skin stretched almost painfully tight. "He's burning up!"

"Help me get him to his bedroll," Rand said to Percy, who stood next to her father and the others, all gathered worriedly around.

Armed with a bowl of water and several clean strips of linen, Cait knelt beside the stricken man, stripped away his jacket and shirt, and began to bathe his neck and shoulders.

Her father hovered nearby. He and the little explorer had become fast friends, and his worry was apparent in the deep lines etched into his face. The little man regained consciousness off and on, and Rand spoke to him quietly whenever he did. Eventually, his eyes slid closed and he didn't awaken again. Within the hour, the other three men had fallen ill.

"Whatever it is," Cait said, replacing the damp cloth on his forehead with a fresh one, "it must be highly contagious." In that light, she sent the others away, but Rand had refused to leave.

He studied Sir Monty's flushed face, glanced over at the other three sick men, and shook his head. "I'm not convinced."

"What do you mean?"

"Late this afternoon, Walpole shot a rabbit. According to what he said, he shared it with one of the porters, who shared it with two of his friends."

Cait searched his face. "And those are the three other men who are sick."

"So it would seem." He turned to Percy, who always seemed near at hand. "Find Maruba. Ask her to fetch the old woman who has been looking after the natives."

Percy nodded and slipped away. He returned a few minutes later with the willowy girl and the wrinkled, ancient woman who had been serving as cook on the journey.

"You want see us, Bwana?"

"I want the old woman to have a look at this man. I think he and the others may have eaten something poisonous. See if she can do anything to help."

Maruba translated for the woman, then smiled. "Visona know much about healing."

The old woman knelt beside Sir Monty and frowned at the slightly gray cast of his skin. She felt his forehead, then opened his mouth and examined his tongue. She said something that sounded like a mixture of Portuguese, French, and the native language many of them spoke, and Maruba nodded.

"She say pink thistle might cause. Sometimes used to poison enemies."

Rand's brows drew together. For a moment his glance strayed to Talmadge, who stood talking to Geoffrey over by the fire. "Is there an antidote?"

The older woman lifted a bony hand and shook the small leather pouch she carried. She gave him a toothless grin and began to chatter again.

"Acacia leaves and the crushed bodies of insects," Maruba explained. "Visona say she make potion. Man drink. If he not die, by morning, sickness will be gone."

Cait's heart constricted. Dear God, not Sir Monty! He was such a dear little man.

"Tell her to do it," Rand said to Maruba, his expression grim. "Tell her to see to the others, as well."

Cait knelt once more beside the usually jaunty, freckle-faced explorer. "Someone poisoned him. Surely Lord Talmadge wouldn't do such a thing."

"Hard to say what a man will do for that kind of money. We're lucky whoever it was didn't try to kill us all."

She rinsed the cloth and sponged the narrow chest, the rag sliding over his curly gray hair. "Why didn't they?"

"Maybe they didn't have the chance. Sir Monty said

he left the rabbit cooking over the fire. Anyone could have walked up and doused it with poison."

"Von Schnell was married to one of the native women. He might have known how to extract the thistle poison."

Rand nodded. "Or Talmadge could have brought the poison with him from Dakar."

"I'm frightened, Rand. Whoever did this wants the necklace badly enough to kill for it. And we are still two days away from the base camp."

A muscle flexed in his jaw. "It's time we spoke to the others. At least they'll know what they're dealing with."

And so he did. Gathering the men together, he told them about the rope being cut at the bridge and that poison had been used on the meat. He didn't say more, didn't voice his suspicions about who might have done it, couldn't since he wasn't really sure.

"Just be careful," he said. "If you see anything suspicious—anything at all—tell me or Percy."

"You think it may have been vun of the porters?" von Schnell asked, his pale blue eyes traveling off toward the second campfire.

Rand shrugged his shoulders. "It could be. I'm sorry to say it could be any one of us. Whoever it is wants that necklace very badly."

The men all eyed each other warily, as if by a single glance they could ferret out the culprit among them. Saying little, they made their way to their respective bedrolls, each preoccupied with his own thoughts.

She and her father sat up with Sir Monty, but Rand also elected to stay. They took turns sleeping, then sitting at the sick man's bedside. By morning, it was obvious his fever had broken.

"I think he's going to be all right," Cait said thankfully.

"Looks like it," Rand agreed.

They let him sleep a little later than the rest of the crew, waiting until they were all packed and ready to leave before rousing him from his exhausted slumber.

The little man accepted the canteen of water Rand

handed him and drank deeply, his Adam's apple bobbing up and down. "Can't thank you enough, old man," he said wearily. "Might have died if you hadn't thought to ask for the old woman's help." He reached down unsteadily for his shirt and Rand helped him drag it over his rumpled red hair.

Her father walked up just then. "Thank God you're still amongst the living." He laid a hand on his friend's shoulder. "The question is, are you well enough to continue this abominable trek down the hill?"

"Rather go than stay up here." He flashed a crooked grin. "I'm still a little weak, but I'll make it."

"Good! Good! Knew you'd say that. Hadn't the slightest doubt."

By now the porters were loaded and ready. Rand suggested the three men who had also been sick leave their packs behind, and though Talmadge grumbled at the waste of supplies, the men were allowed to do so.

The going continued to ease as they descended the mountain. Just one last difficult traverse, where the trail grew narrow halfway up a sheer rock cliff face, and it would be a simple trip the rest of the way down to the base camp.

Cait looked down at the final obstacle she would have to conquer, thought of the dead porter, remembered what had happened to Sir Monty. A tremor of dread ran through her.

TWENTY-SIX

A sullen, iron gray sky loomed overhead. A stiff wind blew in off a turbulent sea, plucking withered blossoms from their stems, lifting fallen leaves and bits of moss, swirling them around Rand's heavy brown boots.

The weather would make crossing the narrow portion of trail even more difficult and yet if a storm broke it would be far worse. At the top of the cliff face, the small group gathered to prepare for the difficult descent, each man checking his gear and simply catching his breath before starting out.

The trail descended rapidly here. By the midpoint, it had dropped to a spot twenty feet above the rocky granite scree piled at the base of the cliff. There it leveled off until it reached the opposite side, where it widened once more and continued on into the jungle.

Rand looked down at the sheer rock wall, at the jagged tumble of granite below the narrow trail, and every instinct in his body told him this would be the place their assailant would pick for his next attack.

He was wrong.

Turning to look for Cait, wanting to be certain she stayed close by as they made the assault, he froze when he saw her standing a few feet away, pinned against Phillip Rutherford, trapped by the choking hold he had around her neck. Talmadge cocked the pistol he pressed to the side of her head, and a wave of fury swept through Rand's body.

For an instant, he could hardly breathe. He hadn't expected this. It wasn't like Talmadge to make a stand out in the open. He was a swindler and a thief. In the past, he had succeeded in his dubious endeavors by using his wits, not his brawn.

Rand's stomach churned with fear for Cait. Apparently the baron had grown tired of waiting and decided it was time to act.

Mentally, Rand went over his options, his glance sliding to his musket, just a foot or so away and leaning against a tree. Too far away to do him any good, at least at present.

He fixed his attention on Talmadge and silently cursed him. He should have killed the son of a bitch the moment he'd discovered the role he had played in the death of his cousin.

"Well, gentlemen . . ." Every man's attention hung on the baron's words. His smile was as vicious as any Rand had seen. "It looks as though this is where we part company."

The professor gaped at Talmadge as if he couldn't trust his aging eyes. "My God, man, what the devil do you think you're doing?"

"Nothing you could possibly understand, Professor. Simply taking what is mine, that's all. What I've earned for the months I've spent on this damnable bloody island of yours. You may enjoy this kind of life, my friend, but I assure you I do not. Now—if you will be so kind as to hand me the necklace, no one will get hurt."

Sir Monty took a threatening step forward. "It won't do you any good," he said, his face flushed red and this time not with fever. "You can steal the necklace if you want, but you won't be able to get it off the island."

The baron's mouth edged up. "Won't I?"

"What about Cait?" Rand asked with a calm more menacing for its softness. His eyes remained on her small red-haired form and he cursed himself for letting her out of his sight, even for a moment. She was shaking, he saw, and so pale the freckles stood out across her nose. But her legs were braced apart and it was clear she was ready to escape the moment she got the chance.

His jaw tightened. Silently, he prayed that at least for the moment, she'd stay exactly where she was.

"Ah . . . Caitlin, yes." His smile was smug and Rand hated him for it. "I suppose—as her loving husband—you would be concerned. It should be obvious, Your Grace, your lovely wife is coming with me." Rand stiffened and Cait's face paled even more, if that were possible. "If you wish her to remain alive and healthy, you will encourage the professor to make haste with the necklace."

The old man was already bending to the task, sliding his pack off a thin shoulder, flipping open the canvas flap, hurriedly withdrawing the necklace he had so carefully wrapped in linen and stored away.

"All right now . . . very slowly, Professor, bring it over here. Open my coat and place it in the pocket."

Donovan Harmon did as he was told, opening the baron's cotton twill jacket and carefully shoving the necklace into an inside pocket.

"My thanks, Professor. Now, I'm afraid it's time for us to leave." He made a faint nod of his head and started to back away, dragging Cait along with him. "As for the rest of you, you will all remain exactly where you are until we are safely away. If I catch even a glimpse of one of you, Caitlin is dead."

She started to struggle, tearing at the arm around her neck, trying to kick him in the shins.

"Do as he tells you, Cait!" It was rare that she ever obeyed him. He prayed she would do so now. "As long as you do what he asks, he isn't going to hurt you." He shot Talmadge an icy glare that held a deadly warning. "Are you . . . Baron?"

The vicious little smile reappeared, tinged with what Rand recognized as a shot of lust. "Of course not. Caitlin and I are going to become even closer friends than we are already. A great deal closer."

Rand clamped hard on his jaw. Helpless rage welled up, the desire to snuff the life from Phillip Rutherford with his two bare hands.

The pair moved backward, step by step, and Rand held his breath. The path across the cliff face was difficult under the best conditions. Moving together as they were would make the journey doubly hard. He watched Cait backing farther and farther away, and a jagged edge of fear cut into his chest. He dragged in a shuddering breath, knowing if he meant to help Cait he would have to stay calm.

He watched them moving down the narrow, treacherous trail, step by careful step, and once more examined his options. Though he couldn't see Percy for the leafy cover of foliage, Rand could feel his presence a few feet away. The others stood silently watching, fascinated and horrified all at once, and silently praying for Cait.

The only one missing was von Schnell.

It was an odd coincidence, if indeed that was what it was. But Rand didn't think so, and he didn't like it. It didn't bode well for any of them.

Still, he waited, allowing the pair to continue along the ledge, reaching the halfway point where the danger lessened, but a fall from the path into the jagged rocks twenty feet below could still break an arm or a leg. Cait made no effort to fight the baron and Rand said a silent prayer of thanks for her sensible nature. They continued to inch along and eventually reached the place on the opposite side of the cliff face where the trail widened out.

He let them disappear into the forest before he turned, dug into his pack, and jerked out his pistol. Grabbing the musket, he tore after them. As Rand started the descent down the trail, Percy armed himself and fell silently in behind.

"I'm coming with you!" the professor called out, taking up the third position. Sir Monty hoisted a musket and followed.

The wind had kicked up. Clouds settled low over the

mountain and a few drops of rain began to fall. The storm was about to break and they needed to get safely across the sheer rock wall. The porters must have realized it, as well. By the time Rand had reached the midway point, the entire party had started down the trail, heading for safety on the opposite side.

Rand climbed slowly along the narrow ledge, placing each foot carefully. The expedition strung out the length of the trail, and Rand's instinct for danger raised the hair at the nape of his neck. Ahead and behind, above the cliff, and in the tangle of boulders below, his gaze searched for von Schnell.

By the time he spotted him, behind a granite outcropping high above the cliff face, it was already too late. Cursing as the first small boulders began to rain down, Rand swung his musket up, slammed it against his shoulder, and fired. The lead ball tore into von Schnell's chest and he staggered backward. Even from a distance, Rand could make out the surprised look on the big German's face. Then his body went limp and he collapsed out of sight on the ground.

But von Schnell had done his job and the avalanche continued to build, larger, heavier boulders beginning to crash around him. On the path behind him, he heard the porters' frightened screams, feared some of them had been swept off the trail by the rockslide and crushed on the boulders below.

There was only one place to go—into the jagged scree below the ledge, a twenty-foot drop where he might find cover from the certain death raining down from above. He spotted a rock that looked flatter than the rest, made the leap and landed bent-kneed on the balls of his feet. Percy landed beside him. They spotted the protective overhang of a huge granite boulder at the same instant and raced to duck beneath it, pressing themselves into the low, tight space and out of the path of the vicious rocks that continued to thunder down.

In the scree not far away, he recognized St. Anthony's

curse, and hoped the professor and Sir Monty had landed safely. When the rocks had finally stopped falling, he and Percy ducked out from under the boulder to find Lord Geoffrey nursing an injured arm, two of the porters who had been higher up on the trail killed by the fall, and another crushed beneath the weight of the heavy rockfall, but the women were safe, and the professor and Sir Monty had weathered the jump with only minor cuts and bruises.

He glanced up at the ledge and saw it was partially blocked by the slide.

"Geoffrey's arm will need to be tended," he said to Sir Monty. "Some of the porters have suffered cuts and scrapes. Can you take care of that?"

The little man nodded.

"You'll have to get round these boulders and make your way back up to the trail on the other side of the rockfall. Do you think you can handle that?"

This time the professor nodded yes.

"All right, then, I'm going after Cait."

Donovan Harmon reached out and caught his arm. "Be careful, son," he said. "And bring my girl back safely."

Rand reached out and squeezed the professor's thin shoulder. "I'll bring her back. You can count on it."

"We'll meet you back at the base camp," Sir Monty put in as Rand retrieved the pistol he had dropped when he made the jump, checked the load, and shoved it into the waistband of his pants. Rand gave a final wave, then he and Percy started their climb through the vicious maze of boulders toward the place where the trail took off down the mountain.

Talmadge had Cait and the necklace, and it was obvious he had a plan to get off the island. If he succeeded, Rand and the others would be stranded on Santo Amaro until the *Moroto* returned. By then, the baron would be miles away and Rand might never find them. God, what would Talmadge do once he got Cait alone?

Fear made his chest go tight. If the man had harmed

one strand of gold-tipped hair on Cait's head, the bastard was a dead man.

The baron's fingers bit into Cait's arm as he dragged her down the trail. "Hurry up!" It was muddy and slick, the light mist becoming a heavy drizzle, threatening to turn to rain.

"What do you think I'm doing? I'm going as fast as I can!" In a way she was, since the pace he had set was brutal, giving her a stitch in the side and an ache in her neck and shoulders. But of course, she was also doing her best to slow him down any way that she could, stumbling over branches across the trail, stepping into partially buried holes and pretending to fall, generally making the going as difficult as she possibly could.

"I don't know why...why you're in such...a hurry," she said, trying to catch her breath as he tugged her along. "You can't get off the island until the *Moroto* comes and that...that won't happen for more than a week."

He jerked her around to face him, making her stumble again. "There is a boat waiting even now—in the cove to the south of the base camp. By tonight, I intend to be on it."

A shiver of dread went through her. *Tonight?* They couldn't possibly make it that far by nightfall—could they? But they started moving again and she realized they were covering a good deal of ground.

"What...what about the rest of the treasure? Surely you don't mean to leave here without it."

He didn't bother to stop, just tightened his grip on her arm and kept going. "We're taking it with us. There is no one left in camp but a few aging natives, a pair of valets and a footman, and that dotty old cook, Hester Wilmot. They are hardly going to stop me."

No, they wouldn't do that. Talmadge was a baron and the man who had hired them. They would probably even help him.

She glanced down at the pistol pressed into her side. So far she hadn't tried to run. Rand had told her to do what the baron said. She believed it was a message telling her to wait until he could catch up with them. For the present, it seemed a good plan.

She spotted a hole partially covered by leaves and purposely stepped into it, giving her a moment to glance around.

Still no sign of him.

Talmadge jerked her upright and slapped her hard across the face. "Do you think I'm a fool? Do you really believe I don't know what you're doing? If you think your bloody duke is coming after you, you are wrong. By now the fool is buried beneath a hundred tons of rock." He shook her—hard. "He is dead—do you hear? Gone from your life for good. Beldon is dead and you belong to me. You had better learn to accept that." The edge of his mouth curled up. "In time, you may even be grateful."

She shook her head from side to side in bitter denial, her vision blurring with tears she refused to let fall. Numbly, she let him drag her along, her cheek red and stinging but barely able to feel it. Rand couldn't be dead. She refused to believe it. It wasn't possible. Talmadge would have had to have an accomplice, someone who would be willing to commit murder—

The thought ended abruptly, the answer coming with a sickening jolt that made the bile rise up in her throat. *Von Schnell.*

Dear God, it was possible. More than possible. Perhaps the German had been responsible for the death of the porter on the bridge. Perhaps he had poisoned Sir Monty.

The tears she had been fighting rushed into her eyes and she stifled a sob, refusing to let him hear it. She stumbled again, but didn't fall. The drizzle had soaked through her clothes and they clung to her skin, feeling wet and heavy, making each step harder than the last. She could see Rand's image in her mind, imagine his purposeful strides, feel his commanding presence as if he were actually there. Her lips trembled with the memory of his fiery kiss.

She took several short, painful breaths, then a long, deep, steadying one, forcing herself to calm.

There was no way to know if von Schnell had succeeded in killing Rand. Even Talmadge couldn't know. Rand had suspected the big, beefy German from the start, and he would be wary. She took another long, calming breath, and forced her legs to continue up the trail.

Rand was alive.

She had to believe that.

And she had to be patient a little while longer. If she was, sooner or later, Rand would catch up with them. He would find Talmadge, and when he did, she would escape.

It occurred to her that she trusted her husband in this, trusted him with her life. Cait drew in a shaky breath and brushed at the tears on her cheek.

She trusted Rand to protect her. Perhaps if he still wanted her, she would find the courage to trust him with her heart one more time.

Dusk began to fall. The night sounds of the jungle crept into the fading purple light, ominous in a way they had never been before. On a branch above the trail, a great white owl flapped its feathered wings, and her heart nearly jumped through her ribs. She could feel the bird's big yellow eyes on her, a soothsayer's silent warning. A monkey screeched a message from the top of a tree and a shudder ran down her spine. A small green lizard scurried across her path, paused at the side of the trail, and hissed its displeasure as they passed.

Look out! they all seemed to say. *You are in danger!*

There was no doubt of that. She had underestimated Talmadge from the start. Even Rand hadn't seen him as the cold-blooded monster that he had turned out to be.

Rand. Her stomach contracted with fear. Surely he wasn't dead. Not Rand. He was so vital, so magnetic. Such a powerful force. He filled her world, made it complete. Losing him had been devastating.

Losing him again would destroy her.

The thought hit with the force of a storm. It was the moment she knew how desperately, how completely, she loved him. No matter what mistakes he had made, she loved him. She always would.

Dear God, let him be all right.

Cait gathered her courage and returned her attention to the trail, which had started to flatten out, the foliage becoming less dense. Familiar landmarks began to appear and she realized they were close to the base camp. By now her boots were covered with mud, her skirt and blouse dirty and torn in half a dozen places. The ribbon at the end of her braid had come loose, leaving the heavy red mass in a tangle around her shoulders.

They rounded a corner in the trail and Talmadge jerked her to a halt beside an acacia tree. For an instant she thought he was merely giving her the rare opportunity to rest. Then she heard the sound of Rand's voice and her head snapped in that direction, her heart slamming hard against her chest. She spotted his tall figure blocking the trail ahead, and love for him swept over her, so fierce it made her giddy.

"Let her go, Talmadge," he warned, his voice hard-edged and determined.

The baron only jerked her more solidly in front of him, his fingers biting painfully into her arm. He pressed the gun more firmly into her ribs.

"It's over," Rand said. "Your little plan to kill us has failed." His mouth settled into a hard, grim line. "I'm still alive—and you still have my wife. Let her go. If you don't, I'm going to kill you."

She heard the ominous click of the baron cocking his pistol.

"You think you can stop me? Try it and she's dead." He was backing away, Rand stalking him like the leopard that had attacked him in the jungle.

Cait glanced behind her, up the trail the way they had just come. A few feet more and Talmadge would encounter the aboveground root she had noticed on the journey down. Perhaps he had forgotten.

Her muscles tensed in anticipation as the chance she had been seeking grew closer, ready for the moment he would reach it and she could break free. She prayed he wouldn't see it if he glanced behind him.

Instead, his entire concentration was fixed on Rand. With a sudden shot of clarity, Cait knew Talmadge meant to kill him, and fear spilled like acid into her stomach.

The root lay mere inches away. Her heartbeat increased. A second passed, then another. The heel of his boot connected with the root just as she had hoped, and for a split second the pistol fell away. Cait shoved him with all her strength, jerked free, and started running.

"You little bitch!" Talmadge shouted from behind her.

She saw Rand aim his weapon, realized the baron pointed his gun in her direction, heard the loud report of a pistol being fired. A glance over her shoulder and she saw Talmadge go down, his chest stained red with blood.

She raced forward. Rand caught her in his arms and for a single second, frozen in time, she felt safe, protected, her world finally right again.

Then time broke into disjointed segments that collided with one another in the span of a heartbeat, yet each passing moment seemed an eternity that would forever be etched into her mind.

Holding her tightly, Rand looked over at Talmadge and must have seen him stir. She heard a softly muttered curse, then he shoved her behind him and stepped into the path of the bullet meant clearly for her. The baron's pistol exploded.

"Raaand!" Cait's horrified scream echoed in the silence of the jungle. At the same instant a musket fired from deep in the foliage, slamming into Talmadge with deadly force. He twitched once and no longer moved, his eyes staring sightlessly upward. Cait scrambled to Rand's side, her breath coming fast, burning painfully inside her chest.

Percy raced toward her as she lifted Rand's head into

her lap with trembling hands and smoothed the dark hair back from his forehead. "Rand," she whispered, hot tears welling, forming a wet path down her cheeks. They dripped onto the front of his jacket and soaked into the fabric, which blossomed bright red with his blood.

Percy knelt beside her and quickly ripped open Rand's shirt. The grim set of the valet's hawkish features made her heart squeeze painfully inside her. She pressed a kiss to Rand's forehead as Percy continued to work, stuffing a handkerchief into the wound to slow the flow of blood, examining the damage the bullet had done.

Cait stroked her husband's beloved face, smoothed his hair back again. "Dear God, Rand . . . why? Why did you do it?"

A shaking hand gently cupped her cheek. The muscles across his chest clenched in pain, yet a soft, sad smile touched his lips.

"Because I love you, Caitie. Don't you know that by now?"

"Rand . . . Oh, God . . ."

"I love you," he repeated. "I would protect you with my life."

"Rand . . ."

"And I would never, ever hurt you again."

His fingers fell away and a sob caught in Caitlin's throat. She lifted his big, sun-browned hand to her lips and pressed a kiss into the palm.

"I wanted to go back with you," she told him. "I wanted to be your wife again. Oh, Rand, I wanted it so badly."

For a moment those fierce dark eyes fixed on her face and there was so much love in them she thought that her heart was surely breaking in two.

"I love you," she whispered.

He smiled with such pleasure, fresh tears rushed into her eyes.

"Whatever happens . . . I want you to remember—"

"No . . ." She pressed her trembling fingers over his

mouth to still the words. "I won't let you say it. You aren't going to die. I won't let you." Her voice cracked on the last and the ache in her throat grew fierce.

His mouth edged up. "Some things are worth dying for. You're worth it, Cait."

She only shook her head, tears rolling in hot, wet rivers down her cheeks.

"You would have . . . gone back with me?"

"Yes . . . Oh, God, yes. I don't want to live without you, Rand. Not ever again."

"Do you . . . trust me, then . . . not to hurt you?"

"I trust you, Rand. And I believe in you. You're the best man I've ever known."

His hand tightened faintly over hers. "If you trust me, then nothing else matters. If you love me, then no matter what happens, we have everything . . . don't we, Caitie?"

The pain, dear God, it was nearly unbearable.

He almost smiled, but even as he did, those beautiful gold-flecked eyes slid closed and the hand that gripped hers went slack.

"No . . ." she whispered, agony washing over her, ripping her heart loose inside her. "Please, Rand, don't die, not now, not when we have so much to live for." She stared down at him, the dull ache of loss already throbbing in her breast. Rand was going to die, she could feel it. Her whole life had been one terrible loss after another. Losing her mother, losing her friends. She had lost Rand once and now she was going to lose him forever.

She pressed her lips against his, felt their fleeing warmth, and whispered his name. Beneath her hand, she could feel the pulse of his life draining away. In minutes he would be gone.

Scalding tears rolled down her cheeks. She thought of all they could have had, the future that loomed before them if only he would live.

Her hand tightened almost painfully around his. "We don't have everything!" she told him fiercely. "We don't have a child. You don't have a son, Rand—the heir you

need to insure your family name. You can't die—not
without a son!" She roughly squeezed his fingers. "We
don't have everything—do you hear? Not until we have
a son!"

Percy gripped her shoulders, tried to ease her away,
but she refused to budge. Instead, she clutched Rand's
hand and told him again that he could not leave her. Percy
left for a moment. He spoke to someone, then the old
woman, Visona, shuffled forward. She stooped down beside Rand, opened his bloody shirt, and began to examine
the wound.

Beneath Cait's hand, she could feel Rand's heartbeat,
faint and reedy, but it was there and she started to pray.
All the while the old woman worked over the wound in
his chest, pouring in a mixture of herbs, packing it with
crumbled leaves, talking to him softly in that singsong
way of hers.

Cait cradled his head and stroked back his hair, ignoring the blood seeping into the front of her skirt. Rand's
blood. Blood he had given to save her life.

I love you, Caitie. Don't you know that by now? In
truth, she did know. Had known it in her heart for some
time. From the moment they had met, everything he had
done had shown his love for her.

All but that one mistake. That one, terrible, nearly un-
forgivable mistake.

Since his return to the island, she had seen the regret
in his eyes, recognized it deep inside him. He had proved
his love again and again, earning her trust once more,
making her ache with her need for him. Rand Clayton
was everything she had imagined him to be and more. He
was a man among men and she loved him as she never
would another.

Sitting on the soft mud floor of the jungle, Cait bowed
her head and began to pray. When she had finished, she
kissed his cheek and watched as Percy walked toward
them, a grim look on his face. He waited for Visona to
finish, then knelt to examine his friend.

"How . . . how . . . ?" She swallowed past the lump in her throat and tried again. "How is he?"

Percy shook his head. "It's bad—I won't lie to you. But his breathing seems to have steadied in the last few minutes, and his heartbeat sounds a little more even. Your husband is a strong man, and he has a powerful reason to live." His eyes came to rest on her face. "I knew even before he did how much he loved you. Now I think he knows how much you love him."

It took a moment for his words to find their way through the fog of her despair. "Are you . . . are you saying there's a chance he may live?"

"A few minutes ago, I would have said no. Now . . ." He felt Rand's pulse again, seemed pleased by its strength. "The lead ball went completely through, which means we won't have to dig it out. He was bleeding very badly, but Visona has managed to stop it. Aye—if we can keep him alive for the next few hours, I believe there's a chance he may live."

Hope rose up and yet she was afraid to grasp it. Instead, she simply nodded. "I'll stay with him."

The ghost of a smile moved over Percy's lips. "I never doubted it . . . Your Grace."

Her throat constricted. She was Rand's wife, the Duchess of Beldon. She would never deny it again. They worked to make Rand comfortable, but didn't dare move him. Percy fashioned a canvas tarp over their heads to protect them from the rain. Cait settled herself in the mud at Rand's side and for the next thirty-six hours, she didn't leave him.

Thirty-six hours and ten minutes after he was shot, Randall Elliot Clayton, seventh Duke of Beldon, opened his eyes, saw his lovely wife sitting there beside him, her head bowed in prayer, her small hand clinging to his, and vowed—no matter what it took—that he was going to live.

EPILOGUE

Ephram Barclay rapped lightly on the ornate front doors of Beldon Hall. Dust flew from his dark gray tailcoat and his back ached from the hours he had spent on the road. He had made the journey with all haste, traveling to the country from London, wanting to personally relay the news he had recently received.

A pair of Beldon footmen, liveried in red and gold, pulled open the door, and the butler, a thin, graceful man with wispy gray hair, motioned him in.

"His Grace received your note," the butler said. "I shall tell him you are here."

Ephram had sent a messenger ahead, informing the duke of his pending arrival, knowing His Grace would be eager to hear the news. The duke and his wife had been in residence at Beldon Hall since a week after their return to England, having left for the country just a few days after the presentation by Professor Harmon—now Sir Donovan Harmon—of the famous Cleopatra's Necklace to the British Museum.

Ephram had read about the nearly fatal injury the duke had suffered on the island. Even after a month of recuperation aboard the ship home from Dakar, he had still looked pale and a little weak the last time Ephram had seen him.

Not today, Ephram saw, stepping through the doors of the study to find him waiting in front of his desk, an arm around his petite wife's waist. He looked fit and trim and stronger than ever. And the lady—good heavens, with her fiery hair and wide green eyes, she was lovely in the extreme. Small though she was, there was a sturdiness about her, a strength of character that was impossible to miss.

She gave her husband a soft, sweet smile before they started toward him, and Ephram knew at once that the stories he had heard were true.

The Duke of Beldon and his duchess were, without question, very deeply in love.

"Ephram—it's good to see you, old friend." Beldon clapped him on the shoulder, momentarily dislodging his wire-rimmed spectacles. Ephram slid them back into place on the bridge of his nose.

"It's a pleasure to see you as well, Your Grace." Introductions were made and the duchess smiled at him warmly.

"My husband speaks of you often. It's good to finally meet you."

They made pleasant conversation for a moment, but Ephram could see the impatience in the duke's dark eyes. It was obvious the man had changed in the days since his marriage—and all for the best. But patience seemed a virtue that still remained elusive.

"Your note said something about information you had received in regard to my cousin."

"Yes. I brought it as quickly as I could." They moved toward the hearth and took seats around it. Ephram settled his flat leather satchel in his lap, opened the flap, and removed the sheaf of papers he had received two days ago from America. He handed the papers to the duke.

"If you recall," Ephram said, "the last word we received of the *Sea Nymph,* the ship was making packet runs along the coast. The owners, Dillon Sinclair and Richard Morris, had managed to slip away."

The duke glanced up from his reading. "Go on."

"According to this latest information, a little over two months ago, the men were apprehended during a dinner party at the home of a rather prominent banker in New

York where they had begun to sell investment ventures again." He smiled. "Interests in a cargo of copra the *Sea Nymph* was to pick up in the West Indies. The profits were predicted to be quite sizable."

The duke looked down at the papers. Ephram noticed his wife had slipped her small hand into his big one. "Where are the two men now?"

"They are incarcerated in some dismal American prison awaiting trial, but that is merely a formality. The men have already confessed their crimes. They have also confessed the name of their accomplice in England—Phillip Rutherford, Baron Talmadge. According to Sinclair and Morris, it was Talmadge who approached them with the idea for the swindle."

"Then it's over." The duke's shoulders relaxed. The duchess lifted his hand and pressed a kiss against the back.

"Talmadge got exactly what he deserved," she said. "It's just too bad it didn't happen sooner."

The duke simply nodded. Those intense dark eyes had swung to his wife's pretty face and a soft smile curved his lips.

When he realized what he was doing, he cleared his throat, returned his attention to Ephram, and came to his feet.

"I appreciate your coming," he said, helping his wife up, as well. "There's a room prepared for you upstairs. You can start your journey home on the morrow, after you've had supper and a chance to rest."

Ephram bowed his head. "Thank you, Your Grace."

The duchess took his hand. "Thank you for coming, Mr. Barclay, for setting all of this to rest once and for all. Even with the baron dead, I know the subject of the swindle and the death of my husband's cousin were never far from his mind."

But Ephram wasn't so sure. It seemed to him, watching the duke so enamored of his little wife, that Rand Clayton had more important matters on his mind than revenge. He had a woman he obviously loved and a glowing future ahead of him. One day he would have a family.

Those were the things that were important.

"I have yet to wish you both felicitations on your marriage."

"Thank you, Mr. Barclay."

The duchess gave him a winsome smile and Ephram began to think that in choosing the little American, the Duke of Beldon had picked exactly the right woman to be his duchess.

A last glance across the room, and Ephram knew that was exactly what the duke was thinking.

AUTHOR'S NOTE

Hope you enjoyed *Perfect Sin*. Rand and Caitlin were such fun characters to write—and what a grand adventure! Their friends, Nicholas and Elizabeth Warring, the Earl and Countess of Ravenworth, appear with Rand in a previous book. If you haven't read their story, *Wicked Promise*, you might give it a try.

After that, watch for *Heartless*, out in the spring of next year. Till then, happy reading and all best wishes.

Kat